Zephyr

ANDREW COOKE

PAGE PUBLISHING, INC.
New York, NY

First originally published by Page Publishing, Inc. 2018

ISBN 978-1-64138-592-3 (Paperback)
ISBN 978-1-64138-593-0 (Digital)

Printed in the United States of America

I dedicate the entirety of this novel to the Holy Trinity, for providing me with a voice, to the Blessed Virgin Mary, for your refuge during my struggles, and to the Cooke family, for your undying love and support. I love you all.

Contents

Prologue

She sat motionless in the car, letting the early winter snow settle upon the clear windows that reflected her sad image. The parking lot gradually emptied as the minutes flew away, but the concept of time paid no attention to her. Rather, Chronos himself wished to stand still and silent, as if the frigid winter air petrified him and held him in its misty grasp. She counted the snowflakes that sprinkled on the transparent portrait of her face and wondered if she would be buried underneath its weight.

"God help me," she whispered. She willed herself to exit the car and allowed the cold snap to invade her lungs. She saw that the lot had completely emptied. Its only companions were remnants of sand and salt from a light snowfall that settled in between each parking spot.

She closed her car door and stared at the ominous vehicle. It was a black Corvette Grand Sport with tinted black windows and shadowed rims. The body was modern yet paid homage to the generations before it. The exterior, drenched in the folds of night, was sleek and broad, with opaque headlights that cast a sinister gaze on whoever glanced at it. The design broke the rules of geometry with its even creases laden upon the entire exterior of the vehicle. The carbon fiber hood relinquished a window, the only glass portal that displayed a powerful supercharged engine that roared relentlessly. She then realized that the engine only mocked her own feral cries and did nothing to truthfully match the sorrow that she had felt these past months.

She walked around the passenger side and examined her throne room. The interior of the car was subservient to her own tastes in style and conduct. Leather seats dwelled within the metallic shell, caressing her as she negotiated turns and high speeds. They acted as ex-lovers who sacrificed their own lives to protect the one they so desired to let live. Her soft hands and long, delicate fingers were the only signatures that the stick shift recognized, and it allowed itself to be choked and jerked in crippling ways. She moved her eyes up to the head unit and gazed at a screen she never used. Her own mind was an organic GPS, with city maps memorized and routes committed to memory. It sat in the car blank and dead; she would never know that it was only a mirror to her own heart. Or perhaps she did and chose to ignore it.

She began to walk down the small, humble lot and looked around the area. There was a couple across the street arguing about someone or something. "Why don't you do something about it?" the woman yelled.

"Do what? It's out of my hands, there's nothing I can do!" he replied.

"He's right," the woman sighed. "Nothing . . . I suppose."

She climbed a set of stairs that stood in front of her. When she reached the top, she placed her hand on the brass door handle and tried to open it.

"Locked."

She turned around and decided to attempt entrance from another position. She descended the stairs and slowly walked toward the front of the building. A pedestrian who looked to be in his early twenties passed her by and turned around to gaze at the Venusian beauty that he had just witnessed: a tall, slim figure with slender feet and small ankles enclosed by a pair of black calfskin boots with quilted leather and a fading heel. Her legs were elegant yet firm, and although they were completely covered by a long calfskin dress, the young man knew that her legs were toned pillars of heaven. The dress relinquished a slit that rose just below her knees, and the young man prayed that the wind would allow him a better glance at the rest of her legs.

He snuck a peak at her rear, disappointed that the god of winds did not grant him his request. He licked his lips at the way her hips swayed from side to side as she walked alongside the building. It was full and spherical, complimenting her thighs tremendously that shook with a model's gait. She had a torso that gave no voice to any complaints the young man may have had; it had a trim waist with a full pair of breasts peering through a white silk blouse. Her arms and shoulders were draped by a black wool overcoat that accentuated her figure.

Goddamn . . . he thought.

The woman stopped walking and slowly turned around. The young man took this as an opportunity to glimpse at her face. He first saw her tapered jaw that housed full pink lips. Then, he saw icicles that hung from each ear and glittered against the vicious cold air. Behind those lovely pair of ears was her long onyx hair, comparable to a black velvet cloth that held up a line of diamonds in a jewelry box.

But when he gazed into her eyes, he flinched and started to rub his chest. The pain was so sinister and so powerful that it felt like his soul was being eaten alive. He immediately turned on his heels and escaped with long, speedy strides. He begged that his attempt to distance himself as far away from the woman as possible would be successful.

He closed his eyes, and the picture of her silver, ghastly eyes traveled back and forth in his conscience.

Black pupils that were nestled upon a hoary iris crept into his soul and swallowed it. He kept walking for what seemed like miles until he was certain that the eyes abandoned his body and allowed his heart to slow its rate. He never saw her again, nor did he attempt to see her again.

The pallid-eyed goddess continued walking the side path until she arrived at the front stairs. She looked up and read Latin inscriptions on the pillars and marveled how the old language shone forth from the building in complete ignorance of the gray snowy sky. She carefully read over the inscription and committed it to memory. She promised herself to ask a priest what the words meant, not because she was ignorant of the dead language but only to hear a pleasant word emanate from a man of the cloth.

She ascended the stairs and wrapped her gloved hand around the old brass handle. She pulled the door open and immediately threw herself inside the dark building. The lobby was dim and melancholic; the only sources of light came from the candles on the walls and from her ethereal eyes. She took off her gloves and thrust them into her coat pockets. She dipped her right hand into a dish full of cold water and made the sign of the cross on her forehead. She took her time blessing herself, keeping her movements nice and slow, as if she resented her own presence in such a holy place. She brushed off her perverse, conscientious thoughts and continued walking until she arrived in the main congregation of the church.

The interior of the church was as empty as the outside. It had a dark-red carpet that had not been vacuumed or maintained in weeks and short pews that were stained in a mahogany shade, which in time faded to an auburn hue desperate for attention. The stained glass windows depicted scenes from the Mysteries of the Holy Rosary. The woman imagined lonely Roman Catholics kneeling in prayer and reciting the rosary in front of the vibrant portals to the biblical past. Their heads were lowered in reverence to God, who in turn gave them comfort and answers to their prayers. She also noticed an altar laden with a golden cherubim and marble stones, tall Ionic pillars that reached up to heaven in a relentless stance, and tiny biblical quotes submerged in a high ceiling.

She turned to her left and saw the booths for the Sacrament of Reconciliation. The priest's stall lay in between each booth, allowing him to direct the absolution to either side of him. The entrance to the confessors' booths was covered by a thick red curtain that draped to the floor. She stiffened her posture and glanced around once more before she entered.

The inside was as black as night, but a small bulb lit up the booth when the woman knelt on a leather platform. She saw a screen that filtered both the sight of her face and the priest's. This privacy gave her more comfort than she had expected. She bowed her head until the priest's voice broke the silence.

"In the name of the Father, and of the Son, and of the Holy Spirit . . . amen."

The woman made another sign of the cross in compliance with the priest. She folded her hands and kept her head lowered. "May I ask you a question, Father?" Her voice was airy and incredibly calm. There was a brief silence on the other side of the screen.

"Uh . . . yes? What is it?" He had a kind voice, almost innocent in its pitch.

"This is my first time participating in this Sacrament, so I apologize if I seem nervous. How shall I address you?"

"You may address me as Father Bonaduce."

If Bonaduce was able to look through the screen, he would see that the woman was smiling.

"Thank you." She cleared her throat and raised her head without opening her eyes.

"Whenever you are ready."

"Forgive me, Father, for I have sinned. It has been a lifetime since my last confession . . . and these are my sins . . ."

I

This particular hospital had a reputation for being an institution contrary to its ideals; it purported rejuvenation but instead gathered death and pain within its walls. It was loneliness. Actually, it was deterioration. It was a mere representation of what it did not support. Perhaps it was a mockery of human nature, with God punishing those who believed they were immortal or invincible. Perhaps the nurses and doctors who zipped by in all directions were really Angels of Death relieving the hospital of its crowded rooms. The wings were carefully folded underneath their white coats, ready to unfold at any moment. A tall man with anguish in his eyes released his stare on the hospital staff and directed them toward the white walls. He secretly wished that he could manipulate reality and swallow himself within that white void. It would be so damn beautiful. Sweet deliverance. Or perhaps he should merge with the floor itself and become a statue. Why not doom his entire body to the confines of sculpture? He was curious to know if he would be marveled or looked upon with disgust. Either way, his pain would end and his thoughts would freeze in marbled stone.

Luis Estrada felt the pangs of fear on three occasions: when he first became Don, when he married Rosa, and tonight. He remembered his heart pounding furiously when Rosa's water broke and during his maddened rush to the hospital seconds later. His associates followed after him, partly due to obedience and mostly due to worry themselves. Don Luis treated his men unlike any other organization. Though he was a firm man, he was also unusually compassionate in his work. No one dared confuse his loyalty to the organization, for he would be kind one morning and ruthless in that same night. He managed this duality with success and diligence, which ultimately led to his lengthy reign over the entire city.

Eventually, he shared his supremacy with the other organizations. The Russians adored him, and the local but powerful Forty-Second Street Gang feared him. Such was the population of the city: crime lords and gangsters. Don Luis never slept without regret for his daily activities involving murder and soliciting. He did come to realize, as most men in his business had knew already, that it was the world he lived in and it would only hurt more if he resisted the environment.

And here he was, justifying his life and recalling every detail of his hideous resumé.

Luis looked to his left and saw a painting of a delicate yellow rose. He saw his reflection in the glass frame and studied the new addition to the piece of art. The rose beheld a square and handsome face, according to Rosa's frequent remarks, with dimples in his right cheek deep enough to swallow her lips. His eyes were brown and tired; Luis wondered if it was a gift of fatherhood or a reminder of his recent agony. His build was slim yet deceptively strong, but tonight, he felt disgustingly frail. He was wearing a black custom-made suit with a subtle pinstripe design and loud Italian style. Luis and Rosa were celebrating their eighteenth wedding anniversary when she suddenly stopped chewing her food. She gave Luis a long, hard stare, and seconds later, he was speeding on the highway to the hospital. He loosened his white silk tie and shoved the silken noose into his jacket pocket.

"Nice job," he chuckled. "Way to celebrate your anniversary, Mr. Estrada."

Luis kept thinking strange thoughts during this seemingly million-year wait. He knew that he could not leave Rosa as a perpetual widower, nor could he leave Pedro in the prime of his youth. Pedro Estrada had the title of being a rebellious but curious seventeen-year-old with more ambition than his father. Often Luis would receive compliments from fellow members of his . . . society: "Your son will take over the family business. You can see it in his eyes. He is strong. Ambitious. Just like his *papi*."

The business. Dammit, that was another thing. He could not abandon it. Absolutely not. There was so much to do. Especially with Pedro—

"Luis!"

The scream that resonated from the delivery room awakened Luis from his daydream. He rushed to the door, but a nurse blocked his charge.

"I'm sorry, sir, but you can't come in here." Her eyes were stern underneath her surgical mask.

"But my wife!" Luis yelled. "She needs me!"

"You have to wait until the baby comes!"

"Is she okay? Rosa! I'm right here! Hold on!"

"Sir! Please wait outside!"

The nurse disappeared behind the metallic doors and left Luis brimming with worry. He began to pace around the doorway and tried not to imagine every morbid thing that was happening behind those doors. Was there something wrong with the baby? Rosa? Was he too late? He remembered stories of mothers delivering stillborn babies, crying and sobbing because their babies could not do the same. Or stories where the father must choose between saving the life of the child or the mother. Or stories where he had no choice at all. Did he have to run in there and hold a small bloody mass of what was supposed to be a newborn . . .

Stop it. Right now. Luis shook his head and punished himself for being a man of thought. He sat down in a nearby chair, lowered his head, and clasped his hands together in prayer.

"If you keep worrying like this, you grow wrinkles on your forehead."

Sitting directly across from Luis was his son, Pedro. He was indeed tall, just like his father, and had a medium build. He was still in his years of priming to become a man but exuded an aura that was more mature than youthful. His hair was long and fell over his face in a disheveled style. His clothes were baggy and dark—he always wore black, possibly as a testament to his own growing pains and anger. His eyes were just as dark, almost black in color and in spirit. He was often cold and reclusive, so Luis was surprised to see that Pedro was carrying a conversation with him.

"Were you this scared when I was born?" Pedro asked.

Luis chuckled. "No. But only because your arrival into this world was expected. Your little brother's or sister's arrival was unexpected, that's all." Luis sighed deeply. "I just pray to God that everything's all right." Luis kept his hands clasped and closed his eyes tightly. Pedro rolled his eyes and slouched in his seat. The plastic chair squeaked as he threw his head back.

"Nothing in this world is guaranteed," Pedro said. "Or expected, for that matter. So there's no point in predicting anything."

Luis raised his head from his hands and stared at Pedro. "That's exactly the attitude that will get you into trouble. Everything has to be predicted, no matter what. If you want to stay alive, you have to—"

"Mr. Estrada?" A short doctor appeared in front of Luis. "You may see her."

Luis quickly jumped to his feet and grabbed the doctor by his shoulders. "How's Rosa? How is the baby?"

"She's fine . . . and so is your daughter." He smiled widely.

"Daughter?"

"Go see for yourself."

Luis dashed past the good doctor and shoved the doors open to the delivery room. He saw a package containing hospital scrubs and quickly threw them on. He washed his hands in a soapy blur before he found Rosa's room.

"Rosa . . ."

Luis recognized the sweet face of his wife despite the muddled hair and her fatigued eyes. Her smile was wide and euphoric, with a dimple in each cheek. She was often described as "Spain's lost flower" and received the attention of every man who was lucky enough to grace themselves with her presence. Her eyes were narrow and bright; Luis had always felt a sense of calm whenever he gazed into them. Her body was curvy and trim, with very little signs of imperfection in her skin. In her arms lay a tiny warm baby with big cheeks and a small round nose. Her hair was silken and moist, and she kept her eyes closed while huddled next to her mother.

"Hey, it's your daddy," Rosa whispered. "Say 'Hi, *Papi.*'"

The little girl opened her eyes and fixed them on Luis. They were big. Curious.

And white.

"Oh my god . . . her eyes . . ." He swallowed hard and kept staring at his daughters pale eyes.

"Don't worry—the doctor says that it's . . . oh, what did he say? 'A normal abnormality.'" Rosa turned her head toward her newborn. "Tell your *papi* that he worries too much."

"She's beautiful." Luis moved closer to the two women in front of him.

"She has your brains. I can tell. Just look at how her eyes shine. Like diamonds."

"Hi, sweetie. I'm your *papi.* Are you happy to see me? I'm glad to see you."

The little girl closed her eyes and burrowed herself in her mother's arms. Luis heard a noise and felt a cool breeze enter the room. Rosa felt the chilly wind wisp through her hair while Luis glanced around.

"What was that?" Luis asked. "There's no window in here."

"Zephyr." Rosa held the baby closer to her.

"What?"

"That's what I want to name her. Zephyr. Like the calm wind that blew through here."

"Zephyr . . . Zephyr Estrada." Luis drew his face near his daughter. "Hi, Zephyr. Hi sweetheart."

Zephyr's eyes sparked a ghostly white when he repeated her name, and in return, she merely blinked.

*   *   *

When Zephyr was born on that brisk, breezy evening, Luis phoned his mother in Spain as soon as he was able to extricate himself from his daughter's magnetic eyes. Raquel Estrada needed to know that her only son was now an official father. When he dialed the number, a sigh of relief rushed over him, as would have happened to any father who witnessed the birth of something greater than his own life.

"*Hola?*"

"*Mami*, it's me! I'm calling from the hospital!"

"Well, no shit! How is the baby?" Raquel exclaimed.

"It's a girl!"

"Oh my god!" Raquel threw her head back in joy. "What's her name?"

"Her name's Zephyr. Zephyr Rita Estrada."

"Beautiful! I'm on my way now!"

"Whoa, slow down! We're in—"

Raquel hung up the phone before her son could tell her the hospital in which they were staying. She was too ecstatic to bother with directions and felt that she would lose sleep if she did not see her granddaughter immediately. She grabbed the phone again and started dialing a series of numbers. After one ring, an operator answered the phone.

"Thank you for calling—"

"I would like to book a flight to America please," Raquel interrupted with unbounded joy.

The operator chuckled. "We can certainly help you with that. Will it be a one-way ticket or a round-trip?"

"I would like to book a round-trip flight, please." Raquel tried her best to remain collected. She could hear the operator's manicured fingers tacking across the keyboard on the other end of the line.

"Okay." The operator paused briefly. "And when would you like to leave?"

"Tomorrow, if possible."

"Okay . . ." she said. "Let me see if there are any available slots for you. I am going to put you on hold. Is that okay?"

"Sure! Take your time!" Raquel lied. She did not want her to take her time. At all. She was so hopeful—and impatient—that it had shown in her voice.

"Thank you, please hold."

Raquel switched hands and patiently listened to the rumba that was playing in the background, all the while imagining what her new granddaughter looked like. She wondered if her grandchild had at least some of her features. She was a woman in her early fifties, with black hair and shrewd, delicate eyes. Her face had hardly a wrinkle on it, and her cheeks were still as full of life as they had been decades earlier. Her body housed boundless vitality that endured time's volleys. Her steps were quick and light, and her touch was soft and comforting. She swore for years that her sense of humor kept her youthful and alive. She succeeded in keeping everyone as content and optimistic as she was, despite the murderous environment that was called life. There was a sudden thought that held the image of Raquel's face and showed a reflection of hidden sadness for the first time in years, and it only made her regret gazing into any opaque glasses informally called mirrors.

"Ah, shit, I'm finally getting old," she whispered.

Next to the mirror was a picture of Raquel and Luis, much younger in age rather than appearance. She had her arms wrapped around him from behind, her face laden with dimples, and Luis had covered his eyes with his hands at the last second. His smiled was adorned with missing teeth and plump cheeks, and Raquel remembered how she would pinch at them with every chance she got. This comedic timing stuck with Raquel throughout her life and with the other lives she had cradled and nurtured. She was glad that she had a new soul to shape and foster.

"Ms. Estrada?" The operator returned to the line.

"Yes?" Raquel perked up from her daydream.

"Thank you for patiently waiting. We managed to find a seat available for you in first class. The flight will depart at six o'clock the next morning. Would you like for me to go ahead and book this flight for you?"

"That's perfect!" Raquel released her excitement and showed no shame in doing so. "Book it!"

"No problem, I'll be more than happy to do that for you." A brief silence pervaded the telephone. "Your ticket has been confirmed—a round-trip flight for Ellipses International Airport has been confirmed. You will be departing from El Prat at six o'clock the next morning and will arrive at your destination at approximately nine o'clock. You may pick up the ticket at the front desk two hours prior to departure. Please call ahead in case you may have to cancel."

"Why the hell would I do that?" Raquel was still ecstatic. "I'll be there, believe me!"

"I'm sure you will . . . is there anything else I may help you with?" The operator could not stifle her smile.

"Nope! That will be all for now! Thank you!"

"Okay. Thank you for your . . . I'm sorry, Ms. Estrada. But you seem so happy. Happier than any other customer I've had. Any particular reason?"

Raquel laughed. "I am so sorry for my excitement, but my granddaughter has just been born, and I have to see the little angel as soon as possible!"

The operator giggled. "Spoil her rotten and send her home."

"Of course! I have to get revenge on my son for his childhood days somehow."

"I'm sure she's beautiful. I wish you two the best in life."

"Thank you so much, the same goes for you!"

"You are very welcome," the operator answered. "Enjoy your flight, and give your granddaughter my blessings."

"That's sweet of you! I definitely will. Thank you again."

Raquel hung up the phone and sprang toward her bedroom. Her remarkable agility did not fail her as she danced gracefully across the floor. The bedroom was large but incredibly clean and organized, with an exotic-style décor that suited her personality entirely. Her bed lay in the middle of the far wall, with simple tan blankets that draped across the mattress. Each fabric had a subtle detail that popped against the earth-toned furnishings that spread throughout the chamber. The makeup table sat to the right of the room, which contained a tall, ovular vanity glass that displayed flawless reflections of whatever the portal captured. The chair in front of the table was placed in a humble manner that did not give justice to its longevity.

Raquel always kept a glass vase full of crimson roses at the left side of the table. She would wait until they were all withered before she switched them out for a different color. All except one rose were replaced: a red frosted-glass rose. It was old but still maintained its high quality and glamour. When asked by friends and acquaintances about this curious glass rose, Raquel would reply, "As long as that single rose lives, so do I."

Raquel reached over to her large dresser and pulled out two drawers simultaneously. She then glided over to her closet and yanked articles of clothing from their hangers and watched them soar onto the bed. She grabbed her suitcases that lay on the closet floor and hurled them with strength that would have surprised any bodybuilder. Raquel emerged from the closet and folded the clothes in a tremendous frenzy while stuffing each item in her suitcases. They were pink Burberry suitcases, one large roller and two medium-sized bags, that displayed the telltale plaid pattern on the fabric. Raquel nodded in pride and closed them. These pieces of luggage could *never* be missed. She wiped the light sweat from her brow and dragged them across the floor to the doorway. Before she exited, she turned around and made the sign of the cross with her right hand. She kissed her fingertips and turned off the light.

Raquel Estrada was absolutely ready to be a part of Zephyr's life.

II

The flight from Barcelona to Ellipses resulted in anxiety and restlessness for Raquel. She repeatedly cast glances outside of her window in the plane, hoping that the gleaming shores of that little island would conjure itself in front of her eyes. She had been to Ellipses before, but the knowledge of Zephyr's birth enhanced Raquel's passion for the city. She breathed a deep sigh of relief, and her anxiety heightened when the plane landed in its runway.

She was the first person to stand up from her seat, paying little attention to the directions the flight attendants shouted through the loudspeakers.

"Ladies and gentlemen, welcome to Ellipses. The temperature outside is forty-three degrees, with newborn Zephyr bringing in a calming breeze throughout the area . . ."

Her new granddaughter occupied Raquel's mind to the point that her name squeezed into each conversation. All Raquel cared for was holding Zephyr in her arms as she rocked the newborn back and forth, singing Spanish lullabies and humming soft melodies in her ear. Raquel giggled lightly and directed her attention toward the upper luggage compartment that hovered over her seat. She inhaled deeply and stretched her back before she depressed the button to open the storage compartment.

"All passengers must remain seated until Zephyr has turned off the 'Fasten Seat Belt' sign . . ."

Raquel looked around and saw that a handful of people had already risen from their seats and proceeded to gather their carry-on luggage. They displayed impatient expressions on their face and dared not heed the instructions of the flight attendants. Finally, the accordion walkway bonded with the exit door of the plane, and the flight attendant twisted the lever that locked the door. Raquel's impatience built up in her hands. She played with the handle of her luggage as if it was a guitar.

"Come on, come on," she mumbled, "sometime this century would be nice . . ."

As soon as the door opened, Raquel burst past the flight attendant and strode down the long walkway. The smell of jet exhaust and cheap cleaning products invaded her lungs, but her resolve to reach the baggage claim helped her ignore the polluted scent. When she entered the terminal, she felt a cool breeze kiss her face and whisk through her hair. She smiled when she felt the cool wind play with her youthful skin, and longed for the wind to prevail on her lips forever.

It suits her, Raquel thought.

She located the escalator leading to the baggage claim and gladly descended to the lower level of the airport. She journeyed to the conveyor belt that displayed her flight name and number. The anxiety that she experienced on the plane returned with a vengeance; Raquel found herself pacing back and forth next to the conveyor belt, hurriedly exchanging glances between the silent belt and her watch. She started to tap her heal against the floor and rolled her eyes at the sign on the far wall that read, "Efficient and fast, because you want it to be."

Suddenly, Raquel heard a noise. She whipped her head towards the hole that led to the outside where the airplanes had parked. The sound of gears whirring sung sweet melodies in Raquel's ears, and the conveyor belt finally danced in front of Raquel's eyes.

"About freaking time," she muttered. The luggage started to appear on the belt and snaked its way toward the passengers. Every second that passed seemed like an eternity for Raquel, who was gazing despairingly at each piece of luggage that was not her own. She saw the joyful faces of a couple who had been the first to collect their luggage, and leered at their departure from the area.

"*Dios.* I hope it didn't get lost during the flight."

Raquel felt her anxiety manifest as the wicked mistresses Worry and Stress. The two women laughed and danced on her psyche, until Hope came along and purged those bitches from Raquel's conscience. Raquel's Burberry plaid print bags finally came into view: one large roller suitcase and the two medium-sized bags she had packed earlier that same morning. An airport security guard, commencing his tour of the area, noticed the curious bags, and the surprisingly young-looking woman carrying them.

"Those are beautiful suitcases, miss," the security guard called out to Raquel as she swung one bag over her shoulder.

Shit, she thought. A *rent-a-cop*. Raquel inhaled quickly and turned towards the security guard's direction with a wide, fake smile on her face. "Oh! Why, thank you! They were a gift."

"Oh really?" The security guard was grinning at her. "A beautiful lady like you shouldn't carry heavy gifts like these all by herself."

Raquel sighed to herself and studied the flirtatious guard. He was a tall man who looked to be in his late forties, with a clean face and a wide body. He wore the typical guard's uniform: navy-blue buttoned shirt with a pleated pair of pants, which sloppily fell over a pair of black, unpolished shoes. His badge was a dull gold metal plate that pierced into an undeveloped chest, and his waist was large enough for Raquel to use as a table for her luggage. He saw her waiting for her luggage from afar and saw this as an opportunity to strike a conversation with her.

"Oh, no, thank you, sir. I'm fine by myself."

"You sure? I would be more than happy to help."

"No, no. It's fine. I can manage." Raquel walked toward the exit that was situated on the far end of the hallway. She grumbled when she realized that the security guard was following her. She could hear his heavy footsteps crash onto the floor and could almost feel his weight crush the earth that lay underneath him. Raquel stopped walking, and she turned to the guard. "I'm sorry, what was your name again?"

"Giovanni. What's your name?"

"Giovanni! Nice name! Stay the hell away from me." Raquel turned on her heel and walked away, snickering to herself. Giovanni scratched his chin and stuck out his middle finger at Raquel. Two seconds later, she turned around and glared at Giovanni. He quickly spun around on his heel once her furious eyes met his and tripped over a nearby garbage pail that halted his nervous retreat. Raquel laughed hysterically when the clang of the trash bin robbed the security guard of his balance.

"Very graceful, Gio!"

Raquel quieted herself when she remembered to contact Luis when she landed in the city. She released her luggage from her grip and fumbled through her purse looking for pocket change. It was filled with mints, ibuprofen, Chanel perfume, rosary beads, a prayer to Saint Philomena, a handkerchief, and a pocket Bible. Despite the "nun's purse," as her son often joked, she managed to fish out enough change to make a phone call. She grabbed her luggage and walked over to a pay phone that sat alone on a wall next to a restroom. Raquel pulled out the handkerchief from her purse and wrapped it around her hand. She then picked up the phone with her swathed hand and dialed Luis's number. The phone rang a few times, and Raquel smiled when she heard her son's voice.

"Luis! Hey! It's *tu madre* . . . uh huh . . . yeah, the flight was okay—if anything, my ass is sore . . . yeah . . . no, I ate on the plane already, so don't cook for me . . . yeah, so how's Rosa? Has she rested? Good, good, and how's my little *nina* doing? She's just staring, huh?" Raquel snickered. "Babies will do that for a while . . . okay, I have to hurry so I can see her for myself. So listen, I'll be there soon. All I need to do is hail a cab and . . . no, no, I don't need someone to pick me up, I told you that back in Spain . . . ugh, you sound like your father just now."

Raquel laughed and glanced at her watch. "Listen, women don't need men for everything . . . yeah, yeah, whatever . . . I'll be fine . . . God help you, you worry too much." Raquel giggled. "Listen, I have to run, I'll see you soon okay? I love you too . . . okay, *adios.*"

Raquel hung up the phone and grabbed her luggage. She walked down the long hallway and made her way outside. The night air welcomed her with open arms, and she felt the same cool breeze that touched her face inside the terminal. She glanced in both directions and saw a bellhop hailing taxis for other visitors. He was the polar opposite of Giovanni; the royal-blue uniform that covered his body failed to cover his lanky frame. She walked up to him and gently tapped him on his shoulder.

"Hi there," Raquel greeted the bellhop. "Would you mind if you helped me carry this luggage? I really appreciate it!"

"Not at all," the bellhop answered. "Shall I hail you a cab?"

"That would be very helpful, thank you!"

"Not a problem." The bellhop smiled and grabbed the luggage. Raquel smirked and followed him to the curb. He raised his arm, and soon a yellow taxi cab pulled to where Raquel was standing. She wondered how he could lift his arm with very little muscle attached to his bone but brushed the thought aside when he dragged the luggage to the trunk of the car. When the bags were loaded, she dug her hand into her purse and pulled out a fifty-dollar bill for the bellhop. "Thank you," he said, hardly raising an eyebrow at the hefty tip he had just accepted. Raquel nodded politely and stepped into the cab. She gave the driver Luis's address and the cab sped off into the labyrinth of the city. The bellhop kept his stare on the vehicle until it disappeared from his sight.

*   *   *

Raquel stared out of the window and daydreamed for an hour about Zephyr until she recognized the land surrounding the estate. The taxi pulled up to a large silver gate, with a guard post situated on both sides. The security guard, much unlike Giovanni, was a rather large man with an athletic build and a sullen face. He wore a black uniform housing no badges or any other form of identification, and Raquel noticed the Kevlar vest hugging his muscular frame. His face was as dark as night, and his eyes were intimidating and narrow. Raquel was too excited to notice the burly man when he approached the window, and she showed no fear when he opened his mouth to speak.

"Good morning." The guard spoke in a baritone voice. "Are you Ms. Estrada?"

"Yes, I'm Zephyr's grandmother." Raquel exhibited her pride in her title.

"We were expecting you. Please go on ahead."

"Thank you."

The guard nodded and walked back to the booth. He couldn't help smiling at Raquel's declaration of her position; nevertheless, he maintained composure and pressed a button hidden underneath his desk. The large ornate gate slid open and the taxi drove through the serpentine driveway. Trees and open fields decorated the area surrounding the Estrada estate, and the sun threw its curtains upon the courtyard. Raquel's eyes were graced with the image of two guards performing their rounds, both men having taut leather leashes clamped to the collars of two German shepherd dogs. This view gave Raquel a premonition of Zephyr playing with a puppy of her own, laughing and giggling as the soft fur tickled her dimpled cheeks.

Raquel saw her immediate family waving joyously at the yellow taxi. She waved back at them, while motioning her eyes towards the tiny figure of Zephyr swaddling in her mother's arms. Her mouth widened when she saw Zephyr's finger grasp the blanket, and she unconsciously paid the driver his fare. The driver nodded and stepped out of the car. It was the first time Raquel had noticed his lanky frame and melancholic face, the result of chauffeuring dozens of people every day. He never looked at her face when he opened the door for Raquel, nor did he welcome her to her destination with a smile. She reached into her purse and dug out another bill for him. The driver felt her delicate hand shove down his beige jacket and land an extra twenty-dollar bill into his breast pocket. Raquel took no notice of the smiling driver when the Estrada family approached her.

"Oh, my boy! It's been too long! Rosa! You look so beautiful!" Raquel hugged and kissed them both. "Oh, God . . . this must be Zephyr!"

"Yeah," Rosa giggled. "This is our little *nina*." Rosa placed the baby into Raquel's arms.

"Hi, sweetie! How are you? I'm your grandmamma. You look so pretty today!"

Zephyr stared at her grandmother.

"Oh! Look how her eyes sparkle! They're gorgeous!"

Luis traced Zephyr's face with his fingertip. "They have a rare color. The doctor said that it was natural and that we shouldn't worry."

"Well, I think they are just beautiful. Don't you agree, little one?"

Zephyr kicked her feet. Her eyes exhibited a friendly glow whenever Raquel tickled her cheeks.

"We better get inside," Luis started. "It's getting a little chilly." He motioned everyone towards the front door to the large home that towered over them. "I would die if Zephyr coughed."

"Don't be silly, she's a strong woman." Raquel rocked her as they all entered the mansion. "By the way, I haven't seen Pedro. Is he around?"

"He left for somewhere," Rosa sighed, "probably to shoot pool with his friends."

"I swear, that boy lives for the unorthodox. Tough luck, he'll just get a slap from me later on." Raquel laughed. "Anyways, come on, Zephyr. We'll show your big brother what he's missing."

"I'll have someone bring your luggage to the guest room. Dinner will be at six." Luis opened the door for the women before him.

"Okay," Raquel replied, "and Luis?"

"Yes?"

"You did a good job. I'm proud of you."

Luis kissed his mother's cheek. "Gracias, *Mami*."

III

Pool halls have the curious tendency of being situated in the darkest crevices of any city. Cars that visit these lonely edifices are crookedly parked because the drivers are usually too inebriated to coordinate themselves or the machinery they operate. These same drunken dregs hobble their way across the lot and somehow succeed in entering the pool hall, only to stagger in front of the bar and order a tall glass of chilled lager. The cigarette smoke permeates through the air and quickly replaces any faint trace of pure, unaltered oxygen, while the tenants vainly light another scented candle to mask the stench. Truckers who have not bathed in days would stretch over the pool table and attempt to sink that last shot. The sounds of their perspiration dripping form their armpits create a solemn melody that is only understood by those who shared its appreciation and practice. Belching, cursing, and sweating only add to the symphony that play in the hall's orchestra. The only dim iota of delicate femininity remains inside the bodies of the bartenders—girls still in their early twenties trudging through community college and trying to mix a daiquiri for intoxicated Neanderthals. The job is manageable until one of the derelicts strives to flirt with one of the bartenders. This usually results in the bouncer dragging the poor bum away from the comforts of his debauchery and into the discomfort of the unpaved gravel.

This was the second home of Pedro Estrada.

He maintained himself in a private room situated in a corner away from everyone else. He paced the billiards table in front of him, pondering his next movements like a Roman general. The cue balls were set in the triangle, ready to be released from their wooden binds.

Pedro left the table as is and walked over to the bar to grab a cool beer. The bartenders obliged to the underaged rebel, not because of his looks but because of the name that preceded his request. He often flaunted his surname to get whatever he wanted. "No one refuses an Estrada," he told the nervous girls. When he received his drink, he took a few sips as he walked back to his private corner. Pedro allowed the foam to dance on his upper lip until he wiped it with his sleeve. He wore a simple white dress shirt with baggy blue jeans, torn and ripped in numerable places. His shoes were brown as a result of dirt, not of color. His hair was thrown across his face in a lazy manner, and he showed his apathy for the conventional in the way he carried himself. He placed his drink onto a nearby table, turned around, and gently lifted the triangle off of the pool table. After throwing it disgracefully on the floor, he took the white, unmarked cue ball and set it on the table in front of the colored cue balls. He grabbed his cue stick and slid the long heavy wood between his fingers. With precision—and arrogance—Pedro slid the cue stick back and struck the white ball with a violent thrust, grunting as the balls spread in a wide arc.

"Looks like you got a solid three and a striped nine in."

Pedro looked up and saw a tall, slender figure in a cheap trench coat standing at the far end of the pool table. His eyes were less menacing than Pedro but housed more of a madness and sick anxiety. He wore a winter cap that covered his head, shaved bald in order to avoid aesthetic attention. He scoured the table and directed his gaze at Pedro.

"Hey, Slim. Just my luck too. I wanted to get them all in." Pedro chuckled.

"Well, if you did that, you'd lose the game. The eight ball's what counts. Get that in on your first try and you are God."

"Yeah, I know." Pedro carelessly threw the cue stick on the table and sighed. Slim took off his trench coat and tossed it on a nearby chair. He rubbed his hands together and licked his lips.

"So," Slim started, "how are you doing?"

"Same. Nothing new. You?"

Slim picked up a cue stick that lay suspended on the far wall. He bounced it in his hand repeatedly, and then he put it back. "Nothing to report . . . this is about twenty ounces."

"You know, those things already have the weight stamped on the sides. Why measure them like a jackass?"

"Because being a jackass is better than being naive. I call solids." Slim positioned the cue stick in his signature grip and lightly struck it against the white ball. It rolled down the pool table and tapped a solid three into the side pocket. "Oh, by the way," Slim said as he paced around the table, "I saw your grandmother today."

"Oh. And?"

"She's a milf."

"Besides that, you freak." Pedro rolled his eyes.

"That's all I wanted to say. Did you see her yet?"

"I will. Eventually. You saw her at your job?"

"Yup. She seemed happy. Gave me a nice tip." Slim sunk a solid fifteen.

"Because of my sister. That's why she's happy."

"Zephyr, right?"

"Yeah."

"Weird name."

"I know."

Slim positioned himself behind the eleven ball, but accidentally tapped the stick against the white ball. "Fuck. Scratch. Your turn."

Pedro grabbed his cue stick and walked around the table. He positioned himself behind the white ball and slid the stick back and forth between the bridge he had created with his hand. He struck it and sunk a striped fourteen in the left corner pocket. "I don't even know what the hell it means."

Slim brought back two boxes of nachos and set it on the table. "It's Greek mythology. Zephyr was one of the gods of wind. It was supposed to be the calm and peaceful breeze, wipe the sweat from your brow, shit like that."

"I never knew my mother was into that shit."

"It's popular."

"Whatever." Pedro threw the stick on the pool table and sat at his corner table to enjoy his beer.

"What's up your ass tonight?" Slim noticed Pedro's surly mood.

"Nothing."

"Aww, c'mon. I'm your boy. Talk to me." Slim smirked as he took a bite of the salty, crunchy nacho. "Want a beer? I have my fake ID with me."

"I'm worried that my father may not give me control of the family business."

Slim laughed. "And who's he gonna give it to? Zephyr?"

"Who knows? Maybe . . ."

"She can barely talk, and her best attribute is shitting in her diaper. The fuck are you worried about?"

Pedro chuckled. "True."

"Listen, in three more years, you'll be able to take over the business." Slim swallowed a mouthful of nachos and lightly burped. "If you still feel threatened by a toddler playing with Barbie dolls, you can always get rid of her."

Pedro choked on his own saliva. "Get rid of her? What are you talking about?"

"I mean kill her." Slim showed no humor on his face.

"What the fuck . . . I can't kill my own fucking sister!"

"Yes, you can. It's obvious that you don't like her, so why not make it easy for yourself?"

"No! Forget it! Drop the topic!"

"It's simple—just pull the trigger. Actually, no . . . smothering will be much easier."

"Shut up—"

"Although you will have to deal with your parents somehow—"

"I said shut the fuck up!"

Slim stared at the crimson-flushed face of his friend. He was breathing hard and fast, and his eyes were shining with anger and fear. "Just think about it," said Slim. "And take your time. You *do* have three years. If you get the business, great, we can pretend that this conversation never happened. If not, well . . . faking amnesia won't be the best thing." Slim grabbed his trench coat and started walking toward the door that led to the main billiards area. "And don't worry," he continued. "You don't have to do this alone."

Slim left the room whistling and humming. Pedro remained still and kept his eyes on the empty mug in front of him.

"Take your time, Pedro," Slim mumbled under his breath as he strode outside the pool hall. He made his way down the narrow alleys; their only source of light was the frigid, ominous moon that descended its veil across the horizon. Those who were daring enough to gaze at its iridescent glow surrendered their spirits to the comforting embrace of the night and released themselves into her treacherous bosom. The night sky brought an arrogant, almost sadistic comfort to Slim. He rarely ventured out into the public during the daytime; part of this habit was attributed to his lust for the clandestine and the dark, the other part he attributed to his love for the Forty-Second Street Gang.

When he first met Pedro as a freshman in high school, Slim had already been a gang member for three years. The gang provided Slim with the comfort and security of brutality and egoism. This was Slim's family, his household, and they, in return, treated him as such. His brothers were men who would stalk a lone woman, grab her, and take turns raping her in an alley. His source of income came from corner stores, which he and his brothers would often rob. Witnesses were scarce in such activities, but they shared the common characteristics of disappearance, dumbness, or death. Slim's bedroom was an abandoned apartment that served as his gang's headquarters. It also doubled as a guest house for the crack addicts and desperate prostitutes, the latter being those who were "bugged." The shroud of chaos and testosterone-driven depravity was his shelter.

Guillermo Nunez was headed for home.

He crossed the street and reached into his trench coat for a cigarette. He managed to fish one out and shoved the stick into his mouth with disdain. He patted down his torso for a lighter, but the small metallic square never appeared to his touch. He thought about asking one of the local heads for a lighter, but they would probably plead him to death for a few bucks, and he did not want to be bothered with those begging fucks.

"Shit, where is it?" He was cursing under his breath as he kept walking. The cold air invading his tobacco-rich lungs were provoking him. Slim looked onward and saw a handful of homeless people crowded around a flaming barrel. Slim approached them and held the cigarette next to the pitiful flame. He held it there until he produced a burn on his Marlboro.

"Ex-excuse me. Do you have a dollar on you?"

He glanced away from the flame and saw a young girl who looked to be in her late toddler years. She wore a pair of blue jeans with a dirty brown fade running down her shins and a large yellow sweatshirt covered by a pitiful wool overcoat that had holes in the lapels. Her face was smudged with car exhaust and God knows what else. Her hair had not been washed in what seemed like years, and Slim crinkled his nose when he inhaled the air around her. Her eyes were a brilliant light-brown, and it was the one redeeming quality she had that whispered remnants of a past beauty.

"Fuck off." Slim took in a big puff and started to walk away.

"Please . . . j-just one dollar. We haven't eaten for days." The homeless girl followed him for a few steps. Slim saw her shadow creep in front of him. He whipped around and clasped his hand around her neck. He tightened his grip until his long fingernails burrowed into her filthy, crusty skin. She immediately grabbed his hands, but she could not pry them loose. The homeless men heard her faint yelp. The malnutrition made them weak, and they could do nothing but stand by with fear.

"I-I'm sorry!" She managed to sputter out a few choked words. Slim grinned at her, his white teeth blinding her tired eyes.

"What's your name?"

The girl couldn't breathe, and she felt her body turn numb. Slim shook her head and jerked her out of her trance.

"I said, 'What's your name?'"

"R-Rebecca," she choked out.

"R-R-Rebecca, is it? Hold old are you? Five? Six maybe? If you want money, at least offer to suck my cock. The way you're choking, it seems like you'll be good at it. Stop fucking begging for free shit! You got that?"

Rebecca let her tears pour down her mud-laden cheeks and land on Slim's hot hands.

"Stop fucking crying! I asked you a question! Do you fucking understand me?!"

Rebecca summoned her remaining strength to nod.

"Good. Now get the fuck outta my sight!" He threw her to the ground and watched her face smack the pavement and bust her lip wide open. One of the homeless men rushed over with godlike speed to help her up. Slim turned around and puffed on his cigarette.

"I hope you cook in hell for this!" The homeless man shouted at Slim with anger in his eyes.

"Whatever." Slim walked off and threw the butt of the cigarette away. The homeless man helped held Rebecca close as she cried in his arms. She felt a strange comfort in his arms, but she welcomed it wholeheartedly.

"Things will get better," he said. "I promise. Let's get you warmed up over here. I'll give you some of my food I've been saving up."

They both walked together, with Rebecca still huddled in the stranger's arms. The memory of Slim's face still burned in her mind, but the calm look in the homeless man's eyes relaxed her, and she buried her face closer into his chest.

"Thanks . . . mister," Rebecca replied.

*   *   *

Pedro sat alone, staring at the empty box of nachos that stood before his blank eyes. He pondered Slim's twisted suggestion since he had left, weighing the benefits and the consequences back and forth. His oscillation resulted in a conversation he was having with his conscience.

"You don't like your sister. You're afraid," it said. "Actually, no—you're terrified that your father would hand over the business to Zephyr."

"But why the jealousy?" Pedro replied. "Seriously, who doesn't give the baby of the family the most attention? Why should my family be any different?"

"Oh, stop trying to rationalize this. Did you see the way your father looked at her? The way he stared in those freakish eyes? Just think: If Zephyr hadn't been born, Daddy dearest would've considered you for the top slot. But oh no, they *had* to have another child."

"Why did Mom and Dad decide to have another child? Wasn't I enough? Why did Slim tell me those things?"

"As if killing your sister never crossed your mind before? You enjoyed it when Slim told you to smother that bitch. You just reacted the way you did out of that 'It's the wrong thing to do' bullshit."

"No! It's wrong! Mom and Dad would be devastated."

"They'll get over it. Or you can just kill them and not worry about it."

"His allies would come after me . . . every gang and hit man . . . Vlad . . ."

"Gonna have to do it somehow, Mister Pedro."

"Somehow," Pedro echoed those words. "No. Shut up. They're good parents. They love me. I had a happy childhood. Why bite the hand that feeds you?"

"Because the hand that once fed you now wants to feed someone else," his conscience replied.

Suddenly, Pedro's thoughts were inhabited by Slim's voice. That demonic sound gave Pedro comfort, and he felt no fear in accepting it. He was cushioned by the deceit and satanic speech that sounded throughout his mind. This gave Pedro a shameful passion that he tried not to douse. He blinked a few times and shook his head, but the idea still lay buried in his mind.

Pedro had to get out. He had to escape. He made his way through the crowds of drunks and smoke, and strode outside. He did not feel like expressing any love, especially if he was considering the murder of his family. But it was wrong. Very wrong. Breaking the Fourth Commandment times one hundred. Pedro decided to purge that idea from his head and look forward to the future. Luis Estrada would hand the business to him when he retired. Tradition rules all.

He had to, no matter what. Pedro felt satisfied with his conclusion, and he took out his keys to unlock the lone Porsche that sat in the parking lot. He entered the dark red car, turned on the radio, and set the dial to the Latino station. Joe Arroyo was blasting through his speakers. Perfect, something to concentrate on. Pedro drove off and kicked a cloud of dust behind him.

He secretly wished that the dust was his conscience.

IV

Rosa sat in the foyer and anxiously waited for Pedro to return. She cast repeated glances out of the window that pointed towards the guard's gate. She wore a simple black Versace dress with a fold of extra fabric elegantly draped across her neck, with matching black diamond earrings and a dark pair of four-inch heels. Her makeup was minimalistic yet striking enough to garner attention from Luis, who delighted Rosa with his awestruck gaze. She insisted on dressing up for the family dinner with Raquel, despite the matriarch's protests and assurances. Rosa was indeed a rare woman who displayed a modest but breathtaking grasp of feminine beauty. Tonight, however, she experienced a numbing pain of concern and worry. Her maternal instincts guided her to Pedro's welfare, but at least some of her worry was extinguished when she saw the red Porsche pull past the guard's gate. As soon as the car was in the driveway, Pedro stepped out of the car and showed a semi-satisfied look on his face. He walked up the sidewalk and pushed open the front door. He entered and saw his mother staring at the floor in a contemplative mood.

"Hey. Sorry, I'm late." Pedro took off his coat and threw it on a nearby chair.

"No problem." Rosa was still lost in thought.

"What's wrong?" Pedro was worried that Rosa somehow read his thoughts, but she remained silent. "You okay, *Mami*? What's the matter?"

"I'm worried about you, son."

"About what?"

"I don't know. I just feel something is upsetting you."

Pedro did his best to conceal his previous meditation. "No . . . nothing's upsetting me."

Rosa looked up at him and grabbed his hand. "Pedro. I know that things have been stressful lately, with Zephyr being born and your grandmother staying with us. So much to prepare for and so little time." Rosa sighed lightly. "I'm proud of you for keeping your reserve and for maintaining yourself. I think that's what we all need . . . and I know that you've been thinking and wondering lately. I don't know what it is, and you don't have to tell me, but I'm here for you. Myself, your father, your grandmother, and even your little sister—we're all here for you. We love you . . . I love you."

Pedro let his mother's hand fall to her lap as he walked away. Rosa watched him back away from her, staring at her eyes the entire time until he disappeared up the staircase. She breathed a long, melancholic sigh and rose from her seat. She listened to the clicks of her heels hitting the tile as she walked to the dining room where the rest of the Estrada family had been located. She took special care to wipe a small tear from her eye before she entered.

*   *   *

Rosa calmly walked into the bustling dining hall after she had succeeded in collecting the remainder of her demeanor. A gleaming silver chandelier (which had definitely reminded her of Zephyr's eyes) hung from the ceiling and blasted its rays out onto the pure white walls and the equally brilliant tablecloth. In each corner lay a marble statue of small angels with folded hands in prayer. Atop their heads were small platforms upon which a small green plant stood. A large case housed the fine china, or at least it used to contain them. They were sprawled all over the table and added such glamour to the already joyful room.

She surveyed the dining table and took notice of each respective family member: Luis was busy polishing the silverware with a large grin on his face, priming the tools for the upcoming feast. Raquel played the part of a clown for baby Zephyr, making silly faces and occasionally blowing against her small stomach. Zephyr's eyes were broad and revealing; each flash of her big silvers satisfied Raquel in her humorous endeavors. Pedro seemed to be in a cheery mood. Rosa swore to God that she caught a glimpse of a smirk that appeared on his face, but it had disappeared as quickly as it had shown itself. *A brief moment of glory*, Rosa thought. *I'll take it.*

The couple of bodyguards that decorated the perimeter of the dining table also took notice of the joy Zephyr exhibited throughout the room and could not help but feel devoted to the wonder and innocence of the newest member of the Estrada family. They watched as Raquel stood the chubby infant on her legs and bounced her gently on her grandmother's hips. Zephyr's little noises were euphoric and uplifting and threw a sense of calm into the guards' hearts.

When the kitchen doors opened, the family turned their heads to greet the plethora of chefs and kitchen aids bearing gifts of fine cuisine. The family decided to head straight to the main course: baked ham battered in a sauce that Raquel insisted on making herself, followed by a fresh salad and spiced rice. An inviting dessert was placed on one of the angel tables. Luis tried to catch a glimpse of the sweet-smelling treat, but Raquel gave him a look that made him shrink back to his meal. He shyly offered his mother a helping of some rare brands of wine and other exotic liquors. She pointed her finger first at her eyes and then at his face.

Zephyr was content with a bottle of sweet milk given to her by Raquel. At one point, Raquel kissed Zephyr on her tiny round cheeks while she was sucking on her bottle, and she spat the liquid out of her mouth. "I guess we won't do that again, *nina*," Raquel joked. She wiped Zephyr's mouth with a napkin, using gentle dabs so as not to stain her innocent beauty.

After they dined, the family ventured into the den, where Rosa took over entertaining Zephyr while Raquel entertained everyone else with stories of Luis when he was a baby. Luis sat in his seat and blushed, while Rosa laughed and teased her husband. Pedro sat quietly and listened to the stories with minor interest.

"And did you know," Raquel continued, "that when Luis was five, he lit a match and burned a hole through the carpet?"

"Your son failed to tell me that little misdeed." Rosa chuckled. "I never knew how much of a little devil you were! Any other adventures you want to tell me about, Mr. Estrada?"

"You mean misadventures," Luis answered. "I still feel that sting on my rear to this day."

"Yeah, Manny smacked that boy's behind so bad that he had to sleep on his stomach that same night!" Raquel giggled as she sipped a glass of red wine.

One of the bodyguards chuckled. Luis took notice and tuned to look at him. The guard quickly regained composure. "See? You even have him laughing at me. Thanks, Ma."

"Sue me," Raquel playfully retorted. "Everyone needs to see the hidden side of the great Don Luis."

"No they don't! I would hate for them to think that their employer is a former arsonist."

"I dunno, sweetie." Rosa rocked a sleepy Zephyr in her arms. "I don't feel like fire-proofing this house."

"See what you did now? Now my own wife is gonna sleep with a fire extinguisher next to her bed." Luis laughed and sat back in his silken chair. He swirled a glass of chardonnay and crossed his legs. "I'll be honest though—I miss Dad."

"Yeah, I miss him too," Raquel sighed. "Although I am enjoying life without his stubbornness. God, there were times when I wanted to slap him until his hair fell off."

"He was the one who knew that Luis and I would get engaged, right?" Rosa asked. "I'll admit that it creeped me out a bit when he told me."

Raquel chuckled. "Oh, he always had a sixth sense about things. Like the time I found out I was pregnant with Luis. He came into our bedroom and gave me the biggest hug I had ever felt." Raquel scooted over to Zephyr, who was dozing off in Rosa's arms, and covered her ears. "The jerk almost flattened my boobs with those bear arms of his," she whispered. "Then he stared into my eyes, you know, like he was one of those pretty boys on the *telenovelas*, and he said, 'I can't wait to be a father! I love you so much!' Then I said, 'Bullshit, how did you know?'"

Luis and Rosa both laughed, along with the eavesdropping bodyguards. Rosa looked down at Zephyr, who was sound asleep.

"I wonder if this little one has the same gift." Rosa brushed the area around her daughter's eyes with the tip of her finger. Luis turned to Rosa and set the empty glass on the end table.

"Maybe she does . . . is she asleep?"

"Yeah, I think Grandma filled up her little tummy so much that it just knocked her out."

Raquel smiled. "Good. That means she's satisfied. No anorexic babies allowed." She combed her fingers through her long hair and closed her eyes. "I think we should follow her lead and get some rest."

Luis wiped his mouth with a silk napkin. "Sounds like a good idea to me. We all need our beauty sleep . . . not that you two need it, you both have enough beauty for the whole world."

"You taught him well, Rosa."

"*Gracias, Señora* Estrada."

The Estradas stood up and walked toward the staircase. Raquel ascended them with ease and grace that was becoming of her enormous vitality. Pedro followed after she had disappeared into her guest room.

"You've been quiet all night, son." Luis patted Pedro on his back and followed him upstairs.

"Yeah, I'm fine. Just been listening to Grandma's stories. That's all."

"Oh, all right. Did you enjoy them?"

"Yeah, you were a hilarious kid, Dad." Pedro rolled his eyes as he continued up the stairs.

"Well, now you know it runs in the family."

"Sure do. Anyways, g'night, Dad."

"Okay . . . night, son."

Pedro smiled and entered his dark room. He closed the door behind him and locked it. The walls were filled with posters of his favorite punk rock band, Mist, and semi-nude posters of his favorite actresses. His desk was a complete mess filled with small textbooks and pieces of loose-leaf paper. He had wood floors that squeaked with each step he took in certain spots. On his nightstand were a red boom box and a picture of him and his family. His father had his arm around him on one side and his mother kissed his cheek on the other. It was a two-year-old photo where Pedro actually looked happy.

He reached underneath his bed and pulled out a tan-colored box. He took off its lid and lifted a full bottle of cognac. He grabbed the flute glass next to it and poured himself a drink. He raised it in the air and made a toast to himself.

"A toast—may the business be passed on to its rightful heir."

Pedro swallowed the drink whole and allowed the liquor to warm his heart along with the ambition laid in it. After he had drunk its last drop, he plopped down on his bed and let his dreams twist and soar in front of his eyes.

Zephyr's nursery was a medium-sized bedroom whose walls heralded the hues of soft pink lilacs and garnet rose petals. Pictures of delicate ballerinas dressed in snowy tutus danced and leaped over a bookcase filled with bedtime stories waiting to be read to the sleeping infant. She had already been placed in a crib filled with sheets softer than clouds and a short quilt wrapped around her tiny body. It had a white center trimmed with a pink border, with little laughing bears playing inside each stitched square. Inside Zephyr's crib lay a large brown teddy bear that measured equally to Zephyr's body. He had a large nose in the shape of a heart and a smiling expression whose warmth matched the softness of his curly fur. The crib itself was painted white, which meshed in well with the entire background of the room. Zephyr's peaceful slumber also blended into the serene environment, which attributed its qualities to the Estrada daughter's demeanor.

"Is she still asleep?" Luis whispered in Rosa's ear.

"Yeah, just like an angel. Isn't she beautiful?"

"Like her mother." Luis wrapped his arms around Rosa's body and kissed her gently on her neck.

"Oh, stop." Rosa giggled and turned around to meet her husband's eyes. They kissed in the only way passionate lovers kiss—delicate, but with a wide flame. Their eyes closed, and Luis could almost feel her heart drum against his broad chest, and she felt the muscles lace across his back. She sighed deeply and pulled away from her husband. Luis noticed a sad expression on her face.

"What's wrong? Is something bothering you?"

"Nothing . . . I'm just worried. That's all."

"About what? Whatever it is, you know I'll take care of it."

Rosa slowly walked to the edge of a rocking chair that sat next to Zephyr's crib and rested her body in it. "Oh no, it's nothing that has to do with *that*. It's just Pedro lately has been . . . I don't know."

Luis walked over to Rosa and knelt down in front of her. "Yeah . . . I know. He seemed to be a little bit distant today. I noticed it too." Luis sighed and lowered his head. "I think he realizes that Passage is coming up in just a few years, and he's wondering what's going to happen with this business I just so happen to love and cherish."

"And we are not, by any way, being sarcastic."

"Oh no. Not at all. I enjoy what I do." Luis sighed. "If it were up to me, I would hand over the business to someone who enjoys pain and suffering."

"Oh, don't say that. Good things always come in times of bad."

"Like what? So many people have died I'm sure my soul is as black as night, and I lost my father, all because of this business."

"But if you never had this business going, no one would be here. We would never have had Pedro or Zephyr, and . . . I would be unhappy."

Luis looked at Rosa and saw the sincerity flash in her eyes. "I would be unhappy too. I . . . I just feel that Pedro is asking for something that is not worth asking for."

"I know. That's how I feel too. But he's strong and responsible. If you can handle it, so can he."

"Maybe." Luis rubbed his eyes. He felt so mentally tired. "Your turn—why are you worried?"

Rosa stroked Luis's hand back and forth. "It's just sometimes I wish he would just . . . talk to me. I tell him that he can come to me about anything, but he never does. Then I think, 'Well, maybe he just wants to be left alone for a while.' But then, I don't want him to think that we're abandoning him either. I just hate that feeling of . . .

you know . . . being a bad parent. Like tonight, he came home from God knows where, and I couldn't even ask where he's been."

Luis reached over and held Rosa's hand in his. Her finger was married to a large pink stone filled with light and strength. He burrowed his eyes in hers and felt the concern stream through his body. "Don't think like that. You're not a bad parent. Pedro's just going through that phase that all teenagers go through. He'll get over it soon, believe me. But whatever you do, don't think that you're doing a horrible job as a mother." Luis kept his stare on Rosa, and she half-smiled at him. "If I had any inkling of you being a bad parent, I would never have proposed to you years ago."

Rosa read her husband's eyes and noticed the conviction behind them. "You're so good to me. I needed to hear that."

Luis kissed her hand softly. "I love you, my sweet rose, no matter how many times you tease me about my child years."

Rosa laughed. "I wasn't teasing you. I was just speaking the truth. You are a little demon."

"You mean *was*."

"No . . . I had it right the first time. Remember when we were sixteen? When you kissed me?"

"Oh, here it comes . . ." Luis rolled his eyes and chuckled.

"And where did we happen to be, oh loving and angelic husband of mine?"

"In my mother's house."

"Where in her house?"

"On her bed."

"Exactly," Rosa playfully asserted. "On her king-sized bed!"

"I distinctly remember you not complaining either."

"No . . ." Rosa reached over and turned off the lamp sitting next to her seat. "I never did."

Luis stood up and brought Rosa out of her chair. They embodied the two teenage silhouettes and danced slowly in their nostalgic waltz. Luis inhaled the perfume on Rosa's neck and buried his head in it.

"Not complaining now?" he asked.

"Never."

"Just don't tell my mother what we did in her bed, okay?"

"Behave and maybe I'll keep quiet."

"You strike a hard bargain . . . but you have a deal." Luis smiled and looked up at the ceiling. He lost himself in his thoughts and turned his gaze on Rosa. "You know what scares me?"

"Failure, snakes, and ringworm. Why?"

"Besides that," Luis said. "Zephyr's going to be beautiful. That scares me."

"Well, yeah!" Rosa rolled her eyes at Luis and laughed. "She'll be fine if you're worried about boyfriends. I know you'll be there to interview each and every one of them."

"You're sounding like my mother now."

"Good, I'm glad. Don't worry, sweetie. I'll personally make sure that she learns how to defend herself. I promise."

"Okay . . ." Luis felt comforted by Rosa's words.

"Now if only I had someone to go to bed with tonight. Hmmm . . . what shall I do?"

Luis chuckled and held Rosa closer to his body. They exited Zephyr's bedroom and turned off the light. The couple walked across the hallway and entered their own bedroom. It boasted a modern vibe, with a broad wooden headboard that stretched about seven feet wide. It was a comfortable king-sized bed, which was especially needed because Rosa had a tendency to roll about until she found a satisfied sleeping position. A nightstand with a small white lamp stood on both sides of the bed. Of course, their bedroom absolutely had to have a walk-in closet where Rosa could store her shoes and where Luis could hang his suits. This was their favorite domain. For one, they could slumber away their anxieties. For the other, the most important other, was that they could enjoy the pleasure of each other's company.

Rosa felt his heart beat against her breast and was warmed by its rhythm. She closed her eyes as he let the charm of his hands massage her into the bed that lay next to them. When her eyes opened, Rosa saw the top of her husband's naked body glide across her body, with her nails clenched around the lining of his tattoo. It was a large pair of angel's wings that decorated each shoulder blade with a tiny halo that settled in between them. It was inked in shrouds of black that refused to submit to the fingers of time. Rosa always wondered about the strange longevity that befell Luis's body. He was in his forties, but his muscular body told his age otherwise. After seeing Raquel again, Rosa concluded that it was simply a result of great genetics. When he sat up, she marveled at the bright shimmer in his eyes more than any other part of his body. A glint of joy finally set in the often-melancholic eyes of the Don, and she noticed her lips widened in a smile. She kissed his neck and rested her neck in his and prayed that her tired husband would keep her held in his arms forever.

V

The next three weeks for the Estrada family flew by in a euphoric blur. Each day began with Raquel waking up earlier than anyone else, usually around four in the morning, and making her way to the kitchen. The chefs and maids would enter the area two hours later to begin preparations for breakfast, but Raquel would shoo them away and proclaim, "You all have the day off! Go back to bed!" They continued this ritual for two more days until Luis finally told them to take off the rest of the month. The workers nodded to him and walked away with large grins on their faces.

Raquel was happy that she was able to cook for her family, especially for Zephyr, who was fed pureed bananas and applesauce made straight from her grandmother's hands. The Estrada matriarch would emerge from the kitchen on two occasions: to feed the entire household and to tickle Zephyr's belly for a few cherished seconds. The toothless smile that shown on her granddaughter's face gave her the joy needed to continue playing chef and also gave Raquel a way to apologize to Zephyr for waking her up at odd hours in the morning. Zephyr was placed in a high-chair so that she could observe the magical creations that her grandmother was performing for her and the family. Her bright silvery eyes swept the stove and the numerous culinary products that decorated Raquel's domain. On one occasion, Raquel left her boiling pots and simmering pans and walked over to the large freezer door that lay atop the metallic refrigerator. She opened the door and pulled out a tub of rainbow-colored sherbet. She closed the door and set the tub on the table next to Zephyr's chair. Raquel dug out a large spoon and tore off the top with her manicured fingers. Zephyr watched as the spoon was shoved into the thick frosty cream. The curious infant's eyes widened as Raquel placed the spoon filled with a thin layer of sherbet closer to Zephyr's mouth. She obliged entry and opened her soft mouth. She sucked on the cold, fruitful cream and looked down at her tiny feet. She darted her head up at Raquel and kicked her feet playfully against the high-chair's bottom while crying out for more of Raquel's treat.

"We'll keep this between you and me, okay, sweetie?" Raquel rubbed her nose against Zephyr's and gave her one more spoonful of rainbow sherbet.

Later that morning, Luis walked with Rosa downstairs and met Raquel and Zephyr in the kitchen. He kissed his smiling daughter on her tiny round cheek, and Raquel secretly prayed that he would not smell any trace of sherbet in her breath. When he walked away to kiss his mother on the cheek, she felt a wind of relief brush through her hair. Rosa outstretched her arms to her daughter and picked her up out of her high-chair. She kissed Zephyr and held her snugly in her arms.

"*Buenos dias*, you two." Raquel continued to focus her attention on the stove and her creations for the day.

"*Buenos dias, Mami*," Luis answered. "Up early again, I see."

"Of course. It's how I stay young. Besides, you know I get bored easily. So Zephyr here is my entertainment. How did you two sleep?"

"We slept very well," Luis said. "How about you let me take over?"

"Nah, don't worry about it. I'm sure you slept like a log. You did make up the bed, right?"

Luis was confused by Raquel's question. "Y-yeah why?"

"Oh, just wondering." Raquel turned off the stove and quieted the kettle of boiling water. "You forgot to fix up my bed when you and Rosa were sixteen."

Luis and Rosa stared at each other in shock. Zephyr kicked her feet against Rosa's cradled arms.

"You . . . you knew about that?" Rosa spoke up.

"Uh, yeah. I was sixteen once too, you know. Except Manny and I made sure that we fixed up the bed after we were done with it." Raquel smiled and walked past Luis, who was still standing like a statue. "Oh, don't look so surprised, son. *Mami* knows everything." Raquel kissed him on his cheek and rested her palm on his face. She grinned at him and lightly slapped his face before she walked away to her guest room. She turned around and called back to the dazed Estradas behind her.

"Food is ready, by the way!"

*   *   *

Zephyr had experienced busy days for herself, and felt the energy that pervaded throughout the Estrada atmosphere, not only from her immediate family but also from the blur of workers and helpers that whipped and whirled around her curious silver eyes. She would receive her morning dessert from Raquel, who casually put an extended finger to Zephyr's lips each time she fed her granddaughter a spoonful of sherbet. This was followed by a tickle on her belly or an Eskimo kiss, both of which succeeded in garnering a wide smile from the happy infant. This was a gift Raquel gladly accepted from Zephyr, and she promised herself that with each smile gained would be a love returned tenfold. One morning, while Raquel performed her routine with Zephyr, Luis walked into the kitchen just before Raquel inserted the cold utensil into the baby's opened mouth. She darted her eyes toward his sleepy build and immediately flicked her wrist to put the cream into her own mouth. She let it slide on her tongue and swallowed hard, feeling it drip and ooze down her throat. Raquel snickered and felt her dimples burrow deeper into her cheeks. Zephyr, in return, kicked her feet and cried out in confusion.

"*Buenos dias, Mami* . . . what's with Zephyr?" Luis reached into an overhead cabinet and pulled out a box full of tea bags.

"Oh, nothing," Raquel choked. "She just probably wants some of this ice cream sherbet I have."

"Why? You gave her some?"

"Of course not! Babies aren't allowed to have this!"

"Just asking. Sorry." Luis shook his head and placed the kettle on top of a burning flame. "Maybe you shouldn't have some this early in the morning. Sugar can make you irritable."

"No, it's not that. I just don't want you to think that I'm trying to poison my granddaughter. That's all." Raquel stood up and closed the lid to the sherbet, winking at Zephyr before she replaced it in the freezer. "Well, she's all yours, son. Make sure she's well-fed, *si*?"

"Uh . . . yeah. *Si.*"

Luis looked at Zephyr with a puzzled look displayed on his face. He turned his sight back to Raquel, but she had already disappeared around the corner. Zephyr opened her mouth and stuck out her tongue at her father. She hoped that he would oblige her some sherbet instead of her grandmother. He laughed and tickled her cheek.

"What? *Papi* will feed you soon. I promise."

Zephyr started to pout when she eventually received mashed apples and formula for breakfast. After her morning meal, she was whisked away from her high-chair by her grinning father, who swung her up and down through the air. She gazed at her father as she felt her feet dangle against the wind Luis created underneath them, and he made sure that he kept his eyes glues to hers. Luis took special care to wait until her food was fully digested before he embarked on his aerial adventure with his daughter. This was a lesson he learned the hard way when he, once before, swung Zephyr through the air in her bedroom and saw the rush of yellow fluid spew from her mouth and land onto his silk pajamas. She merely looked around, despite the stench that replaced any breathable air in the nursery, but Luis could not help but laugh. Raquel walked by and noticed the joyous clamor coming from the Estrada father and daughter.

"I don't know why you're laughing," she said with a chuckle. "You did that to me when you were her age and I almost dropped you from shock."

Common to every waking day with Zephyr was Luis's inability to avoid her hoary eyes. He felt a strange comfort when he gazed into those pair of ethereal pearls, which mirrored his broad face whenever she smiled and drowned in a silver sea of tears whenever she cried. Zephyr became the weakness of the man who could not be fooled nor conquered. However, Luis did not feel remorse for discovering this subtle breach in his personal fortress. He took much delight in the sublime protection Zephyr provided for him. For that, he loved her more than anyone else alive in the world.

If anyone noticed Zephyr's inherent beauty, it was the keen eyes of the Shy Rose herself. Rosa always gave her daughter a fantastic bath full of calming lavender scents and dried off with towels exuding a warm vanilla glow. Zephyr's hair was jet-black and gaining length, ending with small curls humbly rising upward to her clear and slender face. Her cheeks were round and full of dimples, tiny impressions that received attention from Rosa in the form of kisses and gentle pinches. Her lips were round disks that tapered off into thin, delicate ribbons; indeed, it gave her a smile that was as enlightening as it was opulent. Her ears were already pierced at the behest of her mother, and thus a single stud the size of a sugar grain was embedded in each earlobe. Her most powerful attribute convinced Rosa that her daughter was able to see that which was beyond the normal scope of perception. At one point, Zephyr stared at the ceiling of her nursery and kept her gaze pointed at an invisible spot, despite the vain attempts Rosa made to gather her attention. After a while, Zephyr regained her infantile composure and watched her mother. Rosa later concluded to Luis and Raquel that the Estrada infant must have seen heavenly angels dancing and playing in front of her eyes. From then on, Rosa held firmly her belief that Zephyr was gifted both in sight and in observance, and she promised herself that she would keep those abilities forever honed and cherished.

The relationship between Zephyr and Pedro neither improved nor exacerbated. There were those rare moments in which he would be called upon to watch his little sister momentarily while the other Estradas were occupied by the tasks of daily life. During such impedances, as Pedro mentally called them, Zephyr would remain calm and silent while she watched her brother intensely. Even if she had felt her stomach growl from hunger or if her diaper became larger than usual, she would not cry or complain. Her eyes became snowy orbs of curiosity and wonder whenever Pedro carried her from one place to the next. He seemed to take care of Zephyr out of duty instead of love, and the infant took notice of his behavior. A moment of glory appeared when a flash of Pedro's bedridden hair swept across

Zephyr's line of sight. She observed the mishmash of strands and spikes that dominated his skull and the joyful baby could not help but marvel at the image. Pedro looked at the inquisitive infant and felt a smile creep on his face.

"My hair's a mess, I know."

Pedro kept his stare on Zephyr and continued his duties as normal. He found himself warming up to the newest addition to the Estrada family but remained adherent to his natural method of rebellion. However, the delicate eyes of Zephyr often succeeded in making Pedro's modus operandi ephemeral and forgetful, as the older brother found himself tickling and playing with his influential sister. Pedro realized firsthand that his sister could not be ignored nor hated, and he experienced a strange comfort in that fact.

What followed the coming days of laughter and idle amusement was the traditional setting of Zephyr's baptism. Luis himself drove to a nearby shopping mall and set out to find the outfit that he felt was good enough for his daughter to wear. He searched five different stores for what he envisioned to be the perfect baptismal garb. Eventually, he came across a pink silk dress adorned with a quaint peter-pan collar and a short sash around the waist. The dress was decorated with hundreds of cherry-colored beads that gave the outfit a subtle crimson glint whenever a beam of light descended upon it. The sleeves were short and ruffled with a tiny imprint of the designer's signature stitched in each cuff. Luis closed his eyes and conjured the image of Zephyr sleeping peacefully in the dress that humbly lay before him. He smiled at the visual of her feet enclosed in a pair of cotton-white booties with a light decorative lace etched across the rim, and her complimenting the look with a tiny bow in her curling hair. He opened his eyes and grabbed the dress in front of him. He pulled back the collar to check the size and frowned at the number that failed to match his goal. He looked around in the store and located a store clerk folding clothes nearby. He inhaled deeply and approached the clerk.

"Excuse me. I apologize for interrupting, but I was wondering if there was a possibility that you carried this dress in a different size."

The store clerk gave Luis a blank stare. She was a young chubby girl in her teens, with freckles on her cheeks and a beady pair of eyes. "Uh . . . what size are you looking for?"

"Three to six months."

"Let me see if we have it."

"Thank you very much."

The store clerk set a young boy's T-shirt down on the folding table placed in front of her and walked to the rear of the store. Luis saw her punch a code into the door handle that led to the storage room. The lightbulb blinked red twice, and the clerk sighed in frustration. She entered the code again, much harder this time, and the lightbulb blinked green once. She twisted the handle, opened the large metallic door, and disappeared inside. Luis gazed at the floor and hoped that the correct size lay somewhere inside that room. He looked toward the entrance of the store and saw a sea of customers and mall rats cascading past the stores. Teenage couples publicly displaying their affection toward one another occupied the dark and depressed corners hidden between each store. The older couples walked to the far right of the hallways, their slow speed mimicking the nature of slow vehicles moving to the rightmost lane to avoid the onslaught of speedy youngsters and impatient customers. Families chasing after their adventurous offspring dominated the hallways of the mall. The majority of them were dressed in armor decorated with pacifiers, knapsacks, infant strollers, and the occasional toddler leash that presented itself in the form of a child's backpack with a long tiger's tail. This appendage usually ended up within the closed fist of the irritated parent, blood-red and sweaty from the intense grip utilized to prevent the child from sprinting off into the proverbial sunset. Luis chuckled to himself and expressed self-gratitude in knowing that his daughter would never need such a controlling item. However, he could not help but bow his head and fervently pray that he would avoid purchasing a knapsack leash.

When Luis raised his head, he saw a pair of men standing in front of him. The clothes they wore were equally as menacing as the grimaces born on their faces. Each wore a mélange of thuggish clothing meant to intimidate whoever studied them but only succeeded in gaining disgust at the sight of them. Luis smiled and cast a quick glance at the nervous store clerk who had just returned from the storeroom.

"So what can I do for you gentlemen?" Luis reached over and grabbed the dress from the frozen store clerk.

"It's something you can do for us, Don Luis," the first one replied.

"Oh, really? Such as?"

"The reassurance that your recent absence is only temporary."

"Well, be reassured then. I'll get back to my day job soon enough."

"Do we have your word?"

"As always. Now if you'll excuse me."

Luis brushed past the two men and casually walked over to the cashier. He calmly placed the dress on the counter and waited for the stationary store clerk to collect herself and return to the registers.

"By the way, tell Mr. Mal that I do not appreciate being followed. Anywhere. If he is worried about my duty to increase his profit, then tell him to leave. Follow me or any of my relatives again, I will have you shot dead in this store. Do you understand?"

The two men looked at each other for a moment; they then turned to Don Luis and nodded.

"Good." Luis pulled out his wallet and handed the cash to the store clerk. She darted her eyes back and forth between the thug couple and the curiously calm customer. Luis took notice of her anxiety and leaned in close to her.

"Don't worry. I just have impatient clients." Luis winked at her and placed Zephyr's dress inside the quaint plastic bag. He wrapped his fingers through the holes and grinned at the duo that remained standing in front of him.

"Have a good afternoon," Luis said. He let out a small chuckle and strode past them. Once he was out onto the mall walkway, he saw a couple more men waiting for him about two stores down. He rolled his eyes. It was obvious that they made it known to him that they were not going to leave him alone. Luis approached them, dodging the masses of customers that congested the shopping mall, and met their stares with his own piercing eyes.

"Walk with me," Luis commanded. "All four of you."

Rosa had accompanied Luis to the shopping mall and parted ways with him when she noticed the glint that appeared in his eyes after he discovered the infant store. She rolled her eyes and patted her husband on the back.

"I must be psychic," she had said. "Go ahead and get your daughter something. I'm gonna walk around for a bit."

Rosa kept walking while Luis entered the store like a human drawn to an alien spacecraft. He shook her head and kept smiling as she walked down the long corridor. She passed by a number of stores and casually looked into each one. One was a clothing store that exhumed a rotten fragrance the second she walked past its entrance. She scrunched her nose and let out a sigh of disgust before she accelerated her gait. She came upon a candle store and decided to saturate her nose with scents of apples, butterscotch candy, and any other scent that would free her mind from the fragrant memories that plagued her. She walked in and grabbed the first candle in sight. Rosa jammed the base of the wax cylinder near her nostrils and inhaled slowly. Her sigh carried a resonance of relief as she pulled the candle away for her smiling face. She flipped the small scented hero in her palm and read the description of the scent: "Melodious Grape. A journey into the realm of grapevines."

Rosa smirked and placed the candle back on the shelf. She walked along the entire candle section while nonchalantly picking up and sampling each fragrance that piqued her interest. She looked out towards the store exit and saw Luis walking with four men—two men on both sides. She watched them carefully, especially her husband, as he conversed with each one of them calmly and almost jokingly. Rosa picked up a candle entitled "A Midsummer's Daydream" and strode toward the closest retailer. Rosa hardly noticed the smiling clerk ring up the candle while her gaze was on her husband. Her eyes darted back and forth between the clerk's actions and the Don's movement. He stopped directly across the walkway where the store was located and leaned against the banister. Rosa opened her purse and pulled out a twenty-dollar bill to give to the clerk. She then grabbed the candle and placed it within the plastic bag herself, simultaneously telling the clerk to keep the change as she sped towards the exit. Rosa slowed her walk, breathed in deeply, and met the five men with a wide smile.

"Excuse me, gentlemen. Would you mind if I steal my husband away from you?"

"Yes, we do mind. We still have much to discuss with your husband."

"No, we don't," Luis answered. "I will keep in touch. Enjoy your day."

Luis walked off with Rosa's arm within his. They both walked off, leaving the four men leering at their heads. One of them shoved his middle finger in the air and turned around to walk in the opposite direction. Luis kissed Rosa's hand and glanced at his bag.

"How did you know I was around?" he asked.

"Like I said, I must be psychic," answered Rosa. "Just had a feeling that you were around."

"Yeah . . ."

They both stayed silent. She looked at Luis and realized that his eyes were increasingly growing tired and old.

"Everything okay, sweetie?" Rosa looked over her shoulder and saw the backs of the four gang men disappear farther into the mall's horizon.

"These guys get younger and younger every year, you notice that?"

"Umm . . . yeah, they look like college kids."

"They are." Luis sighed and rolled his eyes toward the ceiling. "What a waste of college credits."

"Yeah . . . so is everything okay?"

Luis turned his eyes towards his wife and smirked. "I can't get anything past you, can I?"

"Course not." Rosa looked around and cast quick glances at the surrounding crowd. Everyone had been enthralled by their goals for shopping and did not seem to notice Rosa or the Don. She brought

Luis's ears close to her soft lips and whispered softly in his ear. "Were they concerned about you being absent for some time?"

"Yep. You got it."

"How soon until you return to business as usual?"

"Next week, after Zephyr's baptism and after Mom leaves. I . . . don't want her to see me working."

"Oh . . . okay. I understand." Rosa reached inside her plastic bag and pulled out the candle that possessed her nose. She held it out in front of Luis's nose, and he looked at her strangely. "Sniff it," she said, with the innocence of a little toddler.

Luis shrugged his shoulders and inhaled the perfumed candle deeply. He closed his eyes and let out a contented sigh. "That smells good. Thank you."

Rosa giggled and held Luis's hand for the rest of the afternoon.

When Luis entered Zephyr's bedroom, he noticed her tiny hands rub her small eyes back and forth. He picked up the drowsy baby and began to rock her slowly with the rhythm of his deep humming. Zephyr tried to keep herself alert but could not resist the gentle quivers in Luis's voice. She fell asleep within mere minutes of hearing her father lull her into this oh-so-familiar world.

Zephyr was not a morning person in the slightest. This was evident even on the day of her baptism; she only awakened to let her mother bathe her and put on her baptismal clothing. After her duties were performed, she fell back asleep and remained in her peaceful animation for the remainder of the event. "She had that 'Don't bother me again' look on her face before she fell asleep," remarked Rosa. "Let's keep that in mind thirteen years from now . . ."

Meanwhile, Luis was dressed in a shiny wool suit drenched in a dark-blue hue with a clean white dress shirt and a simple matching tie. Rosa stood next to him in front of a bathroom mirror, each inspecting the other with wide smiles and occasional playful chuckles. She wore a soft lavender business suit that she rarely wore but proudly displayed. It was custom-made for this occasion only, and she made certain that it was pleasant to her daughter's closed eyes. Pedro himself wore a gray tailored suit with polished black shoes and a silver tie. He surprised his parents with his punctuality and his taste for clothing. Rosa smiled at him and felt her heart jump when he showed a grin in return.

Raquel seemed to relish the idea of being Zephyr's grandmother in such that she had bought an outfit that was very conservative and maternal. She wore a white blouse with ruffles at the sleeves that pointed to a royal blue-skirt that reached well over her youthful knees. Her legs were covered with white stockings, and her feet were covered with simple black heels. Luis chuckled when he glanced at her outfit, and she playfully shook her fist at his face.

"Laugh it up," she whispered. "This will be the only time you'll see me wear this."

At the church, the priest walked over to Rosa who held Zephyr snugly in her arms. She was still dreaming and breathing softly in her new outfit that Luis had painstakingly picked for her. Zephyr remained in that state despite the frigid water trickling over her head. The church was empty and carried with it a silent, sublime air. Tall pillars held up the ceiling, which was decorated with shimmering jewels and geometric carvings. The priest himself couldn't help but smile at the precious infant that lay in her mother's arms. Father John Joseph Marie poured another tiny wave of holy water over Zephyr and made the sign of the cross after the last particle of water dripped onto her smooth forehead.

After the ceremony, Luis and Rosa talked with the priest and thanked him for taking the time to baptize their daughter. They were standing outside the church doors and welcomed the calm and cool wind that brushed against their faces.

"It's good to see you again, Father," Rosa said as she delivered the sleeping baby to Raquel. She kissed her nose and cradled her gently.

"It was my pleasure to do it, *Señora* Estrada. I was happy to hear that you and Luis had another child."

"She definitely was a surprise," Luis recalled, "for all of us."

"Your daughter will bring all of you so much happiness and joy. She is the most peaceful child I have ever seen. That is a blessing from God. Take care of that blessing."

ANDREW COOKE

"Amen, Father," Luis answered. "We will."

Father Marie bowed his head to the two parents and ventured toward the entrance of the church. He climbed the stone steps and took in the enjoyment of the crisp air surrounding him. He turned to his right and watched the cool breeze brush through the leaves of a nearby maple tree. The branches rustled and danced in the wind and left a still resemblance of quietude when the wind died down. He turned back and waved to the Estrada family before he let himself inside.

The day of Zephyr's baptism was also the last day of Raquel's visit, and this reminder ran heavily through the minds of Luis and Rosa. After the family returned home, Raquel immediately went to her guest room and packed her things. She attributed her rushed mannerism to fight her reluctance for leaving. Everyone within the household adopted sad expressions and became abnormally silent, speaking only when spoken to and casting vague smiles on their faces whenever Raquel made a joke. Her livelihood and evening tales resonated through everyone's mind, especially her unusual grasp on the proverbial Fountain of Youth. Pedro remained indifferent and reserved while succeeding in showing little reaction to his grandmother's words of farewell. Even Zephyr had awakened after Raquel gently stroked her supple cheeks. Her wide eyes opened, and the pale burst of silver and white emptied from them. She stared at her grandmother, the young Aphroditian beauty who was staring back at her. Zephyr read the air of longing in her grandmother's bright brown pupils and saw the departing future they were going to encounter. Raquel's bags were brought along with her and lay atop the curbside of the church, where she was awaiting the taxi cab to pick her up. When the flash of yellow peeked around the corner, she glanced at it in the hopes that it was for another client. When it pulled up to where the Estrada family stood, her heart sighed deeply, along with her voice.

"You know . . . they come early when you don't want them to," she lamented.

Everyone heard the latch inside the trunk of the cab click open, and the driver emerged from his seat to assist with loading her luggage. He was a rather short man with a gray moustache and a balding head. He nodded to the Estrada family out of courtesy and proceeded to grab the nearest bag. He causally swung the heavy bag into the trunk and performed the same gesture with the remaining luggage. When the last suitcase full of Raquel's clothes plopped inside the trunk, the cabbie slammed the door and quickly walked to the driver's side of the car. He leaned against the hood and looked at his watch, while casting quick glances toward the Estrada matriarch.

"*Dios*, someone's in a rush," Raquel said. "And stop looking at me with all those gloomy faces! I know we're on church grounds, but no one died, okay?"

Rosa chuckled. "We can't help it if we'll miss you, Ms. Estrada." She hugged her mother-in-law and smiled at the curious infant that lay in her grandmother's arms.

"Still so formal after all these years. I don't mind if you call me Mom, you know . . . just don't call me an old lady, got it?" Raquel laughed, although with a hint of repressed sadness. "I'm just teasing you, sweetheart. I'll miss you too. Take care of my baby while I'm gone, okay?"

"Don't worry, Zephyr will be just fine."

"I was talking about Luis."

Rosa laughed. "He'll get the same treatment."

The two women hugged and kissed each other, while Zephyr curiously looked at her grandmother. She saw her walk over to Luis, who slowly approached his mother. Raquel noticed the worry in her son's eyes, as with any other mother who safeguards her children. She placed her hand on his shoulder and carefully read his mind.

"What's on your mind, son?" Raquel stayed silent until he was ready to answer.

"Oh, nothing . . . just dreading the thought of going back to work."

"I see . . . I understand." Raquel stared at the ground for a moment and then she cast a glance at Zephyr. Her eyes were fixated on her father's, giving no sign of directing her silver gaze elsewhere. Raquel noticed her inquisitive granddaughter and lightly kissed her nose.

"Luis?"

"Yeah, Ma?" Luis brushed Zephyr's hair with the tip of his finger.

"I am so proud of what you have done for your family. Your father would've been proud too. I know it. You're a good man. A *good* man. I know I've said this to you a million times, but . . . men like you are rare in this world. Make sure you are just as good for your daughter. She will need you more than anyone else she will ever know. I don't want my granddaughter to suffer like I did . . ." Raquel paused for a moment. She looked up at the sky and counted the clouds that hovered over her head. She brought her eyes back to earth and continued her talk with her son. "May God keep his protection on you and your love."

Luis kissed his mother on her cheek and hugged both her and Zephyr tightly. He caught the glimpse of Zephyr smiling widely when he released his embrace from the two women. The Estrada infant kicked her feet out and bobbed her tiny heels up and down.

"Someone wants her father," said Raquel. She placed the giddy baby in Luis's arms, who then tickled her belly with the tip of his nose. "Children grow up so fast. Make sure you're there to witness it." She turned to Zephyr and gently pinched her cheeks. "But don't grow up too fast, sweet *nina*."

Zephyr turned her small head to meet Raquel and her sad face. Her smile faded as she read her grandmother's mind.

"Grandmamma had a lot of fun with you, sweetie. But she has to go bye-bye now. You be a good girl while I'm gone, okay?"

Zephyr's lips started to quiver once Raquel said "bye-bye." Her eyes glowed bright silver and filled with heavy tears. Her small mouth opened wide, and the once joyful heir to Raquel's love transformed into the precious bride of sadness. Zephyr's wail sent a solemn tremor to Raquel's heart without any sign of calm, and her tears rolled down her soft cheeks and landed onto Luis's arms.

"Aww, it's okay, sweetie . . . please don't cry for Grandmamma." Raquel almost cried with Zephyr, but she succeeded in holding back her tears when Luis handed Zephyr over to his mother. She lowered her voice to a soft whisper and held her granddaughter close to her.

"Okay, okay, Zephyr . . . listen, I'll make a deal with you, okay?"
She rocked Zephyr back and forth in her arms as she spoke. "This is
something we grown-ups call a promise. Do you know what that is?
It's something that can never, ever be broken. Wanna try it out with
me? Yeah? Okay, here we go . . . I promise that I will visit you next
year for your birthday. And the year after that, and the next one after
that. Forever and ever. Is that okay?"

Zephyr quieted her crying and displayed a content look on her
face.

"That's my girl. Every year for your birthday, you'll get to see
Grandmamma. I promise."

Zephyr breathed softly and smiled. Raquel kissed her on her
forehead and handed the happy child back to Luis. He placed a white
pacifier in her mouth. She sucked on it and fixed her big bright eyes
on her father.

"And I mean it, Luis," Raquel asserted. "I'll be back next
October."

"We'll be here waiting for you," Luis answered.

"Okay . . . well, I better get going before I miss my flight."

"Oh," Rosa said, "we would hate to have you miss your plane.
Then you would just have to stay with us. Hint, hint."

Raquel laughed. "Oh no, now I *really* have to go. I'm rubbing
off on you."

Pedro came up to his grandmother and smiled. He opened his
arms to her and was surprised to see that she accepted them without
any ill will or any signs of reluctance. She wrapped her youthful arms
around him and hugged him tightly. He rubbed her back in a small
circle, breathing softly and smiling the whole time. When he let go,
he found himself ensnared still by Raquel's grip. She started to hug
him tighter and tighter, almost strangling him, and he felt his face
turn an awful red hue. He stammered his speech when he gathered
enough air to talk.

"G-grandma?"

"Be good. Do you understand?"

"*Si* . . ."

Raquel released her hold and grinned at Pedro. She placed her palm on his cheek and held his face for a moment. She lightly slapped it and left a red mark when she turned on her heel to leave. Raquel giggled as she waved to the small Estrada crowd and blew a kiss to baby Zephyr before she entered the vehicle. The door closed on the fifty-something-year-old fashion model. She lowered the car window to wave her goodbyes at the Estrada family one last time. As the taxi cab turned the corner and sped off to the airport, Raquel closed her eyes and reminisced on the piercing, wondrous gaze that belonged to a certain young lady. She kept this image in her mind and kept her in friendly company even as she entered the door to her Barcelona home.

VI

The church was as solemn as the infant he had just baptized. Father Marie stood in the doorway and watched the Estrada family through the clear window. They waved their hands to the departing matriarch and kept their eyes on the road that housed her yellow taxi cab. When their sight lost trace of the golden vehicle, the family stood in place and chatted about the joys they experienced while being with Raquel. He saw Luis whisper some words in Rosa's ear. She gave a sort of reluctant nod and let her husband leave. Don Estrada fixed his tie and ascended the stairs that led to the church's front door. Father Marie stared ahead and dipped his right hand into a small dish of frigid holy water. He crossed himself and lowered his head in silence.

"May it be done according to your will," he whispered.

The heavy wooden door creaked open, and Luis followed the sunlight that entered along with him. He tapped the holy water with his right finger and made the sign of the cross. He kissed his hand and turned to Father Marie, who continued gazing at the contented Estrada family that waited outside.

"Thank you for waiting, Father," Luis said. "I hope I did not keep you from anything."

"Oh, no. Not at all. I was just admiring your family. They seem happy."

"Very happy. It's been a long time since I've seen them like this."

"Is that why you wanted to see me?"

Luis stared in the kindly priest's eyes and read the intent buried within them. "Yes. Can we walk?"

"Of course."

The two men exited the lobby and entered the main body of the church. It was wide and open, faithfully evoking the true three-dimensional image that the original architect conjured in his plans. The ceilings touched the sky and held its own against the voids of time and wear. The church pews were newly lacquered in a dark cherry wood color that stood out against the crimson carpet that stretched throughout the building. The light that cast Luis's shadow upon the walls were attributed to lone candles placed alongside each statue that paid homage to the Catholic faith's saints and figures in the Bible. Luis walked by the statue of Our Lady of Guadalupe and gently touched her feet. He promised himself that he would remember to bring her a red rose the next time he visited her.

Father Marie stopped in front of a room that was the size of a small closet, with a red curtain on both sides of the door leading to a tiny nook. The good priest reached into his pant pocket and pulled out a small silver key etched with a crucifix on its handle. He inserted the key and unlocked the door to the priest's end of a confessional booth. He placed the key back in his pocket and nodded toward Luis.

"For our privacy, *Señor* Estrada."

Luis smiled. He pulled the curtain back and looked around himself before he stepped inside. He knelt down on an adjacent cushion and triggered a soft switch that provided him with a dim light. In front of him was a screen that obscured the sight of the priest's face. Luis started to cross himself but caught his motion and froze it.

"Sorry," Luis said. "Reflex."

"It's okay," answered Father Marie.

Luis continued his motion and closed his eyes. He clenched his fists tightly and bit his lower lip. He cleared his throat before he commanded a professional voice, one he had not heard since Zephyr's birth.

"This is what's going to happen and what needs to be done in the future . . ."

*   *   *

Luis exited the church exactly thirty minutes after he had seen his mother depart. He looked toward the street and noticed that his family remained in the same spot he had left them. Rosa was rocking Zephyr back and forth in her arms while Pedro stared at the street filled with passing cars and sullen pedestrians. Luis sighed while he descended the stone steps to greet his wife's curious eyes. She saw the expression on her husband's face, compared it to her own, and playfully stuck her bottom lip out at Luis.

"Aww, no," Rosa complained to Zephyr. "Daddy has to go back to work now. Boo . . ."

"Yeah, well if it was up to me, I would stay home." Luis brushed Zephyr's cheek with his finger.

"Too bad it's the opposite, huh? Well, just make sure you come home sometime soon. Okay?"

"Yeah . . . okay."

"I'll be here waiting."

Luis glanced at his watch. It was fifteen minutes past three, and the sun began to wrap itself in an iridescent light in preparation for burying itself into the earth. "I better get going."

"Yeah." Rosa looked down at Luis's lips that reached to kiss her cheek. She pushed him back with a free hand and held his attention with her eyes alone. She seemed very stern, very focused. This was the Rosa that was hardly seen, the rose with thorns. "Don't kiss me unless you're saying goodbye. I mean it. Get your ass back home, okay?"

Luis smiled. "Of course."

"And don't you dare forget to bring Zephyr some milk. Understand?"

"Understood."

Rosa smiled back at Luis. The thorns had disappeared, thank God. She hummed a soft melody and walked around with Zephyr giggling in her arms. Luis turned toward Pedro, who still kept his stare upon the street.

"Something on your mind, son?"

Pedro took great care to hide his thoughts underneath his tone. "Nothing much. Just thinking. You're going back to work?"

"Yep. Indefinitely."

"I see." Pedro nodded for a moment and rested his head on the cool winter air. He breathed it in deeply and savored the scent of the sharp, thin wind that entered his lungs. "Any chance that it'll end soon?"

Luis lost himself in thought and avoided his son's question. "You don't want to know."

Luis patted Pedro's head and winked at him. He turned to Rosa and watched her raise Zephyr's chubby arm to wave back at her father. He turned to the sky and threw his conscience to the clouds.

I won't need this anymore, he thought.

*   *   *

The sun continued to descend upon the horizon when Luis drove to his destination. He drove his favorite car, a Porsche 911 Turbo that was as seductive as the roar of its engine. The seats were encased in a leather coating that grasped his shoulders and held back his torso as he wrestled the turns between each building. The small but mighty vehicle hurled its dark-blue streaks through the night-lit streets. It finally stopped at the end of a lone alley where a handful of men, young and old, stood waiting for their employer. He was wearing a black wool suit that would have bled into the dark alley had it not been for the golden dress shirt he wore. The men and boys in the alley listened to his Italian shoes stamp on the tiny puddles left on the ground by a previous rain shower. Luis kept his expressions resigned and calm, despite the tense and nervous stares he received from everyone.

"Evening, gentlemen," Luis started. "Did you all eat already? Yes? If not, I can certainly order a pizza to be delivered here—if you want me to, that is."

The alley's inhabitants remained silent and kept no eyes upon Luis.

"Anyone want to fill me in? I'm all ears."

"We don't have shit to say to you, Don Estrada." One of the men spoke up. He was a bearded man who looked to be in his early thirties. He wore a large white T-shirt underneath a red puffed jacket that reached down to baggy blue jeans. It spilled over a pair of tan boots that would have loved to color itself with Luis's blood. "Business is down, and so is our respect for you."

"Oh, really? Seems like you were handling things quite well in my absence."

"So well, in fact, that the guys and I think you should step down." He reached into his jacket and pulled out a sawed-off shotgun. He aimed the gaping hole at Luis's head and walked closer to the calm Don. Luis felt the cold barrel pierce his forehead but refused to move an inch.

"Sure you wanna do this, Lorenzo? It's not going to go well on your end."

"Oh, I think it will. I think it fucking will."

"That's not how I predicted it."

"So you're a fucking psychic now?"

Luis sighed and reached into his blazer pocket. Lorenzo pushed the barrel further into Luis's skull. Luis raised his hands and backed up a few steps.

"Relax, geez. All I wanted to do was grab a piece of gum out of my pocket."

Lorenzo brushed Luis's suit jacket aside and thrust his hand into his pocket.

"Oh, be my guest," Luis joked. "Take a look for yourself."

When Lorenzo pulled out of the pocket, he had a small white piece of paper folded in his hand. He looked at it puzzlingly, all while casting quick glances at the crew surrounding him.

"Go ahead and open it. I have patience, Lorenzo." Luis backed up to a nearby wall and rested his body against it. He looked up to the sky and whistled a soft melody to the stars that encircled the clouds while Lorenzo unfolded the slip of paper and read its contents. His eyes widened in shock, his heart beat out of his chest, and fear stuck her icy fingers down his throat.

"Wh-what the hell . . ."

The crew who surrounded Luis and Lorenzo whipped out their guns from their holsters and aimed the steel cannons at their target.

Don Luis heard the melody of fifteen triggers pulling back to release the swarm of lead that invaded bones and popped blood vessels. Luis closed his eyes and listened to the song of bullets piercing flesh and tearing through wet organs that eventually spilled out onto the concrete. The scent of smoke and plasma poured into the atmosphere, and Luis couldn't help but inhale the deathly perfume and savor its mist. It had been a long time since that feeling became a part of him, and he knew that he had to get back into the habit of enjoying the fumes rather than hating it.

When the shooting stopped, Luis opened his eyes and gazed around the alley. The men who surrounded him lowered their weapons and kept them at their sides. He looked at the ground and traced the pool of blood and sweat to the shivering body of Lorenzo, who clawed at the ground in an ill attempt to reach for his shotgun that dropped a few inches away from his face. He coughed out a globule of blood and felt the hard sole of Luis's dress shoe stamp on his hand. Lorenzo was in so much pain that he did not scream, and let out a stifled grunt instead. Luis bent down and pulled a pair of leather gloves over his hands. The shiny leather blinded Lorenzo as he noticed the Don picking up the shotgun that was meant for him. Luis thrust the metallic barrel against the base of Lorenzo's skull and adjusted his grip to fit the weapon into his strong hands.

"You see, Lorenzo? This is what a rather dangerous gun pointed to your head feels like. I don't like the feeling at all. Do you?"

Lorenzo spat out another ball of blood and phlegm. He turned his head up toward Luis and smiled. "You can . . . go to hell . . ."

Luis turned his face toward the evening sky and pulled the trigger back. The sound of shards burrowing into brain matter and concrete rang throughout the alley. Chunks of skull and skin exploded out on the ground, and blood sprayed in all directions, covering Luis's clothes and part of the men's shoes. He stood up and threw the gun next to Lorenzo's body, letting it float in his blood towards his now-unrecognizable head. Luis sighed and pulled out a handkerchief to wipe Lorenzo's blood that fell on his face. It smeared against the fabric, so Luis decided to give up the attempt to make himself clean once again. He walked toward the men and stared into every pair of eyes that crowded and studied him.

"Sorry to keep you waiting. I'm back." Luis adjusted his collar and thrust his hands in his pockets. "Are you all well?"

All the men turned to one another. They cast a glance at the bleeding corpse that lay at their feet. They nodded to Luis, who smirked in reply.

"Okay. Let's go run some more errands, shall we?"

Luis skipped over Lorenzo's body and stooped down to pick up the bloody slip of paper that casually floated to the ground amidst the swarm of bullets that surrounded it. He shook off the excess blood and dirt while the men created a path for him to exit the alley. He read the contents of the paper and nodded slightly. He threw the slip behind his left shoulder and strode to the end of the deathly corridor. He opened the door to his Porsche and stepped inside without as much as a wave goodbye to the crew. He sped away while they cleaned up what was left of Lorenzo. One of them picked up the note that Luis left behind and unfolded the paper to read the contents: "Pray."

*   *   *

Luis pulled up to a tall gray building with colorful lights illuminating the interior behind black tinted windows. He parked alongside the curb and shut off the engine. He sat back in his seat and fiddled around with his wedding band. The golden circle that hugged his finger gleamed in spite of the calm night that enveloped the city. He leaned his head against the driver's window and began to count each star that materialized in the sky. When he located his first star, he dedicated it first to Zephyr and made a wish in his heart that he would live to see her grow up into a woman whose happiness in life would be greater than his own. At that moment, he turned away from the comfort of his thoughts and concentrated his mind upon a tall young man that approached his car. Luis reached over to the passenger's side and opened the door for him. The man stepped inside the car and stared at the floor while he closed the door. Luis noticed the glum expression in his eyes, even if the young man failed to give Luis the pleasure of his face.

"How's it going, Adam?"

"Nothing much," he answered.

Luis inserted the key into the ignition and turned on the car. The hum of the exotic car caused the young man to sigh deeply and remain in silence for the duration of the ride. Luis kept himself from asking any inquiries on his passenger's mood; however, he did know enough about him to formulate his own conclusions. His guest was a teenager whom Luis refused to call African-American, only because his heritage could only be traced to a birth in a urine-drenched alley. His mother was a prostitute who claimed that she was too young to be a mother and apparently too old to give a damn about the melancholic teenager sitting across from the Don. He ended up in the care of his grandmother, who became the mother that the young teen deserved and grew to love. The young teen received immeasurable adoration beaming from his grandmother to sustain him, but she had always been a struggling parent even before the days of her only daughter's acceptance of prostitution as her basis of income. When Adam was sixteen, he heard from a close friend that Don Luis was a man whose kindness was equaled only by his wealth and that the only way to help his grandmother handle daily finances was to make a deal with the Don. Upon meeting Adam, Luis sensed the same ability that was attributed to everyone he knew; his talent. Adam was a budding lyricist who managed to filter his lifelong frustrations through musical artistry. With the help of Luis's impeccable knowledge of business and promotion, Adam was able to view the realm of stardom that once lay hidden in his wildest dreams but succeeded in keeping his humble roots within the atmosphere that he occupied.

Tonight, Adam's eyes crept toward the same earth that seemed to attack his conscious with very little mercy. Luis's keen sense of mood picked up Adam's less-than-happy demeanor and forced him to break the silence that pervaded inside the vehicle.

"What did Mr. Mal tell you to do this time? Is he still asking you for errands?"

"Y-yeah." Adam stared out the window and counted the lights that decorated the night air.

"Okay . . . what kind of errand?"

"Collection."

"I see . . ." Luis turned a corner and parked the car in a lone alley, wet and shimmering from a brief drizzle. "You're collecting from Lorenzo, correct?"

Adam whipped his face toward the Don in shock. "Yeah! How'd you know—holy shit, man! What the hell happened to—?"

"Oh, I took care of whatever it was that needed my attention." Luis pointed to a spot on the alley ground. "Right over there."

Adam followed Luis's fingertip to a small patch of cracked concrete, filled with tiny crimson puddles that reflected the white moon which hung in the sky. Adam turned to Luis, who kept a stern expression on his face.

"If you continue to do favors for Mr. Mal, you'll end up getting yourself in Lorenzo's situation. Your blood will be splattered on someone else's clothes and face. I left it on just for you so that you could see what could be your future. Don't think that's beyond you either. You're young, but you're not immortal. Lorenzo started out just like you did, and look where that got him. Is that worth it?"

Adam listened attentively and remained silent.

"When I first entered this business, it was out of necessity. Back then, it was better to rely on yourself than the police. I was . . . forced into it, but I managed somehow. At least you have a say in the matter."

"But I can't say no to Mr. Mal, you know that."

"Have you ever tried?"

Adam closed his eyes and shrugged his shoulders.

"If he approaches you for a job again, you tell me about it. He'll get upset, but not at me. He knows I have his balls in a jar, and if he ever crosses you or anyone that has some familiar connection to me, I will shove that jar down his throat."

Adam chuckled and covered his mouth out of embarrassment.

"Okay? I'm serious. Mr. Mal has the largest gang in this city. I'm sure he has plenty of muscle to carry his groceries. You don't need to be involved with him anymore."

"Okay . . ."

"Good." Luis wiped some of Lorenzo's blood from his face. "How's your grandmother?"

"She doing all right, I guess. I spoke to her a few minutes ago, and she told me that the doc says she needs a kidney transplant."

"Does she have a donor?"

"No . . .not yet. She's been put on the list though. For now, she's on dialysis."

"Do you have her medical information?"

"Uh . . . yeah, it's at my crib. Why?"

"Next time I see you, give me a copy."

Adam stared at Luis and tried to read the intent in his mind. The Don's eyes were still fixated on the spot where Lorenzo made his final remark. He did not blink, and Adam wondered if Luis felt compelled by a desire to make amends for each death he helped orchestrate.

"All of life is an industry, and medicine is one out of many. I have connections there . . . I'll make sure that your grandmother gets placed higher on the donor list. All right?"

'You sure about that? I don't want to cause any problems, you know?"

"It's no problem. I'll do this favor for you . . . under one condition."

Adam smiled. "Name it."

Luis moved closer to the smiling teen, with an ominous expression in his voice. "Stay the fuck away from Mr. Mal."

Adam's smile faded to a deep frown. He knew that Luis was serious, and he was more afraid of the Don than ten Mr. Mals combined.

"All right. Deal."

"Good." Luis reached over and unlocked the door. He motioned for Adam to step out of the car. Adam nodded and slowly exited the dark vehicle.

"Walk home tonight, get some fresh air and all that jazz. I want you to think about what you saw here and thank God that you did not witness what I saw an hour ago. Do you understand me?"

Adam nodded. "Yes, sir."

Luis smiled. "I'll see you at the studio tomorrow."

Luis drove off and gazed into the rearview mirror to observe Adam's reflection in the glass. The young man thrust his hands in his pocket and walked in the opposite direction. He kept his face in front of the glowing white moonlight and casually strode down the sidewalk. Luis smirked, content with Adam's acceptance of their oral contract. When the teen disappeared from his view, Luis reached for his car phone and quickly dialed a number. He cradled the phone in his shoulder while he sped off into the empty streets that lay before him. The phone rang on the other end a few times before a calm voice answered, "Stokes residence."

"Hi, Ms. Stokes. This is Luis Estrada."

"Oh, hi! Are you all set to come over?"

"Yes, I'm on my way right now."

"Okay, good. See ya soon then."

Luis hung up the phone and shifted gears. He drove for a few minutes until he came to a broken stop sign that pitifully stood on the corner of a sidewalk. He made a right turn at the Stop sign and stopped at a white house on the corner. It was the only piece of architecture that did not have the telltale broken window or a plot of long, uncut grass. It was situated across the street from two men standing opposite of each other, one spitting out insults to another in a lyrical fashion. The words were as damaging as the street itself, with each syllable sounding off in the minds of those who happened to stop by and listen. The exchange remained violent and filthy yet somehow managed to hold onto a distinct quality of skillful expression without choking what was left of the art form. Luis observed the battle with a content air, while he mentally attributed a soft melody to compliment the furious conversation. He glanced at his watch and decided to temporarily abandon his daydream and pay a visit to the lonely white house on the corner.

He stepped out of his car and caught a glimpse of a silhouette in the living room window. The figure pushed aside the curtains and peeked through the foggy window to survey the surrounding area. Luis waved, and the shadow waved back at him before the curtains flew back to its original setting. Luis approached the front walkway and looked down the road on both sides before he continued his walk. The shadow opened the front door and pushed the screen door wide open to welcome the new guest. The light from inside the home flashed on the silhouette's face, and the eyes of a wise older woman greeted the Don. He outstretched his hand only to receive a warm hug in return. He blushed and wrapped a free arm around the woman, who kissed him on the cheek two times before she let go.

"Hey there, cutie," the woman said. "Come on in."

"Thank you very much." Luis entered the house and the woman closed the door behind them. Luis turned around to meet his warm hostess. She was a tall and slender black woman of an age that betrayed her body. Her face had only a few wrinkles, which Luis attributed to her wide smiles and hearty laughter. She wore a simple blue cotton robe that fit snugly around her torso. Her slippers were miniature teddy bears whose tiny faces stuck up at Luis. He snickered softly, and the woman playfully sneered at the Don.

"Be careful, Mr. Estrada," the woman cautioned. "They do attack when provoked."

"I'm sure they do," Luis answered. "Thank you for having me on such short notice."

"No, no! Thank *you*. The woman glanced at Luis's clothing but said nothing. "How did it go with Adam?"

"Very well, actually. He told me about your situation with the kidney transplant."

Ms. Stokes fixed her eyes on the floor. "Yeah . . . I figured he would come to you and tell you all about it, you being an angel and all."

"God, no! I'm no angel, believe me."

"You helped Adam and me with our troubles. You're an angel in my book." Ms. Stokes walked over to the kitchen and placed a kettle on the stovetop. "Would you like some tea, cutie?"

"No, thank you. I only came by to tell you that he will no longer see Mr. Mal. I know he's been running some errands for him, and I know you know about that. We made a deal." Luis could not hold back his wide smile. "I also promised him that I will see to it that your name will be among the top of the donor list."

"Oh, God bless you!" Ms. Stokes clasped her hands in prayer and held her face to the ceiling. "You don't know how much this means to me. Adam is a good boy, it's just—"

"He gets mixed up with the wrong crowd. I know."

Ms. Stokes turned on the stove, and for a while, she stood in silence and watched as the water in the kettle slowly heated up. "Sometimes I think it's my fault . . . I should've been around him more often. It's just with his mother leaving him like that and with me working full time, it's hard. Damn hard."

Luis walked over and placed his hand on her shoulder. "It's not your fault at all. You're doing more good than what you give yourself credit. He's lucky to have you as a parent. Surrogate or not, you're doing better than most. Other people would've chosen to abandon him, but you chose to stick with it and fight. That's love. No one can take that away from you."

Ms. Stokes nodded and smirked. The kettle whistled and she quickly took it off the burner. She turned the knob and shut off the stove. "Which reminds me," she said, discarding the subject. "Congratulations on the newest member of your family!"

"Oh, thank you. Adam told you?"

"Yeah, he did. Girl, right? Zephyr?"

"Yeah, that's my little cherubim."

"You watch her closely now," Ms. Stokes gleefully warned. "Cherubims are warriors of God, and she'll be a handful for you and that wife of yours."

"Trust me, I'll keep an eye on her."

Ms. Stokes poured the boiling hot water into a small mug with a bag of tea inside of it. "Good. And keep her away from . . . this."

Luis solemnly bowed his head and secretly hoped that his next words would not come to haunt him. "That I promise I will do."

"Very good. Now you better get out of here. Adam should be back soon."

Luis glanced at his watch. "We have exactly six more minutes." Luis reached into his jacket pocket and pulled out a small white envelope. "This is for you."

"God forbid you ever give that to me!" Ms. Stokes brushed the air, as if she was trying to wave the envelope off of Luis's hand. "Bad enough Adam tries to give me some money, now you've caught the charity bug from him!"

Luis chuckled. "Then give it to someone else. It's your money— you can do what you want with it. Right?"

Ms. Stokes looked at Luis, and then she stared at the envelope. She did not know what compelled her to extend her hand and take it, but she held no regret in her heart when she opened the envelope and sifted through the small stash of hundred-dollar bills.

"Thank you, Mr. Estrada . . ."

"You're very welcome. I shall keep in touch."

"Have a good night, dearie . . . oh, and Luis?"

"Yeah?"

"Thank you. Really."

Luis slightly bowed his head and headed toward the door. He twisted the golden knob and exited the warm home. He glanced once again down each corner and examined each person that he saw approach his direction. The unfamiliarity of each individual satisfied the Don as he calmly strode to his car while humming a nostalgic melody to himself. He opened the door to his car and climbed in, turning his head back and forth to make certain that unexpected visitors remained hidden within the umbrage of the night. He then turned the car on and sped down the road, with the next destination firmly set in his mind.

It had already been a less than relaxing night for Don Luis Estrada. He realized this fact once he pulled up to the headquarters of a certain Mr. Julius Mal. The building was more dilapidated than official. The pungent stench of old drugs swimming in pools of vomit and bile saturated the air that Luis breathed. He slightly opened his lips and breathed through his mouth in order to dodge the scent of addiction. He then entered a doorway that severely lacked any concept of a door.

His peripheral vision, however, failed Luis in avoiding the sources of the addictive air. There were a number of men slumped against a moldy wall with six-inch long rusty syringes thrust in the crook of their elbows. Their faces were serene, almost complacent with their impoverished surroundings, and they seemed to not notice the mob figure that walked past them. Luis saw a pregnant teenager hand over a tiny wad of singles to a dealer, who in return filled her empty palm with a small cellophane bag filled with white, uneven clumps of cocaine. As soon as she felt the light touch of powder precipitating on her finger, the teen thrust her fingernail into her left nostril and inhaled deeply. Her expression was disturbingly joyful, and she sniffed the last bit of cocaine that merged with her phlegm. She nodded to the drug dealer, who was busy counting the bills he had recently acquired without paying attention to his expectant customer. The teen shuffled away to a lone corner in the building and sat down in a chair that still reeked of the Dumpster from which it had been retrieved. Luis approached the drug dealer and stood in front of him, waiting for him to direct his attention to something other than his money.

"Help you?"

Luis chuckled. "Where's your employer?"

"Wouldn't you like to know?"

"I would, actually."

The dealer looked up from his stack of cash and met eyes with the person holding the conversation. He saw the ominous glow in the Don's eyes and discovered that the tone in his voice immediately changed.

"Y-yeah. Upstairs . . . second door from the right." He tried to mask his fear with automatic vocal output.

Luis looked at the wad of crinkled money that lay in the dealer's hand. He calmly held out his hand, and the dealer gave it to him in a shivering grasp. Luis took the money, counted it, and stared at the dealer's fearful eyes.

"You're short a couple hundred dollars."

The dealer nervously checked his jean pockets and the interior pockets of his jacket. He gulped in disappointment whenever each pocket had empty air filled in it, and he avoided the stone expression laden on the Don's face.

"Chill, man . . . just chill, all right?" The dealer backed away from Luis and felt the cold touch of stone hit his back. He found himself against a wall, and Luis only inched closer and closer to him.

"Oh, I'm fine. It's you who's nervous. Don't tell me you don't have the two hundred dollars. That's the last thing I want to hear right now."

"Look, I ain't got it, homie!"

Luis cast his eyes up toward the ceiling as if he was briefly lost in a moment of thought. He turned his face back to the dealer, who was breathing heavily and clenching his fists in fear. "Hmm, I need the two hundred dollars . . . but you don't have it. I need to see Mr. Mal, and you told me his location, right?" Luis paced in front of the dealer and counted the empty needles on the floor. "How about this: since I'm a nice guy, I'll give you an extension. And by that, I mean you're in no position to negotiate the terms, *comprende?*"

The dealer nodded and listened attentively.

"I'm going to go up to see your boss. When I come back, I want the money in my hand. No money, well, I can't guarantee that the syringes here won't outnumber the pieces of you."

The dealer swallowed hard and nodded in assent.

"Great! See ya in a few!"

Luis walked away and shoved the money he had received into his jacket pocket. He strode down a long hallway with rotting wallpaper and old yellow glue that stuck relentlessly to the walls, simultaneously collecting bits of dust and ash that floated away from Luis's imposing figure. Pieces of aged wood dropped from exhausted strength that used to be attributed to the ceiling and landed in a path which lay in front of the Don's feet. The carpet underneath his Brazilian leather shoes crinkled and cracked whenever Luis took a step. He wondered if the whole building would crumble from his mere presence and entertained the facile attempt if he ever wished to transform that thought into action.

His thoughts soon abandoned all facilities that occupied his mind when he noticed the corners of the hallways adorned with more addicts wandering in their lost minds. One man constantly folded his arms and rubbed the tops of his biceps to stay warm, while silently humming gibberish to himself and his imaginary audience. He noticed Luis walking past him, and he stared violently at the stoic figure that dared to ignore him.

"Shut up! I said shut the fuck up! The birds are singing . . . they sing quietly. Quietly . . . all night long. Listen . . . I said shut the fuck up and listen, you fucking bastard! Fuck you!"

Luis did not bother to shake his head in shame, feeling that such an expression was not enough to fully describe the horror that sat before him. He kept walking, accelerating his pace to avoid any more unnecessary discussion. A young boy who looked to be eleven years old clawed at Luis's feet and grasped his malnourished fingers around his ankle.

"Hey . . . let me get a fix. C'mon, man . . . I'll do anything for one. Please . . ."

Luis could not help but look into the boy's magnetic hazel eyes, encircled by deep pouches of fatigue and sharp lines of drug-induced insomnia. He was a skinny Brazilian boy with long black hair that had not seen the tender touch of a comb in months. His lips were chapped and split apart from sucking on dry butts of cigarettes and possibly from other activities Luis cringed from imagining. He outstretched his hand to show Luis a palm full of blisters and grime from many nights of sleeping on a frozen concrete floor. They shivered from the days spent without a drug fix as a result of his body trying to reject the poison that the young boy continually forced into his veins. The necessity of food and drink had escaped the grasp of his mind, and Luis frowned at the poor mess of human flesh that had found a home in Mr. Mal's building.

Luis tore himself away from the poor soul and continued walking down the seemingly mile-long hallway. He had finally arrived at the staircase, which led to the somewhat palatial home office of Julius Mal. He placed his right foot on the first step and it immediately squealed from the pressure of his shoe. He hoisted the rest of his body up onto the step, and the whole staircase screamed from the agony of his weight. Luis sighed, stayed in his place for a moment, and continued his ascent up the staircase. The dreadful wails sounded throughout the whole building, barely stirring any of the tenants or interrupting their journeys through the illusions they saw before their minds' eyes.

Luis drew an image of Mr. Mal's office in his mind: white newly painted walls adorned with framed pictures of his numerous achievements in his organized crime history. There was that one photograph, which Luis remembered clearly, of Mr. Mal crouching in front of a park fountain, with each water molecule that spat out of the pipe glistening in the white sun that hung in the sky. His face was large and stoic, almost apathetic, and sat on a wide neck that spilled out on all sides of his shirt collar. He was wearing a dark-red suit laden with bold black pinstripe lines. The width of the suit did little to hide his frame, and Mr. Mal used such failure to full effect whenever the situation called for it. Luis recalled being there when Mr. Mal's picture was taken, which happened to be a week before Zephyr was born.

Wow.

He had just realized that he related all his memories to the birth of his first daughter.

Luis had finally met the bodyguard that blocked the door leading into Mr. Mal's office. He was a stocky older man with large black sunglasses and wore a suit only meant for a funeral. His hands were folded in a formal pose, and his demeanor matched that of the Royal Guard of Great Britain. His bald head reflected the lone lightbulb that hung pitifully from a thin wire. It flickered and flashed with every breath both men took, but the guard did not bother to pay it any attention. Luis stood in front of the doorman, and spoke to him in a relaxed tone.

"Good evening . . . are you new here?"

The doorman remained stationary and refused to address Luis.

"Okay. Not in the mood to talk? Don't worry, I have plenty to say." Luis stepped closer to the guard's face and narrowed his eyes slightly. "You're Lorenzo's replacement, right? Don't act so surprised—I know everything that goes on around here. As a matter of fact, I know what happened to Lorenzo. Aren't you a teeny bit curious?"

The doorman swallowed hard when Luis casually wrapped his arm around his shoulder. He placed his mouth next to his ear and continued his speech.

"You see, Lorenzo was tasked with the delivery of various narcotic-related transactions during my absence. He handled the acquisitions and distributions of roughly twenty thousand dollars' worth of cocaine. He did his job well, so well in fact that he had this crazy idea in his that he should take over my position as chief distributor permanently. Amazing, right? To think that a low-life shit sucker like Lorenzo had the brains and the balls to take over my perfect operation."

The doorman's breathing became heavy with each word Luis spoke. Luis took notice of his apprehension and decided to build upon it.

"You seem like a smart guy. Someone who follows orders without the decency of a thought. I just wanted to let you know that no one—*no one*—can control something that I have created. You cannot fathom what it takes to run my organization, so don't think that some shit clicker with a prison tattoo can handle what I handle."

Luis suddenly reached up to the ceiling and yanked down the wire holding the lightbulb and wrapped the iron string numerous times around the doorman's neck. He broke his statuesque protocol and clenched his fingers around the wire, trying desperately to break the cord that was now burrowing into his neck. Luis wrapped it quickly enough to subdue him, and he held it tightly enough to stifle a bloody scream. He was choking silently, and Luis only applied more pressure to his throat.

"This blood on me? Who do you think it belongs to? If you ever . . . get in my way . . . as much as blocking my way to a doorway, I will string your neck high on this cord until you have seizures . . . do you understand?"

The doorman choked and tried to slap Luis's hands off of the cord.

"Stop trying to fucking stop me! What is it with you people trying to halt my progress? I feed all of you! I put all your clothes on your back! I paid for this goddamned cord around your throat, and you want to stop me?"

Suddenly the door to Mr. Mal's office swung open, and the figure of a large, burly man exited to witness the noise that had been occurring. Luis looked up with a murderous rage in his eyes at the build belonging only to Mr. Julius Mal. He wore a wide yellow suit with a golden tie and a large yellow diamond tie pin shoved in the middle of the silk accessory. His face was dark and menacing, but not nearly as menacing as the face of Don Luis, whose hair was disheveled and wild from his sudden attack on the poor guard. His face was red from anger and full of long veins. Mr. Mal's eyes widened in shock but kept the expressed fear only for a moment, and immediately reverted back to his apathetic attitude. When Luis saw Mr. Mal face-to-face, he switched back to his peaceful demeanor and smiled widely.

"Oh! Mr. Mal! So glad to see you. Your new associate and I were having a friendly discussion about your previous associate."

Luis released his grip from the doorman, and his body slumped to the ground, coughing violently and massaging his ruptured neck. Luis stood up, combed his fingers through his hair, and patted Mr. Mal on his back.

"Let's go in your office, I need to sit down for a while."

Mr. Mal had calmly stepped aside to allow Luis to enter his office, despite the rage and distrust of the Don fully embedded in his eyes. He watched as Luis nonchalantly threw himself in a nearby leather seat and reclined back until his head rested on the platform. He kicked his feet up and planted them on Mr. Mal's desk, sighing deeply and wearing a wide grin on his face. He closed his eyes and started to hum a soft melody, while he slowly rocked his feet back and forth on the pendulum of his ankles. Mr. Mal chuckled and motioned his guards to give the two men their privacy. The guards nodded and took it upon themselves to help the doorman untangle the metallic cord latched onto his throat. Luis opened his eyes and caught a glimpse of dark blood spilling over the frantic fingers of the guardsmen, ripping apart the cord and wrapping a piece of cloth around his neck. Luis smirked and turned his attention toward the silent gang leader.

"You think I went a tad bit overboard, Julius?"

"I got nothing to say," Mr. Mal started, "except that what you did was unnecessary. To him and to 'Renzo."

"Oh, don't get me wrong, I did not enjoy doing that at all. Not one bit. But my point had to get across."

"Really? And what point is that?"

"Simply that, you know, anyone that attempts to usurp my position or my duties will end up like Lorenzo. That's all."

Mr. Mal plopped himself down in his large black leather chair that sat across from Luis's relaxed body and pulled out a tan cigar. He held the cigar next to his nose and inhaled the tobacco mixture deeply. "My ass cannot be held responsible for what my crew does. I'm not psychic, and even if I was, there was no way I could've stopped it."

"You could have stopped it by not letting it happen in the first place. Everyone has something to do here. My absence did not hinder our financial progress, now did it?"

"Our financial progression ain't shit compared to what the streets are saying. 'Oh, Luis Estrada ain't around no more. He ain't running shit right now. The great Don is a pussy.' We can't have that talk going around, feel me?"

"Were the streets saying that, or were you saying that?"

Mr. Mal reached into his desk drawer and slowly extracted an item. Luis watched his hands cautiously as the large gang leader chuckled and pulled out a tiny book of matches. He ripped out a match and struck it against the edge of his desk. He then placed the lit match next to his cigar and produced a decent flame that thrived on the end of the cigar. Luis relaxed himself and glanced around the room.

"What's the matter, Estrada?" Mr. Mal asked with a facetious grin on his face. "Don't you trust me?"

"No." Luis stood up and walked around the room. He stared at a certain spot on the wall and lost himself in thought. The sound of

Mr. Mal's mouth blowing smoke through the air only calmed Luis further. He kept his eyes on the imaginary spot while he spoke. "How much money did Lorenzo bring in? Total."

Mr. Mal stood up and pulled out a desk drawer that was situated on front of him. He took out a small black notepad and opened to the page he desired. "Three hundred thousand, four hundred, and sixty-two dollars."

Luis nodded. "That's not bad, actually. Maybe I should take off more often."

"What's stopping you then?"

"Idiots like you."

Mr. Mal glared at Luis, but the calm Don responded by walking toward the door. "Well, I came by to see how things were going, and you know . . . just to update you on my current status and that of your former employee."

"Go fuck yourself, Estrada."

The Don turned around and calmly stared into Mr. Mal's nervous, yet imposing eyes. Such visual contact destroyed the boundaries that separated reality from the fantastic world and thrust both men in a realm where they saw themselves manifest in their own sprit, spectral forms. The dark and seedy office that used to belong to Mr. Mal seemed to explode within Luis's view and left a large white room after the mist from the destruction dissipated. Luis himself found himself wearing a white suit with a matching tie, shirt, and shoes. Mr. Mal was nowhere in sight, his form not yet materializing in the empty space they occupied, but his last words spoke in a delayed echo that spread throughout this plane.

"Go . . . fuck . . . yoursssselllf . . ."

Luis closed his eyes and walked in a small circle, his steps creating silent noises each time his pale shoe landed on the ground. His breathing was serene and contemplative while succeeding in airing out his frustrations and anxieties.

The white room was without walls or boundaries, no firmament to identify the relationship between sky and earth and no direction to determine left from right, or up from down. Luis opened his eyes and looked up toward what he thought to be the ceiling; the direction of his face only won the image of a mountain completely covered in new fallen snow. The peak of the mountain pointed down toward the Don, who stared at the tip as if it were a sword hung on a thin wire. When he brought his gaze back to his concept of the earth, he saw Mr. Mal standing a couple of inches away from his face. His eyes were bloodshot and warm, with dark circles that puffed against his sagging cheekbones and bade bitter welcome to his dragging lips that hung like weeping willows in a snowstorm. His neck was slashed and decorated by a heavy, silver blade, which was tightly gripped by his tense, stubby fingers. The knife was coated in blood and stifling sweat that dripped to the floor in a torturous speed. Each bit of moisture that splashed into the tiny puddle in front of Mr. Mal's feet made him twitch and lose his breath. His eyes continuously studied the Don in white that stood before him. Mr. Mal held the bloody blade in his shaking hand and pointed the steel point towards Luis.

"Anything for a laugh," Mr. Mal gurgled through his blood, "*Señor* Estrada."

Mr. Mal took the blade off his slashed throat and rotated it in his calloused hand until the flat end faced his stomach. He wiped the blood on his bare chest and formed an *x* with his own sanguine liquid. He let his arm relax on his side while he paced around the white dimension that surrounded both men. Luis had remained in his spot while he observed the marvelous splendor of his rival talking to himself and releasing sudden outbursts of nonsensical fury.

"I am the boss. I am the fucking boss here! He thinks he can push my shit around? Fuck him!"

At that moment, Mr. Mal turned the blade in his hand until the fatal tip directed its hungry attention toward Luis. Mr. Mal inhaled deeply and began charging at Luis. His steps thundered throughout the pale dimension, mimicking the stampede of a few hundred bulls stomping the ground in Spain. His body rushed toward the Don, who stood there with barely a sign of fear splashed on his face. He remained apathetic towards Mr. Mal's sprint and kept his eyes glued on the raged gang leader. Suddenly, he stopped just a few inches in front of Luis and directed his gaze toward his chest. He could almost see his heart beat softly underneath his white suit that was padded with silk and glowing fibers. Mr. Mal let his body act independently of his lost mind and felt his hand point the knife toward himself. He placed his free hand over his enclosed fist and thrust the blade into the x on his chest. He jerked from the sudden pain he felt and gasped at the sight of his blood squirting out from his abdomen. It enlarged the puncture he formed in his skin as it spurted out onto the floor in front of him, creating a small pool that quickly flowed over to Luis's feet.

Luis responded to this sight by stepping back away from the bloody lake, while pulling out his handkerchief and covering his flared nostrils. Mr. Mal's blood bubbled and spurted like a bowl of putrid acid. He burned his hand from attempting to close the wound with his palm. His great body felt fragile and awkward as he stumbled toward Luis, his knees transforming into glass plates that shattered as soon as his legs gave out under his large build. He knelt down in front of Luis, who stared at him with no emotion left in his eyes. Mr. Mal clawed at Luis's white slacks, the blood from his hands dripping and staining his pants. He sputtered out a concoction of saliva and blood when he managed enough strength to speak to the cold Don standing over him.

"I-I want . . . to kill . . . all of you . . ."

Mr. Mal's eyes grew heavy and sagged along with the weight of his fleeting life. He lost all feeling in his chest when his heart became exhausted from beating all the years of his life. It gave in to the comforting embrace of a dark figure that materialized behind Mr. Mal. Luis squinted his eyes to make out the body of a female, youthful in corporal demeanor with the wisdom of age that shone in her eyes. Her hair was blacker than the shards of night descending upon an Arabian desert, her strands cascading down her back and ending at her hips in a graceful, almost arrogant matter. Her face was warm and full of harmonious beauty, but Luis could not help but feel a bitter chill run down his torso when he looked upon her eyes, pale as the reflection of the moonlight on a dark and lonely ocean. She was of a medium height in body but made up for it with her colossal dominance she exhibited when she made herself known to the two men in front of her. The curiosity present in all human beings stirred within

Luis, and he let himself question the presence of the beautiful death goddess in front of him.

"Who are you?"

The figure did not answer him but instead fixed her colorless eyes on her inquisitor. Luis felt a sudden fear creep into his heart when those pair of slicing pupils studied his face and made entry into his soul. He felt the figure search the chambers of his spirit, enveloping Luis and thrusting him into a catatonic state. She continued to remain inside his soul, casually opening one door leading to the depths of his spirit and closing another. Luis stood frozen and unable to command the functions of his body or mind. He was left a mindless automaton so long as she remained inside—a guest appraising a household with little regard for the owner. Luis felt a tear roll down his cheek and land on his shoe. The humble drop of sorrow made the figure blink, and she released her psychic hold on Luis. He felt his lungs absorb air once again, his heart resumed it rhythmic beat, and his eyes drowned themselves in his grief. The figure patiently waited for Luis to gaze at her once again, but he found himself weeping on his knees, his wet face buried in his palms. The beautiful death goddess approached the crying Don and lifted his mournful body off the ground with the power of her will. Luis paid no attention to the gravity that abandoned his body as he allowed himself to be levitated toward the dark figure. He stopped in front of her face and felt the warmth of the goddess's face radiate upon his forehead. He raised his head and reluctantly opened his eyes to the sight of the figure smiling at him. Her teeth were as white as her pupils, stretching out to form dimples on both sides of her cheeks. She kept her stare on Luis, who suddenly felt the fear escape from his heart.

"Zephyr?"

Luis found himself back in Mr. Mal's office. The same moldy walls that surrounded both men reappeared in front of Luis's line of sight. Mr. Mal unfortunately was, Luis had thought, still alive. His body was free of any crimson life source that poured from his chest. No bleeding knives were in plain sight, and most importantly, no goddess of death was to be seen in the room. Luis remembered the face clearly and did his best to hold on to the image of Zephyr in adulthood. Her immaculate face, the shape of her nose, and the subtle slant of her ashen eyes—they all started to fade from his memory. Luis frowned at his loss and could only conjure up the image of his infant daughter laughing and giggling in her crib. However, Luis realized that this picture was sufficient in making him joyful once again, and he caught himself snickering out loud.

"What's so fucking funny, Estrada?" Mr. Mal interrupted Luis's thought train.

"You're gonna get yourself killed one day." Luis slowly approached him, who met Luis midway through his destination. Both men were now inches away from each other, feeling the slow and angry breaths which misted around one another. Their eyes showed no fear or apprehension of one getting killed, and each leader hoped that it would be the other who swallowed a bullet. "See you soon, Julius."

Luis Estrada nodded his head in a gentleman's gesture and turned on his heel to exit the office. He looked to his right and saw bloodstains on the floor where the doorman had previously lain. Luis chuckled and ventured downstairs, leaving Mr. Mal loathing at the sight of his backside facing him.

Luis ventured downstairs and looked around the less-than-living room. He spotted the drug dealer nervously standing in the same corner where Luis found him. Luis approached him slowly, and the dealer swallowed hard when he saw the relaxed Don standing in front of him.

"Did you procure the funds, *Señor*?" Luis held out his palm and smiled.

"R-right here. It's all here. Really." The dealer reached into his pocket and pulled out a wad of bills. He pushed it into Luis's hands, who counted the money front and back.

"Two hundred dollars even. Very nice job. I'm proud of you."

"I-I got the money from my bank account, man. I'm bled dry . . . just take it, all right?"

"Bank account?" Luis pondered this concept for a brief moment, and then he redirected his attention to the matter at hand. "Since when did you have a bank account?"

"What? Everyone has bank accounts, man . . . new policy and shit. Who the fuck cares? The cash is legit, man . . ."

Luis slapped the wad of bills against the back of his hand and wandered away from the dealer. He breathed a deep sigh and slumped against the wall as he saw Luis enter a small room. He slowed his breathing enough to observe the actions of the Don, who was looking around for someone or something. Luis stepped over to a woman who lay in a corner ready to shoot a tube of white hot liquid into her veins. The dealer saw Luis violently grab the woman by her drugged-up arm and smashed the tools she had against a nearby wall. The dealer got on his feet to see Luis pull out the stash he had taken from him and handed it over to the woman. She looked first at the wad of money and then at Luis. She felt enamored by his strong gaze, and yet she was terrified. The dealer saw Luis say something inaudible to her, and her head nervously nodded in assent. Luis stretched out his arm to allow the woman to walk in front of him. She accepted his gesture, and he followed her out the doorway. When she exited outside, Luis turned around and leered at the drug dealer, who answered his look by turning away from his sight. Luis sucked his teeth and followed the woman outside to reminisce on the night air that he had temporarily abandoned.

VII

Rosa had returned to her original once Luis had left her and his children at the church to continue his evening duties. After he had left, she hailed a cab while Zephyr lay sleeping in her arms and surveyed the cab driver when he had pulled to her curb. She first walked around the back of the car to commit the license plate to memory, and then she proceeded to hand Zephyr over to Pedro, who politely obliged and rocked her back and forth in his folded arms. Rosa walked over to the driver's side of the taxi and leaned against it as if she was a police officer performing a routine check of the driver and the vehicle he commanded. Her body was rested against the rear door, while the upper part of her elegant torso slightly bent over to witness the face of the cab driver. She watched his confused eyes measure her face intently and gave him no pleasure of her name or the names of her present family.

"Uh . . . evening?" The cab driver felt awkward and uncomfortable.

Rosa smiled and helped him relax. "Hi, could you take us to this address, please?" Rosa reached into her purse and handed over a small white slip of paper. The cab driver took it and glanced over the contents.

"Yeah, no problem. Hop in."

Rosa nodded and opened the door for Pedro and Zephyr. He obeyed his mother and entered the vehicle with his infant sister still slumbering in his arms. Rosa closed the door on them and walked the same path she took around the car. She came for the infant carrier that doubled as a car seat that she had left on the ground. The asymmetric plastic seat sat in front of her hands, and she obliged its wish to be put to proper use. Rosa grabbed the car seat and opened the door on the opposite side of the car. She cradled it in her bosom and entered the taxi. The car seat was placed in between her and her children before she closed the door.

"Put Zephyr in here," she asked. Once Pedro placed Zephyr in her seat, Rosa directed her attention toward the cab driver. "We're all set. You can drive."

"Gotcha," he answered. He shifted the gear into drive and sped off into the city grid, while Rosa slouched in her seat and relaxed her eyes. She remembered the first time Luis instructed her on specific tasks that required her attention while her husband was away. She heard the serious but calm voice that boomed in her ears when Luis lay next to her, his warm arms enclosed around her delicate body as he kissed her neck between each sentence. Rosa felt the sense of ease Luis gave her whenever he was just a touch away, the distance closing as soon as the tip of his finger glided up her shoulder. He never wasted time with his romantic excursions in bed, nor did he have to, for each sensation he gave to Rosa, each whisper that fell upon her ear, was performed and uttered as if it were his last. Rosa knew that this constant worry was upon his brow, though he did his absolute best to shroud it in smiles and other gestures of joyful umbrage. She could read his mind just as easily as a magazine article, and although she suspected that Luis knew this, neither person admitted their knowledge of loving dishonesty to the other.

Rosa kept her eyes closed and discerned the direction of each turn the taxi cab made, taking extra precaution in determining the validity of the driver's status. She heard Luis's voice whisper in her head as her body shifted along with the force of the vehicle.

"Always check the area for tails, whether it may be a nosy cop or some idiot whom I happened to piss off. I don't want anything to happen that I did not predict."

Rosa sighed in a pleasant manner and opened her eyes. The stream of buildings and pedestrians started to fade off into the past, and the taxi cab continued on the route Rosa provided.

"If you do get a cab," Luis continued, "be sure to check everything: license plates, paint of the car, the driver's profile in the back seat . . . make sure it matches the person behind the wheel. And if you feel that he is something otherwise, he usually is."

"What if there's a tail?" she shyly asked.

"Then you go to this address." Luis reached over Rosa and grabbed a small white notebook that lay on the nightstand. He placed it in her cupped hands while gently kissing her knuckle. She opened the notebook and read the words scratched on the paper.

"Okay."

Luis nodded. He stared off into a space on the wall, contemplating on any information he deemed important to pass on to his wife. When she closed the notebook, it awakened him from his daydream and he continued to instruct her carefully. "Sometimes you will feel that there is a tail even though there is hardly anyone around." Luis sighed deeply and fixed his eyes on those of his wife. "The truth is that there's always someone around watching."

"Who's watching us now?" Rosa wondered.

"Me." Luis smiled and rested his head on her shoulder. His face was still full of stubble that had reappeared after his morning shave. Each individual spike of hair tickled Rosa's soft and supple neck. The memory of Luis's chin scratching against her shoulders released Rosa from her fantasy and threw her back to the leather seat of the taxi cab. She glanced behind her and saw no cars following them. Both sides of the vehicle were also absent of any ambitious police officers or any overzealous gang members. Only a small number of cars remained in front of the car, and they were too far away to be of any necessary concern.

Rosa smirked and watched the wondrous infant next to her. Zephyr was snuggled in her warm blanket and looking around the car. Her cool, silvery eyes eventually met her mother's and displayed a curious expression within those colorless pupils. She seemed to read the subtle worry in Rosa's face and the progressive longing for the husband that should have been hers. She deeply loved Luis but secretly resented the people who made him who he was today. Had circumstances been different, she supposed, he would have been the same husband that entertained his family without a pressing duty on his mind. He would have been the father who was able to tuck

Zephyr in every night and read bedtime stories to her with the silence of a mythological nightingale. He would have been the masculinity Pedro needed as a guide for his budding and oft-tumultuous teen years. Most of all, Rosa just wanted him as her own. She would rather spend long days worrying about his bouts with the common cold instead of his wagers with death. Rosa shook her head and giggled once the taxi cab reached its destination.

"What's so funny?" Pedro was staring out the window as he asked his question.

"Nothing. I'm just gonna kill your father next time I see him."

"Oh. Okay." Pedro blew his breath on the window and drew a smiley face on it. The cab driver put the car in park and pressed a button on the door handle. He looked outside of his window and observed the great mansion that towered in the middle of the field. Home sweet home, Rosa thought. The cab driver turned around and addressed Rosa anxiously.

"Is this the place you want?"

Rosa leaned over and looked out the opposite window next to Pedro. "Yes, it is. *Gracias.*"

The driver turned his head back toward the direction of the road. He held the palm of his hand out without looking at Rosa and waved his fingers to reminisce on the feeling of rough dollar bills grazing against his fingertips. Rosa stared at it for a while, contemplating the source of his rude behavior. She abandoned her thoughts when the driver cleared his throat and continued to let his hand hover in front of Rosa's face. She rolled her eyes and politely obliged his request. "How much do I owe you?"

"Price is on the meter there," he answered.

Rosa glanced at the neon red digits that flashed on the screen. Thirty-five dollars and seventy cents. Rosa chuckled, recalling the slower than molasses speed the driver maintained in the duration of the trip. The unnecessary turns, including the early stops made when the light had just turned yellow, all contributed to the four blinking numbers in front of her eyes. Nevertheless, she reached into her purse and pulled out a bill with Alexander Hamilton's chubby profile stamped on the front. She handed the bill to the driver, who immediately clasped his hand without a word of thanks. Rosa motioned Pedro to grab their things and exit the vehicle, while she cradled her curious daughter. The driver remained in the vehicle, making quick glances in his rear view mirror to see if the Estrada family had left his car. When they did, he put the taxi cab in drive and sped off toward the ends of the horizon.

"Hmph," Rosa mumbled. "Jerk."

She followed Pedro inside the home while she gently kissed Zephyr on her nose. She turned to her left and saw that no one else was around. Zephyr giggled while reading the thoughts contained in her mother's eyes. Rosa smirked and carried her daughter inside the large home.

"One day," Rosa sadly whispered, "I'll have to teach you what your father taught me, little one."

Rosa sank in the lonesome chair that stood in the far left corner of the living room. She ran her fingers through her thick black hair and closed her eyes. She had already lain down the Estrada daughter in her infantile chamber and checked on Pedro, who was busy reading a book. She glanced at the cover of the novel. *Crime and Punishment.* She thought it was great choice for a novel but then worried that Pedro may be sinking into a deep depression due to the nature of his books. No such thing as a happy ending, only a bittersweet end to a tale. She kept the concern in her mind even as she walked downstairs and threw herself in Luis's favorite chair. She always wondered why he took such a liking to this specific piece of furniture. When she closed her eyes and reminisced on the early hours of her day, she realized her husband's proclivity to this throne of thought and accepted its reputation with ease.

The telephone that sat on the opposite side of the room rang. She opened her eyes and stared at the vibrating white phone that sent a shockwave through the table upon which it stood. It was a vintage phone that she had found many years ago at a local yard sale. The family had been preparing for a move outside of the city and wanted to get rid of anything that reminded them of the area that surrounded Beelzebub's Bay. Rosa walked by with Luis the same day and gawked at the white phone, laced with gold trim and adorned with a silver fleur that lay on the handset. It was a rotary phone with an old plastic covering that was specked with yellow hues of usage and age. She smiled widely when her eyes paid homage to its appearance and artistic decadence. When she turned to Luis, he could not help but notice the wish in her face. He capitulated underneath the childlike glow in her cheeks and bought the phone for seven dollars. The price did not matter to Luis, who would have bought the aged communications device for three hundred dollars if it meant keeping Rosa's glee for a few more moments. Those moments eventually turned into years, and Rosa deemed herself the only one who was allowed to answer the phone, not out of selfish pride in acquired materials but for the sheer joy she felt for appreciating art and exercising its glory.

Rosa pushed herself out of her husband's seat and glided over to answer the phone. She cradled the outdated piece of technology in her soft shoulder and spoke into the telephone as she gently massaged her hands. "Hello?"

"M-Mrs. Estrada?" The voice that whispered over on the other line was that of a woman.

"Yes? What can I do for—"

"I need Mr. Estrada! Please!" The voice sounded terrified and anxious.

"He's . . . not here right now. Is something wrong?"

"Oh . . ." The woman's voice remained silent. Her breathing was heavy and stifled. "Okay . . . okay, I'm sorry. Umm . . . th-thank you."

"What's wrong? Whatever it is, I can help."

"But usually Mr. Estrada helps me. With my boyfriend . . ."

Rosa paused and briefly lost herself in a moment of thought. "Sarah? Is that you?"

"Y-You know . . . Mr. Estrada told you about me?"

"Yes. Don't worry about that right now. Where are you?"

"In my apartment . . . wait . . ."

Rosa heard silence on the other end of the phone. She waited for half a minute until her voice restarted the conversation. "Sarah?"

"He's coming! Oh my god, he's coming up the stairs! He's gonna kill me!"

"Stay there! I'm coming!"

Rosa heard Sarah's dreadful wails sound throughout the room. She concentrated on each sound that reverberated to the mouthpiece that apparently fell on the floor. A deep voice yelled at her and screamed profanities at Sarah.

"Fucking whore . . . gonna . . . kill you . . . fuck was that today . . . saw you talking with him . . ."

Rosa felt a strong sense of timing well up in her heart. She hung up the phone and pulled out the table drawer. She grabbed a small red notebook and flipped through the pages until she found Sarah's address inked between two sky-blue lines. She read it over quickly, committed the street address to memory, and tore a blank page out of the book. She reached for a pen, still rolling form the shock of the drawer being opened, and etched a small note. After it was written down, she threw both of the stationery back into the drawer and ran to the bottom of the stairs, praying that Pedro was not asleep.

"Pedro! I'm leaving, I'll be right back! Watch Zephyr!" Rosa waited a few moments before she heard a lazy voice call back to her.

"Okay, no problem, *Mami*."

Rosa thanked God and grabbed a pair of keys that hung next to the doorway. She flung the front door open and sped her way to the car. She came to a dark-red BMW convertible that sat in a shadowed corner in the garage. She hardly drove it, saving it only for occasions that called for it. She placed her hand on the door for stability and leaped over it, while simultaneously landing her feet on the clutch and the gas pedals. Rosa thrust the key into the ignition and twisted it almost forcefully in its crank. When the car finished starting, she stomped on the gas and sped through the winding driveway and entered the streets to make the acquaintance of Sarah's beau.

"Sorry, Luis . . ." Rosa whispered. "I have to do this . . ."

Luis pulled into the driveway and drove along until he reached the garage. He immediately noticed that the red BMW belonging to his wife had disappeared from its usual hiding place, leaving a long black streak in its stead. Luis deduced that Rosa was in a desperate hurry and was not able to wait a second longer to depart from the mansion. Most men would take this view as a sign of infidelity—the lonely wife abandoned by her husband runs off as soon as he leaves to wrap herself in the arms of someone else, no matter how selfish his own ambitions were. But Luis knew Rosa since they were children, and he knew that Rosa was as faithful as a rainstorm in London.

He had Rosa's love to utmost completion, and he cursed himself for those days where he felt her love was forever lost. Any doubts he maintained in his mind, whether such doubts commanded Plato's sense of logic or the irrational thoughts of man, vanished once Rosa's smile greeted him as he walked through the doorway. However, when he had entered the home that they built together, Luis did not find the comforting laughter he had become accustomed to but found a quiet emptiness embrace him and kiss him on his cheek. He capitulated to imagining Rosa stealing time in his favorite lounge chair and ventured over to the living room to pique his growing interest.

The living room remained as quiet and solemn as he had left it. The pillows on the sofa were untouched and carried no wrinkles that clued him in on past visitors. The walls echoed no evidence of soft, delicate hands fixing the paintings that hung from them, as if they were soldiers standing prostrate while they awaited further commands from their presiding officer. The floor always held more tales of visitation for Luis to read; tonight, they only told stories of all who had the pleasure and the privilege of striding across the waxed wooden planks. Luis only found a small dent made into his famed leather chair and jokingly admired the shape that his wife's posterior created when she sat down. His eyes traveled up from the indenture, over and across the other side of the large room, and settled on the old vintage phone that Rosa begged him to purchase with her innocent and pleading face. He casually walked over to the table that supported it and glanced at a small white piece of paper. He recognized Rosa's cursive that slid across the paper, and Luis read the singular word it contained: "Sarah."

He let the paper glide back on the table and sat down in his favorite leather chair. He smelled the sweet scent that lingered behind. He thanked himself for introducing Rosa to the wonderful aromas French fragrances had to offer her. But now, he worried about her but did not let his concern build up. He knew that Rosa was fully capable of handling such matters herself, and he remained confident in her dignity. But, as he learned, he could not ignore the fact that he was here and she was elsewhere. That sense of calm loneliness returned. He never got used to that emptiness that only his wife could fill.

He closed his eyes for a brief moment. He then decided to check on Zephyr and Pedro, perhaps kill some time by spending quality time. As he arose from his seat, he tried to predict the outcome of Rosa's visit. He chuckled and shook his head.

If Luis was afraid, he was fearful of anyone who attempted to get in her way.

Rosa arrived at the address that Luis had written down many months ago. It was a dark street with one lamp post tearfully lighting the path down to Sarah's apartment. She decided to park the car a block away in a gas station, wishing to avoid unnecessary attention and larceny and also to save someone from quick and certain injury should such bad luck befall her vehicle. She found a suitable parking space and parked the car. She exited and strode toward Sarah's apartment complex.

When she reached the building, she heard a muffled scream emanate from the third-floor window followed by a loud crash, like the sound of porcelain hitting human bone, and finally, a heart-crunching period of sobbing. Rosa rushed in without so much as taking a deep breath or mentally preparing herself for the sight she would behold.

The lobby was empty of tenants and full of rodents. Little groups of mice scurried across the green tile floor in search of a tasty morsel of rotting food crumbs buried underneath cigarette butts. The stench was animalistic and heavy, with a slight twinge of dying potted plants that sat in all four corners of the room. Rosa paid attention to her surrounding area as she pushed open the staircase door that led to Sarah's apartment. The thought of taking the elevator crossed her mind, but the sight of the lobby alone convinced her that its appearance matched the condition of the lifts.

She entered the flight of stairs and crinkled her nose from the mixed odors of urine and unkempt cement. The banisters were rusty and decked with year-old pieces of chewing gum, gray and petrified from living in the dry and stagnant atmosphere. The stairs themselves were made out of steel that chipped off in places that were too numerous to count. The walls had so much spray paint left by members of competing gang territories that it was impossible to determine the true color of the wall original tints. She ignored these details and focused on the one that compelled her to bring herself here, one out of many godforsaken homes.

She skipped each step of the staircase with her graceful leaps, honed from many years as a dancer in times past, and commanded her feet to land softly on the floor in order to muffle the sound of any echo that may reach the ears of Sarah's boyfriend. Rosa's heartbeat quickened once she reached the third floor, and her perception of every object and person in the hallway was made known to her. Her natural agility allowed her to weave in and out of the gathering crowd, who also heard the noises vibrate the air particles around them and register as bloody screams in their ears. The crowd became more close and compact as soon as Rosa reached the apartment door, but this claustrophobic feeling only made her push aside the crowd with greater strength and persistence.

One of the patrons spoke up. She claimed that this sort of thing had happened before, but she was too scared to inquire about it because he was such a big guy and she had too many mouths to feed. Rosa let an idea enter her head. She allowed it to make itself comfortable in the creative section of her mind. She knocked on the door loudly and waited for a reply.

"Who the fuck is it?" the door shouted at Rosa. She did not need to figure out that it was the voice of Sarah's angry boyfriend.

"It's your neighbor. Is everything all right in there?"

"Mind your own fucking business!"

Rosa rolled her eyes. *They all say that.* "If you don't stop," she continued, "I'll have to call 9-1-1!"

As she finished her last sentence, Rosa heard a sequence of furious stomps approach the door. The metallic chimes of excited fingers fiddling with the rusty chain that held it closed cued Rosa into retreating to the side where the door would cease to open any further. She let her predictions flash in her mind and combed through any problems that may occur. Would he have a gun? Doubtful, but in case he did, let's act in this manner. Knife? Same way—both weapons do more damage than needed. Bare fists? Most likely, considering the thuds and slams that everyone down the hall heard.

Rosa stood still and waited for Sarah's belligerent beau to grasp the reserves of his sanity to unlatch the door and swing it wide open to properly greet her. She smirked when the boyfriend brought validity to her prediction as he yanked the door open and stuck his head out through the doorway.

"You're not gonna call a goddamned—"

Rosa leaned her body toward the splintered apartment door and placed all her weight behind it. She pushed off with her powerful toes and struck the top of the door against his head. She felt a small shock wave travel from the point of impact through her small body. The boyfriend recoiled more from the surprise rather than the pain itself and briefly held his head in his hand. He seemed to be fighting a stubborn hangover; Rosa took this as a sign that she could have figured out herself. He took his hand down from his head and swung his arm in a wide arc. Rosa ducked underneath his blind swoop and stood back up to thrust the bottom of her palm up his nose. She jammed his nasal bone further into his skull, causing him to drop to his knees and cover the blood that gushed out from it. Rosa could see the tears run down his fingers, but she sped past him to locate Sarah. She followed the occasional sobs to the bathroom, where she found Sarah curled like a fetus in a corner and her head resting between her knees.

Sarah was a young Caucasian girl who was as pretty as she was hurt. Luis had been acquainted with her through an acquaintance of his and . . . his connections were way too deep to think over right at the moment. She rushed over to the poor young woman and gently rubbed her back. Sarah flinched from Rosa's touch, but she kept her hand upon the girl's skin to assure her that it was not her boyfriend trying to "comfort" her.

"Shhh . . . it's okay, Sarah. It's Rosa Estrada. I'm gonna take you out of here. It'll be okay, sweetie."

Sarah slowly raised her shaking head and fixed her eyes on Rosa's calm and loving face. Her eyes were red from crying and black from the constant punching and slapping she received for God knows what. Her arms were deadly hues of blue and purple leading to the dirt-black nails that dug into Rosa's back when she helped her on her feet. Her lips were bloodied and split open from the moment her head landed on the porcelain sink that seemed to tower high above her. Rosa let Sarah hang her tears on her shoulder as the two women ventured into the living room. Sarah tripped on the carpet a few times, but Rosa's strength would not allow her to fall completely to the floor.

Sarah's boyfriend held his head up to stop the bleeding, but the dark-red liquid poured out from his nostrils and rolled down his tattooed forearm. He saw Rosa carrying Sarah on her shoulder and stumbled his way to the kitchen. Loud clangs and sudden crashes of dishes enveloped the entire apartment and resonated throughout the hallway, where the door slightly creaked back and forth from Rosa's hasty entry. The neighbors formed a perimeter around the frame of the door. They watched in paralyzing terror as the boyfriend pulled out a wide steak knife and walked towards the two women. He stopped his pursuit and studied the scene in front of him: Rosa stared at him as she whispered some words into his girlfriend's ear.

"Rest . . . over there . . . I'll . . . be fine . . ."

He cursed himself for his inability to hear the strange guest's words but brushed it off and held onto the hilt of the silver edge that gleamed against his anguished eyes. He flung himself toward Rosa and plunged the knife forward, waiting for the sound of metal and blood merging together to form a sweet melody that would sing in his ears. Instead, he felt a hard push against his arm and a sharp twist of his wrist that sent a loud pain up his forearm. Rosa then grabbed his shoulders and brought a swift knee straight to his scrotum. He felt his delicate organs crush underneath her blunt and disgusting strike. The knife dropped to the floor as soon as his large body collapsed under the weight of pure agony.

Rosa brushed a strand of hair that fell out of place and swept the knife far away from where the boyfriend's body lay. She noticed that Sarah and the crowd that gathered in the hallway were all watching with shocked and wondrous expressions plastered on their faces. "Good evening everyone." Rosa addressed the crowd. "*Buenos noches.*" She turned to Sarah, who quickly wiped the tears from her eyes when she saw her boyfriend holding his testes in his hands and groaning in pain.

Rosa placed her sharp stiletto on top of his hands and slightly dug the point deeper into his crotch. The subtle movement was all she needed to make sure he understood his lesson. He wanted to cry so damn loud, but he was smart enough and vain enough to keep his mouth shut in order to avoid the embarrassment of having others clearly hear him. Rosa twisted her foot to drill the point deeper through his skin. This time, the boyfriend could not help but yell out in pain. After his scream sounded throughout the apartment complex, Rosa took her foot off and let the man roll around in pain. She looked at Sarah, who half-smiled throughout the whole ordeal.

Rosa grabbed his hair and violently yanked it up. The gel he wore had melted and ran underneath her fingernails, leaving a greasy amalgam of white nail polish and cheap grocery store hair gel. His eyes squinted in testament to the excruciating pain he felt when Rosa violently pulled each strand of his hair from his scalp. Rosa took a free hand and pointed to her back leg, showing the spectators and Sarah her intent with it.

Her calves hardened to a dense and blunt weapon, which she used to drive her knee into the aggressor's face. His nose cracked and bled under the sheer force summoned forth at Rosa's call. She saw his eyes turn inside their sockets and his tongue suspend from the side of his mouth. As he fell backward, the base of his skull landed heavily on the wooden floor, letting a loud thud pervade throughout the entire apartment. The bystanders watched in awe, as well as Sarah, as Rosa gently brushed her hair back and examined her fingernails. The nail on her left index finger had chipped off, which made her frown at the sight of the asymmetrical pattern born on her delicate finger. Her frown soon turned into a smirk, however, once she saw Sarah bounding after her with open arms and genuine tears in her eyes.

"Oh my fucking God! That was amazing! The way you kicked his ass! Smack! Eat floor, bitch!"

Sarah was sitting in the passenger side of Rosa's car, reliving and reenacting each moment Rosa performed like an actress pining for a part in a Broadway play. She raised her right knee as Rosa did fifteen minutes earlier while pretending to smash her boyfriend's face again and again. She was smiling and laughing through her baggy eyes and bloody lips, not paying attention to Rosa's quiet and solemn mood.

"You totally kicked his ass, Mrs. Estrada! Ugh! He deserved every fucking blow! Fucking loser . . . you know I would come in after working twelve-hour shifts and all he wanted to do was screw? I mean . . . isn't that some shit? My back hurts from waiting on dozens of fucking tables, and all he can think about is shoving that poor excuse of a cock in my mouth!"

Rosa chuckled and shook her head. "Some men don't care, Sarah."

Sarah turned her face toward the window and kept her eyes glued to the passing blurs of colorful buildings and lonely prostitutes smoking cigarettes. "I remember when we were introduced by a friend of ours. She had set us up on a blind date. Bitch. 'Oh, Sarah! Come meet this guy! He's sooooo cute!' My ass! The only thing about him that was cute was the way his face curled after you kneed him in the face!"

"I was raped once, Sarah."

Sarah jerked her head around and fixed her tired eyes on Rosa. "What?"

"A long time ago. I was sixteen. He was my boyfriend of two years. My parents loved him . . . we even talked about marriage."

Sarah suddenly kept silent and listened to Rosa.

"Well, my boyfriend was a walking bag of hormones—admittedly, like most men. Sometimes he would put moves on me that was only appropriate in the bedroom. I used to say, 'Don't you wanna wait for me?' And he would say, 'I would wait for a thousand eternities, *Mami*. A thousand.' In any case, he knew I was Catholic, so naturally he was already upset at the fact that I was saving my virginity for marriage . . . now that I think back on it, it was most likely the reason he proposed to me. But I was young, I was in love. I thought, 'Oh, he really loves me. He wants to spend the rest of his life with me.' I told all my friends, including Luis."

"You knew Mr. Estrada when you two were young?"

"I knew him since we were five. We used to play in his parents' yard and trample all over his mother's flower garden. Naturally, she . . . wasn't too happy about that. But anyway, Luis never really liked my boyfriend Eric. So when I told him that Eric and I were getting married, he was . . . less than thrilled. Luis flat-out said that Eric just wanted what was in between my legs. I remember I started to tear up, and then I just slapped Luis in the face before I left his sight . . ."

Rosa paused during her sentence. She pulled up to the entrance of a small motel and halted the vehicle. She grabbed the emergency brake and pulled up the rod until the latch locked in place. She turned off the car, sat back in her seat, and continued with her story. "After I had left, I went to the theater where we were all rehearsing for this play. I can't remember which one it was, I did so many plays and recitals . . ."

"You were an actress, Mrs. Estrada?" Sarah's curiosity interrupted Rosa's thoughts.

"Oh, no, no. I was a dancer. It's all I was ever good at. Salsa, meringue, rumba . . .flamenco was my forte. I used to be so good at it."

"Oh wow . . ." Sarah rested her gaze on Rosa, who kept the conversation going with her history.

"One of the teachers sent me to the dressing room to pick up a costume piece that was missing from one of the actresses' wardrobe. The dressing room was a bit creepy because it was so far away from everything else. You could scream and no one would hear you . . ." Rosa swallowed hard, as if she was reliving the moment in her story. "I remember seeing Eric in the dressing room, just standing there, breathing heavily and murmuring words. I asked him what he was

106

doing here, but he never answered. He just strode towards me and threw me on the floor. He shut the door behind us, and he threw himself on top of me. I felt my skirt drape over my head and my panties split in two. Then I felt something hot like a prodding iron rip my legs apart and . . . it hurt so much. So much! I heard my blood splatter all over the wood floors, and he just kept going! I told him to stop, that he was killing me, but he never listened. He kept ramming and ramming so hard that I started to black out from the pain . . ."

Rosa gently rubbed her eyes and looked toward Sarah, who sat still and shocked the entire time.

"Last I remember," Rosa continued, her eyes red from holding back tears of memory lane, "I remember waking up like I had a crazy dream. I looked down at my legs and saw my calves cut and slashed from Eric's fingernails ripping my clothes apart and tearing off my panties. Blood was everywhere . . . and I remember that pulsating pain I felt between my legs. I looked in front of me and I saw Eric sitting on the floor, half-naked, panting like a dog, and just . . . staring at me. I started to cry, and all he did was smile at me . . ."

"Oh my god, Mrs. Estrada . . ." Sarah held her own hands and rubbed her forearms from the image of Eric towering over Rosa with his sickly grin. "What happened after?"

"Nothing. He left."

Sarah displayed a look of puzzlement on her face.

"Sarah . . . sometimes men are out there to see you suffer. They don't want to see you happy, nor do they gain some sort of, you know, chivalrous duty to make you smile. Some men simply get pleasure of seeing you cry. Or worse."

Sarah turned away from Rosa and stared at the floor. Rosa kept talking to the battered teen.

"I think Eric snapped and just beat the virginity out of me. From what I found out years later, he had girlfriends on the side who would give it all up to him, and I was the only one he did not 'conquer.'"

"I-I'm so sorry. I never knew . . ."

Rosa closed her eyes and sighed deeply. "It's all right, sweetie. I just want you to realize that you have to be very wary of the men you meet. They're cute, yeah, but they can be so evil. I was so worried that I wouldn't be able to have kids after that whole ordeal. What's worse is that I have to look at Luis every day, until death do us part, and think, 'You are not my first.'"

Rosa moved closer to Sarah and caught the full attention of her eyes. "Looking at the one you love, knowing that he was not your first . . . is the emptiest feeling in the world."

Sarah felt frightened at Rosa's gaze but understood the seriousness contained in them and nodded.

"Since then, I have been very protective of my body, and so should you."

"Okay."

Rosa nodded and pulled out a small golden wallet that lay on the side of her car door. She handed the wallet to Sarah, who reflexively opened the wallet to count the wad of bills that spilled out from the opening. She fastened the zipper on the opening and closed the wallet back. Rosa assumed that Sarah was already cognizant of the routine given to her by Luis so many times in the past.

"I guess you're all set then. I'll tell my husband what happened when I see him."

"Okay . . ."

Sarah opened the car door, but before she exited the car, she reached over and wrapped her arms around Rosa's neck and gently kissed her on the cheek. "Thank you so much for coming for me," she said. "I don't know what I would've done without you."

Rosa smiled and watched Sarah as she closed the car door and entered the lobby for the motel. Rosa observed the speedy exchange between the motel hostess and Sarah and remained in the parking lot until Sarah waved back at her and disappeared in the hallways. She waited for a light to turn on within the tiny row of windowpanes and a slim silhouette to darken the atmosphere in the motel room. Rosa breathed a sigh of relief when an old yellow light flashed on in the window seven rooms down and a figure veiled in a dusky umbrage threw herself down on the bed. Rosa nodded to herself, turned on the car, and let out a long sigh before she drove off to meet the remainder of her evening.

Pedro stood over Zephyr and watched her as she lay in her crib and played with the white and pink mobile suspended over her curious white eyes. She observed the tiny pink pony that rocked and bucked every time she cutely slapped it with her left hand. She smiled widely when the pony reacted to a subtle kick she made, galloping and bouncing on the string that it used to float over her. Her innocent giggle and the star that beamed in her eyes made Pedro smirk and tickle his sister on her belly. If she had teeth, her grin would be wide and marvelous, able to melt the sun with her bright glee. He looked at a nearby bookcase that housed Zephyr's toys and stuffed animals, and grabbed one light-tan teddy bear with a laurel crown on his head, a staff in his right paw and wings on his feet. Pedro stood it up in front of Zephyr and walked it toward her smiling face.

"Hello there, *Señora*! My name is Hermes! Can you say *Hermes*? Huh? Can ya?"

Zephyr started to laugh, and she tried to grab the teddy bear from Pedro's playful grip.

"Oh, no, no! You have to say my name first!" Pedro blew a kiss to Zephyr, who kicked her feet and laughed out to her brother.

"Looks like you and your sister are getting along."

Pedro placed so much of his concentration in Zephyr that he failed to notice the tall figure of Don Luis Estrada standing in the doorway. "Oh, Dad! I . . . didn't hear you come in."

"It's okay, son. I didn't have the heart to disturb you. You two look so cute together!"

Pedro chuckled. "Oh geez. Now *I'm* officially embarrassed. Thanks."

"You're very welcome." Luis walked toward Zephyr's crib and leaned over to stare at his daughter's happy face. She gleamed when the large face of her father hovered over her small, chubby body. She outstretched her arms and legs for Luis, and he obliged her wish to pick her up and carry her in his strong arms. He cradled her gently in his hands and began to walk out the doorway. He sniffed her torso and scrunched his nose from the pungent aroma that wafted from her diaper.

"Guess I have to tend to this little princess," he said. "She left me a small gift as soon as I picked her up."

"Sounds like a job for *Papi*," Pedro joked.

"Uh-huh. You two were inseparable a couple of minutes ago."

"I let something nasty and unclean come between us." Pedro smiled and gently patted his father on the shoulder. As he quickly strode past him, Pedro realized that he failed to gain a proclivity for changing his sister's diapers, but he nevertheless made certain that such a pattern did not get interrupted. When he left his father behind to tend to Zephyr, a slight feeling of guilt crept into his chest and rested on his heart, but each step that took him farther away from any responsibility of caring for his baby sister pushed the feeling away from his bosom and let it fall to the ground to rot in an acidic puddle.

Pedro made his way downstairs and began to head outside. As he opened the closet door to put on his jacket, he stopped himself and stood in front of a tall grandfather clock. It was a mahogany tower of a clock that brought itself out from the depths of the cream-colored walls. It had an imposing fleur-de-lis molding situated in the grand wooden architecture and a large ovular face that housed a crystal white dial and long dark blades that signaled the current time. A black reed ticked its way past the Roman numerals buried underneath the curious reflection of Pedro Estrada, who studied each component of the clock with a steady gaze. He forced his eyes to resist blinking, wishing to keep each image of the grandfather clock as fresh as possible in his mind. When his heavy eyelids started to tweak and twinge from the gravity of his body's needs, Pedro shut his eyes tightly. He felt a lone tear drop down his cheek, but he could not determine whether it was sadness that compelled his eyes to moisten themselves or if it was pure frustration from the constant self-deception he had to uphold.

His hands clenched until his fingernails dug deep into his soft palms. His lower lip tucked underneath his teeth, and his eyes succumbed to the madness that invaded his heart. Pedro's forehead began to form massive beads of sweat, and his chin shot upward to a God he felt had abandoned him. His mouth opened to yell in overwhelming anguish, but no sound shot forth from his vocal chords. Only a dreadful silence sought the reserves of his sanity, and his heart took a sinister pleasure in welcoming the agony that took over his soul.

Pedro opened his eyes and stared into the reflection that faced him once again. He saw a shadowed spirit dressed in a black suit place his frigid hand upon Pedro's soldier and squeeze tightly. In return, Pedro placed his shaky hand upon the figure's and smiled once the figure allowed a dim spectrum of light to flash on his face.

"Hi, Pedro . . ." The figure spoke in a cold and ghastly voice. "We're friends, right?"

"Of course we are," Pedro answered. "Close friends . . . and by the way, it's good to see you."

"Oh, it's good to see you too. It really is. But . . ."

"But what? Tell me. You can tell me anything."

"We can't be friends just yet."

The dark figure paced around until his essence entered the face of the clock and stared straight into Pedro's wondrous eyes. Pedro now saw himself, the dark figure, hovering over the dial of the clock and frowning. The figure's eyes were puffy, and his pupils were as black as the midnight ocean. His face was slashed with wrinkles and spots created from smiles inflicted by the torment and despair he inflicted upon others. The hair on his head was shaved off and replaced with a large tattoo of Beelzebub sticking his tongue out at the heavens, mocking their nature and cursing their existence. Pedro felt a strange comfort when the figure spoke to him. His words were like a poetry recital; each syllable hummed soft melodies into his ears that drove him closer to the figure's message.

"Oh woe to us," the figure continued. "We can't be friends right now. Not as long as she still breathes . . ."

Pedro felt a heavy piece of metal slide down his throat. "What are you talking about?"

"Don't be coy. You know exactly what I mean. We must kill . . . kill now. If not now then later, but we must kill. Your hands hunger for infant blood, yes?"

"Yes."

"Your heart beats faster when you stand over her, yes? Just imagine wrapping your strong fingers around her fragile little neck and squeezing . . ."

Pedro closed his eyes and imagined Zephyr's body quaking and passing away in his grasp, her cold white eyes losing its grip on mortality and succumbing to a fit of jealousy.

"See?" The figure smiled widely as he spoke. "You're getting excited from the thought of it alone. Why don't you run upstairs and taste it yourself? The flesh of the infant underneath your fingertips . . ."

"Flesh . . . blood . . . infant . . ." Pedro repeated the words to himself and snickered as he opened his eyes.

"Kill her . . . kill them all . . ."

Pedro felt his eyes drown themselves in tears and pour down his face, but he refused to let his smile disappear from his face. "But I-I can't . . . kill her . . ."

"Stop fucking around! You keep telling yourself that everything will be fine, that all is hunky-dory. You'll tell me, 'Oh, I'm not able to kill my baby sister! She's not gonna do anything to me! *Papi* will pass the business down to me! Waah!' Shut the fuck up! If you're a man, if you have the right to own the floppy sag of shit you call testes, then get your ass upstairs and strangle that bitch!"

"Shut . . . the fuck . . . up . . ."

"You know what? Forget it. You're a pussy."

"What? No, I'm not . . ."

"You're a big blubbering piece of shit!"

"Stop it . . ."

"Oh, are you gonna cry now? Fucking vagina. Go ahead and fucking cry! You can't handle this business if it was handed to you on a shiny fucking platter!"

"I said shut the fuck up!"

Pedro clenched his hands and threw his fist at the figure in the grandfather clock. He shattered the glass barrier that shielded him from the figure's dimension, and the shards fell to the floor and cracked as he withdrew his fist. The figure still remained within the realm of the glass, who laughed hysterically at the tearful young

Estrada male. The figure kept laughing for what seemed like hours upon hours of relentless mocking, all directed toward Pedro's remaining sanity. He stomped his foot on a shard that held the partial image of the figure's laughing image and watched it split into hundreds of tiny crumbs of glass. The sonorous cackle of the dark figure found momentary comfort within Echo's arms and rested its head in her bosom until her fickle hands released his voice and condemned him to the dungeons of night.

Pedro wiped the remnants of tears from his face and listened out for anyone who might have heard his sudden burst of outrage. He looked on all sides of him and found no bystander plagued with the case of curiosity. He stared back at the grandfather clock in front of him and found . . . nothing. No damage. No evidence of one-hundred-year-old glass shattered on the floor or of any images residing within the glass reflection other than his own. Pedro found himself satisfied with the empty result he received once silence greeted his ears. He combed his hair with his fingers and took in a deep breath before he exited his home.

"Infant blood," he muttered.

Slim stood outside his favorite pool hall and rested his body against a nearby lamp post. The night sky always paid close attention to Slim's demeanor and thus allowed itself to wear a dark frigid veil whenever his face entered the moonlight. Slim enforced the cool sprinkles of rain to drop on all things except his cigarette, which he puffed and puffed until the orange glow ceased to appear on the tip any longer. His black trench coat dragged against the moist concrete, leaving streaks of wet dirt every time he paced back and forth from the pool hall entrance. His eyes never looked higher than an inch above his head, nor did they emanate a calm glimpse of joy when he smiled. His sinister smirk and his pretentious gaze gave purpose to the existence of his dark soul, which was always on the hunt for sweet innocence to corrupt. He licked his lips whenever a couple walked by and showed no shame when the boyfriend cast him a dirty look. Slim would just chuckle and shove his middle finger in the air as the couple walked away faster, partly to avoid unnecessary conflict and partly because they somehow knew that Slim had been in fights before and won. Years and years of living on the streets helped Slim hone his combat skills, and he developed his own fighting style that incorporated knives, guns, steel pipes, tire irons, and anything lethal that his hands could reach. His lanky body, although lacking in physical strength, was ample enough for the speedy maneuvers he had to apply to dodge haymaker punches or long arm hooks. He was able to provide enough endurance to last the fight without feeling drained of oxygen, and once his opponent was reeling from the energy he (more often she) had expelled, Slim went for the throat and turned the proverbial statement into something agonizing and real.

His prowess in street fights showed through his eyes, and a slight smirk was enough to stave off any false senses of heroism each beau may have wished to display. Slim flicked a finished cigarette into a puddle that reflected his apathetic face and look ahead. He saw a small figure grow larger as it approached him, and he smiled once the lamp post light flickered a brief moment to show the pale face of Pedro Estrada.

"Pedro!" Slim called out to his friend with a smile on his face. "What's up, man? What brings you to this side of town?"

"Hey, Slim . . ." Pedro walked up to Slim and glanced on all directions surrounding them. "I need to talk with you . . . just for a sec."

"Yeah, yeah, sure! Let's go somewhere where there's no bitches sucking off for money. They come later."

"Yeah . . . okay." Pedro followed Slim to a small corner where only a homeless man slept soundly. He had a half-full bottle of cheap vodka that rested on his lap and a wide sheet of week-old newspaper flung over his legs. The stench that radiated from his grotesque, almost inhuman body carried its heavy fragrance toward Pedro's and Slim's sensitive nostrils. Their noses squeezed up once their brains registered the scent of something close to dying and accelerated their gait to a corner free from his impoverished oils and vagrant snoring. When the sounds of his depressive slumber only reached their ears as the remnants of an echo, Pedro felt it best to proceed with his discussion.

"So . . . are you close with your gang friends?"

"Yeah, they're good buddies of mine. Look out for each other, nice little feeling of camaraderie, stuff like that."

"Forty-Second Street homies, right?"

"Yeah . . . why you ask?"

"I may need you to talk to them soon." Pedro sighed deeply and stared at the ground. "Believe it or not, I . . . have a job for them."

Slim smiled widely and threw his arm around Pedro's shoulder. "Holy shit! Big man has a job for us! Did your cock grow bigger overnight or something? This has gotta be something special for you to need our little help."

"It is . . . in a sense. It's something pretty big."

Slim waited for Pedro to look up from the ground. His friend kept his eyes fixed on a small puddle that held the reflection of Pedro's sad face. Slim darted his eyes around in confusion and felt that Pedro was expecting something to appear within that puddle. "So . . . this is the part where you tell me what type of job it is."

"We'll get to that eventually, right now I just need you to talk to your gang buddies . . . and have them talk to Mr. Mal."

Slim's smile faded away fast when he realized that Pedro was not adding comedy to his words. He studied Pedro's face and could find no indication of wavering eyes or a slight smirk appearing on his mouth. Pedro kept his sight on the pimply ground, full of cigarette butts and dirty rainwater left behind from a day-old shower. The water reflected the pale moonlight that hung in the evening sky like a melancholic chandelier suspended in a lonely dining room. Slim chuckled and wrapped his skinny arm around Pedro's shoulder.

"Don't you worry 'bout a thing," he reassured his friend. "I will personally talk to Mr. Mal myself. He's a good guy once you get past his size, you know? But you'll have to come with me for the meeting, is that okay?"

"Sure. Whatever. It's fine by me."

"And you'll have to come with me to see him tomorrow night."

"What? Why tomorrow?"

"It's the only time he's available this whole week, and by the tone of your voice, I'd say that you want to meet with him as soon as possible. Right?"

"I-I guess so."

"Listen, Mr. Mal is a serious guy. He's not like one of these wannabe gangsters who stand in the corner of an alley smoking blunts and thinking they're the hottest shit around. Your dad deals with him, right? Then he's serious shit. This is Michael Corleone league, understand? If you have an idea for him, it better be something that's a bit bigger than knocking over an ATM machine."

Pedro continued to stare at the ground and nodded his head slightly. "Yeah . . . yeah, I understand."

"So your head is still on Earth, right? You bringing your A-game with us, right?"

"Right. Nothing to worry about."

"Okay, good." Slim looked around the area before he continued on with his conversation. "I'll come see him tomorrow morning, just to give him a heads-up that you're coming to speak with him. And when he's ready for you, I'll contact you. Make sure that you have no other plans, all right? When he wants you there, you better be there. Okay?"

"Yeah . . . okay."

"Excellent! And don't worry, we got this. Just lay on the charm and tell him what your big idea is. I'm sure he'll like whatever you're cooking up."

"Sure hope so . . ."

Pedro walked toward the opposite end of the alley, with Slim following close behind. The Estrada male kept his forehead pointed toward the ground and remained within the confines of his thoughts. He glanced at the yellow newspaper that floated by, carried by a calm breeze that swept through the alley. He heard murmurs coming from Slim but paid no attention to the excited and ecstatic gangster that crept by his side. His words were mere shadows that lived underneath the folds of whatever brainstorming that occupied Pedro's mind. He fought the urge for such a long time, dodging each obstacle and ignoring each voice of maleficent reason that seemed to invade his ears. He laughed and felt his chest rise up and down from the joyful tremors, which seemed to take firm hold of his logic and sanity. He stopped walking and threw his head between his thighs, while his mouth opened wide to allow the laughter to escape his body. Slim stopped with Pedro and stared curiously at him. He smirked and felt a sudden air of discomfort embrace his body.

"So . . . what's so funny?"

Pedro caught his breath and braced himself against a nearby brick wall. He wiped the tears from his eyes and addressed Slim's question with what little he had left of his sanity. "Nothing . . . nothing, I just feel . . . better."

"Okay . . . you're scaring me a bit, bro."

"Oh, don't be a stiff-ass. I'll buy you a beer."

"Okay . . . sure."

Pedro still laughed and shook his head as Slim loyally tagged along. He found himself chuckling in brief moments, partly to avoid embarrassment but mostly because he had never seen Pedro this happy in a long time. Slim failed to answer his curiosity and decided to wait patiently for another twenty-four hours until Pedro unveiled his idea to Mr. Mal. As the trail of laughter disappeared around the corner, the homeless man that made himself invisible to Pedro's and Slim's suspicion decided to open his eyes and fling the bottle of vodka against a nearby building. He stood up, brushed off the dead newspaper that covered his torso, and slowly walked onto the bright sidewalks that graced the city block.

Luis cradled his wife within his large arms and squeezed her with a calm but tight grip. She had returned from her infamous adventure starring Sarah and her less-than-hapless boyfriend. She walked right past Luis and winked at him, making her way toward the guest bathroom that sat in the corner, heeding the slight pains Rosa felt each time her feet touched the floor. She bent over and pulled out a small gray tub that lay in the bathroom cabinet and set it aside. She stood up and stared at the mirror in front of her, placing her hand on a small latch that jut out from the reflective glass, and pulled it open. She saw a large white box with the words "Epsom Salt" emblazoned in blue letters. It almost begged Rosa to free it from its reflective prison and use it for whatever purpose she needs, whether she had to use its entire contents or a portion. Rosa obliged its wish and grabbed the box before she shut the mirrored cabinet.

She opened the spout on the box and poured a small handful into the tub. She then carried the tub over to the sink, turned on the faucet, and filled the gray container to the brim with hot, steaming water. A cloud of magnesium sulfate rose to her nostrils, which tingled her slender nose and widened her eyes. Rosa placed the misting tub on the counter and twisted the water until it shut off. She walked back to where Luis sat in the living room and set the tub in front of him. Rosa caught him flinging off his slippers and playfully scolded him before he got the chance to use the therapeutic concoction for himself. After he rolled his eyes, she threw her body onto Luis, purposely digging her elbow into his stomach and laughing softly. He pinched her bottom and quickly wrapped his arms around her before she got a chance to retaliate.

"So finish the story," Luis began. "What did she say?"

"She hardly said anything. She just stared at me dumbfounded the whole time. Her boyfriend hardly said anything either."

"Yeah, well . . . I wouldn't have much to say with a stiletto in my hand, personally. I kind of think you enjoyed it a bit much."

"Hey, the bastard deserved it. He broke my nail."

"I can't argue with you on that." Luis breathed in Rosa's perfume; the sweet smell of mandarin oranges and jasmine petals erupted in his nostrils. They seemed to penetrate any memory he had prior to this night he spent with his wife and filled his mind with visions of Barcelonan streets and the people that granted them daily occupation. "By the way, what fragrance is that?"

"Coco by you-know-who."

"Feeling French today?"

"You could say that. Didn't have much time to freshen up once I got that call."

"As long as you're okay, I don't care what you wear."

Rosa rested her head on Luis's broad shoulders. His large deltoid served as a pillow that not only comforted her tired body but also acted as her own protective shield, ready to react should the need arise. Luis took notice of her sudden feeling of sentiment and decided to carefully approach her solemn mood.

"What's wrong?"

Rosa closed her eyes and buried her head deeper into Luis's shoulder. Her soft, cool breath slid against his arm and fell into the moody atmosphere that wrapped around the two Estradas. "Luis . . . I told her about Eric."

Luis stopped his breath and clenched his lower lip. "You did?"

"Yeah . . . I kind of wanted to . . . I don't know, steer her away from the path she was running down."

"I know, I understand."

"But I didn't tell her what happened *with* Eric."

"Might as well keep it that way, although it wouldn't really matter now."

Rosa nodded and kept her head deep within the crook of his shoulder. The couple remained silent, their slow breaths filling in the pervading silence that encompassed them. Their eyes were pointed on the famous spot on the wall, one attempting to read the mind of the other. Luis kept alive his stare on the tall bookcase that stood next to a small green houseplant. He glanced at each piece of literary masterpiece that decorated each shelf. He recalled each author with a glint of fondness that shone in his eyes. Oscar Wilde, Ayn Rand, William Shakespeare, Alexander Dumas. Each person who enabled the ingenuity of their craft to be written onto paper sent a solemn message to Luis, a reminder of how one's true abilities can be exalted upon grand thrones for mankind to worship once they are exercised.

Luis wondered if his call to destiny was to be where he is now, where he always had been. A leader. A criminal leader. *Criminal.* Luis had not thought of that word for years, possibly because he avoided the term as if the letters that formed the word themselves were shrapnel fired from a shotgun. These shards struck his heart in all the sensitive cords which held up the hardened organ, leaving behind erratic slashes and deep indents that burrowed deeper into his marbled spirit. He blinked himself away from his thoughts and turned his attention toward his contemplative spouse.

Meanwhile, Rosa kept her eyes closed in the hopes that her memoirs would not bleed out of her large brown pupils. She kept the flashing images inside her eyelids, leaving her able to focus on the collection of snapshots without any inquiries being made. At the same time, she hoped that Luis would shake her out of the sadness she saw in front of her eyes: the sight of Eric's shadow spilling out onto the floor behind the stage, the shadow growing larger and longer once his towering eyes met those of young Rosa, as shy as the crimson flower that embodied her name. Rosa remembered the strong gust she felt once he threw her dress over her face and shoved his hot, angered body in between her fragile legs. Dark red blood poured out of her stomach, slowly oozing toward Eric's knees and passing through his naked legs, all while hot tears and bladed anguish poured out from Rosa's eyes. Her brown pupils dilated with each aggressive thrust Eric made, and all she could see through the mist of her silent cries was his angry yet satisfied expression on his face. Her body crumbled underneath the weight of her forced humiliation, and the shadow of the former love of her life was finished.

Rosa felt her cheek tingle when Luis's cool breath dried a lone tear that dropped from her eye.

"I know," Luis said. "I know."

Rosa wiped her face and lifted her head. "Sorry . . . I'm sorry. Let's not be nostalgic anymore—wears me out."

"Me too." Luis kept his concern on Rosa and did not put it to rest.

"I'm gonna go check on Zephyr."

"Sure . . . okay."

Rosa gently kissed Luis on his forehead and walked out of the room. Her mind was filled with memories that seemed to escape their chains, and she struggled to bind the tiny demons back to their cold, stone walls. As she walked up the tower of stairs before her, she saw the miniature red imps dancing upon the banister with tiny red tridents in their grasps. They jabbed the bleeding forks into her sides and twisted the metal throngs as it split open her muscles. She merely pulled out the steel branches out of her solar plexus and continued her ascent. The laughing devils encompassed her body and jeered at her stoic expression, ignorant of her resolve to imprison them and coerce their suicide.

She reached the second floor and turned that all-too-familiar corner where Zephyr's bedroom lay. The devils continued their attacks on the Shy Rose, stripping her of her thorns and pricking her fragile arms. She counted the steps she made that led to Zephyr's nightly chamber. The demons saw Rosa's feet enter the bedroom, and their attacks came to a sudden halt. A battalion of angels reinforced the doorway where Rosa stood, golden holy spears that filled every tiny space in the room, all aimed toward the filthy hearts that dared to infect the Estrada woman with their presence. As Rosa approached her daughter's crib, she heard the sounds of a hundred spears rip through the flesh of every demon that harmed Rosa. The hellish plasma splashed on the wooden floor and evaporated into the heavens. The demons fell to their knees with one blow and were soon executed with a heavy swipe of the angelic weaponry. Zephyr opened her silver eyes and stared at the calm face of her mother. When the Estrada daughter smiled, the last demon fell to the ground and cried out in agony before its voice was silenced forever.

Rosa kissed Zephyr on her soft cheek and gently placed the tip of her nose on her forehead. She took Zephyr's tiny hand and kissed it, letting her lips stay on Zephyr's little appendage for a long moment. She felt the infant smile and squirm underneath her lips, and Rosa stood up and gazed at her daughter.

"What's that? *Dame un beso?*"

Zephyr replied with a wide smile. Rosa kissed Zephyr's belly and blew into it. Zephyr's face lit up, and she could not hold back her laughter. Rosa blew into her stomach once more and watched Zephyr giggle and smile at her playful mother.

"Little one, I pray that you never have to experience what I lived through."

Rosa brushed Zephyr's face with the tip of her finger. She studied each feature that belonged to Zephyr and imagined it enhanced to a complete and beautiful form once she was an adult: long midnight-colored hair that covered her head with a twinge of curls falling over her shoulders, a graceful jaw supporting plump red lips that only allowed elegance and ingenuity to escape its confines, and a slender nose that tapered off to a gentle slope, which hung beneath her piercing eyes. Rosa focused on that ghastly pair and concluded that they were to be Zephyr's most powerful asset, able to see what was, what is, and what will be. Her gift of sight beyond sight was housed in Zephyr's gaze. Rosa immediately said a series of quick prayers to bless her daughter's future. Zephyr heard a sequence of steps approaching her bedroom, and she giggled loudly and kicked her feet.

"How is she?"

Rosa listened to the strong voice behind her as she kept close watch on Zephyr. She felt a hand rest on her shoulder and a long arm wrap around her back. The smell of sweet tobacco and sandalwood filled the air and settled on Rosa's nose. Zephyr saw the source of the voice before Luis entered the room, feeling his presence and sensing his personal atmosphere.

"She's fine. I'm just watching her for a bit." Rosa tickled Zephyr's belly and gently brushed her chin.

"Yeah . . . you know, I was just thinking, she's going to be a teenager."

Rosa turned around and placed her hands on his chest. "Aww, is big, strong Luis worried about Zephyr's boyfriends?"

"Yep . . . gonna have to kill 'em."

Rosa gave Luis a mean stare and froze his facetious remark.

"Rosa . . . I'm kidding."

"Just making sure." Rosa smirked and turned her attention back toward Zephyr. "I was thinking," she continued, "Zephyr is going to be absolutely beautiful. Especially those eyes . . ."

"I know," Luis said with a sigh in his voice, "and I'll bet she'll know that too."

Zephyr continued to watch her parents study each part of her body, making their own conclusions of their use and function. They would point to her feet and mumble a few words that the Estrada infant could not yet understand, but at the sight of white teeth and joyous glints in their eyes, Zephyr could not help but join in with the soft laughter that filled her bedroom. She embraced the loving kisses they gently placed upon her cheek and sadly stared at them when her mother and father turned around to leave. Her eyes narrowed, allowing only a tiny slit of silver light to gleam through her eyelids. Her father shut off the light to her room, and her mother blew a kiss through the darkness.

Zephyr laid on her back, cushioned by a soft cotton blanket decorated with pink elephants and white ponies dancing in a carefree pattern. On top of her body lay a cherry-colored blanket, light in weight and comforting in material. It did well in keeping the infant warm and content as she slept past the lifetime of the starlit night. Her mobile hung a few inches above her head and obeyed any command Zephyr made once she nudged the item with her hand or, if she was feeling aggressive, give it a swift punt with her small feet. The mobile would quickly spin and light up the entire crib, leaving tiny dots of light that shown on the nearby walls. The encircling M&Ms taped to the walls orbited Zephyr, and she beheld each colorful sparkle with wonder and glad observance. The sparks that flew about her room started to slow their rotation, and once it slowed to a complete standstill, Zephyr's eyes became increasingly heavy and weighted with the proverbial bars of lead. She breathed deeply and let the lead bars fall in place, and the mobile continued to spin in a peaceful motion rivaled only by Zephyr's slumber.

VIII

Luis drove into the driveway, gave the usual greeting to the guard posted ever so vigilantly at the gates of his home, and sped on until he reached the front steps of his retreat away from his career. Four years had passed on with a queue of events laid present for any and every family that were worthy enough to witness their occurrence. For the Estradas, their sight remained as keen as it had been years earlier, and their minds continued to remember what was most important to commit to towering museums of memory, and to forget all that was ephemeral and agonizing. Yesterday's spirit gave little remnants of joyous occasion to be remembered but was generous in their helpings of anything, which caused sharps pangs in Luis's chest and halted his breathing. Rosa would naturally worry about his condition and had threatened to drag him by his nose to the hospital if she had to. The thought of an angry Spanish wife dragging a grown man—anywhere at all—was enough to scare him into making an appointment with a doctor he had not seen in years. Luis now sat in the car in front of his home, just returning from the same stranger who concluded that it was just stress and that he needed to take it easy for a while. The doctor smiled widely and sent the Don on his way. Luis chuckled and thanked the doctor for his time and "professional opinion that could only be rendered by someone of your stature." The doctor nodded his head, maybe because it was something he either was used to hearing or that he was obliged to hear any accolades thrust upon him, well-deserved or otherwise. Luis left the office, paid his monetary respects to the nurse, and walked slowly to his vehicle parked at a nearby garage.

Luis thought of the growths that had accompanied his life in the seasons that passed. The business he had fostered ended up maturing into something substantial and reckoned by rival gangs, usually those who were envious of his power. Don Estrada managed to enact a sort of treaty with other criminal organizations and syndicates on the East Coast, as well as succeeding in establishing a trade agreement with his associates over on the West Coast. His East Coast brethren comprised of the various isolated Latino gangs stuck on a financial plateau with the uncommon phenomena of gaining little profit despite their reputations which preceded them. Luis took notice of their characters and held a conversation with their bosses, who in turn felt comfortable in Luis's proceeds and decided that an alliance would be wise for both their financial ambition and their higher placement on the criminal food chain. Luis's sales pitch was simple and engaging, which gave testament to his method of obtaining goods for the black and gray market. The other Latino gangs were entranced by his promises of substantial wealth and limitless strength, one which they could use to allow their empire to flourish with virtually no hindrances.

Following that, Luis made contact with his *vory* comrades in Ellipses, a tie he kept severed for many years. Vladimir "the Impaler" Kandinsky was a local club promoter and restaurant owner, a close friend of Luis whose friendship can be traced back to Luis's first day in the United States. Vladimir was a resource to whom Luis's father reluctantly mentioned as a contact to visit within American shores, after the young Estrada male made up his mind to leave beautiful *España* with Rosa.

The circumstances of his departure remained a mystery to those lucky enough to be acquainted with his presence, only because Luis forced his memories of leaving away from his mind. Some people, he thought, were proficient in locking away their nostalgia and trashing the key. But Luis tied up his memories, lined them up in front of a brick wall, and plastered that same wall with the blood of things too painful to be reminisced. He slaughtered his memories; they were too cruel to be kept alive in a black dungeon full of mold and vermin.

Despite his executioner's attitude, he did owe much to the kind Russian who took in the Don and his wife, in their early twenties at the time, and treated them like his children. Vladimir's own wife, Anna, loved the thought of, as she once put it, "Having more life to nurture instead of constant death." Rosa herself was still as shy as a newborn flower but felt comfortable around Anna's twin daughters, Natasha and Katherine, who treated Rosa no less than their own sister. Rosa taught them how to be a performer of Latin dances, and they were amazed that someone so quiet and reserved was brimming with so much artistic talent and finesse. Sometimes they would forgo their evening supper just to watch Rosa practice her famous Flamenco stomps on the restaurant dance floor. Rosa, in return, enjoyed the genuine attention she received from them and was glad that, for once, people appreciated her dancing ability without envy or hatred. Her numerous performances in front of the Russian twins melted her shy demeanor over time, and she enjoyed the time she was able to spend with the Kandinsky family.

Luis felt a surrogate connection with his caretaker, and although Vladimir never admitted it, he enjoyed having a son that he often imagined being his own. Since Luis was twenty at the time of his arrival, Vladimir realized that there was not much of maturation left to administer, but he nevertheless managed to foster a sense of duty in the young Estrada male. He saw a certain potential in Luis that was suited for leadership and motivation, and so he introduced to him the elements of management and promotion in the world of music. Luis quickly caught on to the concepts of keeping a promise to the entertainer and the entertained, as well as improvised on surprises and the unseen occurrences that often plagued the business. Soon afterward, Luis became the personal assistant of Vladimir and stood by his surrogate father with loyalty and admiration.

Vladimir never asked why Luis decided to leave Spain with Rosa, leaving behind his mother and father to constantly wonder and worry about his well-being. The prior Don Estrada entrusted him with the care of his only son, and Vladimir did well not to question the request of a dear friend and once comrade in criminal warfare. He promised himself that he would only discuss the details of Luis's flight if Luis initiated the conversation. On one particular day, while Rosa was busy entertaining his twin daughters, Vladimir asked Luis to come sit with him and Anna in the kitchen. Luis entered the room and took a seat next to his surrogate mother. Anna's tall, graceful figure seemed to match her welcoming gaze, a mere reflection on the warmth contained in her heart. Luis shyly smiled at her, and her eyes twinkled bright blue whenever her cheeks rose to smile back at him. He turned his head toward Vladimir, who had a serious atmosphere surrounding his face. He stared at an imaginary spot on the large mahogany table, clearing his throat before he opened his mouth to speak.

"Luis . . . when your father contacted me, I did not ask questions regarding the terms of your arrival. I did not ask because I would have given him the same courtesy if it were my two little girls . . . I extend that same courtesy to you. None of us will ever ask you about anything, only until you talk to us yourself. That okay?"

Luis bowed his head and closed his eyes. He heard the playful laughter of Rosa and the Russian twins approach the table. He felt Rosa's moist lips land on his right cheek and the tickle of her long hair against his ear. The scent of her dancing and laughing with her new sisters slid away from her body as she walked toward the kitchen. She slowed her steps when she realized that Luis and the Kandinskys were unusually somber. She saw how deep his breathing was, and how he could not bear to look at Vladimir or Anna. Natasha and Katherine were rummaging through the cabinets searching for snacks that the ladies could eat, giggling while pulling out large white bowls and tall glasses. Rosa only listened to the silence that suddenly graced the presence of everyone sitting at the table, but the silence broke once Luis's quivering lips forced out an utterance that Rosa thought she would never hear again.

"I killed someone."

Luis forced himself to awaken from his daydream and concentrate on present matters. He often found himself wondering about his daughter, now in her playful and curious toddler years, and remembered the many moments that kept his face full of smiles. She was the reason for his happiness, the purpose in his life to continue on without regret or remorse. Luis was surprised that he was able to commit to the numerous meetings, which included other leaders of criminal organizations, for he gained a recent notoriety for canceling any appointment just to play with Zephyr and tickle her until her stomach hurt from laughing. That was it, he realized. Her laughter. The sweet melody of innocence he had not felt for so long. A song of pleasure that lifted the rusty, heavy chains off his soul and drove his heart deeper into the arms of Zephyr's tiny, warming arms. After each bout of laughter, Zephyr would let out a comfortable sigh, brought forth by a glimmer of her breezy voice, and smiled at her father until her cheeks became drowsy. Luis made every effort to keep the innocence locked away in Zephyr's eyes and bid a fond farewell to the troubles that caused his heart to pang.

Luis chuckled when he remembered the moment Zephyr spoke her first words. He was playing with her one day when Zephyr paused and stared into her father's eyes. Luis remembered being in the kitchen with Zephyr, and he had turned away from her gaze for a brief moment to glance out the window. He remembered how the sun had thrown its golden beams onto the edge of the horizon, blessing the city with the hope of a new, better day. He turned back to his daughter and noticed her lips moving. He froze his breathing and waited in hurried anticipation for her voice to break his silence. His hands were shaking, and he felt his heart thump violently against his throat. Zephyr then stopped moving her lips and giggled at her father. Luis sighed, somewhat out of relief but primarily out of disappointment, and stared once again out the window. He thought for a moment, and then he smiled at Zephyr before he spoke.

"You are such a tease, you know that?"

"Daddy!"

Luis flew out of his seat and grabbed Zephyr in a joyful swoop. He giggled uncontrollably as he danced around in a circle with his daughter, who was laughing throughout the ecstatic waltz. Rosa had been in the living room reading a new romance novel while sipping a cup of hot coffee. Luis suddenly burst out with laughter and shocked Rosa so much that she spilled the black liquid all over her right thigh. She winced in pain and waited for that sudden surge of agony that usually accompanies an initial burn. When it finally came, she lifted her leg and absorbed the torment while silently yelling at her husband for making such a ruckus. She breathed heavily and thanked God that she was wearing her thick cotton robe instead of the thin silk nightgown she would normally wear. She stood up and placed her mug on the table that stood next to her. She threw the book against the chair that she had just been tortured in and walked toward the kitchen.

"*Dios*, Luis! What's the matter with—"

"She spoke! Zephyr said *Daddy*! She said *Daddy*!'"

"Zephyr! Oh my god, she spoke!" Rosa screamed louder than Luis had done and danced along wither husband and perplexed daughter. Her eyes gained a sudden luminescence that shimmered in her silver pupils, and her dimples grew deeper as she saw her parents laugh and dance around her as if she were an idol. After a while, Rosa skipped to the telephone and punched in the buttons to make a call. Luis was still dancing with Zephyr in his euphoria and forgot everything he knew about the outside world. After a few rings, a cheerful voice picked up on the other line.

"*Hola*?"

"Zephyr spoke! Zephyr said *Daddy*!'"

Raquel screamed out and laughed along with her daughter-in-law. She put her hand over her mouth and tried to slow her breathing so she could talk like a normal human being. After both women calmed down, Raquel giggled before she was able to speak in a coherent manner again.

"You make sure that she says *Grandma* when I see her for her birthday! Do you hear me? Grandma."

Raquel then asked about Zephyr's voice, in which Rosa handed the phone over to Luis, but not before she had to pry her husband away from the happy infant. He walked backward toward the telephone, staring at Zephyr while tripping over a nearby garbage pail. He finally reached the phone and talked with his mother.

"Her voice was soft . . . breathy. Like the sound leaves make when a breeze blows through it . . ."

Raquel said a quick prayer whenever Luis described the pitches and subtleties in her granddaughter's voice—well, concerning the one and only word she had spoken of all day. She also told Luis to go thank Rosa for picking the name Zephyr and not a name that sounded like a horrible disease.

"I know mothers are drugged up their asses during labor," she said, "but they need to stop naming their kids Chlamydia or Rebel just because it sounds cute. 'Oh, I wanted to name my son after his great-grandfather, Hieronymus.'"

Rosa stayed on the phone with Raquel, talking about how much Zephyr would be talking and how they would enjoy every minute of it. Luis had calmed down as far as laughing was concerned, but his smiles were glued to his face and showed no relent in fading away. Raquel decided not to keep Rosa too long and promised to see Zephyr on her birthday as she had always promised to do. Raquel exchanged her joyful farewells and hung up the phone with dreams of what Zephyr may say next.

Young children who speak their first words naturally have a tendency to continue speaking for hours on end. A little over a year after Zephyr addressed her father, she started to speak fully cogent sentences and express herself with innocent eloquence in her voice. She was not arrogant in her speech; rather, she displayed a full understanding of each word that ventured out of her mouth and did her best to follow its literary law. She maintained her childlike voice, but a shadow of maturity slowly emerged within her speech with each passing day.

Raquel was overjoyed to hold a conversation with Zephyr, sometimes asking her granddaughter questions on purpose just to hear her relaxing voice speak once more. They would always sit down at the kitchen table every evening with a large bowl of rainbow-colored sherbet, and Raquel would tell Zephyr many stories as the little Estrada gazed at her grandmother with her big silver eyes. Raquel's tales of grandeur ranged from biblical events—which Zephyr regarded the Wisdom of Solomon as her absolute favorite— to Raquel's adventurous youth back home in Spain. She told Zephyr about the intertwining streets of Barcelona that was so confusing that a woman got lost trying to get to her house. She told her that the reason Barcelona was so baffling was that the mayor who built the city had a daughter so beautiful that every man in *España* wanted to have her as his wife. So he devised a plan to make sure that the man who would marry his daughter was worthy enough of her love.

"So," Raquel continued, "he pulled out a big, big drawing! This drawing was a blueprint of the whole city, and it had lines going through here and ending there and starting back up here again! He made the city into a maze so deep and so puzzling that it took the team of construction workers months just to figure out where to start building! Once they figured it out, the mayor got up on a tall stool and said to the crowd, 'Calling all the men! Calling all the men! I know all of you want to have my daughter as your wife! But you have to prove to her and myself of your devotion! After this city is built, I will place my daughter in a small house with pink windows at the edge of the city! I will then place you all here where I am standing, and you must travel through the city to find her in that house! I will have my guards accompany you, in case you give up the search. They know the way and will guide you back home! Only if you succeed, will I accept you as my future son!'

"And so all the men agreed to the mayor's deal, and they all went home to prepare for their journey. They waited and waited for the city to be built, writing letters to the mayor's daughter showing how much they loved her and how happy they would make her if they succeeded. They went to the Spanish gardens to pick out the most beautiful flowers to give to the mayor's daughter. They even practiced getting on one knee to propose, reciting their lines as if they were poetry. Each one was convinced that he would be the new husband of the mayor's daughter."

Zephyr kept her wondrous eyes on Raquel the entire time she narrated the creation of Barcelona. Her spoon was full of melted sherbet, but she glided the oozing ice into her mouth and swallowed the sweet cream. A little bubble of sherbet settled on her lower lip, and Raquel reached over with her handkerchief and gently wiped Zephyr's mouth with a lightly perfumed cloth.

"And so the city was finished! The mayor had secretly hidden his daughter away in the small house with pink windows, located in a place only he knew. He then called all the men to the main square and stood up on the same tall stool he used before. He said, 'Men! Go and search!' And all the men of the city and the guards that accompanied them scattered in a tremendous stampede! The ground shook and quaked with each step they made! A storm of petals flew from the bouquets of flowers they all grasped in their hands! Cheers and applause erupted from the crowd—even the mayor was applauding the men! They all set out to find this beautiful woman and make her their wife!

"They searched and searched, but they all got lost in the crazy labyrinth the mayor had built. Some men almost starved and had to eat the bouquet of flowers to survive. Some men gave up and asked the guards to guide them back home. Those who gave up returned with sad expressions on their faces, and the mayor was sad too. He wanted his daughter to be married and be happy, but the men were so quick to give up their search. Months and months had passed on, and the large number of men trickled down to just a handful. Soon, a handful turned into a few, and a few turned into one. To this day, no one has ever found the mayor's daughter in the mystifying maze of Barcelona, but legend says that she still exists, waiting for a worthy man to take her as his wife."

Zephyr stopped eating when Raquel finished her story. Her eyes were wide and curious, begging her grandmother to tell her another story. Her face was round with deep dimples burrowed into each cheek. Vermillion lips adorned the rest of her face, with a pair of ears that gracefully sloped against her straight dark hair. Raquel saw Zephyr's mouth open, and her heart jumped at the sound of Zephyr's sweet voice.

"Grandma, can I visit you in Spain?"

"Of course you can, sweetie! Just be sure that you ask your *mami* and *papi* first." Raquel was happy to hear that request from Zephyr.

"Yay!" Zephyr bounded down from the chair and let her tiny legs quickly carry her toward the kitchen exit. Raquel raised her eyebrow and realized what her granddaughter was thinking.

"Wait, wait, sweetie! I meant later, not now!" Raquel was chuckling when Zephyr froze in her tracks.

"Oh . . . okay . . ." Zephyr stuck out her bottom lip and pouted. She walked slowly back to the table and climbed into her seat. Raquel felt touched by Zephyr's sudden disappointment. She quickly hatched a plan in her head

"There's one teeny, tiny thing you have to do first."

Zephyr's silver eyes lit up with curiosity. "Okay! What's that?"

"You have to read me a story."

"Like a bedtime story?"

"Sure. Or any story you like. It's your choice, *nina*."

Zephyr looked down as if she was lost in thought. After a moment, she sprung out of her chair in delight and ran to the other side of the table where Raquel sat. "Okay! You have a deal!" Zephyr stuck out her tiny hand to Raquel. She took Zephyr's soft palm in her own and shook her hand.

"Deal!" Raquel said with a laugh.

"I'm gonna go practice now!" Zephyr nodded her head and quickly sped off to her bedroom.

"Okay, *nina*, have fun!"

After a few seconds, Zephyr ran back with a speed gifted only to those as young as her. She stretched out her small arms and gave Raquel a big, warm hug. "I love you, Grandma!"

Raquel felt a surge of energy well up inside her heart. She stopped the water from flooding her eyes and succeeded in holding back tears. Zephyr's hugs were always full of emotion, and that love was always enhanced once Zephyr touched someone.

"I-I love you too, sweetie."

Zephyr loosened her embrace and ran back to the bedroom. Raquel listened to the footsteps fade away upstairs until it paused in a certain spot.

"You're too powerful, *nina* . . ."

*   *   *

Zephyr entered her bedroom with a large smile painted on her face. Her bedroom paid great homage to a princess's chamber, decorated purely by Rosa, who had insisted on the current style that lay before Zephyr's twinkling eyes. It was a small room surrounded by four soft pink walls with portraits of grand cities around the world. On one side hung a picture of the Eiffel tower piercing the night sky as it floated upon a sea of lights and life. Directly opposite of that structure was the famous church of Santa Maria del Mar, photographed at an elaborate angle where the building towered over the entire continent. It was Zephyr's favorite site in her bedroom, partly because of her grandmother's stories about Barcelona, which added to her already wide imagination. Another cherished site of hers was the bookcase that sat directly in front of her, filled with children's tales of adventure and anthropomorphosis. She skipped over to her bed, a platform full of white plush pillows, which supported a small, caramel-colored teddy bear with a foam scepter in one paw and a pair of wings on each foot. She grinned and climbed on top of her bed to grab the stuffed animal.

"Come here, Hermes! You're gonna help me find a book!"

Zephyr dragged Hermes all the way to the entrance of the room and sat him neatly in front of the bookcase. She patted his head and sat right beside him. They both stared at the bookcase, with one of them vicariously looking for the best book to practice. Zephyr motioned through each child's book, calling out their titles based on pure memory. She knew each book from when her father narrated the titles and also by recognizing each different color and cover design. She was quick to associate each certain design with a specific book and attributed each book with a keyword she created for herself.

"Okay, let's see . . . the duckling book or the fire engine book? Or how about . . . the piggy book?"

Zephyr studied each recognizable pattern and recollected her father's voice. She looked at Hermes, his tiny black eyes glued to a spot on the bookcase. She rested her own eyes on a book that caught her attention.

"Oh! I'll pick this one!" Zephyr reached for the "piggy book" and pulled it from the bookshelf. She looked at it for a moment and nodded in assent of her decision. She held it close to her heart and ran out of her room.

"Now I just have to find someone who will read it to me!"

Zephyr grabbed Hermes by his paw and skipped down the hall-way. She was hoping that Rosa was downstairs so that mother and daughter could share a story about three little pigs and a wolf. She noticed that Pedro's bedroom was ajar, and she could hear voices emanating from within. She tightly clenched the small book and held her breath. Her eyes, once joyful and curious, were now sad and worrisome. She remembered how she tried to get her big brother to play with her many times, but he always had something else to do. If it was not that, he would tell her to "Go ask *Papi*," or "*Mami* isn't doing anything right now, ask her." Zephyr always wondered if Pedro hated her or if he did not want her as a sister anymore. Nevertheless, she maintained her stubborn sense of hope and always acting on a pure, almost blind faith. Who knows? Maybe he would actually read with her this time.

She walked towards Pedro's room and saw him lying on his bed reading a magazine. His eyes were glued to the heavily inked pages and did not seem to notice the shy Estrada girl standing in the doorway. His really skinny friend was flipping through channels on Pedro's television. Zephyr allowed her timid eyes to enter the room before she did.

"Umm . . . Pedro? Will you read a bedtime story with me?" Zephyr tried to sound as adorable as possible when she spoke.

"Not right now. I'm busy. Maybe later, Zephyr." Pedro kept his eyes on the magazine page and did not look at Zephyr.

"Oh . . . okay." Zephyr lowered her head and frowned. Her hopes were crushed along with any joy she had. She turned around and started to walk out of the bedroom.

"I'll read a story with you, cutie." Slim stood up and called out to Zephyr, who paused for a moment. She sighed and continued walking out of the bedroom.

"Hey! I said I'll read with you!"

Zephyr turned around and glared at Slim with her ghastly, fro-zen eyes. "My *mami* said to never talk with strangers."

Slim looked bewildered. "But I'm no stranger!"

Zephyr rolled her eyes, letting her silvery orbs rotate in her eyelids. She paid no attention to Slim's maleficent stare, which attempted to burn a hole in her forehead. Instead, she turned around and swiftly ran downstairs, disappearing into the living room. Slim sighed and sucked his teeth.

"What a bitch."

Zephyr ventured into the den and found her mother's graceful figure in a large red leather chair. She was reading a book, and Zephyr could tell that her mother already did not like the story. Rosa often shook her head when a storyline did not make any logical sense. Her long dark hair flowed nonchalantly over the left side of her face as she held her forehead in disappointment. Zephyr stared at her for a moment and studied how her mother's long, wavy hair wisped itself away on the cool autumn breeze that blew in from a nearby open window. Each strand of hair seemed to rest on a wave of hair and accentuate Rosa's humble yet beautiful face. Her eyes quickly scanned every letter on the page, deciphering their meaning once combined with a similar symbol and moving on to the next set of words in a smooth, elegant pace. Zephyr closed her eyes and prayed in her tiny heart that she would one day read as well as her mother, and she also prayed that she would grow to be just as beautiful and graceful as Rosa.

As soon as Zephyr opened her eyes, Rosa had just closed her book and dropped it on an end table that stood next to her. She looked up and saw Zephyr slowly approach her. Rosa noticed that Zephyr held worry and sadness in those lovely silver spheres.

"What's the matter, sweetie?" Rosa asked. "You look sad."

"*Mami* . . . will you read a bedtime story with me?"

"Of course I will! Come to *Mami*."

Rosa held out her arms to her smiling daughter and let her climb up on her lap. Zephyr relaxed herself on her mother's bosom while Rosa pulled out a drawer in the end table and took out a bright yellow blanket. She wrapped it around Zephyr and herself, and once the light cotton cloth touched Zephyr's dimpled cheeks, she snuggled deeper into Rosa's comforting embrace and giggled. Rosa smiled and opened the book to begin reading along with her daughter.

"Once upon a time, there were three little pigs . . ."

*   *   *

As Zephyr offered her utmost attention to the story about a trio of miniscule pigs battling an aggressive canine, Luis remained sitting in his car, a blue Porsche Carrera that strangely supported a subtle humility rather than indulging in unnecessary extravagance. He opened his eyelids, heavy from the constant burdens he witnessed on a daily basis and looked at the reflection in his rearview mirror. The medley of lights that twinkled against the abyss of the city threw him deeper into his meditation. Each light that blinked onto his mirror seemed to snatch a hue out of the spectrum and flicker their color of choice once the moon allowed the sun to rejuvenate his golden splendor. It was as if the moon was the conductor of the sparkles, its silver light maintaining the timing of each red, pink, and blue glimmer that shot across the sky, traveling through the voids of the night sky and finally resting their journeys upon Don Estrada's mirror.

He wondered if he was the lunar master standing atop his podium addressing the faint glows of the audience. Or perhaps he was the lights themselves manifested in flesh and sorrow, forced to follow the dictations of the conductor. He thought about his career, the one side of him that managed to remain legitimate as a music producer. He wondered if manipulating sound to produce a pleasant melody was what he was meant to do or if managing a crime syndicate was his true calling.

Thinking about the hours spent in the studio with Adam—he never called him First Degree—in comparison with the time he gifted to his criminal background only made Luis despise his history even more. He admitted to himself, however, that it was his choice and his choice alone. There were no cold barrels held to his head that foretold his life splattering on the table, which weighed more than the mass of bullets hidden inside the chamber, waiting to shoot out of the gun like horses anxious to exit the stables during a race. There were no threats upon him or those he loved, no warnings of death, or worse yet, bodily harm that promised enduring, lasting pain, be it mental or otherwise. He had every opportunity and skill available to him that may have led him away from the life of constant deception and actions thrust under cloaks of roses and rays of light. These cloaks, he realized, only cast shadows upon his evil deeds, covering what was not meant to be seen, forever relegated to buried treasures, which contained venomous serpents rather than shimmering piles of precious stones.

"I killed someone."

Luis found himself repeating those words out loud, to himself, with an emphasis on *I*. He was no longer in his car but back in the kitchen where Vladimir and Anna sat staring at him, in complete shock and sadness, a medley of emotions, which seemed to reach out from their own hearts and accumulate in the room. Natasha and Katherine froze in place and barely managed to turn their heads to glance at the calm, stoic eyes of their father. Anna herself swallowed hard but did not seem to flinch at Luis's words. She heard those words countless times before and found herself becoming more accustomed to it as her years progressed. Rosa's mouth, once pressed together to kiss her love on his smooth forehead, now were clenched together in preparation for the next words, which would pour unsteadily from Luis's mouth.

"She—Rosa—was raped by a boyfriend of hers, and she . . . told me . . ." Luis's eyes tightened to stave off the flow of tears that fought to make themselves known to the world. He clenched his fist and opened his bloodshot eyes to meet Vladimir with melancholic honesty. "I was so angry that he would do this to someone like her . . . someone who would sell her soul just to see someone smile again! I hated him!"

Vladimir kept looking at Luis. He did not blink for fear that if he did so Luis would end the conversation and leave the table.

"So . . . I saw him walking home one day, and I had a shard of broken glass in my hand . . ." Luis stopped. He remembered how hard he clenched the glass blade in his palm. He remembered the faint sound of blood dripping onto the pavement as the blade cut deeper into the folds of his hand. He remembered how he ignored the pain, constantly reminding himself that Rosa felt worse. The way he threw her on the floor, pinning her down, slapping her face and forcing himself inside of her. A virgin destroyed. A man satisfied. Eric must have laughed after he abandoned Rosa on the floor, her blood oozing out from her legs, her hot tears drying on her beaten face. When Luis finally saw her that evening, when they met on an old, wooden bench to take their usual walks within the Barcelona maze, her face was resting on her chest. Her chin was implanted between the nooks of her bosom, and her eyes were studying every tiny rock and pebble on the ground. Luis followed the path her eyes took, and his eyes started to water once he realized that she wore a red skirt when it was supposed to be white.

"I-I haven't been home yet," Rosa stammered, her body convulsing in the cold night air. "I'm scared to go home . . . I don't want to explain . . . why my dress . . ."

Rosa opened her mouth wide and buried her face within Luis's open arms. Her body was still shaking, and Luis could tell that she was trying to wail, but no sound came out. Only the ear-piercing shriek of silence pervaded through the air. Luis held her tight, his heart quickening from the unique amalgam of anger and regret. Regret for not being there when he should have. When he could have. He felt Rosa inhale deeply, and then she let out a dreadful cry that reached heaven and stopped the angels from trumpeting songs of humor and joy. Her cry prolonged itself, almost like a funeral song, a layered threnody that reached its climax after only a few seconds. Her small sobs allowed her tearful chorus to finally die down. She inhaled again, and her wail continued to shoot forth from her bloody, paralyzed body. She cried hard—she made herself cry hard—for she wanted to make Eric hear her screams. She wanted him to hear her constant pleas to stop hurting her after all she has done to support and love him. She wanted him to feel what she was feeling.

Luis lifted her chin up to brush her wet hair away from her face, her eyes blackened when Eric slammed his fist into her face as she struggled to get up. She closed her flooded eyes; she did not want to look into Luis's eyes and have him see what she had hidden all these years, even as they had begun their maturation into adulthood. When he whispered her name, a calm wind blew against their huddled bodies, cooling her hot cheeks and drying her heavy tears. She opened her eyes and saw that Luis had cried just as hard as she did. She forgot about the whole event, the rape, Eric—everything. She sniffled and rested her body on Luis's comforting grasp.

It was then that she knew she truly loved him.

Luis looked up and saw Vladimir's hand raised up, showing the young Estrada male the wrinkles and slashes created from his years in the Gulag. Vladimir was known to have exceptionally rough hands, the kind that would scratch a woman's face if he wiped a tear from her eye. At the same time, they held a soul of warmth within his palms, something that Luis was able to notice despite his tears blurring his vision. Vladimir rested his hand and opened his lips to speak in his calm yet commanding voice.

"Do not say any more."

"I'm sorry . . ." Luis was addressing Vladimir as well as everyone in the room.

"Don't be . . . are you hungry?"

Luis gave him a bewildered look. The only emotion present in Vladimir's voice was that of stoicism. "W-what?"

"Are you hungry?"

Luis moved his mouth and frantically looked at each person in the room. He first looked at Rosa, who stood just as dumbfounded as he. Her face seemed to have lost all memory of what she had been doing in the kitchen, and her breathing was both stuttered and heavy. Luis then glanced at Anna, who placed her elbow on the table and held her chin in her tiny hand. He could see the blood drain from her slim wrists as she bore the weight of convalescence once more. She moved her tired eyes toward Luis and seemed to speak without moving her lips.

"Men need to eat . . . don't they?"

Luis shook himself out of his dream and found his body back in the physical realm he was originally, supposed to occupy. He blinked a few times before he opened the car door and stepped out to inhale the bitter autumn air. He closed the door and started on his short hike to the front door.

He entered his home, the castle which he had built upon blood-stones, and saw the two Estrada women snuggled together in a reading blanket. The large title adorned on the book covered a portion of Zephyr's jaw so that all Luis could see were her bright snowy eyes glancing over each word that Rosa spoke. Zephyr seemed to follow the rhythmic pace and the intricate utterances contained in every word, as if she was reading just as well as her mother. Luis chuckled, allowing it to travel to the ears of his daughter. She gasped, leaped down from Rosa's lap, and ran into her father's open arms.

"Daddy! What took you so long?" Zephyr wrapped her tiny arms around Luis's neck.

"Sorry! Sorry! Next time I will take you with me! How's my girl?"

"Good! I'm reading a story with *Mami*!"

"Oh really? What story?"

"'The Three Little Pigs!'" Zephyr kept her smile on her face and her eyes on her father.

"Oh wow, that's great!" Luis picked Zephyr up and carried her over to Rosa.

"You're home early." Rosa stood up and began folding up the reading blanket.

"I missed you two." He reached over and kissed Rosa on the cheek. Zephyr observed this small gesture and closed her lips together tightly. She placed a gentle kiss on Luis's cheek and smiled at him.

"You get one from me too." Zephyr beamed.

Luis laughed. "Oh! 'Tis an honor to receive such a glorious blessing from an angel like you." Luis inhaled deeply. "And this little angel needs some sleep."

Zephyr rubbed her ethereal eyes. "No . . . I'm not sleepy . . ."

"Uh-huh. Daddy will play with you tomorrow night. I promise."

Zephyr stared into Luis's eyes. At the moment his eyes read hers, he felt a sudden feeling of imprisonment, as if she succeeded in capturing the remnants of his damaged soul torn asunder by his constant wagers with death and the devil. But he knew that Zephyr did not see the blood in his memories nor the sight of demons dancing and laughing in his conscience. She only saw the mist of his being, the air that gave him the hope, the courage to live for someone, rather than end the life of another. She easily grasped his soul with her eyes alone, her most powerful allies, and Luis dared not fight her possession.

"You promise?"

"I promise, sweetie."

"Okay! I'll sleep now, we'll play later!" Zephyr tightened her hug around his neck, letting the musky sting of his cologne tickle her nose. He let her down, and she skipped over to the foot of the staircase. She turned around and waved at her parents.

"Good night, Daddy! I love you!"

Luis smiled as he watched his joyous daughter sprint upstairs and turn the corner to enter her bedroom. Rosa glanced at Luis and read every word of worry that was painted on his face.

"You know . . ." Rosa walked to his side and placed her delicate hand on his face. "Your daughter had the exact same expression in her eyes when she walked in here. What's wrong?"

"Next week is Halloween . . ."

Rosa let her hand drop onto his chest. "That's right . . . I forgot."

"Are the numbers in the same place?"

"Yes."

"Okay. Let me know when everything is arranged."

"Sure."

Rosa felt his hand slowly wrap around the nape of her neck as he pressed his lips against hers. It was a sad kiss, a kiss saved for a soldier who waved goodbye to his wife as he sailed off to war. It was a kiss displayed in the romantic novels Rosa often read, where the couple finally showed their love for one another, eyes flooded with hot, angry tears, fighting the heavy load of affection they felt, up until the last moment where they collapsed, bodies contorted within each other and dead in their arms. Rosa inhaled deeply, suddenly feeling the sharp pain of regret in her spine. She shook it off and continued to walk upstairs with her husband and silently prayed for the sleeping Estrada girl in the nearby bedroom.

When Rosa stripped off her clothes and climbed into bed, she felt her head spin around the room and flip her house upside down. She shut her eyes, hoping that they had some hidden power to still the room and force her away from fantasy. When it felt safe to open them again, her eyes fell upon a large wooden dresser which stood across the bedroom. Sitting atop that dresser was a large mirror that reflected her toned body and the wide silhouette of Luis, his chest rising and falling from his gentle yet heavy slumber. She stared at the mirror, studying every object it held in its alternate reality. She wished that she was a part of that world, a mere reflection of what was true, a set of doppelgangers free from emotion and fear. She smirked and peacefully sighed to adjust her body in the bed.

She moved her fingers to grab the sheets and twisted her torso to turn over slowly without waking Luis. She struggled and caught herself panting heavily. She relaxed her grip and slowed her breathing for a moment. When her heart sped up again, she dug her nails deep into the sheets and tried to move herself again. But her body was strapped to the bed in frozen, heavy chains. She saw wide links of steel slide across her torso, constricting her full breasts and crushing her heart. Another chain pierced the bedroom floor and slid over her ankles, scratching her bone and slicing open her skin. As the blood poured from her feet and merged with the metallic hues of the chain, another chain sprung from the ceiling and wrapped around her neck. The cold noose grinded against her throat as she tried to scream out, but her voice was choked by the heavy weight of the dark shackles. Terror possessed her eyes, as vicious as the bounds crushing her body. She hurriedly glanced around the room, but all she could manage to see was the tall mirror that hung proudly over the dresser.

Okay . . . okay, she thought. *What is it you want to show me?*

She reluctantly closed her eyes and allowed the heavy black chains to squeeze her body tighter and crush her torso. Her chest snapped and cracked underneath the pressure, while the jagged bones pierced her lungs. She felt her larynx implode from its unholy weight. Her skin ripped open from the friction of the cold metal, while her eyes beheld the blackest light, an enveloping shroud that choked her vision and blinded any conscious thought. A loud scream stabbed at the air, but Rosa knew that it did not come from her lips. They were glued together, as if the muscles in her jaw failed to obey her mental command. They resisted her whims, gave no attention to her volition, and revenged her wish to move by slicing her spinal cord and paralyzing her entire body. Her body only granted her permission to drop a single tear down the left side of her face. The hot droplet squeezed out of her closed eyelids and slid down her cheek, creating a wet streak which refused to dry.

Rosa opened her eyes and found herself standing on a beach, chainless and breathing again. It was nighttime, cool and pacific, with the moon casting its silver resplendence on the pulsing sea. The sound of the waves crashing upon the cushioned shore rang in her ears, a loud yet pleasant melody which gave necessary requiem to her fears. She looked down at herself; she was naked and warm, with a soft glow kissing her toned frame. When she looked up, she saw a white piece of silken cloth float toward her waist and wrap around her body. It hugged her torso, once crushed by tenacious chains, now brushed by soft air that solidified once it contacted her skin. It rested across her full breasts and draped over her soft, supple thighs. It encircled her neck and let its excess cloth flow elegantly down her back. Only her face, arms, and feet remained bare. Rosa inhaled softly and marveled at the beauty that became her, less than a narcissistic enamoring of herself but more of an appreciation for the detailed perfections of her body.

She felt a joyful breeze brush past her face, allowing her to breathe in the cool midnight air and accept the smile that formed on her face. She closed her eyes once more as the wind combed through her hair. The wispy, wavy strands of her black hair flowed outward from her head and rode the current—the same wave of air that brought Rosa's heart to final sanctuary. She giggled as a cool touch of moisture from the sea landed on her neck, sliding ever so calmly down her clavicle. She opened her eyes, and the image she saw held her mouth open in astonishment.

"Zephyr?"

Zephyr appeared along the coast, letting the soft waves relax its tiresome journey upon her feet. She was no longer a toddler but a full-grown woman, and she succeeded in capturing every aspect of Rosa that all would call "beautiful." Her hair was long and wavy, blacker than the starred firmament that hung above their heads. It blew in the oceanic breeze, showing a glimpse of her face to the Estrada mother slowly walking toward her daughter. Zephyr's face was circular in shape, with sharp cheekbones and a dainty chin. It was a face of rare beauty, not breathtaking nor murderous but calm and confident of its inherent and opulent femininity. Her lips were blossomed, full of vigor and glittered with pink lip gloss. Each speckle of light reflected the moonbeams and lit up her face amidst the darkness that surrounded her. Zephyr turned her head and stared into Rosa's eyes, and she beheld a pair of eyes that forever humbled the moonlight. They were silver and bright, with black pupils sitting upon the hoary iris as if there were small pods coasting along a gentle current. They sparkled and fought for dominance of being the source of light, and Rosa could not bear to deny that Zephyr's eyes had won the skirmish.

Zephyr wore a strapless silk dress, as white as her eyes and as soft as her glow. It served as a piece of wind that wrapped around her slender body and froze on her skin. Tiny particles of star and moon flickered on her dress, and her body seemed to breathe along with the cloth that hung on her full breasts. Zephyr inhaled deeply, and her breath seemed to be the source of the gentle wind that blew across their bodies.

Zephyr turned to Rosa and smiled. Her dimples burrowed deep into her cheeks and her wide smile reached all the way to her ears. Streams of bright diamonds cascaded down her earlobes, and a silver necklace was suspended across her elegant neck. Rosa stared at the necklace closer and noticed that a small, empty case had hung at the end. It needed a jewel. A small jewel worthy enough to house itself atop Zephyr's lavish torso. Zephyr placed her hand and gently massaged the empty case.

"Isn't this a beautiful view?"

Rosa walked up to her and held her daughter in her arms. Zephyr rested her head on Rosa's shoulder, closed her eyes tightly, and exhaled.

"I miss *Papi* so much . . ."

Rosa let go of Zephyr and brushed a strand of hair away from her cheek. She looked out to the sea and noticed a dark figure rise out of the horizon. The waves stopped its movement, the wind froze in place, and all that Rosa could hear was a deafening silence. Rosa continued to stare at the figure that slowly approached the two Estrada women. It did not walk; rather, it seemed to glide across the stilled ocean, all while ignoring the worried expression on Rosa's face. She turned to Zephyr, who remained passive despite the mysterious figure that stopped time.

"He's here . . ." Zephyr said. "I've been waiting for him for a while now."

Rosa felt an enveloping aura chill her back, as if a ghost stood behind her and begged her to purge him to Purgatory. She turned around and saw Pedro, a grown man himself, but his head was completely shaven. He wore nothing but a pair of cotton slacks, blacker than abysmal space, and he bore tattoos everywhere on his body. These pieces of torturous art acted on their own autonomy, projecting themselves out of his skin and moving about in a sinister altered reality. The snakes branded on his neck slithered and lashed out at unseen prey; his face merely smiled at the green, devilish serpent, and it seemed to smile back at Pedro. He had black teardrops on both sides of his face, a sword on his right forearm and a shield on his left, a skull over his heart, a naked woman on his right bicep holding rosary beads, with his initials arching on his shoulder. "P-A-J-E." Pedro walked past Zephyr and Rosa, and his mother could see a large "QD" tattooed on his back, in large gothic letters that seemed to bleed with agony and arrogance. She thought long and hard as to what those letters meant, but her pondering submitted to vanity.

When Rosa took her eyes off her son, the dark figure appeared in front of her face. She opened her mouth to scream, but she could not find a face at which to shriek. He had no face, only blackness that took the form of what a face was supposed to be. A nose, a chin, but no eyes nor a semblance of a mouth. All she saw was a dark servant of the sea, bathed in the night and relishing in his umbrage.

Rosa glanced at Zephyr and saw no fear in her cold, pale eyes. No apprehension of the figure was displayed. No, Zephyr was not afraid at all. She brushed back her long hair and sighed softly. She smirked and chuckled. Zephyr was . . . content.

The figure knelt at the Estradas' feet and waved his hand over the white and tan crystals of the shore. One by one, the small particles of sand repelled each other, revealing a trio of gray wrinkled oysters. Rosa stared at them, arranged in a triangle, and glanced at Zephyr and Pedro. They both were smirking, fully confident of themselves and of what they would find. Rosa looked back at the dark figure, who spoke in a deep, whispered tone.

"Each of these oysters I place before you, in them contains pearls. One is of absolute knowledge, one of immortality, one of madness. Do know that neither will bring happiness but all will bear fruit. Choose."

The figure turned and slowly walked into the ocean. His departure was as ominous as his arrival, gently gliding into the sea and letting the waves fade his being into abysmal waters.

Zephyr bent down and picked up one of the oysters, letting her black hair fall over her shoulder and rest on her bosom. "Zephyr, wait . . ." Rosa heard herself speak out, but Zephyr smiled and said, "It's okay. Trust me." She opened the oyster and saw a brilliant white pearl sitting atop its tongue. Zephyr took it out and held it up against the moonlight. "This is absolute knowledge," she said. "Glorious knowledge. I can feel it . . ."

Rosa felt anxiety creep into her heart but fought off the evil mistress and decided to match her daughter's courage. She bent down to pick up her oyster, but Pedro brushed her hand aside, impatient to receive his reward, and ripped it open. Rosa watched in shock as Pedro laughed hysterically and danced along the shoreline.

"This is . . . fucking . . . beautiful! Can't you see this? Oh! But my pearl can see! It sees everything . . . everything it sees. Pearl . . . pearl! See the pearl! See the pearl! Look at my pearl! I said, 'Fucking look at my pearl!'"

Pedro screamed at no one, cursed at nothing, and belittled some unseen being that stood beside him. And yet he was overjoyed at the pearl in his hand—a black, ominous orb of dark matter that screamed out in mutiny against Zephyr's own pearl. The white, brilliant sparkle of her pearl was a direct contrast to the void contained in Pedro's palm. He smiled once more as he juggled the pearl from one hand to the next, biting his tongue to stave off his laughter. The madness was forever his.

Rosa stared at Pedro while he obsessed over his prized jewel. She felt shame for the choice he had made. Rosa turned her eyes toward the ground, and saw the oyster that lay before her flip open on its own. She gazed at the calm, blue aura it emanated, peaceful and comforting in its resonance. Rosa picked it up and tried to look deep inside the pearl, to see where this aura originated.

"See?" Zephyr walked over to her mother and placed her hand on her shoulder. "I told you. Welcome to eternity."

Rosa chuckled and held the pearl between her index and middle finger. The pearl lay still between her fingers, almost as if it found itself at home with Rosa Estrada. Rosa closed her hand and let the pearl fall into her palm. She held it against her heart and breathed deeply.

"It's beautiful, sweetie," she said.

Pedro felt something buzz at his head. He stopped playing with his madness jewel and stared hard at the two Estrada women. He glanced at their white and blue pearls and felt a sudden rage creep into his chest. His eyes widened, and his mouth clenched as he called out to his mother.

"I like your pearl . . . I want it."

Rosa's hand quivered once he began to approach her. Zephyr's eyes glowed with white light as she stepped in front of her mother, protecting her and her wanton treasure.

"You chose your own. Live with it. Die with it."

Pedro laughed and pulled out a gun. His tattoos were slithering wildly out of his skin as his muscles clenched against the trigger. Rosa tried to place herself in front of her daughter, but a wall of vigor blocked her from reaching Zephyr. Rosa then realized that Zephyr created the wall herself just by standing her ground, a lioness preparing to kill her prey.

"Move, Zephyr! That pearl is mine!"

Zephyr shook her head and smirked. She spoke only in a voice that threatened the softness of a whisper blown into a child's ear. "Darling. No. The madness is yours alone."

Pedro shoved the barrel against Zephyr's head and twisted the barrel into her skin. She remained stationary with nary a flinch or a speckle of fear.

"So . . . shoot me. I will still be here. My life is inevitable."

Pedro smirked and pulled the trigger. The discharge of the cold, metallic bullet left the gun and sprayed blood over Zephyr. Her pale eyes remained open, her smile never faded, and her body was relaxed. Rosa heard herself scream out, and the wall that was placed between mother and daughter had fallen. The blur that surrounded her blinded her eyes so much that she had to grab Zephyr to guide herself out. She yelled Zephyr's name, a long melody that traversed the black night sky, and clasped her daughter close to her chest. The pearl that she had held fell to the sand, and stood staring up at its tearful owner. But she did not hold a dead body. Zephyr was breathing calmly and continued standing in her place. She brushed her hair away from her face and allowed a cool breeze to kiss her warm, dimpled cheeks.

"I'm not dead, *Mami*."

Rosa smiled for a brief second and tasted a teardrop that fell into her mouth. She followed Zephyr's eyes to where Pedro stood. His body had slumped to his knees; his head had burrowed deep into his chest, as his tattoos fell dead to the ground and his blood oozed from his left eye.

Pedro had shot himself.

IX

It had been raining all evening. Hard enough to completely drench Rebecca's hair and leave her strands pasted onto her wet face. She ran through the dark streets of Ellipses and was curious to know if anyone heard her feet slam against the soaked pavement. She held her arms over her head to vainly shield her already-drenched body from the heavy rain, while she carried a small cardboard box full of stale French breads and cold, expired cans of tomato soup. She knew that every little bit of food and comfort she received was precious and so endearing. Like a letter from a loved one to a soldier of war. She saw herself as that poor soul who stands near the mailbox every day, in between battles and times of peace, praying to every deity she knew, that her love would send her a letter detailing how his heart rose to the top of his chest whenever she was away from him. How he would fall asleep and dream of her sleeping next to him, her breath sliding softly over his naked chest. Or how he thought about her every day or how she crossed his mind once in a while. Or simply that she was a name that a friend mentioned in a casual conversation. A mere recollection of her name would make her heart quintessentially soar to the heavens or make her eyes water from sheer joy.

But she did not have anyone to stand near a mailbox to await her. She did not have anyone pray for her safety and eventual return. No one dreamed of her, nor was there anyone to fantasize about her body rubbing against his. She did not have a boyfriend, she thought, or any friends for that matter. The only reason her heart was soaring was because she was out of breath from running in the rain. Her eyes watered from the dirty raindrops pouring into her eyelids. Or maybe it was real tears after all.

She finally ran inside an alley, a shallow and narrow cave where abandoned houses lined the row. The buildings were hollowed and eerie, with a piece of broken glass hanging in each window begging to be broken off and laid to rest among its brethren. The roofs had large gaping holes where the rain poured in like waterfalls. One could hear the stairs inside each home creak and echo throughout the alley whenever someone climbed them. It seemed as if they threw themselves deeper into depression as they rose within the interior of their newfound home, as dilapidated and as empty as they were. Their shelter was their sadness, their agony personified. No one complained about their dwelling, but no one did anything about it either. Everyone figured that the last resort would be suicide, to venture out into the city streets and dive in front of a moving truck. "The Parish," as they named it, was a step down from death, and that in itself was an unaffordable luxury.

Rebecca ran inside the last house on the left and stopped running once she got inside. She stood in the middle of the lonely foyer, set the box down in front of her feet, and squeezed the water from the hem of her shirt. She looked down at her soaked jeans and decided not to even bother squeezing them as well. She bent over to pick up the box, and let her soaked black hair fall away from her face. Droplets of rain and soot landed on the box and splashed against the corners of the tin cans of soup. She sniffled and tasted the acidic mucus that slid down her throat, closed her eyes, and breathed a long sigh of relief. Rebecca was home.

"Mister! I got some food!" Rebecca called out to her only friend, the only one who comforted her when a handful of nails pierced her throat and made her cry so long ago. He hugged her, held her, gave her some food, and talked to her in a soft voice until she slept against his bony, solid shoulders. This time, Rebecca thought, she would return the favor. She knew Mister liked French bread, and even though they were stale and rock hard, all Rebecca had to do was make a fire and let the rainwater soften the bread as it heated up. The same could be done for the soup, but she was worried that it may taste funny from being so cold. High maintenance was something one did not attribute to the homeless, but for Mister . . . he deserved some form of wealth. She smiled as she climbed up the stairs and called out to him.

"Guess what? I walked by the bakery earlier today and I got the owner to give me some of his bread. French bread! He said that they were stale, but I didn't give a shit. It could have rats crapping all over it, but as long as it was French bread, it's still good, right?"

Rebecca reached the top of the stairs and turned to the bedroom where they usually sat down and gave air to the dreams they held in their hearts, warming them as a fireplace warms a couple on an iced morning. She closed her eyes and deeply inhaled the French bread, savoring what little scent it had left within its dry, crusty shell. She smiled widely and opened her eyes.

"And of course I got our usual tomato—"

Rebecca froze her speech and suddenly felt her arms carry a hundred-pound weight. The box of food and bread she carried crashed to the floor and crumbled on the rotted wood and disintegrating in front of her feet. She became deaf, unable to hear her own screams and the outburst of tears that flowed down her red face as she saw the bloody, lifeless body of Mister dangling from a cord. His eyes were still open, his mouth agape, his toes pointed toward a dark circle of hell. Rebecca sprinted to him and hugged his waist as she frantically wailed against his torso. She still could not hear a thing, only the squeaks of the cord rubbing against the wooden beam bade a soft requiem. She shook his body, trying to hold onto some semblance of a miracle that he was still alive. Rebecca looked up at him, gazing at his limp body through a window of flooded eyes, and buried her face against his leg. She shut her eyes and held his leg for what seemed like an eternity, cursing herself for not being there for him when he needed her most. No favor for her to return. A debt forever unpaid. She kept her arms clenched onto his leg and kept her eyes closed as she spoke.

"Someone help me get him down . . ." Rebecca was afraid to open her eyes and see her best friend dead before her. "I said help me get him down! Get him down! Somebody!"

Rebecca already imagined a text for an obituary that no one would read. He would not be visited by family, for he did not have one beyond Parish and Rebecca. No church to house his skin and bone and no soft ground for his burial, Concrete, poisoned water, and the sounds of rain splashing on tiny glass drug pipes—those were his processions.

But he was a somebody.

He was a somebody who was as mysterious as his name suggested, but his gifts of skill and humble demeanor were without comparison. Nor could there be any sort of competition with his knowledge of life and the pursuit of survival, which Mister often said was the more important of the two.

Although Mister was a man unknown, he was a resourceful human being. After he had healed Rebecca from Slim's torturous grasp, he sat her in a corner with a torn cloth hanging over a pair of old curtain rods. To most, it was an unacceptable lodging even for the poorest soul, but to Mister and everyone else in Parish, it was sustainable, therefore acceptable and therefore full of wealth.

"Have some soup," Mister said to Rebecca. He pointed to an old rusty pot that hovered over a pitiful flame. Rebecca was fed a warm spoonful of tomato soup, just enough to calm the maw in her stomach. Once she finished sipping, Mister gave her another helping. No one showed her so much kindness in her years of solitude in Ellipses. Mister was different, she realized. His kindness was purchased by her own, and neither asked for it.

"I . . . I'm sorry," Rebecca managed to say.

"For what?" Mister asked.

"I didn't mean to take your food—"

"Never apologize for something that was out of your control. It only invites misery."

"O-okay . . ." Rebecca took another sip of Mister's soup. "Are . . .are you gonna have any?"

Mister chuckled. "When you get to my age, you'll find that eating less saves room for helping someone else."

"Okay . . ." Rebecca managed to smile. "Thank you for the soup."

"What's your name?"

"Rebecca."

"Rebecca. You might as well keep calling me Mister. It fits me."

Rebecca laughed. "What kind of a name is Mister?"

"A good one!" Mister smiled and motioned over to his personal tent. He pulled out a large wool blanket and wrapped it around Rebecca. "So," he continued, "what's your story?"

Rebecca paused. "It's . . . a long one."

"I understand."

"I mean, it's pretty boring . . ."

"Well, welcome to Parish, where nothing is boring. Nothing bores us when we're in this . . . condition."

Rebecca smirked.

"How old are you anyway?"

"Nine. I'll be ten next month."

"Where's your family?"

"Dead."

"That was a quick answer, Rebecca."

She realized that Mister was more intelligent than his surroundings would suggest. "Yeah . . ."

"Look, if you're going to stay here, you need to know some things."

"Okay . . ."

"Number one: don't talk to anyone except to me. Number two: everything you find is precious. Number three: learn to defend yourself."

"I've . . . never been in a fight before. I mean, I took karate when I was six, but I forgot how to do everything."

"Throw that shit out."

Rebecca was confused. "Wait . . . what?"

Mister sat closer to Rebecca. "I said 'Throw that shit out.' Martial arts with too much form and shit will get you killed out here. When I say that you need to learn how to defend yourself, I mean use everything in sight. Bottle caps, rocks, fucking soda cans if they're nearby."

"Kinda like street fighting?"

Mister smiled. "Exactly."

Rebecca adjusted herself and buried her shoulders deeper in Mister's blanket.

"Also," Mister continued, "learn to deduce. You know what that means?"

"Understand the crap out of everything?"

"Smart girl. Never stop thinking, and always bear in mind that you environment is your weapon, your friend, and your snitch. Got it?"

"Got it."

"Number four—"

"You mean number five. The whole thing about the environment and stuff was number four . . . right?"

Mister gave Rebecca a friendly nudge. "You're a natural. Number five, develop an iron stomach, but I don't have to worry about teaching you that if you're eating my soup."

"Why? What's wrong with your soup?"

"I had to stretch out the broth with gutter water."

Rebecca stared at the warm red slop and immediately spat it out. She coughed and sniffled once the traces of liquid exited her taste buds.

"And you have to develop an iron mind. You were enjoying the soup until I said something about it."

Rebecca wiped her mouth with her torn sleeve. "Okay, yeah . . . I got it."

Mister taught her these things over a period of four years—eight years in Parish time. The town would accelerate your education faster that what could be taught in schools. Mister would talk to people, but Rebecca stayed silent. He brought "home" stale food and old meat, but Rebecca never questioned their source nor did she purge them from her stomach. She happily ate whatever was placed in front of her, with the understanding that what she was feasting upon may not be there tomorrow. Or the next day.

He also showed her the city of Ellipses, confident that walking the streets and all that is hidden will serve her better than any map known to man. He would send her out to such and such street and return with anything of value. If she got lost, then she had to relocate herself. Sometimes, Mister would not see her for hours, and though he would grow worried as a father does for his child, he still believed in her abilities. His faith always answered him in the affirmative when she returned with double of what was expected.

If someone wanted to mug them for God knows what, Mister would step aside and allow Rebecca to defend them both. She remembered standing straight with her arms by her side, and Mister would punch her as hard as he could. Anyone outside of the slums would have contacted the military if they ever saw Mister's brutality, but it was necessary, he often said. Rebecca's tears would mix with the blood on her cheeks, and she would flinch when the salty streams of water covered her wounds, but she was commanded to not make a sound. If she did, she was hit again.

"Life will treat you harder than I'm hitting you," Mister said, "so you should be grateful and take this punishment as charity."

After a while, Rebecca only moved her head when the blow connected with her face, and she even smiled at one point. When Mister saw that grin, he stopped his assault and questioned her.

"What's so funny?" he asked.

"You hit like a baby girl!" Rebecca answered.

Mister smiled back. "Lesson over."

As a result, the young teenager was adept with her low blows and dishonorable conduct and acted within the comforts of a savage fighting style that could not be matched nor expected. Her movements were natural and yet so brutal and unpredictable that she gained a reputation for being Mister's devilish bodyguard, despite her young age.

All of these things were taught by a nobody.

Rebecca's hearing came back, and she heard herself scream out to everyone, but no one was around—at least no one wanted to be around.

"Get him down! Please! Help me! Oh my God, please help me!"

Her only words were pleas, mere inquiries to relieve her anguish. No relief came. Once again, there was no one to comfort her. Once again, she was alone. Only the kind dead granted her company. A nameless friend. An insignificant hero. But only a martyr for whom one lonely girl mourned. She cried until her chest hurt, and she could only force out tears if she cried out of short spurts. Her breathing jerked and shook her body, and she finally went silent, praying that she would die as well.

She let go of his body and stared up at the noose. It turned out to be an old lamp cord chewed up by a dog that used to call this forsaken place a home. She traced it away from Mister's neck and saw the lamp itself hanging on a short loose end. The light bulb was still in its place, and the lamp itself remained intact. A dark red stain graced the side of the lamp. Blood. New blood. She dried her eyes with her murky hands and examined the lamp itself. Small chunks of flesh remained glued to it. Rebecca mustered up the courage to look at Mister one last time. She did not hold back the tears that started to well up in her eyes as she walked behind Mister's body. A large wound sat on top of his skull, where a small hole dripped blood all over the floor. His gray-streaked hair married the colors of his blood and remained plastered to his beaten skull. Rebecca's mouth quivered in anger, and she immediately sold her soul to dark resolution, to deep vengeful infernos that made her forget the cold, rainy night that awaited her. She looked up at Mister, and she turned away from him to grab a chair from the opposite side of the room.

"Things will get better," he once said. "I promise."

"Thank you . . . Mister."

"One day," he once began, "I was standing in line at a store. This guy comes behind me and decides to cut in front of me. Now I was pissed. I wanted to slap him silly. I just kept staring at him with this angry-ass look on my face. Well, he bought his stuff and walked off without so much as an apology or even giving a shit about cutting in front of me."

Rebecca sniffled and let the cool breeze dry her eyes.

"You know the point I'm trying to make?" Mister asked. "Sometimes you get mad at people, and you want to say something to them. You go home and you relive that little show over and over again in your head. And guess what? That guy who pissed you off? He forgot about it when he walked out that door. So why bother?"

"Why bother . . ." Rebecca heard herself ask that question as she climbed the chair to free Mister from his noose. She found the knot and fiddled around with it until she was able to loosen the cord and release it from his neck. His body dropped onto her, and she felt the air kick out of her lungs as she supported his husky frame. She pivoted and let his body crash on the floor, making a loud echo throughout the building. She caught her breath and climbed down from the chair. She walked over to his body and rested her hand upon his forehead. Her fingers gently closed his eyes, and for a moment, she was glad that he finally looked peaceful. She turned around and walked over to the box of food. She knelt down, picked up a crumbled piece of French bread, rearranged the soup, and stood back up. She then walked back over to Mister as if she was in a funeral procession, slowly and calmly, marching to an angel's piano that only she could hear. She reached his body, and then she carefully placed the items next to his head. Rebecca wiped a final tear from her dark eyes and crossed herself. She turned on her heel, walked out of the room, reached the staircase, and slowly descended from the second floor. She ignored the stares of the other homeless citizens and ventured out into the alley. When she was on the main streets, she looked to her right and noticed a pay phone rusting away on the side of the brick wall. She picked up the phone, started to dial, and waited for an operator to answer her.

"9-1-1 emergency."

"My friend is dead, I . . . I think he . . . he was murdered. Oh God . . ." Rebecca cleared her throat. "The address is Sketch Lane . . . it's the last house on the left."

"Ma'am, what is your name—"

Rebecca hung up the phone. She stood by it and waited for the police and coroner to arrive. The rain had slowed to a light mist, cleaning her tired face and wiping the sweat from her forehead. She leaned against the wall and she felt the chill from the bricks crawl up her spine. She shivered, not for the cold but for the sight of Mister hanging from the ceiling and for the talks they would no longer have. Rebecca shook her head and sighed.

"Block it from your mind. It'll be there . . . when you're ready to see it again. Just open the box and pull out your forgotten treasure, right?" Rebecca whispered to herself, her own voice keeping her company as the flashes of blue and red lights graced the alley.

She observed a pair of officers emerge from their cruisers and scan the area. Rebecca noticed their bright gold badges shining against the colored alley. They reminded her of large gold bullions that she once saw in a historical magazine, glowing with its own source of light and swiftly abandoning any need for divine resplendence. When one of the officers approached her, she read the tiny digits that were punched on the top of his badge: "Detective." Rebecca liked that title. It informed everyone surrounding him that he was smart. Collected. A Spanish noble who exuded a calm and quiet aura of prestige. He neither flaunted his status nor did he bid any sense of inferiority to it. She heard a mumbling, a slow drone in her left ear, but her eyes remained fixed on his personal gold bullion.

"Hey! Miss! I said, 'What's your name?'"

Rebecca shook herself out of her enamored trance and cleared her throat. "Rebecca . . . Rebecca Ortega."

The detective whipped out a small notebook and a fountain pen. She admired the slim design of the pen and thought it looked like a feather quill encased in a classic, black shell. He looked Italian, sporting beautiful dark hair and a handsome face. He also had a sort of depressed look in his eyes, with small sacks forming underneath them. He looked to be in his early thirties, so she was wondering why he looked older than necessary.

"I'm Detective Bernini, I need to ask you a few questions."

"Okay." Italian indeed. Nice job.

Detective Bernini looked up at her and noticed her youthful face "How old are you?"

"Thirteen."

"Home address?"

"Here."

Detective Bernini stared at her, and then he nodded. He scribbled more notes into his pad and continued the conversation without looking back at her. "You were the one who made the 9-1-1 call?"

"Yeah."

"What's your relationship with this person?"

"Friend."

"What time did you discover his body?"

"I'm . . . I'm not sure . . . I don't keep track of time anymore. It was while it was raining hard, that much I do know."

"Okay . . ." Detective Bernini drew a line in his notepad. Rebecca kept her eyes on his badge and wished that she could hold it for a while and study it some more.

"Show me where his body is." Detective Bernini waved his hand to the coroners and watched as the other police officers sealed off the surrounding area with yellow tape. Rebecca led the detective through the alley, being careful to retrace her steps exactly as she first walked them. She could tell that Detective Bernini was used to crime scenes in dark alleys; he curiously scanned each fallen piece of broken glass, the holes in the rooftops, and even the bands of the homeless huddled together to keep warm. They knew that the police were in their small city, but they paid them no attention nor did they care.

Rebecca entered the house where she and Mister lived. As she climbed the stairs, she felt a dark shroud follow her back, blowing an evil chill on the back of her neck. Her hands quaked, her legs felt weaker and weaker as she walked. Her breathing quickened, and her heart had difficulty keeping up. Rebecca turned around and saw Detective Bernini calmly standing behind her. He gave her a confused look that was more awkward than perplexed.

"What's the matter?"

"Nothing . . . it's through that room."

They both entered the gravesite of Mister. It was a barren room that smelled of dried blood and rotting wood. Detective Bernini coughed as he reached into his suit jacket pocket and pulled out a dark-blue handkerchief. He pushed it against his nose and inhaled deeply. Rebecca raised her eyebrow at him, wondering why he needed to do such a thing. She then grew angry at him, disrespecting Mister like that, and she suddenly hated his badge. Rebecca looked at his face, and despised how his nose crinkled against his dirty cloth, how his eyes darted back and forth across the room, and especially the way he slowly approached the body as if it was seething with disease and poison. Rebecca felt an urge to rip off his badge and slam it on the floor. "He was my best friend!" She wanted to scream out those words until his ears bled. She knew, however, that she had to maintain herself.

"God, it stinks in here, doesn't it?"

Rebecca gave Detective Bernini a cold stare.

"Oh . . . sorry. Stand back for a second."

Rebecca stood in her spot as he examined the scene. He kept the handkerchief close to his nose as he circled Mister's body. He examined the cord, the lamp attached to it, and the body that lay on the floor, mouth still open, and his eyes shut hard in coerced sleep.

"Was he like this when you found him?"

"No . . . I took him down from the lamp cord over there. He was hanging from it."

"Oh, Christ . . ." Detective Bernini hung his head in frustration.

"What's wrong?"

"It really helps if you don't touch the body until the authorities arrive. Now this crime scene's inaccurate. Nice job."

"What was I supposed to do?" she snapped. "Leave him hanging there like a fucking mannequin?"

"Watch your language." Detective Bernini stared at the body. A medley of footsteps was heard behind the two, and a small pack of uniformed officers entered the room. They looked at Rebecca, her face moist and red, and they turned to the detective, who kneeled down beside the body.

"So what's the word, Detective?" one of the officers inquired.

"Well, I wanna say that this poor sap was killed, but Miss NYPD Blue here took the body down."

Rebecca's eyes narrowed for a second, but then she started to chuckle.

"I see nothing funny about this," said Detective Bernini.

"You're an idiot."

Detective Bernini quickly stood up and glared at Rebecca. "Say that again."

"I said, 'You're an idiot.' Look at the body. *Obviously*, he was killed. Look at the lamp cord. Look at the bleeding lamp up there." Rebecca pointed to each object she was identifying. "If you carefully lift up his head, his skull is cracked wide open. Then if that still doesn't convince you, then look at his neck. Look at those small indentures in his skin. Unless, you know, he knocked his head open with the lamp, wrapped the lamp cord around himself, and then hung himself. But since *you're* the brilliant detective, then you go ahead and tell me how wrong I am."

One of the officers followed her words and all of her hand gestures, then shrugged his shoulders and shook his head. "She's right, Detective."

Detective Bernini slowly leered at the officer, who felt embarrassed at agreeing with Rebecca. But the detective looked at the body again. Something was strange about it. He studied each item Rebecca had mentioned: the cord, the bloody lamp, the scarring around his neck. He pulled a pair of latex gloves and carefully burrowed his fingers into the floor and scooped up Mister's head. He saw a partly dried spot of blood on the back of his head. He looked closely and saw a gaping hole where the blood poured out. The hole was in a spot that made it extremely difficult to self-inflict. Impossible, even. The little bitch was right, he realized.

"The blow," he began, "was inflicted right here." He pointed to the exact spot on the back of his head. "Try getting a lamp and hit yourself right here. Can't do it. We're gonna have to call it—"

"Call it what?" Rebecca interrupted. "Murder?"

"Yes." Detective Bernini was irritated and humbled at the same time. "Murder."

Rebecca did not nod in agreement. She was still staring at Mister's body lying on the floor. Once he was standing on thin air, neck dislocated, those eyes staring at nothing. Now here he was, facing the empty ceiling while a group of cops questioned his death. The mumbles and quick snickers angered her, but what more could she do? Mister was gone, along with his gentle hugs and stories of times past, which were spoken when he was not comforting Rebecca like a father soothing his daughter. She thought they would have more time, but maybe it was time for her to murder her own condemned life.

"What did you say your name was?" Detective Bernini addressed her while he glanced over Mister's body once more.

"Rebecca Ortega."

"Anything else you can tell us about him, Miss Ortega?"

Rebecca stared at a floorboard for a moment and then she turned her eyes toward the rude detective. "He mentioned one time that he was in the Korean War." *Damn, had to give away that secret,* she thought.

"Fantastic. That narrows it down." Detective Bernini bonded his speech with sarcasm. "Any other brilliant deductions?"

"Leave it alone, Detective." One of the surrounding officers spoke up. "Let's just get what we need to get and get the hell out of here, all right?"

Detective Bernini stared at the floor for a moment and lost himself in thought as the coroners bent down to lay a long white sheet on the floor. They moved to Mister's body, with one man at his feet and another standing at his head. The coroner at the feet looked toward his partner. Rebecca read their lips as they counted to three, then Mister's body was hoisted and carried toward the white sheet. He was laid upon it—a soldier wrapped in a white cloth—and hovered toward the hallway. Rebecca followed him out of their room, still tasting the smell of blood and sweat that dripped from Mister's suspended corpse. *Strange,* she thought. His stench was neither pungent nor stifling. It did not cause her to bury her nose in a white handkerchief or make her sound off complaints of a rotten fragrance that permeated through a place she called home. It was her sanctuary. Rebecca then realized that Mister was gone. The room was empty as it always had been, except now she finally noticed that it truly was an empty shell—a discarded remnant of an occupied crevice that continued to rot and crumble.

Detective Bernini walked past Rebecca without saying a word to her. He followed the coroners out and brought the surrounding officers with him. One of them delayed his stride, turned around, and addressed Rebecca with a smirk. He was an older man who reminded Rebecca of those wise gentlemen often described in the classical literature she used to read with Mister. The covers were bent and destroyed, the pages were ripped at the ends, and the titles were worn and faded. But the books still had the smell of a calming musk and still maintained glorious hours of vacating away from her life. She felt that this mature officer was the direct manifestation of those books—traditional yet still relevant to modern society.

"You should be a detective someday."

Rebecca smiled, the first time she smiled since she discovered Mister. "Really? I . . . never really thought of that before but . . . thank you."

"And don't be shy. The real you showed itself when you talked to Detective Dipshit over there." The old man placed his hands to the side of his mouth and closed his fingers together. "And between you and me," he whispered, "he deserved it."

Rebecca giggled and nodded to him. He chuckled and started to walk backward.

"Come downstairs when you're ready. They're gonna ask you some more questions at the station."

Rebecca nodded and stared at the weak ceiling for a moment, branding her mind with the memory of her home and resolving to never forget the background that she was determined to never return. When she brought her eyes down from the wooded sky, the officer was gone. She brushed her hair back with her grimy hands and walked out of the room. She ventured down the creaky staircase and saw Detective Bernini standing among his fellow officers. She looked around for the kindly old officer, but he was not anywhere to be found. Rebecca tapped a nearby officer on his shoulder, and he turned around with an annoyed look on his face.

"Don't worry, cutie, we'll get you to the station soon enough."

"No, it's not that I was just wondering . . ." Rebecca stopped herself from stammering. "There was this officer, this older guy that was here. Where did he go?"

"What older officer?"

Rebecca looked around in bewilderment. "An older officer."

"The oldest officer we have here is Detective Bernini over there. The oldest guy we have here is in his thirties. Maybe you should be a better judge of age, huh?"

The officer turned away and left Rebecca to think inside her confusion. She stared at a star that dotted the black sky. She wondered if Mister was the star that shined just for her, pushing her and encouraging her to keep her resolution. She chuckled. He always did say to "jump on opportunity before it jumps onto someone else." That quote remained in her head as she looked at the officer in front of her, tapped his shoulder, and waited for him to turn around and allow himself the pleasure of her audience.

"So . . . when are we going to the station, Officer?"

Rebecca stared in awe at the city lights that gleamed through the back of the cruiser window. One of the police officers volunteered to take her to the station, but she knew that he was bribed with a round of drinks at a local bar if he volunteered. She didn't care. She wanted to gaze at the buildings adorned with golden bulbs of light that towered against the night sky. A couple walking on the sidewalk were laughing and hanging onto one another. It seemed as if they were holding each other up, supporting one another, braving themselves to face the morning that will always rise to challenge the misty evening. This was the same city that Rebecca grew up in and lived, but she bore witness to the same city through a different pair of eyes. They belonged not to the Rebecca who ran to the Parish to shield herself from pouring rain. It was not the eyes of a young girl who ate stale French bread and cold cans of expired tomato soup. They only housed themselves in Rebecca Ortega, a person who once had eyes to see but no vision. She lived in smog—no air to breathe nor a hope to grasp. Was this the world outside? Suddenly she longed for a report or some sort of summary of all the events and happiness she missed in her open prison. Rebecca had no walls to trap her. No reptilian creatures thirsting for human flesh nor any wizards to cast hexes upon her. She built her own walls; she provided her own blood-lusting creatures, her own sorcerers to curse her. She was always independent by virtue of her nature, and she was so independent that she refused anyone to contribute to her sadness except for herself.

The cruiser pulled into a long driveway that led to a short building with the letters "EPD" etched across the entrance. Rebecca looked through the rear car window to scan the multitude of police cruisers in the large parking lot. She liked the color scheme of black and white painted on the sides of each cruiser. She felt herself smiling—a characteristic that was hardly seen when she was alone. Her mouth stretched out to show a set of yellowed teeth thick with plaque and old bits of food. Her lips were chapped so much that blood could be seen crawling out of their thin crevices and dropping onto her chin. She had large bags under her eyes which almost sagged to her cheeks. But she still smiled, and that joy alone made her look beautiful.

"Hey, Officer . . . how many cars are out there?"

"Hell if I know."

"It looks like a lot! Like two hundred of them!"

"Mm-hmm."

Rebecca ignored her disinterested driver and waited in excitement for the cruiser to pull up to the entrance. She gazed at the large letters blazing its neon blue lights against the atmosphere. EPD. Ellipses Police Department. Her eyes studied the sign as if it were a marble statue created by Donatello himself. Rebecca's body jerked forward as the cruiser came to a full stop. She was anxious to jump out of the vehicle and run inside the building. She wanted to be her own personal tour guide. She waited impatiently for the driver to climb out of the cruiser and walk over to her side to open the door for her. She stepped out not as a homeless young woman slamming her foot onto cold, wet pavement, but as a Hollywood screen goddess who greeted the press with wide smiles and graceful waves. Her clothes suddenly were not ripped to pieces, barely draping over her shoulders and hanging upon naked threads. Her shoes were not as thin as socks that made her feet feel every small pebble as she ran through the rain. Her body was now not infested with open sores or layers of dirt and soot, nor was her hair darkened by grime. Rebecca was now a model of couture fashion: she wore a stunning gray suit made from Carolina Herrera, tailored to match and conform only to Rebecca's frame. She wore a soft white blouse that made room for her full breasts to tease those who glanced at them. She wore a pair of sharp stilettos that strapped itself around her manicured feet and accentuated her toned calves. Her skin was flawless—no blemishes, no signs of it ever touching dirt. It glowed with nary any assistance from the surrounding light. It was almost angelic, the way she strode inside the building, looking around the area for her audience to rush out and beg their hearts out for a small semblance of an autograph or to seek her unmatched ability to discern what cannot be seen, the aptitude to command sight beyond sight.

When she walked toward the front door, she suddenly felt a surge of regret creep beneath her skin. It slithered its way toward her heart, and she had to control her stammered breathing. She missed Mister. She wished that he was the one driving her to her dream, a dream she had never thought of until a few moments ago, as she felt the cold rain splash against her face. Her stride became noticeably slower, and she soon came to a complete stop. The ground stared up at her, taunting her to cry once more, but her resolve held back her tears. Her resolve took the form of anger, directed at the one who hung her source of joy. Her eyes narrowed, her teeth clenched tightly, and her lips curled to a sneer. This dream, this desire. It only came alive with someone's demise.

"Hey, c'mon! I can't wait the entire goddamned century for you!" the driver shouted at Rebecca.

"Yeah. Coming."

Rebecca entered the building and was immediately surrounded by everything ominous and official: high walls of brick pasted with a row of photos detailing the most wanted criminals in the city. A poster illustrated with the EPD logo set atop a blue background hung high on the wall like a flag too precious to display outside. She listened to the telephones singing melodic rings to the administrative assistants speaking in their professional voices. Once they hung up the phones, they reverted back to their vulgar dialects, saying things like "I need a fucking drink" or "My ex-husband makes me wanna smash my head into concrete . . . repeatedly." Rebecca snickered and realized that her driver was gone. She frantically looked around the area and jogged towards a large metallic door. To the right of her sat a guard, who stared at her without uttering a word. Rebecca shyly walked over to the guard and swallowed hard.

"Excuse me . . . this officer drove me-"

"He's already inside." The officer then smiled at her. "Don't let him bother you—we have a department of jerks here." He pressed a button hidden under his desk and the metal door buzzed loudly. He nodded to Rebecca, and she pulled the heavy door with both hands and entered.

The door slammed behind her and made her jump. She calmed herself down and looked around for her chauffeur. She saw him standing in what seemed to be a break room, talking to a female officer. She was pretty; her hair was tied in a high ponytail that showed off her sharp cheekbones and wide, naive eyes. He talked with a smirk, brushing his eyebrows occasionally as he continued his speech. Rebecca started to walk towards him, but she saw Detective Bernini sitting at his desk, staring hard at a pile of papers shuffled all over his desk. She approached his desk and stood in front of him for a moment. He ignored her. She cleared her throat loudly to gather his attention, but he only addressed her while he pulled out a blank sheet of paper and grabbed a pen.

"Have a seat," he grudgingly said. Rebecca noticed a plastic, beaten chair and sat down in a dainty, feminine manner. She sat up straight and waited for him to address her. "All right . . . full name?"

"Rebecca Anna Maria Ortega."

"Age?"

Rebecca was annoyed that he forgot about her age already, within a time span of a half hour, but she controlled her feelings of displeasure and answered his question. "Thirteen."

"And you're homeless?"

"Yes."

"For how long?"

Rebecca paused a moment and stared hard at a piece of paper scribbled with notes. She could not make out his handwriting, but she continued her conversation with the detective, her voice laden with whispers. "Must have been . . . four years."

"Where did you originally live?"

"I thought we were gonna talk about Mister's murder."

"No. We're not. You first. Where did you originally live?"

Rebecca sighed. "Down on Berry Street, in the Sill Apartment complex."

"Where are your parents?"

"My dad died when I was five. My mom has been drunk ever since. *Now* can we talk about Mister's murder?"

Detective Bernini averted his eyes away from the sheet of paper in front of him and looked at Rebecca. "You ran away, didn't you?"

"Damn right I did. I'd rather live out on the streets than deal with my cunt of a mother."

"Do you want some soap for your mouth, young lady? I'll be glad to give you some."

"Whatever."

Detective Bernini stared at Rebecca for a moment. He was trying to read her mind through her eyes, but all he saw was a quieted fury buried deep within her subconscious. "All right, so who is this Mister? What's his real name?"

"I . . . really never knew. No one in the Parish asks each other's background. I mean . . . we were all in the same little situation—what was the point of asking? We were there, that's all that mattered. So no one cared if I called him Mister. And he didn't care either."

"You mentioned to me that he once said he was in the Korean War, right?"

"Yeah . . . but it was maybe only one time."

Detective Bernini nodded his head a bit. He raised his eyebrows as if he was happy about something. He smirked, not in a clever way but with an implicit manner of sarcasm. "Well, finding out his info will take some time. We can get some fingerprint analysis done, and maybe we can find out his real name."

Surprise and joy made Rebecca quickly lean over and smacked the palm of her hand on his desk. "You serious? Really?"

Detective Bernini chuckled. "Yeah. There's a catch."

Rebecca felt her heart sink into her chest. Her smile faded slightly, but her eyes remained hopeful. "What catch?"

Detective Bernini lain back in his chair. Rebecca could hear it creaking to support his body weight. "You gotta go back home."

Rebecca leered at the detective and clenched her open hand into a fist. "Horseshit! No way!"

"Look, I know this doesn't sound like a fun trip to the mall, but technically you're a runaway. A missing person. It's my duty to take you back home to your mother."

"No! Don't you understand? I ran away for a reason!"

"And what reason is that?"

Rebecca slouched back into her seat and submitted her joy to despair. She clenched her lips and shot up out of her seat. "Fuck you then!"

She walked away from Detective Bernini and headed toward the door. She outstretched her arms to push the door open and run out of the station. She did not care if she had to hurl her body against the door to open it. Her exit was in front of her. As she braced herself, a pair of uniformed officers appeared in front of her escape and formed a barrier in front of her. They were both over six feet tall, overweight but solid in all respects. They locked themselves in the floor, and Rebecca realized that not even a sledgehammer would break their ground.

"You have no choice, Miss Ortega," Detective Bernini called out from his desk. "You're going home."

Rebecca turned around and glared at the detective. She held her evil stare, but Detective Bernini did not seem afraid of her furious eyes.

"Look at me like that all you want, I don't care. And by the way, thanks for the address you gave me. Now stop bitching and let's go."

Rebecca ended her angry gaze and sighed. She lowered her head towards the ground and sniffled. When she looked up at the detective, a tear was seen rolling down her face.

"If I go home . . . do you promise to give me Mister's info?"

Detective Bernini smirked. "Of course."

Rebecca stepped away from the pair of officers and walked back to Detective Bernini. She sat back down at his desk and snatched a piece of paper that sat on his desk. He watched in curiosity as she grabbed the pen that was in his hand and slammed it against the sheet of paper. She pushed it in front of him and watched the pen rock back and forth from the force she so angrily applied.

"I want it in writing."

Detective Bernini chuckled. "I just told you that I promise to—"

"And I told you that I want Mister's info. So stop dicking around with me and write it down."

Detective Bernini snickered and reluctantly picked up the pen. He slid the paper to himself and began to write. Rebecca watched him intently as he scribbled his statement on the paper. When he laid his pen down, she leaned over and took the paper from him. She smiled and stood up from her chair. She held on to the paper like a thief holding on to his robbed goods. She walked over to one of the officers that blocked her way out and held the statement in front of her.

"Can you come with me to Detective Bernini's desk, please?"

"Uh . . . sure."

He looked at his partner and shrugged his shoulders. He followed the ambitious young woman back to the detective's desk. He was still sitting down, bewildered with Rebecca's methods. Once she reached him, she handed the paper to the officer.

"Can you please read this out loud?"

The officer nodded and began to read the statement to the detective and the teen. "I, Detective Gregorio Bernini, do hereby swear to give Rebecca Ortega the information of a murdered victim, dubbed as Mister. She will receive this information upon completion of analysis and upon her return to her original place of residency. Any violations on my part or on the part of Miss Ortega will void this contract and result in penalties not yet outlined. Signed, Gregorio Bernini."

Rebecca smiled and thanked the officer for reading the statement. The officer handed Rebecca the paper with a grin. She took Detective Bernini's pen and scribbled her signature underneath his own. She then looked up at the detective. "Where's your copier?"

"It's over there," he said with a frustrated sigh.

Rebecca turned to her left and saw a large white copy machine pushed back against the wall. She strode over to it and lifted up the cover. She carefully placed the paper down on the glass surface and lined it up perfectly. She closed the lid and pressed a green button on the bottom right-hand corner. The bright-green light glided from the right and shut off once it finished its scan. She heard a rustling of papers inside the machine and was overjoyed to see a white sheet of paper with the detective's exact handwriting painted on it. She grabbed the copied paper and lifted up the lid to pick up the original. She walked back to Bernini's desk and gladly handed over the copied paper to him.

"Try not to lose this," she said. "If you do, I can make another copy for you."

Rebecca rode in the back of a cruiser once more, only this time she was dreading the trip rather than rejoicing in it. She barely looked out the window, failing to notice the bright street lights beaming against her face and shedding its radiance upon her melancholic eyes, nor did she pay attention to the soft glimmer of the stars shining on the moist roads. It looked like the sky had dropped a large bag of glitter on earth, and the wet streets absorbed each sparkle into every crack, every loose rock and pebble that lined the sidewalks. Rebecca leaned her head against the window. The nostalgic views of the city streets and the skinny grocery stores made her heart beat faster. She memorized this area, as do those who once lived in a place where they despise and curse its very existence. It was a thought best lobotomized out of their skulls. She imagined that a screwdriver was sitting on her lap, waiting for her to grasp its handle and burrow into her temples. Her only escape, her refuge, was to be the one swinging by a weak cord that crushed her neck.

Almost there, she thought. She wondered if she should escape. She wondered if she *could* escape. The windows were too hard to break with her head, and she was already tired and sore from her long jog through the rain. She was especially sore from discovering Mister floating over her wet eyes. She rested her chin on the ledge that jutted ever so slightly from the door. The subtle pricks of old leather scratched at her skin, but she ignored each tiny needle as if she delighted in it. It was better than seeing *her*, she thought. This was a pain she would withstand for a decade. Gladly.

Rebecca placed her hand on her thigh and felt something crumble beneath its weight. She slid her fingertips over the object and remembered the contract she had Detective Bernini sign. She chuckled at her own clever attitude she upheld when she asked him to pin his covenant with literature and how she promptly walked over to the police officer and made him witness. Maybe the cop she met at the scene of Mister's murder was right; being a detective was . . . comforting.

She then felt like crying. Her thoughts returned to that scene, an almost unholy tragedy set upon a stage, where she was innocence exalted and a fool entitled. Why did she not imagine her future before? Did she see herself amidst the people domiciled in a vagrant alley? No one told her to leave. No one told her to stay. Her schizophrenic choice was hers alone but still one that was spliced. Rebecca only knew how to survive today and worry about the bleak morrow when it entered her room, a room she shared for almost two years. Her thoughts, her very being, lay dormant in Mister's hollowed body.

Rebecca froze her thoughts once the police cruiser came to a stop. She refocused her eyes and saw a short apartment complex through her fogged window. The deformed red bricks that lined the building remained as depressing and as pitiful as she had remembered it. The sign that read "Sill Apartments" still lacked the decorative endeavor that other complexes would invest in their buildings. The shameful edifice that stood before her—albeit with a vain attempt to discourage her from entering—did not change at all. She took this vision as a bad omen; however, what lay before her on the outside was only a vague reflection of the inside.

"We're here." The police officer glanced at his rearview mirror.

"Yeah . . . thank you."

The police officer placed the cruiser in park and opened the door. He looked around the surrounding area and shook his head. *Oh, now you understand*, Rebecca thought. He then walked over to the rear of the vehicle and stood on Rebecca's opposite side. She scooted over as he pulled the door open and she got out of the car.

She met the chilled air that surrounded the building and inhaled it into her lungs. The officer could tell she was readying herself for whatever demons she left behind those two years ago.

"You live *here*?" he asked.

"Yep."

"Damn."

"Yep. Thanks."

The officer watched as Rebecca climbed the steps and pressed a button embedded on a nearby wall. The buzz was still loud enough to wake up the city block. She was met with silence. Rebecca grew impatient and pressed the buzzer again. The speaker crackled and sputtered before a voice answered her.

"Hello? Who's this?" A woman's voice answered with irritation in her voice.

"It's me."

Silence greeted Rebecca once more. She pressed the intercom button and spoke clearly. "*Mami* . . . it's Rebecca."

"Oh my god! Rebecca!"

The door buzzed. Rebecca pulled open the glass door and briefly waved to the officer as she entered. He nodded and slowly walked back to the cruiser. She could hear him turn on the engine and drive off into the lonely city streets.

The first floor of the apartment complex was where she once lived. Rebecca never thought that her mother may have moved to another floor. Change in any way did not fare well with Ms. Ortega, and she would rather throw herself off a cliff than move even a hundred feet away from her current residence. Rebecca wondered if anything had changed once she ran away. But her thoughts quickly reverted back to the sight of her mother, her face stricken with sadness but still holding a glimmer of youth and beauty in her eyes. She remembered the long curly hair streaked with silver strands here and there, a pair of lips as crimson and as full as Rebecca's, and shoulders that tapered off into a thick but desirable body.

When Rebecca marched down the long tan hallway, she heard a door open in front of her, and a shadow of a tired woman spilled out onto the hallway floor before Ms. Melissa Ortega ventured out herself.

The two women watched each other. Rebecca had stopped walking once her mother's eyes froze her in place. It was a sort of cold snap that held the Ortega daughter in place and refused to grant her freedom of movement. There they stood, two women separated by circumstances schemed by the demon himself.

Melissa Ortega ran out of the doorway and threw her arms around her lost daughter. She was crying, and such an emotion only made Rebecca angrier. Her eyes narrowed, and her lips clenched shut. She tried to move against her mother's embrace to give her a clue that she no longer felt safe in her arms, but Melissa would not budge. She held her tighter and let her tears cascade down her cheeks and land on Rebecca's shoulders. When she finally pulled away, she saw that Rebecca was devoid of all emotion. Her daughter only looked at Melissa, who smiled through her blanket of wrinkles and blotched face.

"I missed you so much! Oh my god, I missed you so much!"

Rebecca only stared at her mother with no feelings of remorse for escaping her home.

"Oh, thank you, God . . . thank you, God." Melissa hugged her again and swished her body from side to side. She managed to pry herself away from Rebecca and held her against her bony shoulder. They walked together through the hallway and passed through the doorway.

Rebecca was home.

"Are you hungry, sweetie?" Melissa must have asked her for the fourth time. "Here, I heated up some soup earlier. It's your favorite: chicken noodle. You still like chicken noodle soup, right?"

Rebecca only stared at the table where she sat. It was an old cream-colored table that wobbled on one leg and squeaked whenever she leaned on it.

"I have a bowl for you . . ." Melissa kept her smile the entire time she grabbed a large white bowl that sat on the counter. "It has a stain on the outside, but don't worry. I cleaned it as hard as I could. I used that bleach I always keep down here. You remember, right?"

Rebecca remained silent.

"I know you do. You were so good at keeping things locked up in memory. Like you had a . . . gift. Yeah. Are you thirsty? Do you want some orange juice? Or apple? I went shopping this morning. I only bought a few things, but it should last for the next few days. Do you remember that grocery store down the street? I used to take you there when you were little. You had so much fun. Remember?"

"Where's Santo?"

Melissa became silent. She looked down at the floor before she answered. "He . . . left."

"Oh. What happened between you two?"

"The soup is still warm . . ." Melissa's hands were shaking.

"What. Happened?'"

"Rebecca . . . baby . . ."

"Answer me! What happened to Santo?"

"I made him leave!" Melissa screamed out and slammed the bowl on the counter. "I kicked him out that day when you left—"

"You waited that long to kick him out?"

"I was scared!"

"He touched me! He—"

"He was gonna kill me! If I said anything—"

"I'm your daughter! Why didn't you—"

"He hit me, Rebecca! Do you understand? He'd always hit me!"

"He was molesting me! I was fucking nine!" Rebecca's eyes grew moist and red. "Why didn't you try and stop him?"

"I-I tried to—"

"Why didn't you stop him, *Mami*?"

Melissa walked in a stammer and placed her hands on Rebecca's shoulder, but she brushed off her mother's quivering hand. "I . . . I was scared. I was so scared . . ."

"How did you think I fucking felt? You don't know how much it hurt me!"

"I-I'm so sorry—"

"Do you know what he did to me?"

"I tried to stop him, Rebecca! I came into your room when I heard him! You don't remember, do you? I saw him and he . . . he got off you and walked toward me. He grabbed my neck and threw me to the floor. He said that if I said anything that he would . . . he would just . . ."

Rebecca's eyes were streaming with tears. She saw that her mother's tears rushed out so much that the bags underneath her eyes began to swell up.

"Why did you think I ran away? My own mother just fucking stood there!"

"He said that he would kill you too, Rebecca! It was the only way I could keep you alive! Baby, I . . . needed you in my life! I love you!" Melissa dropped to her knees and began to slam the floor with her fist. She kept slamming and slamming until blood started to spill on the floorboards. She stood up on her knees and looked into Rebecca's wet eyes.

"When you left, I was so . . . angry. This man made my daughter leave. He made you leave, Rebecca! Not me! I wanted to kill myself . . . you don't know those nights when I cried myself to sleep! I wanted to die! I wanted to die so bad!" Rebecca sniffled and continued to listen to her mother. "But I got out of bed and I ran to the kitchen . . . I grabbed that large plug for the cake mixer in there . . . and I beat that bastard in his sleep until he screamed! Then I kept beating him and beating him! I wanted him dead! I wanted him to feel my pain! I wanted him to feel your pain! Not a day goes by when I didn't think about you! You were my whole life . . . you were the reason I stayed alive . . ."

Rebecca's eyes widened in shock. "Did you . . . kill him?"

Melissa dropped her head into her chest. "No . . . I called the police soon afterward, and they took him away. But . . . oh, Rebecca, you don't know how good it felt to see him like that . . . I watched his eyes open wide while I fucking beat him! I fucking beat him and beat him." Melissa's mouth stretched to a grin. "I was so glad to do that to him! I wanted to keep going until all his blood drained out of him . . ."

"Oh, God . . . *Mami* . . ."

"He took you away from me, Rebecca! He took you away from me! My only child!"

"*Mami . . .*"

"Oh, sweetie, I love you so much! I'm so sorry!"

Rebecca ran to her mother and collapsed into her mother's arms. They both cried on each other, their tears mixing and pouring at the same speed.

"Why didn't you kill him? Why? Why?"

"I'm so sorry, baby! I'm so sorry!"

They cried for what seemed like hours. They refused to let each other go—they both feared that they would lose one another again, to become lost to the void that swallowed them both. Rebecca did not ask how her mother did it. She did not ask her what became of Santo. Melissa did not ask where Rebecca was all this time. Neither of them cared. All that mattered to them was the embrace they felt, after so long . . . so many nights alone crying, cursing themselves, and wishing they were dead. All those nights they spent staying awake—Melissa hoping that her daughter would walk through that door and ask for some soup, Rebecca hoping that her mother would walk through the Parish and find her eating stale bread in that alley. Here they found each other and released that agony that grew inside of them. They were both happy; a bittersweet regret lay in their tears. The smell of sweat and blood permeated the room, mixing into a sweet, warm fragrance that settled on their faces. Their wet, puffy faces. And as Rebecca held her mother, and as Melissa kissed her daughter on her forehead, they became relatives once more. Mother and daughter, once separated in anguish, now together in tears.

Forever.

X

Raquel woke up in the middle of the night to hear a soft, muffled voice speaking in the adjacent room. The voice was not disturbing at all, but she did hear her loud conscious forcing her to get out of bed, to struggle against the comfort of dreaming and escaping the reality of her surroundings. She opened her tired eyes and hated herself from lifting her head off the pillow, that weightless cushion of feather and air, which supported her long strands of hair and kept the beauty laden in her face. She laid her palms flat on the bed and pushed herself into an upright position. She sat still to let her body remind itself that it was now awake, the slumber had ended, get back to reality, and enjoy the memory of what it was like to sleep again. Raquel sighed a bit too loudly; she was hoping that someone would hear her and apologize wholeheartedly. She wanted someone to burst through her bedroom door and serve a warm cup of mango tea on a cedar wood tray, decorated with petals of . . . anything—just something that illustrated the regret of simply making her torso vertical. "Oh, Raquel! I'm so sorry for waking you up! But you looked so beautiful that I couldn't help but awake you to see how your eyes shine!" Raquel looked over to her right and slammed her fist down on her husband's chest. When her fist landed on the mattress instead of a wide, hairy chest, she chuckled and forgot that he was not there to be beaten . . . playfully beaten. Although sometimes, she remembered, she teetered on casual folly and desired injury. Raquel made a playful smirk and slammed her fist down on the mattress again.

"Just so you don't forget what you're missing, you idiot."

Raquel chuckled and threw the covers off of her. She rotated to the side of the bed and slipped her delicate feet into a pair of pink, fuzzy slippers. Zephyr had once sneaked into her bedroom and tried them on herself. When Raquel walked in, she saw her granddaughter shuffling around, stopping often when the oversized slipper came off her foot. She would just retrace her tiny steps and slip her foot back in again, then she continued shuffling about the room, giggling at how the small, pink fur would wave against the air. Zephyr froze in her steps when she turned around and saw her grandmother standing in the doorway, watching her every move and giggling at her attempts to make the slippers fit snugly on her feet. She stared at her grandmother with her wide platinum pair of eyes. Her mouth opened to form a small *O* that showed the shock in her body. Her mouth closed and her bottom lip stuck out ever so slightly. Her eyes pointed toward the floor, and her chin descended into her chest.

"Grandma . . . I'm sorry . . ."

Raquel looked at Zephyr and could not help but condemn herself for catching her granddaughter in such a joyful mood, then ceasing it from continuing. "It's okay, baby . . . you can have them. Just let me wash them for—"

"No . . . it's okay. I'll put 'em back."

Zephyr slid her feet out of the slippers and squatted down to pick them up. She held it in front of her chest and walked over to Raquel's bedside. She looked so disappointed and envious of Raquel that she could slip into the pair of shoes easily without any signs of struggle. Raquel stepped over to Zephyr and placed her hand on her slim shoulder.

"I'll find you a pair of your own. That way you can practice. Is that okay?"

Zephyr's face swelled up with delight. "Okay!"

Zephyr dropped the slippers on the floor where she had found them and bounded toward Raquel. She hugged her leg and ran past her to go to her room. Zephyr loved hugging and would hug a tree if her arms were long enough to wrap around its thick base. Raquel cherished each hug as if it were a silk cloak that draped over her naked body and softly clung to her skin. She wished that Zephyr would hug her tonight and wake her body enough to stand up in her bedroom.

Raquel held the memory of Zephyr's embrace in her mind as she finally stood on her feet. She walked across the bedroom and opened her bedroom door. She always kept it ajar to allow a lonely stream of light creep into her room. This time, she noticed, there was no light to spread itself inside the bedroom. The hallway was as dark as the night sky, draping its abysmal curtains over the entire mansion and made Raquel squint her eyes just to see through the blinding air.

She followed the gentle waves of the murmured voice to a guest bedroom. The only source of light Raquel could see in the bedroom was the pale moon seeping through the open curtains. She peeked inside the room and saw Rosa sitting up in a corner chair, her back turned to Raquel. She had a small phone pressed against her ear, the plastic covering clicking occasionally against her tiny diamond stud in her ear. She kept her voice whispered and low as she spoke into the receiver.

"So it will be next week, on Saturday . . . yeah, that's right. I know! Of all days, right?" Rosa laughed and gasped suddenly when she realized that her laugh was a bit too loud. "Oh, she's doing just fine, still reading everyone bedtime stories—to the point where we all can memorize them all, hee hee. But she's too cute to resist, you know?"

Raquel stood in the doorway and patiently waited for Rosa to finish. She saw how Rosa smiled as she spoke to the person on the other line and how her smile faded quickly once she listened to the voice that whispered in her ear. Rosa sighed, sent off her farewell, and hung up the phone. She grabbed a black fountain pen that lay next to her and scribbled something on a notepad in front of her. Raquel gently tapped the door with the tip of her fingernail. Rosa quickly turned around and breathed a sigh of relief once she saw Raquel in the doorway.

"Oh, I'm so sorry, sweetheart," Raquel said. "I didn't mean to scare you."

"Oh, no, no, it's okay. Did I wake you up?"

"Nah, couldn't sleep anyway." Raquel took a step outside and let her silhouette ease further into the bedroom. "Besides, I would've been yelling and banging against the wall if you were too loud. Nicely, of course." She chuckled and waved to Rosa as she began to leave.

"I was on the phone with Vlad," Rosa whispered as if she was preparing to open a healed scar. "Just now."

Raquel halted her slow trot. "You're kidding."

"No."

"He contacted you or did you contact him?"

"I contacted him . . . Luis asked me to."

Raquel strode back into Rosa's room and sat on the edge of the bed. Rosa turned her body away from the desk to meet Raquel's worried stare. Raquel dropped her chin in her chest and closed her eyes. She spoke to Rosa without looking up at her. "That time already?"

"Well, all Luis said was to contact him."

"You know . . . I remember when Manny asked me to do the same. I hated setting up those meetings. But it was okay, since we made a deal—I set up the meetings. he sleeps on the couch. I kept saying, 'Do it yourself, you jackass!' But you know . . . tradition and all. Except during my time, there was no Forty-Second Street or whatever the hell it's called." Raquel combed her fingers through her wavy, disheveled hair and sighed softly. "Not to say that I married into an angelic family organization myself, but . . . you know what I mean."

"Yeah," Rosa said, "I know what you mean."

"I wish Luis wasn't involved with them. But . . . I'm not the boss."

"I know . . . I wish the same. But they bring Luis a lot of money."

"Does he still tutor that young kid? Adam, right?"

"You got it. He seems nice from what Luis describes."

"Well, if he can guide him in the right direction, then maybe Luis would tutor me as a musician. Watch me—tomorrow morning I'm going out to get a tattoo. The big number *42* hovering barely three inches above my ass. I'm gonna get drunk first and not buzzed drunk—I'm talking shit-faced—then I'll do it. Then I'll have the artist draw an arrow pointing downward that says 'Place lips here.' You laugh, but watch me! I'll walk around in a tight skirt where everyone can see. And I bet you my jewelry that once they see a sixty-year-old woman with that ink, they'll turn the hell around and join a semi-nary . . . either that or see an optometrist after they're blinded by my glory!"

Rosa covered her mouth and muffled her laugh. Her eyes twinkled in the little bit of moonlight that did enter the room. When her hand left her face, her smile started to frown once a new thought entered her mind. "I'm worried about Luis . . . I told him about this dream I had, and he just said, 'Call Vlad.' No explanation, just told me to call him. And I'm not one to ask him why or 'What do you mean?' But this time I did. And . . . he had the saddest look on his face. I . . . haven't seen him like that since we moved here."

Raquel nodded her head and stared at the floor. She curled her lips together and sighed. "Luis wants to pass on his title."

Rosa quickly sat up. "What? How—"

"Trust me. I know. He wanted you to call Vlad for a reason. Did you have to call whatshisname too?"

"Who? Julius Mal? No, he told me to not worry about him."

"I see . . ." Raquel paused her speech for a moment before she spoke again. "When is the meeting?"

"Halloween," she sighed. "Of all days."

"Well, don't quote me on this, but it does sound like he wants to pass his title to Pedro."

"What? No! He's only eighteen! He's too young!"

"Luis was sixteen when you both got here. Only two years was all he needed to get to where he is now."

"But it's Pedro!" Rosa slammed her fist on the mattress and forgot how loud her voice suddenly became. "I'm sick of this! Does Luis have to do this?!"

Raquel only sat silently and listened to Rosa's hidden anguish that finally resurrected itself.

"Why my son? Why! Does this shit ever end?"

At that moment, a soft moan was heard across the hallway. Both women turned their heads to study the sound, and their gazes fell upon Zephyr's sleepy body shuffle into her parents' bedroom. She was rubbing her calm silver eyes, and Raquel could not help but smile after seeing her granddaughter in her white pajamas decorated with pink, grinning elephants. Her feet were bare, and her hair was ruffled on the sides. She approached her mother, still rubbing the sleep away from her eyes.

"*Mami*, are you okay?" she asked, with a small wind of innocence in her voice. Rosa picked her up and laid her across her lap, gently stroking her wavy hair and waiting until Zephyr closed her eyes again.

"I'm okay, *nina. Mami's* okay."

Zephyr's breathing calmed into a peaceful sleep once more. Her body felt limp in Rosa's arms as she brushed her finger across the slope of her jaw.

"I asked myself the same thing years ago," Raquel said. "I remember yelling and screaming and cursing maybe a few months after I dated him. I didn't want him to get hurt. I didn't want to go to his funeral . . . ever. I told him, 'End it! I don't care what you do! I love you! I don't want you taken away from me!' But despite all of that, I never left him. I couldn't. You know why?"

Rosa looked at her and shook her head.

"He only told me three words: 'It never ends.'"

Raquel stood up once Rosa placed Zephyr back into her bed. She walked back into her bedroom and sat next to Raquel again. Rosa had the look of a thirst for comfort, a longing to be held for no reason. Just an escape that everyone wished for in life. She had no destination to reach, no place to be. She only wanted to sit. And to her, sitting was the best thing for her to do at that moment. Her only motion was to tilt her eyes toward Raquel as she continued to speak.

"No one wants to see their son as . . . that. I know. I never wanted Luis to do what he wanted to do. I'm sorry . . . it's what he *had* to do. I . . . regret it every day. I wanted him to have a normal life, you know . . . be a teenager. Date you. Get acne. Marry you, and give me a soccer team of grandkids. He did all that, well, except the whole soccer team thing," she said with a chuckle. "Except that his job is . . . not what I wanted for him. But I remember the circumstances all too well—just as much as you, and I realize that things do happen for a reason." Raquel sighed. "I guess all I'm trying to say is to keep praying to God. Pray that He keeps Luis safe. And Pedro. That's all we can do."

Rosa nodded and continued to stare at the floor as Raquel spoke.

"And pray to God that Zephyr will never have to go through this with her children. Ever. She's such a sweetheart; I never want to see her cry. She does not deserve it."

"Yeah . . ."

Raquel nodded and leaned over to rest her elbows on her knees. She closed her eyes and bowed her head toward the floor.

"Why us?" Rosa asked. "Why. Us."

"I wish I knew. But we're strong women. In a way, *we're* worse than any criminal out there . . . because we can take it."

"You're right."

"You're strong, Rosa. Continue to be. And to be honest, I still believe that this will all end. Somehow."

"Thank you. I . . . needed to hear that." Rosa sighed. "We better get some sleep . . . big day coming soon."

"Take care, dearie. I'm here if you need me. I have experience, damn it all."

Rosa smirked as she stood up with Raquel and hugged her. They held each other longer than expected, as if they both needed to be understood. No one was around to listen—to feel their daily agony—and yet they embraced each to share their spirits. Such a cathartic release gave them enough strength to carry on, and they were the iron spears that adorned the shadows of the men in their lives. The sharp blades were aimed at everyone. They either held their long blades and stood them against the sky above or slashed them through the air as they pointed to their targets. Raquel was right; they were stronger than their beloved businessmen. They transcended the bitterness in their hearts that were aimed at the business, and they became immortal, divine beings. When they released each other, they were both smiling. They rode in the same boat, and the company was cherished as they threw their paddles into the water and rode the current. When Raquel walked back into her room, she crossed herself before she climbed into bed. She slept through the whole night, occasionally uttering prayers in her sleep. Each silent request to God was for the mother who slept in the next room and to the young woman who would inevitably grow up to be just like her father. When that thought entered her head, she cried. Raquel knew—somehow she knew—that Zephyr would step in her father's shoes but walk along a whole new path created for herself. Raquel turned onto her stomach to wipe her tears on her pillow and breathed softly before she fell asleep once more.

XI

It was All Hallows' Eve, the day of spirits long abstracted or forgotten, brought back to life by the mimicry of the living. People were seen out on the streets dancing and striding on the sidewalks, imitating models gliding down a runway. They all imagined groups of media moguls scrambling inside a thick crowd in order to snap one picture of them—a single shot that froze their glory into a crystal of time. People dressed in masks, witches, skeletons—they all loved their one day, their one ability to express themselves in the guise of someone—or something—else. They donned a shade of errors and lies that covered their bodies and sent streams of joy through their hearts. Music was heard in the alleys; haunting operas whose voices echoed throughout the skinny alleys. Buildings sparkled with dark oranges and crimson bulbs laid inside jack-o-lanterns and black demon eyes. Even the sky itself seemed to emanate an unnatural hue, some unholy shade of red that appeared only in the night sky that hung over this screaming earth.

The Estrada mansion was set as a background for the long line of cars and SUVs that lined the curvaceous driveway. Out of each vehicle came an ominous man, dressed in tailored suits and shoes shined to rival mirrors. Their eyes were always narrow, their lips were firmly closed, and their smiles were fake and arrogant. They ignored Rosa, who pulled out one of her best evening gowns that hung from her full breasts and glided slightly over her delicate toes. She directed each boss to the dining room, where Luis sat at the middle of the table, refusing to acknowledge himself as the head of anyone. He smiled politely and gave a short nod to each criminal that walked past him. They remained ignorant of his presence not because of uncouth behavior but because they feared him. The same hand that waved each boss to their designated seats was the same hand that summoned blood to spill out of their chests and crush their very skulls. This hand was a hand with both curative powers and the ability to perish with a simple gesture—this schizophrenic appendage silenced any ill thoughts they have had of King Luis before they even pulled up to this castle he called home. They were afraid of him, but more than that, they were afraid that he was cognizant of their fear.

Each man sat at the table and waited for silver platters of food to be placed in front of their faces. Their hands shook before they opened the shining silver lid that housed their dinner; legend went that Luis once had the head of a low-level thug decapitated then served it at the dinner table of a rival crime lord. No one knew if this legend was actually a story of truth, but at the same time, no one was foolish enough to confirm or deny its existence.

When one crime lord was brave enough to open the lid, a scent of spices and tender beef wafted up to his nose. He smiled, and the lords and their captains all followed suit, opening their lids and breathing a sigh of relief when food—and not heads—greeted their grumbling stomachs. They all took hold of their silver utensils but halted their journey toward satisfaction once they saw a large, gout shadow seep into the dining room. They all dropped their forks and knives back into their silken napkins once Mr. Julius Mal entered the room.

The crime lords often asked themselves why they were apprehended by a brief feeling of fear, less than what they felt by Luis Estrada but more than what they normally felt by their nightly activities. The men, the slaves, the weapons, the drugs, the gambling—all were done almost with reckless abandon. No feelings were expressed, nor were they forcefully repressed. The best way, they knew, was to not feel at all. Adopting a stoic approach to their crimes was the best way to live with their consequences—to live with them by not living with them.

But there was something terrifying about Mr. Mal's large frame, his custom-made suit, his square-toed shoes, and the long cigar in his mouth. He puffed on the scented plant until he produced a decent cloud of smoke. The tobacco that drifted from his mouth seemed to hurriedly mist to the ceiling. A clever boss noticed this antic and thought, *Geez, even the smoke is afraid of him.*

He walked with an arrogant gait, hard and cruel, as if he was stomping his foot on the floor to collapse the house around everyone—and leave himself standing amidst the ruins of what he wished to create, what he needed to create. It was one of many things he had always wanted—a fortress that would house his family and assimilate those willing to call him *Father*. He had already formed a mental portrait of the foyer and the hallway that led to the dining room. He brushed past Rosa and glared at her kind and gentle face, but she did not flinch. At all. Her eyes remained coolly fixed on his own, neither showing any sign of fear or a worry that he could crush her skull with his hand alone. This serene gesture unsettled him. Everyone else was afraid of him—why not her? She should be shaking in her panties! She should have stuttered her speech and directed him to the dining room with a quivering hand. But she didn't! Then Mr. Mal realized that she was married to the one man whom even Mr. Mal had no choice but to worship. The strength of the king was merely a mirror of the strength of his queen.

He surveyed the stares of every criminal in the room and smirked. He felt better. The fear he received gave him comfort. *Now this is more like it*, he thought. An empty chair was reserved for him, and if it was not, he would take it regardless of its true owner.

He walked over and dropped his body into the seat. The table slightly quaked, and Mr. Mal greeted everyone with a small smile. His teeth flashed white through his black lips as he slowly looked down at his plate. He lifted the cover and crudely dropped it on the table. It clanged against the soft white tablecloth and twirled and teetered until it came to a stop. He chuckled and picked up his fork to eat the tender roast in front of him. No one dared to tell him to wait, partly because of fear but mostly because of avoidance. No one wanted to start an argument simply because they knew it was a vain battle.

"Couldn't wait for the rest of us, Julius?"

Mr. Mal threw down his fork and turned his head toward Luis Estrada. His eyes were just as calm as his wife's, and Mr. Mal hated Luis all the more. Luis remained in his place and raised his chin to address everyone in the room.

"Gentlemen, thank you all for coming. We are currently waiting on one more. As soon as he gets here, we will begin. For the moment, enjoy what you have in front of you. Please excuse me."

Luis stood up and exited the dining room. Each boss nodded his head to him and began to engage in casual conversation with the person sitting next to him—not including Mr. Mal, of course. They always felt at ease with Luis Estrada around, taking refuge with the thought that he will secure their welfares, monetary and physical. With him around, they were able to act as themselves and ignore the large angry man that sat among them.

Zephyr was upstairs in her bedroom when she heard footsteps ascend the stairs. She hopped out of her bed and poked her head in the hallway. There she saw a tall man with sad eyes glancing at the top of the staircase. *He must be lost*, she thought. Her naivety made her venture out of her room, and her little steps took her to the tall man. He saw her approach him, and he stared at her everlasting silver eyes. Instead of despising their hue, he thought they were beautiful. Her cute face combined with her shy voice made him smile for the first time all day.

"Umm . . . hi! Are you lost?"

The tall man could not help but lie to her. He actually wanted to use the restroom upstairs, but he wanted to hear her speak again. "Yes I am," he said. "The dining room is down over there, right?"

"Yeah! It's down the stairs, take a right, pass by my mommy, and the dining room with all those mean men are there."

He chuckled. "Thank you, dear." He turned around and started to descend the stairs.

"Hey!"

The tall man froze in his steps. Did she look past his lie? "Yes?"

"How come you look so sad?"

The tall man buried his chin in his chest. "Oh, I'm just a bit sad. That's all."

Zephyr continued holding his eyes with her gaze. He now felt afraid and felt his heart quicken. "But why are you sad? Didn't your mommy give you some gummy bears?"

"Huh?"

Zephyr smiled and ran back into her room. He heard a rustling of plastic bags before she ran back out to meet him again. She handed him a small bag of store-brand gummy bears. The plastic bag drooped over her small palm, and he smiled widely as he took it from her.

"Now you won't be sad anymore!" Zephyr said with a smile. "I didn't want to go trick-or-treating tonight, so my mommy bought me a bag of gummy bears." Her eyes shone brighter every time she spoke. "So here! They're good!"

"Thank you . . ." he answered.

"Now just remember—down the stairs, take a right, pass by Mommy, and you should see the dining room. You'll like it!" Zephyr outstretched her arms as she described the size of the room. "It's big and they have lots of food. Daddy made pies too! He said that he would save me a piece. But if you don't get one, I'll give you mine!"

"Sweetheart," the tall man said chuckling, "you can have the pie. I won't take it from you."

Zephyr's eyes narrowed in pity. "Please?"

The tall man sighed and smiled. "Okay."

Zephyr grinned walked backward toward her bedroom. "Okay!" She waved him goodbye and turned around. He saw her enter her bedroom and heard the mattress squeak when she hopped onto her bed. He bounced the bag of gummy bears in his hand and smirked. He turned his body around and descended the stairs.

He saw Luis walking past the bottom of the stairs. The tall man quickened his descent and called out to him once he was back on the first floor again.

"Luis!"

Don Estrada turned around and stared at the tall man for a long second. The tall man did the same. Both men felt their eyes water, but they held back tears as they did not want to show their signs of weakness. Luis and the tall man walked toward each other in a slow gait, and they both extended their hands to shake one another's. When their fingers clenched, so did their hearts—but their formal greetings were interrupted by their memories. They immediately hugged each other and held one another as a brother held a wounded soldier in his arms.

"It's good to see you, Luis."

"It's good to see you too, Vladimir."

When the Impaler entered the dining room, every conversation was immediately silenced and all the bosses stared at him. He was missing in action for such a long time that they at first did not trust their vision. They threw their napkins on the table and stood up in unison as he walked to his seat. Don Luis Estrada nodded to Vladimir and looked around the room. Each seat was taken, and Luis wanted this to happen. He moved over to a bottle of French wine that sat atop a small bar table. He picked up a white napkin and draped it over his forearm. Luis then grabbed a silver corkscrew that shined against the golden light beaming from the ornate chandelier. He had a gentleman's precision with his motions: a slight tilt of the bottle, a strong yet gentle insertion of the corkscrew's point, a subtle twist, and finally, a smooth pull of the rubber cork. He set the bottle on the table and carried the screw with the cork in his hand. He calmly walked over to Vladimir Kandinsky, who sat at the far end of the dining room table. He held the cork close to his nose so that he could receive a glimpse into the olfactory dream he was minutes away from experiencing. He inhaled the scent, and a smile formed on his face. He nodded to Luis and then turned his head to nod toward the other less-than-gentlemen in the room. Luis chuckled and walked back over to the bar table and set the screw down on a small white plate. He placed the bottle back in his hand and began to walk around the table. He personally served each boss the wine, talking as he made his way around the room.

"Gentlemen," he began, "I only bring out this bottle as a celebration. It would be rude of me to ask someone else to serve you this pleasant drink, and as your host, it would especially be rude if I did not commemorate your visit personally. This glass I pour for you is my special way of saying, 'Welcome.'"

Luis poured a glass for Mr. Mal, who loudly sucked his teeth and rolled his eyes. When he received his share of the wine, he downed it in one gulp and cleared his throat. "Good wine, Mr. Estrada." Mr. Mal spoke with a hint of insolence in his voice. "Almost better than the wine I usually get. Almost."

"I'm glad you like it, Julius."

When Luis finished making his rounds, he grabbed a lone flute glass that stood on the bar table and poured himself a taste. He stood at the entrance of the dining room and held his glass high. It glimmered and sparkled in the chandelier light, and the bosses could not help but appreciate the fine quality of the glass and its owner. "Gentlemen, I welcome you all. Cheers."

They all nodded to Luis and politely sipped the wine. They sighed in contentment and placed their glasses back on the table. One of the men had a confused look on his face. He was a representative of a small gang that was exceptional at producing gambling rings throughout the city.

"Are you going to have a seat, Don?" He began to stand up and offer his chair.

"Thank you, but no. I do things for a reason."

The man nodded and made himself comfortable in his seat.

"I am not here," Luis continued, "to discuss our achievements. We all know what we do, and we all know that we are proficient in exercising our ability to . . . win. Methods which separate us from what others may perceive as wild or unstructured. No. Our abilities are very organized, very logical. We have no competition except for those of us who dine with me tonight. And competition does not exist among us since we all get along . . . I hope."

Luis smiled as he said those last words. He inhaled slightly and continued his speech. "Our knowledge stems from what we received as a birthright, from our fathers and from our relatives who precede us. The only exception here is Mr. Vladimir Kandinsky, who gave me a great privilege of having me make the pleasure of his company. He is of original wisdom, for no man precedes him. His knowledge is purely his own, and for that I revere him. You are a deity, sir, and we are all overjoyed to see you again. Welcome."

The men in the room lightly clapped for Vladimir, who smirked and nodded his head in assent to each person in the room. Mr. Mal was the only one who did not clap—he only stuffed his mouth with more food.

"I also extend a most respectful welcome to Mr. Julius Mal." After hearing his name, he put down his fork and finished chewing his food. "He was once a small part in an even smaller group, just a simple mob hand with nowhere to go. And now here he is—the reigning leader of the largest gang in this city. As such, I welcome you."

The table clapped while Mr. Mal raised his eyebrow at Luis. He did not know if he was being cheered by Don Estrada or insulted.

"All of you, those of you who are essential for our own survival in this city, I send you my greatest thanks. You are the foundation upon which we have built our empires. Without you, we are less than nothing. You are deserving of thanks from all of us. I *especially* welcome you to this meeting."

The men around the table clapped louder than before, acknowledging Luis's praises as well as their own accomplishments. Luis gazed at the floor for a moment; everyone knew the real reason for his organization of this meeting. It was not to serve them expensive bottles of wine or to hear him sing song of praises—praises that they have heard from others and themselves. When Luis spoke again, they were waiting for his confirmation of their thoughts.

"Gentlemen . . . it is customary to announce the heir of our thrones. We all know that this life we choose is like the life of a monarch. We cannot end it ourselves, nor can we choose just anyone to continue our reign. As the kings of our nations, we must administer to our people, right? We must always raise our shields to those who threaten our kingdom and hold our phalanx until time kills us all.

"That being said, we cannot avoid this event much longer. You all knew this conversation before you received the notice. I must hand down my title as Don to my child, born into this life that I have . . . created."

All the men in the room looked to Luis for an answer. The silence in the room could be heard throughout the mansion. Rosa was sitting in a chair that was situated deep within the foyer. Her long, toned legs were crossed over, and she felt her heart quickening when there were no words yet spoken in that dining room.

When Luis finally spoke again, his words forced a breeze that blew her gown over her knees.

Mr. Mal rode in his large SUV in a jolly mood—so jolly that his driver often looked in his rearview mirror with a perplexed look on his face. His face crunched in confusion as Mr. Mal's chest shook up and down in laughter. His white teeth kept revealing themselves in the nightlight, and he occasionally inhaled long, deep breaths in order to continue his eccentric burst of glee. He calmed himself down and shook his head as he smiled until his cheeks hurt.

"Luis, Luis, Luis . . . my man!" Mr. Mal chuckled and sighed. "Ain't you a trip . . . you're something else."

The driver and the passengers only listened without question, though they kept their inquiries to themselves despite the urge to voice their thoughts. They only felt Mr. Mal's baritone voice echo throughout the inside of the car. The large metallic vehicle sped its way on the dark highway, with quick streams of light illuminating the tinted windshield. The frigid air blew inside the radiator and wisped itself through the vents in the car, but it was too warm to assimilate itself into Mr. Mal's icy soul. While his escorts rubbed their biceps and blew their hot breaths onto their hands, Mr. Mal welcomed it into his lungs. He loved the feeling of something cold and lifeless entering his bloodstream and tightening his skin. The rush of absent heat made him feel immortal, like a son of Hades who preferred to bask in icebergs rather than comfort himself in torturous flame. Mr. Mal took to heart that famous adage: "What does not kill you makes you stronger." The sharp twinge of pain he felt when the frosty wind brushed his naked face, the brief sense of pain when his skin collided to form cracks and abrasions—all were pleasant to him. All were attributed to his vitality. His masochism was not a result of the absence of pleasure, but rather, it was the abundance of agony. He sought the destruction of his own body and made his heart resilient enough to exhibit no emotion. That was it, he thought, he was a statue. Cold. Unfeeling. Inhuman. He thought of those words as the car pulled up to his home. His heart quickened when those words spoke softly in his mind. And he liked it.

Mr. Mal stepped out of the car, and the suspension of the vehicle seemed to breathe a sigh of relief as it bounced back to its original position. He stood in the middle of the driveway and pulled out a large tin container from his breast pocket. He opened the silver lid and a short row of cigars lined up for his choosing. He pulled out one cigar that sat in the middle of the tin container and shoved it into his mouth. He closed the lid and placed it back in his breast pocket while an underling rushed over with a lighter to conjure a decent flame for the cigar. Mr. Mal chuckled and blew out a cloud of gray smoke. It twirled and danced its way up toward the heavens, dissipating into the cold air and losing its substance forever. Mr. Mal compared the smoke to Luis Estrada—a man who was once a solid entity, now a mere memory disintegrating into the black October sky.

When he entered his pool hall, a grand residency compared to the row of crack houses and slums that plagued Ellipses, he loosened his broad tie and threw it on the floor. One of his underlings stooped down to pick it up and folded it in his hand. Mr. Mal kept his smile as he ventured over to the bar. The bartender noticed his large frame eclipsing the bar stools in front of him, and he handed Mr. Mal a tall glass of beer. He nodded to the bartender and grabbed the cold mug. He pressed his lips against the rim and felt the cool, refreshing froth slide down his throat.

A sharp crack was heard at the far end of the room. Mr. Mal gulped down another mouthful of ale and walked toward the sounds of heavy sticks slamming against cue balls. The melodies of snaps and profanity signaled his eardrums. But one particular sound was memorable—a signature push. This fingerprint perked his ears, and he was satisfied to see that his recognition proved to be correct.

"Hmph. Is this all you boys do?"

"Mr. Mal!" Slim almost laughed out of joy when he saw his employer.

"Oh . . . hey." Pedro looked at Mr. Mal for a brief moment and averted his attention back to his pool game. He leaned over and struck the cue ball harder than necessary. When the ball scooped itself down the hole, Pedro stood up and placed the cue stick up against a nearby wall. Slim shrugged his shoulders and began playing by himself.

"I just saw your *papi* tonight."

"So?"

"Don't you want to hear what he had to say?"

"I really don't care."

"Yeah you do." Mr. Mal licked his lips and stood closer to Pedro. "He had a lot to say . . . and yet he didn't."

"Well, that's my dad." Pedro rolled his eyes and turned around to grab his jacket that hung on a hook on the wall. "I can't speak for him."

"Well, his ass spoke for you."

Pedro displayed a look of confusion in his face, a sense of bewilderment wedded to curiosity. "What're you talking about?"

Mr. Mal chuckled. "You ain't getting shit."

"What?"

"You. Ain't. Getting. A goddamned. Thing. The business, the legacy, whatever the fuck you call it. Mr. Estrada decided to call it quits. He's retiring."

Pedro's jaw dropped to the floor, and his eyes started to conjure tears. Slim smacked the ball in the wrong direction and stood back up with wide eyes.

"A shame, really," Mr. Mal continued. "I had high hopes for you. I mean, I know we had our casual conversations on what we would do if you were boss. The cartels, the girls, the takeovers . . . but not in this lifetime." Mr. Mal sighed. "Ya know, none of us ever thought about retiring, I mean, maybe some of the older bosses thought of it, but definitely not me. I'm here until I'm dead. Know that for sure."

Pedro kept his eyes solely on Mr. Mal's words. His heart quickened, and all of a sudden, he felt like killing himself. Shoving the cue stick down his throat and choking on the chalk sounded precious to him. He wanted to kill . . . something, even if it was himself. He looked at Slim, and although his best friend interpreted his gaze as despair, Pedro was actually silently begging Slim to murder him.

"But . . . it was supposed to be mine . . ." Pedro did his best to exercise his tongue to speak those chilling words.

"Oh, I feel you, man."

"He promised me . . ."

"He promised all of us. I know, man."

"Shut up . . ."

"Hey look, he did it to protect you—"

"Shut the fuck up!"

Mr. Mal smiled. He had gotten what he wanted from Pedro. Slim was just a bystander, a simple witness who absorbed the facts surrounding themselves amidst the smoke and ash present within the pool hall.

"Look, talk to Daddy dearest. Convince him to change his mind. Nothing is set, right? He won't hear me—he's got his attention on you and whatnot. Look, how about this: meet with me next week, we'll talk it out." Mr. Mal grew quiet. "You'll get over it. It's best for you."

Pedro could not smile. He could not have any feelings that protested his sudden stoic demeanor. He looked at Slim, who shrugged his shoulders again. He then looked at Mr. Mal, and he swore that he saw a subtle smirk in his face. Pedro knew that he had to go home and talk to his father.

He left Slim with Mr. Mal and decided . . . no . . . he *needed* to think out loud. He planned out the entire conversation: "Why would you do that to me, your only son? Break tradition? You're tired of it? No! No one gets tired of it! All those men you invited to our house were not tired! Why you? This isn't fair! No . . . shut up. I said shut up!"

Pedro heard his own dark conscience shoot doubts and questions into his head. He started to paint events in his mind that calmed him down: Luis standing in front of his office window, looking upon the city that, technically, if you really studied the layout, was his—his mother reading a smut novel in her favorite chair, Zephyr sleeping next to her teddy bear. His thoughts dissipated from his mind . . . except for . . . Zephyr! Yeah! Her damning eyes! What freak has silvery eyes? She's not normal. Is that . . . is that why you wanted to leave the business, Dad? For her? For a fucking little girl? She doesn't matter!

"She doesn't fucking matter!"

Pedro repeated this phrase until he arrived home. His mother was cleaning up the dining room, and his grandmother, whom no one had seen all day, was in the kitchen wrapping up the leftovers in aluminum foil and rearranging the inside of the refrigerator to fit everything in its place. She saw Pedro staring at herself and his mother, and she addressed him with a warm smile.

"Hi there, sweetie. Are you hungry?"

"No . . . not really."

"See, Rosa? I told you cigarette smoke kills the appetite. That crap will give you cancer, Mr. Estrada Junior." Raquel shook her head, and Rosa answered with a tiny smile.

"I'll be okay, Grandma. I'm just gonna go upstairs and get some rest."

"Okay, but if you hack up a shitload of tar, don't yell at me."

"*Mami!*" Rosa playfully snapped at Raquel, who continued to rearrange the shelves in the refrigerator.

"What? I'm telling you the truth. Secondhand smoke is a leading cause of death! I read it in the paper the other day. I should show you pictures, Pedro. But I'll be nice—I won't give you nightmares tonight. But take it easy in that pool hall, got it?"

"Yeah."

"Pool halls do not make men look good, and they do not make women look pretty."

"All right."

Raquel stared at Pedro with a slight smile on her face. "This is the part where you say, 'Oh, *Abuela*! That's why you're so pretty!'"

Pedro chuckled. "You are very pretty, *Abuela*."

"Well, no shit—I already know I am, but thank you anyway." Raquel laughed. "Get some rest dear. I'm gonna be right here playing Tetris with this freakin' food."

Pedro nodded and made his way up the stairs. He climbed the steps slower than usual, thinking that maybe his slow ascent into his bedroom would prolong his depression. He hung his head by his neck and sighed deeply. His eyes began to water up, but he absorbed it back into his sockets once he reached Zephyr's bedroom.

She was sleeping soundly, hugging her teddy bear, Hermes, in her small arms. Her chest gently rose up and down in a smooth, rhythmic motion. Hermes stared at Pedro with his large black eyes sitting atop his large nose. Zephyr often rubbed the tip of her nose against his, giggling at how his soft fur would tickle her cheeks. Her smile could charm the earth to reverse its rotation, and her eyes were cold enough to freeze the wind. *A strange paradox*, he thought. The warmth of a joyous smile in constant battle with the floating iceberg in her eyes.

He examined the pillow that slightly elevated her head. It was as soft as the brand had once bragged on television commercials. A brief moment of joy overwhelmed him, but his smile eluded his face once the black soul inside of him decided to blot out whatever purity he had left in him.

"Stop smiling, take the pillow, and smother the bitch."

Pedro shook his head to force his thoughts to leave him.

"Yeah, she may struggle, but who doesn't? She's what? Four? Five? Still a toddler. You can handle it right?"

Pedro grabbed his skull and dug his fingertips deep into his temples. *The thoughts are in there*, he told himself. But they stuck to his mind, siphoning sanity from his mind as ticks suck blood from a homeless dog.

"What's great is when her face gets red when you first cover her damn nostrils. Her arms flail around, she tries to call for help. Thank God pillows muffle out screams, you know? Then, after a while, her arms kind of slow down, her voice is barely heard, then that redness turns to a bluish gray. Oh, don't worry—you'll know it when it happens."

Pedro whispered words to himself. "Stop it . . ."

"And then she finally dies. Takes a while, but patience is a virtue! The best part is when you touch her forehead and it is ice cold. Oh! And don't forget to lift up her arm and let it drop. It falls like a rock! Priceless! You should definitely take a picture and frame it.

I'm serious. And get that goddamned teddy bear away from her. It's fucking stupid."

Pedro fell to his knees and started to sob. He felt his body jerk with every tear that fell down his face. He ignored the sudden bolts of pain in his knees and slammed his fists on the floor. His head rocked back and forth. His mouth was wide open to let the rage emanate from his dark soul.

"Zephyr . . . Zephyr . . ."

Pedro started to crawl on the floor, scraping his knees on the rough carpet just to get to his bedroom. He stood himself up once he entered his doorway and inhaled the stench of old clothes and dust that settled on the walls. His room was always a mess, a simple reflection of his own mind and the conflict with himself. He saw himself as two individuals, one born out of systematic union between two beings, the other born from self. A creation made to extract the option of mental life from Pedro. This vampire dug its demonic teeth into his soul, slashing through the endangered firmament of white space and leaving behind a path of dark mire to fill the void of his spirit. Pedro felt his arms outstretch in front of him to feel the soft linings of his bedspread, and once they touched the cushioned fabric, he collapsed on the bed and burrowed his face in his pillow. Pedro inhaled, and the choking pressure of the pillow blocked his airways, like an astronaut taking off his helmet on the bright side of the moon. Only the comfort of the lifeless air entered his nostrils, and oddly, he welcomed it.

Pedro felt his lungs stretch and implode when they begged for air. His tongue started to slide deeper in his throat. He felt his head shake; his hands gripped the blankets, all while he forced tears to drop from his eyes. Death accompanied him. Pedro felt a sharp gleam on the blood-soaked scythe shine on his back. A cold shiver blew over his hair, and a curiously soft touch grazed against his leg. He was almost there; he could feel the dark apparition lift his scythe in the air to slice through the strings that kept him bound to this physical world.

"Pedro? Are you sleeping?" Rosa was walking past Zephyr's room and saw her son lying face down on the bed.

"No, I'm still up," Pedro said, with a brief sigh of disappointment. He rolled himself over to lie on his back and look at his mother.

"Are you sure you're not sleeping?" Rosa chuckled as she entered his bedroom. "I just wanted to come in and check on you . . . see how you're doing."

"I'm fine, Ma. Just tired."

"Yeah," Rosa said, "we're all drained. Setting this whole thing up wore me out."

"Yeah . . ."

Rosa cleared her throat. "Sweetie, um . . . I know that you're sad, and I know that there's a lot that you're not telling me. Maybe it's school or . . . maybe it's me. I don't know. But all I want to do is see you happy." Rosa began to show more emotion in her voice. "I don't know what I would do without you. I was so happy when you came into my life, and . . . I don't know how I would survive without you. I love you so much, Pedro."

Pedro felt her arms hug him close, and she laid her head on his chest. He felt drops of tears fall on his T-shirt. She was sobbing. Why was she crying? No one is dead.

"I'm sorry . . ." Rosa sat back up and wiped her face. "I just don't want to see you sad anymore. I feel like . . . I feel like it's my fault, like maybe I didn't hold you more or if I didn't—"

"*Mami* . . . I love you too. I'm just . . . down."

"About what, sweetie? About what?"

"Just things. That's all."

"Oh . . ." Rosa lowered her head. She held Pedro's hand in hers and gently squeezed his fingers together. "It's okay . . . you don't have to tell me right now. But, Pedro . . . you can talk to me. I'm here for you, baby."

Pedro nodded and sat up in his bed. He wrapped his arms around his mother, and he could feel her smile over his shoulder. He could not help but smile along with her, but after a minute of embrace, his smile fell into a frown. She let him go and she ran her finger through his hair.

"You're such a sweetheart. Please smile for me. Not now but . . . soon. Okay?"

"I will, *Mami*."

"Okay." Rosa stood up and began to walk out the door. "Your father is out meeting with an old friend of ours. He should be back soon, but get some rest, okay?"

"Okay . . . . good night, *Mami*."

"*Buenos noches*, Pedro." Rosa blew a kiss to her son before she left the room. Pedro fell back down on his bed and stared at the ceiling. He chuckled a bit and closed his eyes. He thought about tonight, the events and the words that he experienced. Mr. Mal's words and the words of his mother danced in his head. He sighed. He was tired. Pedro relaxed his breathing and submitted his body to the comforts of sleep.

XII

The weeks passed on as a leaf floats upon a silent stream, rocking back and forth toward a destination known only to great Fortune herself. Should she choose to spin her wheel in favor or in hindrance was a mystery to a man such as the Don. He usurped the time allotted to him to reflect on events transported backward through time. He stared out the window of his quiet corner office and thought of the sweet breezes that he was fortunate enough to feel with his family—revisiting his filial bond with Pedro, opening cherished moments with Zephyr, and making reminiscent love with his wife. She felt his body glide up and down in an almost melancholic motion, as if he had to do it out of duty. His movements were controlled, hindered, slightly planned and losing the values of spontaneity. Rosa still held on to his back and slid her nails down his spine once he was done. He rolled over on his back and puffed out a long sigh. Rosa stared at the ceiling as she pulled the sweaty sheets up to cover her breasts. She could not help but read Luis's breathing patter, noticing and analyzing each inhale he made and recording the time it took him to release the bubble of air. She sighed herself. She did not know why she acted this way. She had to listen to each breath, each tiny grunt he made when he turned on his side to sleep. It was the absence of conversation lovers make after they entwined one another in a brief moment of bliss.

"Luis?" she asked. "Is something wrong?"

"As a matter of fact, yes."

"What? Tell me."

"I'm not used to sleeping next to you."

"Oh, so you're used to sleeping next to someone else," she joked.

"No . . . I just miss being here in my bed. During the night. With you."

Luis did not look at her as he spoke, but he could tell that Rosa was smiling at him. She turned over and gently kissed his hot shoulder, and then she lay flat on her back to fall asleep next to her retired husband.

*   *   *

Pedro often wondered what would happen now that his father had declined his life. His questions seemed to answer themselves as they buzzed in his head. Would his rivals come after him? No, he has none. Why not? Because his rivals are either part of his organization, his friends' organizations, or dead. What about Mr. Mal? Mr. Mal, as badass as he thinks he is, is a wet cold puppy coming in from the rain. What about us? The family? Already set to go. We're all taken care of. Pedro was worried about his father, and he expressed that concern one day when him, and Luis were playing pool in Pedro's favorite spot.

"Dad, what's gonna happen now?"

"Same as always, Pedro . . . except that I will be here more often. To do things like this. Is that okay?"

"Yeah . . . it's always okay."

"Good to hear. Your turn."

Pedro smiled and took the next shot. He missed the ball on purpose; he wanted his father to win. For once in his life, he wanted to take care of his father, to let him take charge and not be afraid of losing to anything or lose anyone.

Zephyr ran into her parents' room one night to read a bedtime story to *them*. She threw the book onto their bed and hoisted herself up to fall into their open arms. She usually made it to Luis first, since he was always on the side where Zephyr happened to toss the book. She smiled at them, and opened the cover to begin their nightly adventure into a fantasy world in which they all wished they were living.

"Bye-bye, Mama! Bye-bye, Papa!"

Zephyr felt her eyelids drop heavily on themselves. Her head drooped down to her chest and she slightly tilted against her parents. She shook her head a bit and forced her eyes to open. A second later, she closed the cover and fell back in between her parents' bodies. Luis pushed off a section of the comforter and wrapped it around the sweet angel that was too tired to finish her story.

"Now she knows how it feels," he joked to Rosa.

*   *   *

If Luis made any nightly excursions, it was to visit Adam and his grandmother in their home out in the ghettos. He was sitting down with First Degree one night, sipping an exquisite cup of hot tea. Both men slouched back in Adam's couch, enjoying a night that was spent outside of the studio and, more importantly, outside of Mr. Mal's reach.

"Adam . . . why are you still here?"

"Say what?"

"I mean why are you still living here?"

"Because there is nowhere else for me to go."

"But you have the money. You could take your grandmother away from this area, maybe go to a nice neighborhood a few miles away. You won't be far from the studio, and plus, it's away from here."

"Like I said, nowhere for me to go." Adam had a depressed tone in his voice. "Let's face it—I won't fit in with those nice neighborhoods."

"Is that what you really think? Really?"

"Yeah . . . really."

"But other musicians, they've escaped from their bad areas and they still top the music charts."

"But that's the point. That's what I rap about. I rap about what it's like to live here. I rap about the struggle . . . you know . . . the pain, the sadness—all of that. Take me out of here, and there'll be nothing for me to rap about. I can't rap about singing birds or blooming flowers or little rich missy Sally playing with her Barbie dolls. That's why I won't fit in, Mr. Estrada . . . I won't let myself fit in. I rap about what's real."

Luis nodded. He took another sip of his tea and swallowed it while he looked up at the cracked ceiling. "I know what you mean, Adam. I really do. But keep two things in mind: your grandmother would love to leave here, and the memory of this place will still be with you, no matter what. You can carry that memory no matter where you go, even if it's in the suburbs with Sally. That memory will force you to carry it. The passion you have for music transcends its location, never forget that."

Adam looked at Luis and did not have any words to add. He was silent, a trait seldom seen in his music. Luis finished his tea and placed it on a saucer that sat on a nearby end table.

"I speak from experience," Luis continued. "No memory ever fades."

*   *   *

Luis also visited Mr. Mal, who sat rather quietly in his chair as the retired lord stood across from him, his words heavy and stoic.

"Julius, all my assets are separated from you. I know you're making great deals with your own gang, so my leave should not affect you so much."

Mr. Mal sighed. "But you were always my best source of income."

"You have the largest gang in the city. Your manpower is enough to keep you comfortable for years. You don't need me."

"But I do . . . I like you."

Luis raised his eyebrow. "Come again?"

"You have the balls to do what no self-respecting boss would ever do. You're the type of guy who sits on a pot of gold with dancing tits in your face and one of my girls here chewing on your neck. But you give that fucking pot of lucky charms gold to some poor piece of shit in an alley, and you put my girls in a goddamned Catholic school. I respect that, I do."

"But it's not something you would do, right?"

"Hell no. I like gold. I like tits. And if it was me, I would have that girl suck on my neck and on other places. What can I say? I'm addicted."

"You know what? You are. Be careful, Julius. Those tits will kill you."

"Then what a way to go. I'll let you know when it happens, brother dear."

*   *   *

Luis recalled the memory of his midday meals with his mother, the one woman who knew every detail about him and was not shy in pronouncing them to everyone. It was her last day visiting her family, and she was enjoying her last afternoon with her son before she left for Spain that same evening.

"I think I made this tea a bit too sweet," Raquel said, with a twinge of disappointment in her voice.

"I think it's fine, *Mami*."

"Well, you always had a sweet tooth when you were little, just like your daughter. Remember the time you opened the oven door to get that pan of brownies I made?"

Luis laughed. "Yeah, I remember getting my hand burned."

"You're lucky that you didn't get your ass lit on fire."

"*Papi* took great care of my ass later that night."

"He sure did."

Luis stared at his mother for a while. He noticed how she held her small cup of tea in both hands, gently squeezing it as if it would slip out of her grasp at any moment. Her eyes were fixated on the fragranced steam that rose up to her nose. She was unusually quiet, almost choosing to be a silent comedienne.

"Why are you staring at me, Luis? Yes, I promise that I will send you some of my homemade brownies. But only because I love you."

"Nothing, it's just . . . you seem quiet."

"Oh, I'm always quiet whenever I think about your father."

"Yeah?" Luis tried to be as stoic as possible.

"Yeah. Oh, don't worry. It's nothing big—I just want to slap him silly even after all these years."

"You always do, *Mami*."

Raquel smiled and sipped her tea. "Wow."

"What?"

"This tea is perfect."

*   *   *

Luis thought of all these things as he stared out of the window. A cool shudder kept hitting his spine, but he did not turn around to face the wind head-on. He counted the stars, imagining himself to be Abraham who was briefly instructed by God to count the multitude of stars that were to be the reflection of the multitudes of offspring his name will bear. Luis felt that the stars shining before him were the fruit of his indecent labors. Offspring born not of man and woman together in a holy embrace but the result of imps and demons riding on each bullet he had fired, each stab, each choke. The smothering, the hanging, executions in the alleys—all of these were his children. They were slimy, forsaken children begot from his choices, but he embraced them as his sons. They buried their noses in his chest and nibbled at his heart, and for some odd reason, he desired it.

Luis had visited his old Russian friend the night after his retirement ceremony had ended. Vladimir Kandinsky was sitting in his favorite chair in the restaurant situated in the far right corner of the room. The gentle hues of red and gold splashed throughout the room, highlighting Kandinsky's prestige and enhancing the wise wrinkles on his face. He held a shot glass of inexpensive vodka, often saying, "If it's good, I will drink it, whether it costs ten dollars or a hundred." He always had one ice cube that floated in the middle of the jagged glass, and Luis wondered if the small frozen square was reminiscent of Kandinsky's mysterious past, a small remnant of what he used to be. Or perhaps, what he wanted to be. Luis approached the kind man and took a seat in front of him. The two men looked at each other as they studied thoughts and perused their eyes.

"It is good to see you, Vladimir."

"Likewise, Luis Estrada."

A waiter came by and served Luis a shot of tequila with two ice cubes. Luis studied his own drink and believed that the two ice cubes clanking against each other was the symbol of two people: Luis the younger and Luis the leader. He held the glass between his thumb and his index finger and swallowed a taste of his past.

They never talked to each other—they did not have to. One had grown accustomed to enjoying the other's company without speech or utterances of royal sentences. Formality, to them, was the simple expression of thought. They drank their liquor and smiled at certain moments. The silence was wed to the gentle hum of the radiators throughout the restaurant and the occasional laugh of Russian men watching a soccer game on a small television and spotting tall, beautiful European women cheering in the stands. The sounds of Luis's glass being set in the table told Vladimir that he was glad to visit an old friend. Vladimir's ice cube had melted in the glass with traces of vodka still skirting over it. This told Luis that his company was both appreciated and missed and had reminded Vladimir that even those who commit acts that are pleasing to the devil still have a place next to the Divine One in paradise.

*   *   *

Luis appreciated the glamour of the thin streams of light that illuminated the streets below. He analyzed the bustle of people hurrying through the crowds as they carried a unique instance of emotion: anger from a pimp procuring money for his employee and procuring money *from* his employee; a newlywed couple laughing arm in arm as they pranced along the sidewalk while ignoring the despair surrounding them. Luis could not see that far into the city streets, but these emotions are what he felt. He touched the parallels between anger and hope that lay within the Pandora's Box of Ellipses. He was glad that there was some joy left in the world, as one glimmer of a smile was enough to destroy an army of dread.

At that last thought, he turned around and smiled at Pedro. He was standing behind his father with sweat dripping from his cheeks.

His eyes were widened; his breath was quickened. He could not talk at all. He was paralyzed entirely, an invalid in the highest regard. Luis smiled at him, knowing that there was nothing he could do to save his son from this dominating paralysis.

"Where is everyone?"

When Pedro asked this question, Luis closed his eyes to think. It was hard to imagine the past hour he lived through, especially when a pair of eyes and ears warned him of what had happened the other evening.

"The other night, I saw Slim and . . ."

"And?"

"And . . . your son."

Luis nodded his head, partly in understanding and partly in defeat. "What were they discussing?"

"Pedro . . . wished to speak with Mr. Mal, although he didn't say about what." The homeless man outside of the pool hall regretted informing Luis of his only son's conversation, but he knew of and respected Luis so much that he had to fulfill his reporting duties, even if it concerned his employer's kin.

"I see . . ." Luis closed his eyes and shut off a flow of tears who absolutely begged to be released.

He remembered the tears he created within himself and in Zephyr. The way she rubbed her eyes and sat up in her bed, warmed from her gentle and small body—this was so endearing to him. He cursed himself for waking her up; she looked so peaceful sleeping with Hermes. The poor teddy bear was clutched in her arms like a choke hold, but Luis understood that it was Zephyr's personality—to never let go. Luis gently stroked her long black hair and let his finger drop down her soft cheeks. She opened her eyes and froze Luis with her slicing gaze, her Medusa's stare, except it was comforting to him and not petrifying.

"Hi, Daddy . . ." Zephyr whispered.

"Zephyr, go pick out your favorite things and put them in your pink backpack . . . you're going on a trip."

Zephyr's moon-colored eyes did not move away from her father's face. "Where are we going?"

"To Spain, to see your grandmother. Doesn't that sound great?" Luis expected Zephyr to smile, but she remained curious and moved closer to Luis.

"Are you coming with me?"

Luis was glad that the shadows of night covered his face; if not, Zephyr would have seen long strands of tears streaming down his face.

"Daddy, you happy?"

"I'm fine, sweetie." *I'm hurting, sweetie.*

"Why are you crying?"

Luis grabbed Zephyr's shoulders and brought her to his chest. He wrapped his arms around her body and held her tight. He cherished each breath she made, especially the touch of two tiny hands that tried their best to reach across his back.

"Don't cry, Daddy! I'm sorry if I made you sad . . ."

"No, no, Zephyr. You never make me sad. Daddy was the happiest man alive when you were born . . ."

Zephyr's body was shaking. Luis clenched his teeth in anger for making his own daughter sob in his arms.

"I wanna come with you!" Zephyr said. "Please let me go with you! I'll behave, I promise!"

Luis released Zephyr from his arms and felt the same pain one feels when flesh is ripped away from bone. "Zephyr, listen to me. I'll meet you in Spain. Daddy can't leave now, but he will see you when he does leave . . . okay?"

Zephyr sniffled and looked at her father with drenched eyes. "Will you be in Spain in time to read a bedtime story with me?"

"Yes . . . I will."

"You promise?"

"I promise. Now wait for me until then, okay?"

"Okay."

Luis kissed Zephyr on her forehead and stood up to leave the room. He forced himself not to turn around and look at his daughter pack her things. But the sounds of her nose sniffling in the dark room made him look once more. She was so beautiful and yet so sad. How could this happen? Why?

Zephyr had pulled out a pink plastic drawer and grabbed her Barbie doll backpack. She unzipped it and stuffed all of her books in it. She then climbed back on her bed and grabbed Hermes. She jumped back down and wiped her nose with her forearm. She walked out the door, telling herself that she shouldn't look back. Just like Daddy did.

Luis met Rosa downstairs and saw a pair of eyes he had not seen since they moved away from Spain. She had two large suitcases packed and a smaller carry-on bag. When Luis approached her, she was holding back her tears while she talked to him.

"Is Zephyr coming down?" she plainly asked.

"Yes . . ."

After a few moments, Zephyr was seen walking downstairs with her Barbie backpack and Hermes in her hand. She walked over to her mother and felt an arm wrap around her body to comfort her.

"Are you all packed, sweetie?" Rosa asked.

Zephyr stayed silent and looked at Luis. He was at a loss for words. He exchanged glances between both Estrada women standing before him. He could barely open his mouth to talk and had to pry his sentence open with his mind.

"Rosa, I . . . I'm just . . ."

Rosa chuckled. "You said the same thing when I told you I was pregnant with Zephyr."

Luis snickered. For a brief moment, they shared a moment of joy, but they both knew it to be a transient euphoria. "I love you both," he said.

Rosa sniffled and opened her tears to him. "I don't care if it takes you a century. You meet us back in Spain, you got it?"

"I will . . ."

"I said, 'You got it?'"

"Yes. I will."

"Good."

Luis bent down and held out his arms to Zephyr. She ran into them and started to cry again. "I'll be okay, Zephyr. Daddy will read you a bedtime story when he gets there. I promise."

Zephyr let go of her father and held out her teddy bear to him. He told hold of it and looked at its brown, fuzzy head.

"I want you to have Hermes . . . Mommy put some holy water on it . . . so it will protect you."

Luis kissed Hermes's forehead and held it close to his heart. Zephyr stood on the tips of her toes and kissed her father on the cheek.

"I love you, Daddy."

Zephyr wrapped her arms around Luis's neck and refused to let go. The strength she exhibited at that singular moment, the way she gripped the base of his neck, Luis could not pry himself away from her. She possessed him with will alone. Her strangulation was begotten from her eyes, as Samson's strength was begotten from his hair. Zephyr was the only enemy of Luis. She was the one person who was able to subdue him. She conquered His Highness King Luis Estrada, self-exalted heir of his dominion, once a past semblance of a monarchy, now reduced to a peasant shoving his nose in a pile of mud.

She let go of him and Luis breathed a sigh of relief, partly because he was glad to grab a pocket of air that would sustain his spirit and save it from living through another minute of agony. The other part of him, the large portion that grabbed the sky for a miracle, hurled daggers through his heart. But he was so stripped of his legendary armor that his naked body was vulnerable to any frozen arrow that Zephyr chose to shoot. Her eyes grew deeper in tone. Her silver hues drowned in the hot tears that flooded her face and curved down her plump, round cheeks. Whenever Zephyr laughed, whenever she cried, a small dimple was always seen burrowing into the left side of her cheek. This time, her dimples housed Zephyr's tears as a small lake. They were hot and dense droplets of sadness sparkling beneath Zephyr's pale eyes. She sniffled and wiped her nose with her pajamas sleeve. She inhaled a breath of air for a moment. Zephyr knew she had to be strong, though she was too much of an innocent spirit to be burdened with the responsibility of strength.

A taxi cab pulled up to the front of the house just as he had planned earlier. Both of the Estrada women grabbed their luggage and gave Luis a beckoning look, more of a soulful plea to accompany them. When Luis hid his emotions, they knew that such a request was pinned down by impossibility. But his eyes hinted that he would return when he was able to, and the glaze of reassurance in his eyes comforted Rosa and Zephyr.

When they entered the cab and drove off, Zephyr's face had shown through the glass. She stared at Luis as they car pulled off, and the last image Luis saw of his daughter was the way her hair fell across her sweet, melancholic face. The car exhaust blocked his view of his family. Only the red brake lights peered through the smog. When the lights blinked off, Luis stared at the floor and sighed for the last time.

Luis thought of all these things as he absorbed the calm night that surrounded his home. The trees waved toward the flight of the wind. The stars were out but refused to appear, as if even a cluster of celestial glitter must have respected Luis's sadness and paid homage to the death of his joy. He heard nothing, he saw nothing; he embraced ignorance and turned himself into a frozen man. He was now an emotionless being who stared out the window, wondering about the women in his life and the joy of being with them once more, in a future undetermined by temporal distance.

He was supposed to feel the hot shadow of Mr. Mal smiling behind him. He was supposed to hear the clicks of guns readying to purge Luis's heart out of his body. He was supposed to turn around and feel a deep sense of sadness when Pedro and Slim stood in front of his view, one man smiling as the other shook in fear.

"Evening, gentlemen."

"Evening, Don." Mr. Mal raised his hand to relax the aims of his gang members. He approached Luis and laid his hand on his shoulder. "How are you feeling?"

"Just fine. Actually, I feel great."

"Really?"

"Yeah. I'm sure you've noticed something."

"I've noticed a lot of things; like there are no guards around. No boys to keep us company with bullets."

"Of course not. I don't keep around what I don't need."

Mr. Mal's smile faded when he tightened his grip on Luis's shoulder. His large hands were crushing his shoulder, but he refused to show any signs of pain. "And where is your family?"

"Not here."

Mr. Mal squeezed Luis on his collarbone and felt the fragile bone through his fingers. Luis clenched his fists and flinch in pain, but he did not make a sound.

"I'm gonna ask you again: where are they?"

Luis only smiled and shrugged his eyebrows. Mr. Mal released his grip on him and allowed Luis to clear his throat and catch his breath. Mr. Mal stepped behind Luis and reached into his breast pocket. He whipped out the one gun he was saving for Luis Estrada all these years. He cleaned it and polished it every day, afraid that it may not go off correctly or that it was jammed after so much time of neglect and abandonment. When the barrel of the gun was finally pointed at its rightful target, Mr. Mal felt his heart beat faster. His hand gripped the handle perfectly. His aim was sharp and precise. He knew, at that wondrous moment, that he was not going to miss.

He wrapped his arm around the Don and flexed his bicep against his throat. He placed the cold barrel against his left temple and twisted it so that it would not slip from his skin. Luis smiled, addressing Mr. Mal as the mob boss stared at his eyes.

"You're funny, Julius. Worried that the gun will slip from my head?"

"Not at all, brother. I just want you to know that I won't miss. Now where is your fucking wife?"

"Shopping."

Mr. Mal cocked back the gun. "Stop fucking with me!"

"You sure you have bullets in that gun? You better make sure."

Mr. Mal took a step back and shot Luis in the arm. Pedro flinched at the sound of the bullet flying into Luis's shoulder. He was afraid. He did not want to be here, but he needed to watch his father suffer for what he refused to bequeath to his only son. Slim, however, was laughing and enjoying his leader inflicting progressive amounts of anguish. Slim clapped once and licked his teeth.

"I think he likes this, boss. What do you think? Another shot?"

"Shut up, Slim! Where are they, Luis?!"

"Are you enjoying this, Julius?" Luis asked with annoyance in his tone.

Mr. Mal shot Luis in the same shoulder. This time, Luis screamed out in pain and grabbed on to his bleeding arm.

"Where the fuck are they?"

"You see this, Pedro?" Luis looked at his son. "You see this? This is what happens when you're in the business! *This* is what I was trying to save you from! I was looking out for you!"

"Dad . . . where are they?"

At that moment, Luis felt his shoulder heal itself from the bullet that lodged its hot finger deeper into his bone. The pain he felt from Pedro's inquiry stung him more than the lead projectile itself. Luis could only question Pedro's intent with his eyes wide open. At the same time, he wished that it was the bullet that killed his threshold of pain and not the three men standing in front of his bleeding arm.

"You really want to do this, don't you? You really want this?"

Pedro remained silent. His mouth quivered itself open, as if he had something to say. But it only stammered in movement.

"Answer me, son. Or is it because you have absolutely nothing to—"

"I just want to know where they are," Pedro interrupted.

"Oh, c'mon!" Slim walked toward Pedro. "Just shoot the answer out of him!"

Slim snatched Pedro's wrist and slammed a small revolver in his palm. The heavy chrome pistol weighed as heavy as Pedro's beating heart. He gripped the thick leather handle and bounced the gun in his hand until he mustered enough courage to wrap his sweaty finger around the trigger. He kept the gun pointed to the floor, all while worrying that the gun will accidentally discharge and kill someone he was reluctant to kill.

He thought of the quick way Mr. Mal smiled when he approached the large man and told him how bad he wanted the don hood. He remembered the wide grin on his face when he picked up the phone that sat at his desk. It seemed like it was waiting a decade for it to be used for this moment, for this joyful occasion.

He placed the receiver against his fat face and spoke rather softly into it. He hung up the phone and nodded his head to Pedro. A minute later, Slim walked into his office and pat Pedro on his back. He was smiling as well. These two men were unusually glad to see Pedro, and they showed their strategy in their laughter and their idle celebration. Mr. Mal hung up the phone and slouched back in his chair. Pedro remembered how the chair squeaked and screamed out when he rocked back and forth in a subtle amusement. He pulled out a desk drawer that lay to his left and grabbed a chrome pistol. It shined against his white, smiling teeth; Pedro could almost see his own reflection on its barrel. He felt his throat clog up with saliva once Mr. Mal pocketed the gun in his breast pocket.

"Don't worry. You'll get to do the honors," he whispered.

Pedro realized that this was a discreet premonition to what he would experience for himself: the mass of lead and chrome that crushed his palm, the scent of oil and musk that steamed from the leather grip, and the aura of pain that seared deeper into his father's shoulder. The room he stood in —the same room where he had sat on Luis's lap as a child—was now a strange place. Unrecognizable. As distant as a lonely spirit who haunts a lonely bedroom.

Luis stood up. Suddenly, Pedro's visions were cleared from his mind once he saw his father brace his shoulder together. He almost felt Luis's hot blood pour through his fingers. It stained everything he wore and merged itself within the tight fibers of his wool suit jacket.

"So what did they tell you, Pedro? That they can help you get my position? That the title is all yours? Did they tell you that?"

Pedro stayed silent. The gun in his hand was trembling. Luis took notice and let go of his shoulder.

"Son . . . don't."

"Why'd you give it up, Dad? You know I wanted it."

"I wanted what's best for—"

"Shut up! Just shut up!"

Luis held out his hand and walked slowly toward his son. Mr. Mal, the Forty-Second Street posse, and Slim sold him rights for his attention, but Luis refused to purchase it.

"Put it down."

"Better stop right there," Mr. Mal joined in, "or I will have to kill you myself."

Luis glanced about the room and noticed that the small group of men that had accompanied Mr. Mal and Pedro were terrified. Sweat was falling off of their chins. Their arms were weary from holding their weapons in the air for so long. Even Slim, a young man supposedly devoid of emotion, was darting about the room, waiting for something to happen. His anticipation manifested in a deathly fear—that what he expected to happen was in a direct refusal of his foresight.

Luis held his pursuit of Pedro's gun in place and let his arm drop to his side. He stared at the floor and saw images of ghosts in the shining wood. They were the tortured spirits of those he murdered—or had murdered. The victims of past and present all raised their cold scaly hands to him, enticing him to join them in their everlasting cyclone. Their mouths were moving—some were laughing; some were crying sinister tears of joy once they discovered that their destroyer of corporal bonds to this realm was to succumb to their own anguish in purgatory. He heard them yell to him, "Here! Here is where you belong! One of us! Welcome to oblivion, dear Estrada!"

Luis closed his eyes and tried to shut out the spirits. They all disappeared into the haze from where they observed the oft-envied world of the living. Only one soul stayed behind to watch him stand for one last moment. He opened his eyes and saw the silhouettes of the men in his office. The guns blended into the black auras that surrounded him. Zephyr stood in front of him, a young embodiment of innocence. She walked toward Luis, and each silhouette that stood before her shattered before she even reached their vicinity. They broke into pieces like rocks thrown through a stained glass window. Some burst into shards while other silhouettes justly collapsed into themselves. She kept breaking apart each person that stood in his office, in this very room that he feared to be his gravesite. And here she was, a sweet girl born from the sky, defeating all his would-be killers with only a single thought.

She stood in front of him and smiled. She could have smiled a thousand times at Luis and he would never grow tired of it. He welcomed it, even as he faced down these men. He smiled back and started to laugh heartily.

"Why the hell are you laughing?" Mr. Mal spoke out and interrupted Luis's dream.

"Because there is absolutely nothing you can do to me."

The room fell silent. Any noise made was muffled by extreme quiet. Luis stared at Pedro, keeping his eyes on his teary son, his gun still pointed at his heart. Slim kept glancing at the gang members standing by. Mr. Mal stood as a statue stands in a square, seeking attention from the small crowd but failing to receive it. Luis inhaled deeply and smiled. Slim sucked his teeth and pushed Pedro aside.

"Fuck this."

Slim aimed his gun at Luis. A heavy bullet flew at an ungodly velocity and speared Luis in the middle of his chest. His heart filled with blood and spilled throughout his lungs. The sudden burst of the gun startled the men around the room, and Pedro heard all of the guns open fire on him. His body jerked in odd positions as each bullet shredded his torso to pieces. Mr. Mal himself was frightened and he had to duck over to the side of the room as each bullet was unloaded into Luis's body. A rumble of shell casings rained and flipped through the air before they dropped to the floor. A trace gunshot sounded off as the mist settled down to the floor. The lifeless body of a royalty undone was drowning within his own lake of blood and sweat. Pedro kept his gun in the air and looked out the window; he kept his eyes on his reflection assimilated into the background of the city lights. The night air enhanced each wrinkle on his face, every bead of tears that ripped through his cheeks, and all motions of his quivering fingers. He hated the image, and he pulled the trigger back to blow out the window. The gun clicked to kill the image reflected in the truthful glass.

But he had no more bullets left in his gun to shoot.

*   *   *

Adam was sitting at home and watching a movie with his grandmother. It was an old movie that was way before his time but still within the time of his grandmother. She shook her head at certain moments in the movie and told her grandson how this world used to be like this, full of sophistication and grandeur. Men like John Barrymore and Cary Grant, who exuded a debonair attitude when they were seen in public. Or women like Mae West, who brought wit and humor that was clean and yet still sharp enough to slice a man's heart wide open. She especially shook her head when she saw a gentleman and a lady dancing in a ballroom, with her evening gown flowing away from her small ankles, her eyes fixed on her leading man.

"When I was your age, your grandfather dressed in a suit every time he took me out on a date. Oh well, you kids need to have fun, I suppose."

Ms. Stokes laughed when she saw Adam sigh and roll his eyes. He saw her face crinkle with joy, and he could not help but join her in her moment of glee. It was yet another evening, he thought. Another trip into the past with his nostalgic "mother."

She shook her head again when she heard a car pull up in front of their house, hip-hop blaring through the stereo and punishing the piece of sonorous equipment with each beat and curse word. Adam turned down the volume when the car doors shut and two men were heard talking with each other. He froze his eyes on the front door, and he could hear their heavy nubuck shoes stomp up the steps.

"Adam, what's the matter?"

"Get in the bathroom."

"What? Who—"

"I said go! Go!"

Ms. Stokes never heard so much insistence in his voice, so it was a sign to her that she needed to do what she was told. She immediately went to the bathroom and locked the door.

The front door knocked, and Adam felt his heart skip a beat. His hands were shaking when he grabbed the remote and turned off the television. He stood up and had to force his legs to carry himself across a room that he could traverse blindfolded. Everything around him was suddenly foreign and frightening: the walls curved towards the floor, the bookcase along with it, and it whirled around him as he walked to the door. The carpet rose and fell like waves upon an ocean. The ceiling descended to the floor and ascended back to its original place whenever Adam shot his eyes back at it. His hands reached out for the doorknob and turned it. His world slowed to a halt when he saw two Forty-Second Street gang members standing in front of him with smiles on their faces.

Adam could barely remember what had happened after the two men grabbed both his arms and nearly dragged him to the car. He only remember sitting between two gang members who smelled of sweat and traces of blood that he knew did not belong to them. The driver had his window rolled down, his left forearm swinging outside the car, a lit cigar in his hand. He cast occasional glances at the rear-view mirror. He kissed Adam's reflection, and this gesture only made Adam fear the driver more than the destination.

The street lights blurred past his view while the car sped through the empty night. Adam stared straight ahead, afraid that he would disturb his companions and start an unnecessary fight. His hands clasped each other once the road in front of him jogged his memory. He remembered the turns and the stop lights that graced this particular road, the timing of each light change on all sides of the road, and especially the landmarks that graced the borders of the street. An old gas station sat in a lonely manner at the far right corner of the street, begging someone to choose him as their source of fuel, and not the more popular fuel station further down the road. He saw the corner store that, for its small size, had every grocery and produce one could imagine a normal grocery store would contain. The same homeless men and women sat within the concaves of the buildings, warmed by the frigid winds and shivering against the air of regrets they carried on their backs.

Adam could not hold himself together any longer. He cleared his throat and opened his mouth for a second before he spoke out. "Where are we going?" He addressed his nervous inquiry to the driver.

"Estrada's place."

Adam was surprised that the driver did not tell him to "shut it" or say, "None of your business." It was then that he realized that they were being honest and open for a reason. Such veracity led his heart to tremble.

Adam closed his eyes to throw himself into his wishes, all while silently cursing these men for thrusting him into this horrid situation. When he opened them, he found himself in a driveway filled with black vans and cars that were most likely stolen. He saw the mansion that towered over his eyesight, and he knew that the driver was not lying in his expected destination. The driver pulled up behind one of the vans, stopped the car, and then turned his body around to address Adam.

"Out."

Adam's escorts both exited the vehicle, and they stood in the path of the doorway in case he conjured the suicidal thought of running away. In case he still had such inklings to escape, one of the guards lifted up his white T-shirt and exposed a silver gun tucked in his waist. Adam could hear his heart pump hard against his chest. He shifted himself to the left side of the car and managed to climb out. It was an ordeal to force himself to stand up and view the Estrada house, and it was equally as hard to venture up the steps and enter the house. But he did not surprise himself when he saw Mr. Mal standing in the foyer and laughing with his fellow gangsters.

"Adam! First Degree himself! How ya been?" Mr. Mal had an eerie jubilee in his voice. "You came just in time. I was meeting with your manager earlier ago. As a matter of fact, he should be coming down right now."

Mr. Mal turned his head toward the flight of stairs. Adam followed his gaze and saw two men carrying what looked like to be a rolled-up carpet. They held it in such a rude manner that when they descended a couple of steps, they grew tired of carrying such a heavy load that they ended up swinging it back and forth in one motion, then they threw it down the stairs. It landed with a solid thud that shook the floor upon which Adam stood, and he already knew that it was the lifeless body of Luis Estrada, even before Mr. Mal walked over and lifted the cover.

Adam did not cry. He only stood in his place and read each bloody mark that was painted on his body. They assimilated themselves in his face, dead putty barely clinging to his skull. His suit was punctured by bullet holes and colored with dried blood. His mouth was open; it made Adam wonder if Luis spoke any last words, maybe a family member's name. Maybe his daughter. Zephyr—the sweet piece of joy that whispered away Luis's burden.

"Where's . . . everyone?" The sudden thought of the living Estrada family entered his mind.

"We're looking for those two bitches right now," Mr. Mal answered, with a breath of disgust in his voice. "Luis here failed to tell us. But we'll find them."

Adam did not hear Mr. Mal speak at all. He only kept staring at Luis's dead body. Mr. Mal's hand landed on his shoulder and made him jump.

"We're a bit busy, so I need a favor from you." Mr. Mal motioned Adam to walk with him for a few steps. "I need you to get rid of the body. You're a strong guy, right? I'm sure you can handle it. Understand?"

Adam nodded, although it was stuttered and not fluid in motion.

"Good, good." Mr. Mal slapped Adam's back. "Get to work. I have pussy waiting."

Pedro was a statue. A good one, at that. He did not blink, nor did he show any signs of breathing. If anyone did not think better, they would say that he died standing up. But that was the exact feeling he was experiencing at the moment. Death and the loss of one's soul. Especially for him, a young man committing patricide out of temptation. The glory of the position, the rewards it bequeathed, all these business perks enticed him to pull the trigger more times than anyone in the room could count. He wished he was a statue, just a cold, emotionless being that stood in a courtyard, noticed by a few but loved by no one.

Slim stayed with him in that room, upstairs from the foyer, on the opposite side where he and his sister slept. He shook Pedro fervently in order to make him come out of his brief past and to look forward to the dark future that lay ahead of them.

"Holy shit man!" Slim kept clamoring and patting his back. "Holy fucking shit!"

Pedro became a mute at that point.

"Pedro, you officially have a nut sack to hold on to. I mean, fuck! Not even I would do something like that. I mean yeah, I've thought of it. But I never actually *did* it. You're my hero!"

"What . . . did I just . . . did I?"

"You did it, man!"

"Is he . . . is he dead? Is he—"

"You unloaded a whole fucking clip into his body. I'd say that he's dead. No one survives that. Even miracles would haul ass somewhere else."

"What did I do, Slim?"

"Er . . . you grew a pair."

"What did I fucking do?"

"Yo. Calm down. It's not that serious."

"What do you mean, 'It's not that serious'? I fucking shot my father!"

"Pedro! Pedro!" Slim grabbed both of his shoulders and held on tight. "You killed your dad. You pulled off Ancient Rome shit. Done deal. Move the fuck on."

Pedro jerked away from Slim's grasp and paced the room. The gun was still in his hand, hot and sweaty from his palms. He held it up to his temple and slammed the shaft against his head over and over.

"Oh my god, oh my god. I fucking killed him. Oh my god . . ."

"Pedro! Just chill, man! Think about it, just hold off and think about it: Your dad's dead. Okay? Yeah it sucks cock, but it happened. But you gotta look on the bright side! You're now the king, man! It's you! You're Don Fucking Estrada now!"

Pedro ceased his pace and placed the gun in his mouth. Slim saw this movement and only stood still and watched. Pedro pulled the trigger. It only made an empty click. He pulled it again. Nothing. He screamed while the gun was still in his mouth, and he pulled the trigger four more times. He took the gun out of his mouth and let it drop on the floor.

"Look, bro," Slim said with a chuckle, "either you would kick ass at Russian Roulette, or there are no more bullets in the gun. You used them all, man . . ."

Pedro cried. But he forced himself to cry. In all honesty, he thought, he was happy. He cried because people who lose their fathers were supposed to cry. They were supposed to feel and express remorse for a person who was no longer of this world. But there was nothing that held back his joy. He shed his invisible tears, his dishonest tears, and before he turned to Slim, he wiped droplets of nothingness from his face.

"You're right," he said. "What's done is done, right?"

Slim breathed a sigh of relief. "Thank you! Can we go downstairs now?"

Pedro followed Slim out of the room. He smirked as he exited the doorway and went down the stairs. The room was a graveyard to him now, but he still felt as though it was not meant to be an office at all. He shrugged his shoulders. If it was truly a cemetery, Pedro thought, then he had just urinated on his father's grave.

*   *   *

Two hours passed by as Mr. Mal and his men discussed future plans for themselves and Luis's usurped business. They exchanged frequent laughs and nodded quite often, retelling the sudden fate of the former Don.

"He deserved it," one man said to another.

"Now things can really get started." Mr. Mal lit a cigar and swallowed the short end with his lips. "It'll take some time, but I got plans that will put us on the map."

"What about all the other gangs?"

Mr. Mal puffed on his cigar and talked through his teeth. "No one is dumb enough to fuck with us now that the King is dead."

"What about the Russians?"

"Fuck 'em. If they want a war, then they'll get one. And lose. If Vlad is smart, he'll stay the fuck out of our way."

"All right . . ."

A white light brushed past the front door and illuminated everyone that stood in the foyer: Mr. Mal, Pedro, Slim, a handle of men, and a few splatters of blood that still stuck to the floor. The light shut off, and a moment later a car door slammed shut. A set of footsteps reverberated across the front stairs. The men who stood by instinctively placed their hands inside their chests and held on to their guns. The doorknob jingled. It pushed open and Adam stepped in the doorway. He had blood all over him, as well as a splash of dirt and soot on his clothes. His eyes were red and swollen. It was obvious that he was crying during the whole ordeal, but it was difficult for him to tell if the men in the room did not notice his dried tears or if they saw them and simply did not care.

"So?" Mr. Mal asked.

"H-he's in the bay. I . . . tied some heavy stones to his ankles and shoved him over."

"You didn't bury him?"

"No . . . I didn't have a shovel."

Mr. Mal nodded his head and stared at Adam for a while. He read the blood on his shirt, the mud on his shoes, and especially the wet pants he currently wore. It was a result of a mad tailor who pressed Adam's clothes with supreme anguish, and there was no way he could make it through life alive without the consult of his mentor.

"Nice work." Mr. Mal took out his cigar and tapped the ashes away from it. He turned around and walked past his men. Pedro was stationed in his spot, while Slim looked around the house and admired the décor.

Mr. Mal stopped in the middle of the room and flicked away what was left of his cigar. He reached into his jacket pocket and extended his arm toward Adam. His gun shot off a loud bullet that pierced Adam's left lung and splashed an ounce of blood into the floor. Adam staggered backward and tripped over his deathly stride. He fell to the floor and landed on his back. He saw a large shadow creep over him, and found himself staring at Mr. Mal.

"Well, Adam . . . sorry. I just don't want you squealing to anyone. It's a shame that you were a good kid."

Mr. Mal pointed his gun at Adam's head. He pulled back the trigger and fired another round into his skull. Adam's body jerked from the impact, and then it fell into silence. Mr. Mal bent over his body and watched as Adam's soul lifted itself out of his eyes and ascended to heaven, where he would forever view the conquests of Mr. Mal and the Forty-Second Street Gang.

*   *   *

In that divine realm, he noticed that Pedro was still emotionless. He noticed that Slim glanced at him once, then turned away to further appreciate Luis's home. He saw his own body being abandoned in the foyer, as a pool of blood seeped toward the doorway. And as the blood stopped flowing, the lives of Luis Estrada and Adam Stokes were ended by the same gesture of a finger, observed of their death with cruel stares and by the same architect of their failure to live.

Zephyr was unusually quiet during the whole plane ride. But then again, Rosa had realized, she was acting like a normal person. She stared out the window, her silver eyes and her stoic face giving off a partial reflection on the white clouds below her. She did not look at the stewardess when she made her rounds in the cabin. Rosa quietly waved the stewardess off so that Zephyr can concentrate on what she was leaving behind. The hum of the jet engines did not lull her to nap on the flight to Spain. The dry air that circulated throughout the cabin did not cause her nose to make the slightest twinge. Rosa held Zephyr's hand and squeezed it gently, and she was glad that her daughter entwined her fingers in her mother's. Zephyr was alive. She was alert and safe. But she was emotionless. The plane experienced a number of unexpected turbulence, and although other children in the cabin yelped and thrust their heads into their parents' laps, Zephyr barely noticed both the bumpy air, nor did she pay attention to the resulting juvenile clamor.

Rosa saw Zephyr counting the clouds with her cold, sad eyes, and she swore that she saw a lone tear slide down her soft cheek. But Zephyr must have read her mother's mind, for she quickly wiped her face with her sleeve and continued to watch the sky. Rosa so desperately wanted to cry with her daughter, but she forced herself to stay strong. She gently brushed Zephyr's hair and closed her eyes.

When the plane landed, Rosa breathed a lonely sigh that she had not felt in years. The Spanish city that shot forth on the horizon had not changed at all. The airport still emulated the colors of the sunny coast line. The air was warm but not stifling. It was an unusually dry winter, having no signs of rain or even a dark cloud in the sky. Here was her home, foreign yet familiar, like a soldier retuning home after a lengthy war.

The two women stepped off the plane and walked across the runway to enter the air-conditioned airport. Zephyr tightly held Rosa's hand as they walked across the sunlit ground. Rosa saw a dimple form in Zephyr's cheek and her eyes crinkle in the sun. *She's smiling*, she thought. But Zephyr became stoic once again. Rosa nodded her head in despair and continued walking with Zephyr to the baggage claim.

"C'mon, sweetie. Let's go see your grandma."

They weaved their way through the European crowds and arrived at the baggage claim. The conveyor belt was already full by the time they found a spot to wait for their luggage. Zephyr's eyes glowed with a subtle anxiety once her pink and white Barbie backpack revealed itself. She broke free of her mother's grasp and ran to her dainty piece of luggage. She grabbed the backpack without hesitation, swung it around her shoulders, and calmly walked back to her original spot.

"Her books," Rosa realized.

After Rosa retrieved her bags, they both walked amidst the busy crowds and arrived at customs. Rosa dropped her bags in front of her and glanced around the room. Long lines of guests and former residents of beautiful *España* were inching closer and closer to the customs agent. They were all anxious to get back home, a direct opponent of Rosa's anxiety to hop back on the plane and see Luis one last time. Her wish was forgotten when she spotted a sign marked with the name "Estrada" in bold, black letters. She wondered if the sign was truly meant for her—after all, there were plenty of Estradas with that name in the city, let alone in the entire nation. But she studied the person who held up the sign, a dark Spaniard dressed in a black suit and a black tie resting on a crisp, white dress shirt. His demeanor indicated that he was waiting for Rosa and Zephyr. She did not hesitate to pick up her bags, take Zephyr's hand in hers, and walk toward the man.

"Rosa Estrada?" he asked.

"Yes."

"Come with me."

Rose nodded and followed the man outside. A black car that was designed purely for escorting important figures was parked outside, waiting for the two Estrada women. He opened up the back door and waved them to enter. Rosa started to walk, but Zephyr stood like a statue and refused to budge. Her eyes gleamed with a bright silver hue, and her stare made the man flinch when he looked at her face. Her eyes could stop his heart from beating, and he knew this at that immediate moment.

"It's okay, Zephyr," Rosa encouraged her. "We can trust him."

Zephyr nodded and released the man from his paralysis. She followed her mother to the car, and as soon as they were both inside, he shut the door and walked around the back of vehicle. He climbed into the driver's seat, turned on the car, and sped off into the golden streets ahead.

They drove past a number of corner markets full of customers doing their absolute best to haggle down the prices of the seller's fruits. Their hand gestures and the curls of their mouths were traditional in every sense of the word, bearing no movement toward the modern while paying a great deal of homage to good times passed. A large woman selling loaves of bread stood on another corner as the car spun around the bend. She held out a bright tan loaf of bread while shouting out prices to pedestrians. The soft aroma of sugar and dough enticed pedestrians brave enough to walk past her. She seemed glad to have customers flock to her lonesome stand. The bread she baked was as sweet as she was, and she greeted each person with a wide smile as she joyfully latched onto each bill of money they handed her.

A tall man was seen on the opposite side of the street with a beautifully tailored suit and a subtle yet classy fedora. The fabric in his outfit shimmered against the bright roads, paved with sparkled gold and bronze. He had a number of copies of his suit suspended on cedar hangers, waiting for a distinguished gentleman to assert his position and purchase a piece of clothing. He stood with an arrogant pose, his chin in the air and his fingers clasped in front of his waist. He expressed nothing, even when a man stopped by to glance over his selection of suit jackets. When the customer took a suit jacket off of the rack and pulled out his wallet to buy it, the suit seller did not blink as he took the money from him. He only nodded in assent and maintained his poise. He was confident with the fact that his suits sold themselves; if he spoke, then his suits would forever remain on the same cedar wood hangers.

The entire trip on these roads answered Zephyr's silence. Her eyes were fixated on the surrounding area. She remembered her grandmother's stories of the young woman who was hidden from her suitors in a labyrinth, never to be found by those unworthy to see her face. She remembered the honeyed breads gifted from God that attracted everyone with a taste for the fine and the perfect. Zephyr hoped that Raquel would give her a personal tour of the city with a bowl of sherbet in her hands, melting over her fingers and dripping on her lap. This brief glimpse of joy faded when she thought about the hours that had passed. Luis would always read a bedtime story to her before she closed her eyes and drifted along her dreams. Her face slumped into deeper sadness when she realized that this would be the first time she would ever read to herself.

"We're here. Are you excited to see your grandmother, Zephyr?" Rosa's maternal instincts sensed her daughter's melancholic expression from the minute they entered the plane.

"Yeah . . ." she answered sadly.

"Are you okay, sweetie?"

"I'm okay . . ."

Rosa nodded. She returned to her own window dreams, except she imagined where Zephyr's life would turn from now on. Would she return to America and seek the hollow rewards of vengeance, or would she stay here in Spain and try to move on? There was no way in heaven that she would return to her original home anytime soon; Pedro would find her easily. And Mr. Mal. And the largest gang in the city. Besides, she thought, she needed resources to fight. Of course, she could not do it if she wanted to, since there is no such thing as a female boss, not in this realm they currently occupied. Tradition, even among those who were the least bit honorable, always won the skirmish.

But on the flipside, would Zephyr really be happy living here in Spain? "Keep her happy or die trying." Rosa continued to mouth off those words. She halted her repeated prayer when the car finally stopped its drive.

Raquel's house was a large and asymmetrical home painted in a peach hue with white outlines around the front door and the windows. Zephyr looked out her window and studied the optimistic house with her depressing white eyes. She smirked at the color of her grandmother's less-than-humble abode. She slinked back into her seat; there was nothing else to study. It had windows, a wide door, and a roof. It had a gated driveway with black fences equipped with sharp spears. She felt lazy. She did not want to look at any detail that did not involve the musky scent of her father's chest.

Rosa and Zephyr climbed out of the car while the driver opened the trunk. He grabbed their luggage and curiously watched the women ascend the steps of Raquel Estrada. Rosa inhaled deeply before she knocked on the door. After a few moments, Raquel peeked through the door window and opened her home to her two favorite women. She smiled widely but quickly made it fade away once she saw the expressions on their faces. Rosa and Raquel talked to each other without speaking a word. Rosa said that they arrived for a reason. Raquel said that she knew and that Luis had called her a week ago to tell her everything that would, and did, happen. Rosa cried. Raquel cried along with her. But here they were, trading silent thoughts and expressing them as cordial actions. Raquel motioned Rosa and Zephyr to enter.

"The driver will bring in your stuff."

The driver walked in through the doorway afterward and set the luggage down in the foyer. Raquel thanked the driver and waved goodbye to him as he exited the house. Raquel then turned to Rosa and tightly hugged her.

"I know . . . I know."

Rosa held back her emotions, but she could not help but allow a lone tear to fall from her eyelash. She turned away and walked deeper into the home. Raquel bent down to hug Zephyr, and she felt a sweet pair of fingers wrap around her neck. She felt Zephyr's heart pang with agony, and it broke her heart to see her granddaughter so sad.

"Hi, Grandma . . ." Zephyr looked at Raquel with sad, snowy eyes.

"Hi, honey, how are you doing?"

"Okay . . ."

"Did you miss your grandmother?"

"Yeah."

"Are you hungry, sweetie? I have some food on the stove for you. I even got us some sherbet we could share."

"No, I'm okay . . ."

Raquel looked at her granddaughter with sympathetic eyes. "Are you sure?"

"Yeah . . . I'm tired."

"Do you wanna go to bed?"

"Yeah . . ."

"Okay . . . rest well, sweetheart, okay?"

Zephyr nodded and ventured up the stairs with her backpack in the crook of her arm. Rosa and Raquel watched her walk up the stairs with a gait that was as sad as her spirit. Zephyr kept in mind Raquel's stories of her home, so she had no trouble in finding her guest bedroom. She opened the door and immediately plopped onto her bed. She unraveled the blankets and wrapped herself in a tight ball. She shut her eyes and did her best to sleep off the memories of the day.

The evening passed in silence and solitude for the Estrada women. Rosa sat across from her mother-in-law at a table, both women clutching a cup of hot ginger tea in their hands. They hoped that the spicy yet relaxing scent of ginger roots combined with the dim stars in the evening sky would relieve them of their depression. The cat gripped both of their tongues for a long moment.

Then they heard a soft whimper upstairs.

"What was that?" Raquel shot up from her seat.

"Zephyr!"

Rosa burst out of her chair and followed Raquel as she ran upstairs to Zephyr's bedroom. Thousands of thoughts rushed through their minds all at once: *Oh God, what happened? Please be safe, oh God, please be safe. No way they could've found us! Oh God, why us? Please, please . . . not my baby . . .*

They entered the doorway and glanced around the room. They found her lying in bed, breathing with her face was pressed into the pillow. When Rosa looked at her face, she saw a constant stream of tears rolling down her chin. She was sobbing with such a heavy heart; her mouth was open as she cried and trembled in her bed. Her fingers were clenched onto her pillow. She was praying to die, to somehow join her father by ending her own life. She wanted to flood the room with her tears and drown in their warm baths. Zephyr had sadly delighted in suffocating in the same room where her family stood. She gasped for air, her chest stuttered when she breathed again, and she burrowed her cheeks deeper into the pillow.

"Why isn't Daddy coming? Why did they take him away?"

"Oh, Zephyr! Oh my god . . ." Rosa ran to her side and tightly held her in her arms. Zephyr rested her head on Rosa's bosom, still wailing and crying.

"Why did they take him away? Why?"

Rosa knew this feeling. This feeling of repetition—the hopes that a divine figure would descend from the sky and grant her an answer. Over and over, she asked that question: "Why?" Zephyr was praying for relief, to see her father again, with his warm smile enlightening the silver speckles in her eyes. He was now only an image in her mind, as a faraway island is visited but once, an experience remembered but not lived.

Raquel ran to Zephyr's side with swollen eyes, holding the last two women in her life in her arms. They all cried at once, a melancholic symphony, playing only for the dead spirits that floated across the earth. Zephyr's voice had awakened them, and her audience could not help but weep with this poor, innocence-lost soul.

"Oh my God, oh God . . ." All Rosa could do was rock back and forth with her. She kept her eyes clenched to shut out the tears, to dam them up from seeping out of her eyes, and also to save herself from the image of having her only daughter suffer at such a sweet age, to be too young to understand depression.

"I miss Daddy so much . . . I miss him so much . . ."

Raquel and Rosa held sweet Zephyr Estrada in their arms, crying and crying for what seemed like years. This painful night, Zephyr's shivering wails—all was left in their memories and brought up again only as a reminder of what they had lost. They held one another in such a way that they were afraid of being separated. The house they left behind was now a mausoleum. It was now a tomb inhabited by its own architects: a son, a friend, a dictator, and an army. Not one of them were worthy of keeping a heart; rather, they sold their souls to the snickering demon and he gave them a murky flame in return. Thus they stood as usurpers of a throne.

And yet Zephyr was here with her family—her angels—the same ones who held her as she wept. She felt her mother's heart beat against her forehead, and such tenderness comforted her. Her sobbing slowed, her sniffling became rarer, and her tears were completely frozen on her cheeks. She halted her breath and buried herself within the crook of her mother's elbow.

Rosa felt Zephyr move within her arms, and she let her take a moment to breathe in new air. When she released her desperate grip, she raised Zephyr's chin and almost flinched when she examined her face. There was something different about Zephyr's eyes. The vacancy of color, what little of it remained, was now gone. As silvery as they were, they had always exuded warmth. But Rosa frowned when Zephyr looked at her with her pair of evaporated eyes. Her daughter had lost her frailty—her sweet, innocent spirit—and matured too early, too late. And in that moment, as Rosa sadly looked back at her daughter, she realized that Zephyr had abandoned all memories of joy that were prevalent in her life and replaced them with an ill comfort in the memories which she destined herself to create. Zephyr had thus chosen to be Fortune incarnate—a seamstress who spun her wheel in favor of her loved ones and to damn those who did not deserve her coveted sense of mercy.

"My baby," Rosa lamented. "My baby . . ."

*　　*　　*

Part Two

I

The world had decided that two decades was too ample of a time-frame to pursue change, so it transformed itself in exactly seventeen years. By shying itself three years, it allowed each global city to shed shells of yesterday and wear coatings of morrow in its stead. Abandoned were the grocery stores owned by a family who inherited such a market from an immigrant grandfather. Accepted now were the chain superstores that offered discount cards and speedy checkout lanes. Before, cash was the only acceptable form of currency; now, they were frowned upon in a world of hurries and rushes. If a simple corner market was gone, so was the innocence of the city that held it.

These seventeen years played a host to a construction of new corporations that wanted their piece of heaven on earth, except that such divine property was purchased rather than gained. Silver and black towers shone above the city streets, glimmering underneath the golden sunlight, daring anyone who walked by to ignore their ransomed grandeur. Behind the tinted windows were men and women dressed in tailored suits. They walked in a uniformed motion—a motion of chaos, however—as each person shot across the office floor, bumping into one another but with neither the time nor the decency to apologize for their collisions. They just moved forward, a direct result of the constant progression of the world.

Inane still were the amounts of trash and rats that crawled underneath the sewer gates. But the bestiality presented in such vermin was also hidden within the deep souls of the surface. The dwellers that walked and cursed upon the pavement were judicious, to say the least, in their perspectives of the city.

"This place is going to hell in a hand basket," an old man said.

"What else is new?" a young lady replied.

Stenches of soot and baked liquor rose among the sidewalks. The bile that wafted to the citizens' noses did not give off a scent that made them curl in disgust; rather, they ignored it. Either that or they had grown so accustomed to it and considered it to be natural air. No one gave mind to a large rat scurrying along a sewer gate, nor were any eyes averted to the duo of young teenagers standing next to one another, nervous and full of anxiety, as they spoke quickly into a tinted car window while casting speedy glances around them.

A sudden flash of black and gray split up the transaction between the two teens and the dark vehicle. One of the teens saw a young gang member sprinting down the sidewalk, leaping over a box full of garbage, and tripping over a poor man's tin bowl. Hundreds of coins and a bundle of dollar bills tinkled across the sidewalk. No obstacle stopped him, but it did slow him down. And that was exactly what Officer Rebecca Ortega wanted.

She sprinted down the same path where the gang member had lain before her, passing by the teens and the car and successfully avoiding each remnant of garbage and coins the runner left behind. She was in her full uniform: utility belt with a pair of handcuffs, a sidearm, a nightstick, and a few pockets of ammo. She was dressed in black, with silver gleams of light shining from her badge. She was very fast for someone carrying all that gear, but then again, she refused to believe that she was carrying any weight at all.

Her hair was more brown than black but was still dark enough to contrast against her bright brown eyes. She had matured into a beautiful young woman, with a slim nose, a gentle face, and a filled body. A body that was in excellent shape, that is. Her years of struggling in Ellipses had paid off. She was confident. Or arrogant. It was hard to distinguish it most of the time. But no one questioned it any further and simply accepted her as a woman who just got shit done.

Rebecca saw the runner turn a corner and speed down a narrow alley. She stopped her pursuit and paused for a millisecond to think. She glanced at her right and noticed a rare family grocery store. The door was wide open; she thanked God that it was. She ran through the opened door and entered the store.

It was a small grocery store, but it was long. She shopped there often and knew the layout by heart: the dry goods section, bottled juices, and a tiny produce section that offered only a select variety of fruits and vegetables. She weaved her way through the aisles, apologizing to each patron as she did so, and she made her way to the back door where the loading dock was located.

Rebecca pushed in the long handle of a metallic door that led to a back alley. She whipped out her nightstick and hugged the wall to the right of her. She closed her eyes and calmed her heated lungs. She heard someone's faint footsteps approach her, then it became increasingly louder as they neared her location. When the steps became loud enough, she stepped out of her hiding place and smacked her nightstick against the runner's face. He fell on his back and yelped in pain. Rebecca threw the blunt weapon on the ground and stood next to the runner. He clenched his face and rolled back and forth on the ground. She paused for a moment and then gave him a swift kick in his side.

"Are you gonna stop running away from me now? Huh?"

Rebecca flipped him on his stomach with her foot and grabbed each of his wrists with one hand. She took her free hand and pulled out a pair of handcuffs. She slapped the cold holes of iron on his wrists as she read him his rights.

"You have the right to remain silent. Anything said will be held against you in a court of law. You have the right to an attorney . . . if you cannot afford one, an attorney will be appointed to you."

"Fuck you, bitch!" The runner spat on the ground and felt his body being forced to stand up.

"You wish you could!"

Rebecca walked with him to the street across the alley. Police sirens were heard approaching her. Once she stepped out onto the sidewalk, two police cruisers met her angry gaze. One car door opened first, and a tall, disheveled man exited the car.

"You all right there, Officer?"

"Not really. This dickhead gave me a workout."

"Not like you needed it, right?"

"Good answer." Rebecca handed the suspect over to the officer and placed her hands on her hips. The gear that wrapped around her waist was slowing her down, too bulky to be flexible. She sighed and patted her hair that was tied in a bun. She glanced around the group of cars.

"Where's Bernini?" she asked.

"I'm right here, Ortega."

Rebecca turned her head and saw her superior officer calmly approaching her. She held her tongue when she saw his graying hair giving room for a fresh field of skin to form on his head. Detective Bernini did nothing to hide his apparent baldness. Sure, there were men in the department who were also bald, but Bernini made no attempt to deny it. He accepted his genetic malfunction, more so with defeat rather than confidence. He hated being middle-aged, slim in every place except for his stomach. He had charm, but only its remnants. It was still successful, but Rebecca was the only woman he knew that remained disinterested in him, and that failure not only disgusted him but it also turned him on. Greg only liked to chase girls that he could not have, and this recent pursuit made him concentrate on succeeding in seeing the inside of her bedroom. But for now, he had to contend with her recent convict.

He looked at the suspect Rebecca had to thoroughly chase down. He saw the annoyed and defeated expression on his face, with large beads of sweat pouring over his eyelids. He sat in the cruiser, anger in his eyes, infuriated with the fact that a young, pretty little officer like her would be the one to give him the most anguish. He yelled inside the car at Rebecca, and she could read the words that shot forth from his lips. She was glad that the windows drowned out his words because, had it not been for that glass shield, she would have forced the silence on his mouth permanently.

"Gave you a good run, didn't he?" Bernini fumbled in his pockets for a cigarette.

"You're the second person to say that to me . . . and I thought you were quitting."

"Tomorrow."

"My ass."

Bernini pulled out a wrinkled pack of cigarettes and smacked the bottom of it to force out a single cigarette. "Do you smoke, Ortega?"

"If I did, I wouldn't have been able to run down this jackass, now would I?"

Bernini gave her a menacing look. He was surprised to see that Rebecca did not flinch. Her expression was stoic and as lifeless as a boulder that sat atop a crumbling mountain. He abandoned his leer and continued on. "I want you to come with me."

"For what?" Rebecca was hesitant to ask. God only knew what he wanted her for.

"Something that detective hopefuls should see."

Rebecca released a joyful smile that shot forth from her cheeks. She nodded to Bernini and she followed him back to his car. He pointed her to the passenger side, and he unlocked the doors with his car key. She opened the door, sat inside, and waited for her moment to learn, as a young girl waits for Christmas Day to arrive.

The cruiser turned on streets that Rebecca knew like the back of both her hands, but the thought of becoming a detective occupied her mind. Everything around her was a blur, lines and shadows that melded together to form something without a body to give it shape. A sheet of green water appeared over the horizon, a sort of color that gave it a deathly hue. Beelzebub's Bay, everyone called it. An older officer—a man who looked to be around five years past retirement—told her of an urban legend that claimed that the disease-infested bay was formed when the gates of oblivion opened, and all the bile and rotting flesh of the corpses of hell seeped through and entered the water.

"Huh. Kind of silly. Could be sewage flowing through an old pipe. Or algae."

"That's not it," the officer replied.

"Then what?"

"Something . . . sinister."

Rebecca did not have an answer to that, but she was ready to believe the old officer once the car pulled up to the shore. The water today was as unholy as ever. Rebecca saw a number of police cruisers and ambulances line the area. Long yards of yellow tape surrounded the crime scene. A few detectives in old suits smoked their cigarettes and discussed everything but the crime scene itself. They were balding, fat, and unhappy with their married lives. At least that's what she noticed. Their gold wedding bands were faded and chipped, much like the men who wore them. They saw Bernini in the driver's seat and waved to him. He stopped the car, and Rebecca was the first one to exit.

A bloated man lay on the edge of the shore, covered with wet pebbles and a pungent stench that rose from the open wounds on his back. His radius was enclosed by a yellow ribbon that curiously shined in the sunlight. Bernini coughed and held a handkerchief against his nostrils. Rebecca walked with him to the body, and she stooped down to examine him.

"You don't smell anything?" Bernini asked through his handkerchief.

"Not at all."

"You have a cold or something then?"

"No. Just breathing through my mouth."

The man was dressed in a black suit with a once-white dress shirt and a heavily bloodied tie. His eyes were still open—a pair of lifeless orbs that hung onto nothing but wind and sand. Rebecca moved closer and studied his face, being careful not to let her fair skin brush against the corpse. He had a day-long stubble on his cheeks, as well as an outline of a tattoo on his neck.

"What is this?" she whispered. Rebecca reached into her belt and pulled out a simple black pen. She nested it between her fingers and pushed back the collar of his dress shirt. "Number forty-two. I didn't know these guys were suiting up now."

"Well, their management has been doing well lately." Bernini sniffled and wiped his nose with his handkerchief. "He must've done something to piss them off."

"Or maybe they were just bored." Rebecca released the hold on his collar and placed the pen back into her belt. She stood up and sighed. "Gee, I wonder who did this to him?"

"Don't get smart, Ortega. It's not what you know—"

"Right, right. Is this all you wanted to show me?"

"More or less." Bernini called out to the coroners. "We're done here, guys. Drag this poor bastard out of here."

The men dressed in depressing uniforms nodded to Bernini and brought their stretcher to the dead body. Rebecca stared at the sand for a moment. She felt a small nudge against her side. She turned and saw Bernini direct her toward the body with his eyes.

"Oh shit! Wait! Wait!" She jogged over to the body and pulled out her pen again. She stuck it under his suit jacket and flipped it open. She looked at the inside and saw a bulge in the inside pocket. "Hey, can one of you get me a glove?"

One of the coroners nodded and walked to the ambulance to retrieve a box of clear sanitary gloves. He held the box in front of her, and she pulled out a single glove. She smiled at him and began to put it on. She then reached into the pocket and pulled out a thick leather wallet, wet but intact. She opened the wallet and sounded off its contents to Bernini.

"Got his driver's license. William Theodore Glasson . . . wow, what a name. Anyways, let's see . . . an American Express card, a video store card, a grocery store discount card and . . . fifty dollars in cash. Nothing else."

"Nice job, Ortega." Bernini smiled at her and waved the coroners on. He pulled out a clear evidence bag and let Rebecca drop in the wallet. She raised her head toward the sky and closed her eyes. She breathed softly and let her head fall back into her chest.

"What's the matter?" Bernini asked.

"Tired. Just tired."

"Welcome to the club."

"One question, Detective . . ."

"No, it does not end."

Rebecca opened her eyes and stared at the ground. She nodded her head as if a spirit would rise from the sand and comfort her. She chuckled. She walked past Detective Bernini and made her way to the police cruiser.

"Thought so," she said.

*   *   *

Slim had shoved his nose against her thigh, white and pale from the cocaine he spilled. He licked her knee and snorted the cocaine that ran up to her waist. He coughed, almost uncontrollably, to the point that even his paid guest displayed a face of concern. He stopped coughing and cleared his throat. He started to laugh and rubbed his nostrils with the back of his hand.

"Seven inches!" Slim sniffled and rubbed the corner of his eyes. "Oh, damn . . . that's a record!"

The girl laughed and wrapped her thigh around his neck. "I think there's more to lick, baby."

"Hang on. I need one more line. This is some good shit, Pedro."

Pedro was sitting in a chair facing Slim and the girl they had recently purchased. He was still the same Estrada male, with a faint look of sadness in his eyes. They were red and forever puffed from months of sleepless nights. He kept seeing his father, the great Luis Estrada, entering the room with his back turned to him. Even as Pedro saw Slim slide his wet tongue up the girl's thigh and settle on her navel, he saw Luis staring out a window. Sometimes he heard him talk, sometimes speaking to the window and not to Pedro. He merely carried on a discussion with a reflection of what Pedro used to be, while avoiding what Pedro became.

Pedro rolled up his shirt sleeves and bore his tattoos that were implanted in his forearms. They were so colored and so detailed that it was impossible to discern what images and symbols he had decided to engrave in his skin. Pedro himself did not even know. It was just one of many ways to cope with the loss of his humanity, if he had even been born with one.

He brushed his cheek with his hand and looked in a mirror that lay on his desk. Pedro saw his reflection amid the crumbs of powder. His face was tired and wrinkled; his nostrils were as red as the blood he had spilled on his hands when he pulled that trigger all those years ago. He looked down at his palms and he could still see the smears of dried plasma that crept between his fingers. He shook his head and combed his fingers through his spiked hair. He was old, and deep down, he knew he deserved it.

"Mr. Mal wanted to know when we were gonna share the wealth."

"Fuck him." Slim kissed the girl on her neck.

"He needs the money, Slim."

"And you need to come join me here. You gotta taste this sugar while it's still on her skin. I'm not joking, man—it adds flavor."

Pedro stood up and rummaged through the desk drawers. He pulled out a small leather bag and flipped it upside down. He watched a small, pitiful rain of money fall on the desk. He threw the bag down on the floor and counted the stack of bills that sat in front of him. He got to the last stack and let it slide off his hand. "We owe him three grand."

Slim was already inches towards the girl's inner thighs when he heard Pedro's heavy sighs. He dropped his forehead in her crotch and breathed a long and annoyed sigh. He shot up from the girl's pelvis and stood on his feet.

"Go on. Get the fuck out." Slim brushed her away with his pale hands. The girl had a confused look on her face, but she shrugged it off and began to grab her clothes.

"I said get the fuck out!" Slim grabbed her arm and made her yelp in pain. He lifted her off her feet and threw her at the office door. Her head slammed against the frame and split open her upper lip. She was crying already. Slim stooped down to pick up her clothes and hurled them at her face. She held onto the clothes like a screaming child holding on to her security blanket and sprinted out the room. The door slammed shut behind her. Slim rolled his eyes and walked back to Pedro.

"Give that bitch to him. Should cover it." Slim plopped himself in a nearby chair. He let one leg hang off the armrest as he stared at the ceiling.

"That won't be enough, you know that." Pedro paused for a moment. "Give him what's left of that."

Pedro pointed to a small box that sat in a corner in the room. It was bursting with tiny clear bags of cocaine. Slim followed Pedro's finger and immediately sneered at what resulted from its direction.

"Fuck that!" he yelled. "That's hard-earned sugar there! Give him something else!"

"Slim." Pedro walked slowly to the open box. "He got rid of that snitch for us. Without that, we—"

"Will had it coming!"

"*We* almost had it coming. Look, let's just give him that and maybe he won't bust our balls."

Slim lied down on his back and lightly hit his head against the floor. He repeated this three times, all while cursing under his breath. "Fine."

Pedro nodded and picked up the box. He did not bother closing it as he walked out the door. A guard was stationed outside the door, dressed in baggy jeans and a long white T-shirt. He sat in a chair that faced the hallway. It was still the same hallway with old paint and a stench that could only be described as "empty." It was dead, unloving, and with no substance. Pedro once inhaled the air—to try and catch a glimpse of a scent—and still, nothing. The mansion was as dead as Luis Estrada. Whereas Luis's body was decomposing in the bay, the mansion was polluted with drugs and cheap hookers.

Pedro handed the box over to the door guard. He thrust his hands into his pockets and sighed as he talked. "Take this over to Mal. He'll know why."

The guardsman nodded and stood up. He set the box on the floor before he reached underneath his large shirt and pulled out a handheld radio. He held it to his mouth and spoke in a deep, blunt voice. "Yo, Vince, watch the door right quick."

The guardsman waited until a gang member dressed as his twin approached him. They nodded to each other, and the original guard picked up the box and walked away. Pedro turned around and walked back inside the office. Slim was still on the floor, sleeping. Pedro shook his head and threw himself in his office chair. He laid himself back and closed his eyes. He felt his head drop into his chest, and he strangely wondered if his father had felt the same weight of skull land upon his own when he died.

*   *   *

The mirror was framed by a golden medley of roses and leaves. Some thorns were seen etched within a miniscule gap, but only if one studied the mirror frame with dense study. Some of the gold plates had chipped off in the corners, most likely due to the excess of moisture in the washroom. But despite the faded corners, the mirror was as beautiful as it was many years ago, still raising the torch of beauty and decadence to heaven's gates. The golden hues were just beams of sunlight that never escaped the roses; the thorns had pricked away at the sun and let droplets of yellow blood slide down its prickly needles.

Zephyr studied these details every time she entered this particular bathroom with such depth, such amazement. She especially gazed at the image shown before her: strands of wavy black hair creeping around her shoulder, like tendrils of a dark room dripping over her infallible face. Her lips were full but not plump, holding a balance between exceptional beauty and humility. They sparkled with a subtle lip gloss that was colorless in its function. She smiled in the mirror, letting the same dimples she was born with burrow even deeper into both cheeks. Her smile suddenly ceased its existence, never fading or giving a clue that she was not going to smile anymore. It was quick, sharp, like a knife wielded by a thief's hand.

She cupped her breasts in her hands and shifted them in her dress. It was a simple silk outfit with a pair of straps that swung neatly over her shoulders. The fabric that reached across her chest created a natural wave in front of her cleavage. Zephyr had a figure that was toned and tanned underneath the compassionate European sun. Her body was as warm and comforting as a sea breeze, but it was just a blanket meant to cover her frigid heart.

Cold were her eyes, those pair of silver orbs that peeked out of her black, gloomy eyeliner. Her eyelashes did nothing to cover her most valuable assets, nor did she allow anything to obstruct her piercing vision. Zephyr was unashamed of the shocked stares of people walking in the streets whenever they glanced at them. She flaunted them with such narcissism, such self-confidence in their magnetic powers that she grew accustomed to bending others' wills to her own.

She smirked in the mirror. She picked up a thin stick of mascara and gently combed it through her eyelashes. Her nails matched her eyes perfectly. She watched them hover past her face as she went from one eye to the next. She set the rod back into its container and inhaled, but not as deeply as anyone else would inhale. She knew that there were others who would breathe in the air as if it was the last piece of atmosphere available to them. Everyone else would have done so.

But, she thought, no one else was like her.

Zephyr blew herself a kiss and walked out of the washroom. She bent down and tightened the strap laced around her ankle. She wore a pair of black pumps that formed a horizontal line around the base of her toes and split off into two more strands that reached around the rest of her foot, finally ending behind her small ankles. The only jewelry she wore was an earring in each ear—icicles, rather. They were an element that befitted her soul, and she chose these because of this eerie analogy. She brushed her eyebrows with the tip of her index fingers and walked down the stairs. Zephyr was a beautiful woman encased in a glacier, a maiden forever entombed in an icy coffin.

"Honey, are you ready?" Rosa's soft voice called out to her daughter from the bottom of the stairs. Zephyr descended the steps and smiled at her mother. Rosa did little to age, although there was always a wrinkle of sadness around her eyes. She smiled with Zephyr and held it there for a moment.

"Yeah . . . I'm ready."

Zephyr talked with a whispered voice that seemed to travel along wind currents. It was a soft breath best described as a calm wind that dried the brow of a farmer toiling in the fields, underneath a vindictive sun. She reached Rosa and threw her arms around her. Rosa held her tight and chuckled.

"You look so beautiful, sweetie."

"Thanks, *Mami*."

Rosa stepped back and remained silent.

"What's wrong?" Zephyr asked.

"Oh . . . it's nothing." Rosa stared at the floor before she looked back at Zephyr. "I'm just worried, that's all."

"I'll be okay. It's . . . what I need to do."

"I know, Zephyr, I know . . ."

Zephyr hugged her mother. "I promise—everything will be all right."

Rosa did not say a word. She only held Zephyr's face in her palm and smiled. Zephyr held her hand and nodded.

"Is *Abuela* in the car?"

"Yeah, she's there."

Both women stepped outside and saw Raquel patiently waiting in the back seat of a taxi cab. She did not age either, claiming that it was the oranges and grapes she ate every day that kept her youth. A few spots of gray sneaked themselves into her hair, but they were merely a sign of mortal maturation. But her spirit was as youthful as ever, bringing a bright light into the household, so much that the shine almost blinded the Estrada women. She cared little; it was her way of streaming comedy into years of tragedy.

"*Dios!* What took you so freaking long? I've been waiting out here for twenty years! Look at me—I aged because of you!"

Zephyr laughed. "I didn't mean to keep you waiting."

"I'm surprised you're still alive! I thought you drowned in that long shower of yours. How long does it take to bathe anyway?"

"It's not bathing, it's meditation." Zephyr kept smiling. Her eyes were twinkling with joy.

"Well, I was meditating on leaving without you." Raquel laughed and walked over to Zephyr with open arms. "Oh, honey, you know I'm kidding. You look so beautiful."

"Thank you . . . so much." Zephyr squeezed her tight. Raquel kissed her granddaughter on her cheek.

"C'mon and get in so that people will think a supermodel's in the car."

"I'm far away from being a supermodel, *Abuela*."

"You? I was talking about me!"

Zephyr laughed and shook her head. She entered the cab with Raquel. Rosa waved them off and let the taxi carry them off to their destination.

"Are you ready?" Raquel asked.

"I'll be honest . . . I am a bit nervous."

"Relax, relax . . . I'll take care of it, angel. All you have to do is look pretty and be yourself. They'll love you the minute you enter the room."

Zephyr nodded and stared out the window. She let the towers of stress pass her face, with the glare of the blue sky and pale clouds shining on the windows. Raquel's words echoed in her mind, and she let them accompany her the entire way. She looked over at her grandmother, and she curiously wondered why she winked at Zephyr. She smiled and closed her pale eyes until they arrived.

The ride was memorable, Zephyr thought, or at least it should have been. The streets were recognized yet easily forgotten. Her mind was concentrating on the event ahead—an interview that she could no longer procrastinate. It had to be done if she ever hoped to return to the country that she had abandoned.

Zephyr looked at her grandmother. She was smiling as she stared outside the window. Zephyr curiously wondered about her joyous expressions, but she could only pretend to be a mind-reader. But she did recognize those optimistic eyes that watched over her as a child. If Zephyr tripped and fell, she was there to dust off her knees and kiss the wounds. If she read a bedtime story, Raquel was there to listen despite her heavy, sleepy eyelids. Most of all, if Zephyr cried, in memory of her father passed on, Raquel would be there to remind her of the joys of life, of the happiness deserved by everyone. If it was not for her grandmother, Zephyr thought, depression would strangle Zephyr and crush her lungs until she eventually gave up her reason for living.

Zephyr memorized Rosa's wave when the taxi drove away. It was bathed in reluctance, to see her only daughter leave home for a new future. She gave Zephyr the knowledge of women and, more importantly, the wisdom of a gifted queen. She trained Zephyr in all aspects of form: the elegance of physical movement, the poise of emotions, the attainment of knowledge, and the cleansing of spirit. Rosa felt that these attributes were necessary for a woman to reveal herself fully unto this world. "Ease is not a luxury," Rosa once told Zephyr. "If you want things to be easy, then make it so."

Zephyr echoed this thought even after the cab pulled up to a curb. Zephyr looked at the building without blinking, studying it with quick yet detailed glances. It was a simple restaurant geared towards attracting the tourist crowd. It had a quaint lobby that sat behind a set of frosted glass doors. She squinted her eyes and noticed a group of men walking around the room and laughing occasionally. Their hairs were grayed, their suits were tailored, and their knowledge was apparent on their wrinkled faces. These were the *originales,* she thought. These were her father's precursors—the men of crime.

Both women exited the cab and met the warm spring air with closed eyes and deep sighs. Raquel walked toward the glass doors as Zephyr followed. She opened the door for her granddaughter with a smirk on her face.

"Age before beauty," she joked.

They entered the restaurant and noticed a lone man cleaning the bar. He stood in front of colorful glasses of liquor that reflected the soft light of the restaurant. Raquel approached him and spoke a few words with him. He nodded and continued to wipe down the bar with a dry cloth. Raquel then returned to Zephyr.

"He said that everyone is ready and waiting upstairs."

Zephyr nodded. She walked toward the staircase that stood to the side of the bar. Raquel stayed behind and watched her slowly ascend the staircase. Zephyr had a look of strength and confidence on her face. She showed no fear or reluctance in her gait, and she kept her cold white eyes on the goal in front of her. Raquel ordered a glass of champagne and prayed underneath her breath.

"God, keep her safe . . ."

*   *   *

Zephyr walked through a long, white hallway filled with decorative vases and cushioned seats. There was a pair of two large doors at the end of the hallway. She chuckled. *So clichéd*, she thought.

As she walked, she felt a handful of eyes stare at her back. Some men had followed her as soon as she had ascended the staircase. Zephyr knew that they were simple guardsmen, an army communed to protect. She stopped walking and turned around to meet their glances. They flinched at Zephyr's pair of haunting eyes, glaring at them with such ferocity that the men slammed their hands against their chests, perhaps to confirm that their hearts were still beating. She remained stoic as she turned back around and continued her approach, but the men refused to follow her further.

Zephyr stopped in front of the doors and placed her hand on the doorknob. She inhaled deeply, and then she smoothly exhaled. She slightly jerked her head to flick a strand of hair away from her face. She entered the room and approached three men who immediately observed her air of confidence and, especially, her cold silver eyes.

"Good evening, gentlemen," she said in a whispered, almost windy voice.

"Welcome." One of them spoke first. He was a tall man adorned with a lanky frame and a bald head. He wore a custom-made gray suit, possibly to hide his rather emaciated body.

"Thank you for this audience," Zephyr replied.

"Please, have a seat," said the second man. He was the complete opposite of the tall boss, a heavyweight man who looked to be in his early seventies. He had wrinkles all around his eyes and at the peaks of his forehead. He had a full head of hair, but it was the same color as Zephyr's eyes. She was surprised that he was still alive, but she realized that he may have actually been middle-aged. He was a man forcefully matured by the life he led and followed.

"It is not often that we congregate like this," said the tall man, "especially for someone of your . . . stature. However, you will receive the same treatment as others before you."

"I promise that your time and energy will be spent well."

The tall man nodded and ended his introduction. The second boss observed Zephyr for a moment before he spoke.

"From here on out, we will inquire you about anything that is relevant to our interview. You will answer with the utmost honesty."

Zephyr kept her posture in her seat, as if a steel rod was in place of her spine. "I understand. All my answers will be infallible."

"State your full name."

"Zephyr Rita Philomena Estrada."

The third man flinched in his chair. Zephyr glanced at him and saw a boss who was past his middle age but still maintained a glimmer of youth. He must have found a way to resist nature's bond, Zephyr thought. He quickly regained his composure and continued to listen to his associates' questions.

"Religion?" the first man asked.

"Roman Catholic."

"On what day were you born?"

"The seventeenth of October, twenty-two years ago. It was a Friday night."

"Which hand do you write with?" the second man inquired.

"Left."

"Are you a virgin?"

Zephyr paused for a moment, as if the question was inappropriate and irrelevant to her succession.

"I meant in the sense that you haven't committed any crimes."

"Not yet," she calmly answered.

The three men were silent for a moment. The third boss broke the silence; his speech was unusually low and halted.

"Who is your father?"

Zephyr looked at the floor and briefly lost herself in thought. She answered his question with an air of mourning. "My father was Don Luis Vicente Miguel Estrada."

"I see . . ." The third man cleared his throat and continued his questioning. "How did he die?"

"Murdered . . . by my former brother: Don Pedro Alberto Jose Estrada."

He fell silent as he stared at the floor. The first man resumed the interview for him.

"You want to be ascended, to exact revenge?"

"Yes." Zephyr did not hesitate in her answer. "I do."

"Why? It will not bring—"

"No," Zephyr interrupted, "it will not bring my father back. However, I want the same amount of blood to shed from my brother's veins. He did not deserve the title of Don, nor did he even deserve to live even today. Perhaps it is my anger that drives me, but nevertheless, I will pursue him and restore honor to my father. That I promise."

"That was very rude of you to interrupt me, Miss Estrada. I did not give you permission to speak."

"I am not being rude. I simply answered your question before you finished."

"So you preempted me."

"Exactly."

The first man nodded his head and smirked. He motioned with his hand toward the second boss. He sat up straight and spoke to Zephyr.

"You will kill him, is that correct?"

"He is no longer my brother. He revoked his birthright the moment he pulled the trigger. He will die in the same manner that my father died—cold, alone, and surrounded by those who hate him. I often imagine the blood pouring out of his chest and spilling onto the floor—hot, steaming blood spilled by my own blade. I do not care. This thought entertained me from the moment I set foot on this soil. I have had dreams about this for years, and I woke up crying because it was a dream I had yet to realize. But I digress. The fact, gentlemen, is that Pedro did not care. He only cared about being a Don. And nothing drove him away from his lust. Now all he does is rule an empire stolen from the true king and claiming the throne as a laughing jester. Even now he is smiling. Even now, as we sit here, he is smiling at my father. More importantly, he is smiling at me. He is mocking us both, and that is intolerable. And that is where I find myself, gentlemen. I desperately want to spill his blood. Oh, if you only knew how much I lust for it. In all honesty, I want him to die slowly, painfully . . . and when it seems that he will pass on to the next realm, I will revive him back to full health. I will thoroughly mend his wounds, down to the last scar on his finger. I will tell him how sorry I am, how regretful I am for causing him pain. I will buy him new clothes, send money to his bank accounts, and even hire a prostitute to give satisfaction to his hungers. I will do anything to make him better. Anything.

"Then I will repeat my torture. I will personally burn the clothes off his back and throw him to the floor. I will have my men take knives in their hands and slice the skin off his legs. I want his wounds healed with salt. I want him to look into my eyes and beg me to stop. And that is when I sever his strings that bind him to this life. I want his soul out of his miserable body. Right now, you are possibly looking at me as a sick-minded woman, someone who is not mentally well. A sadist, even. But let me assure you, gentlemen, that my mind is sound. Perhaps I am a monster for speaking these words, but my actions are charitable compared to what others before me have done, including you." Zephyr paused and looked around the room. "We all have black souls, do we not? Have you confessed your sins, all those immoral acts you have performed for the sake of profit? Have you dropped to your knees and *implored* God for forgiveness? Neither have I. But I have promised to bring myself back into the sight of God, if He deems me worthy to acquaint his presence. Until then, these things I will do. And believe me when I say that I can do much worse to him. Oh, the plans that I have . . . but I am magnanimous in my strategy, for I am still a child of God. However, this is indeed what I want, and I will *not* apologize for it."

All three men seemed to swallow hard at the same time. The first man rubbed his arms as if he was naked in a Russian winter. The second boss had his mouth slightly opened in shock—no words came out of his mouth or a subtle breath of air. The third man only looked at Zephyr. He just studied her eyes and the way she spoke. She was not lying, he realized. She knew what she wanted, and she was straightforward with it. Zephyr turned her blank eyes toward him, and she was surprised that he showed no sign of fear, but he did exhibit a wondrous expression. His gaze was curious yet controlled. Zephyr smirked at him, and he blinked himself out of his deep trance.

"We will reconvene tomorrow evening," the third boss said, "Miss Estrada . . ." He nodded his head, as if he understood her every word and purpose.

"I appreciate your audience, gentlemen."

She uncrossed her legs and stood up on her heels. The men acknowledged her wish to exit and stood up with her. She bowed her head and walked out of the room. Zephyr kept her cold eyes straight ahead and maintained her peaceful poise. She knew she had done what she could. She descended the staircase and met her grandmother at the bar. Raquel gulped down the last sliver of champagne she had in the glass. She smiled at her and motioned her to sit.

"How'd it go?"

"Okay, I suppose," she answered. "They said that they will get back to me with an answer tomorrow."

"Well, that's good. At least they're considering it."

"That's what I figured. In any case, their decision won't affect anything I had planned. I just need the title as the salt on my meat."

Raquel looked at her granddaughter with sadness. "I know, sweetie . . ." She became silent, but quickly regained her speech. "So tell me . . . none of them were staring at what you got, right?"

Zephyr chuckled. "What're you talking about? I've nothing."

"Hey, don't lie. You know old men's habits die hard. You're not exactly ugly, thank God. You have good genes in your system."

"Yes, and those genes came from you and *Mami*."

"Smart girl." Raquel got out of the bar stool and walked with Zephyr out the door. "So you knocked them dead?"

Zephyr giggled as she waved the bartender over. "I decided to keep them alive for now."

*   *   *

The three bosses were still inside the hotel room when Zephyr left them to think about her chilling words. It felt as if the cold air she brought with her had never faded from the walls. Each boss paced the room and kept his stare toward hell. The first boss cleared his throat before he spoke to his brothers in urban arms.

"So . . . any thoughts?"

The second boss walked over to a table that raised a family of liquors towards the room light. He picked up a bottle of scotch and poured the tanned drink into a short glass. He downed the drink in one motion and gasped for breath as he poured another helping. He drank it slower this time, but he had to catch his breath again.

"Jesus, Antonio, take it easy."

"Well, shit! What do you think I'm trying to do? Didn't that bitch freak you out?"

"Yeah . . . she did. Those were the weirdest eyes I've ever seen. The minute I saw those things . . . I don't know."

"She swallowed your soul, Benito?" The third boss sat in a chair and spoke to his comrades, but he did not face them. He did not want them to look at the fear on his face.

"I felt like she did."

"Anyone else want a drink?" Antonio asked. "I will drink this whole damn bar away if I have to."

"I'm okay," the third boss answered. "I need to be sober for this."

Antonio poured another glass of scotch and sat down in a nearby sofa. He sipped a little of it then sighed in satisfaction as he slouched into the sofa. He looked at the third boss and chuckled. "Emmanuel, you've been quiet. Still thinking about her too?"

"I am . . . actually." Emmanuel became silent for a moment. "She's beautiful."

"I'm not gonna lie," Antonio said. "She did take my breath away."

"You sure it wasn't a heart attack?" Emmanuel joked.

"Well, if it was, I wouldn't mind dying over her at all!"

"But you'll die over anyone that is marginally pretty."

"She's different—she's not marginal."

"I have to agree with him," Benito said. "She is exceptional. She spoke as if she didn't care about our decision, as if she would've run out and killed anyway. I felt she was a bit arrogant, but . . . damn, I forgot what I was gonna say. I keep seeing those goddamned eyes in my head."

"And that's why I'm getting drunk tonight," Antonio said.

Emmanuel nodded slightly and pulled out a cigar. He put it in his mouth without lighting it, losing himself in thought with a large strawberry-flavored cigar between his lips.

"What's on your mind?" Benito asked.

"Oh . . . nothing. Just thinking."

"About?"

"Zephyr Estrada."

"No shit. I mean what about?"

Emmanuel shrugged his shoulders. "Maybe it's just me, but . . . did you notice something about her eyes?"

"You mean besides the fact that they're whiter than a snowstorm?"

"Not just that. They were . . . intense. Almost magnetic. I managed to sum up some courage and stare at them. I saw so much power and raw ambition in them. As you said, they robbed me of . . . something. Maybe it was my soul, I don't know. But for some odd reason, I wasn't afraid."

Both Antonio and Benito looked at Emmanuel with blank looks on their faces. They wanted to pin their thoughts with words, but each felt a feline's paw slamming on their tongues.

"I'm sorry," Emmanuel continued. "I guess I need some rest." He chuckled nervously, but no one laughed with him. "If I have to make the final decision, I'm gonna need as much sleep as possible. But we all know how it will turn out."

"Well," Benito started, "I think she's pretty sincere about killing someone. Maybe we'll have to discard tradition for once and employ a female as a member of our group. Zephyr will—"

"Fuck that!" Antonio spoke out loud after he gulped down another drink. "We're only allowed to promote people with normal eyes, for fuck's sake."

"Oh, just get drunk already. Emmanuel and I will discuss things with you tomorrow morning." Benito turned to Emmanuel with a smile. "I'll see you in the morning."

Emmanuel nodded and walked past them both. He reached the hotel room door, but he paused for a moment and spoke over his shoulder. "Zephyr was right when she said that we've done much worse than what she plans to do. I think we should give her that much."

"She's still an arrogant bitch," Antonio pointed out.

Emmanuel chuckled and turned the doorknob. "Probably why I like her."

*   *   *

Zephyr returned home with Raquel and had a quiet dinner with her mother. Rosa had been cooking the whole time while she was home alone. Her feast was brimming with sweet scents of love and effort that filled the entire dining room. She had made a batch of yellow rice with tiny dots of red and green peppers in the mix. A plate full of fresh mixed vegetables sat to the side of large pieces of chicken breasts, stuffed with a white sauce of which Rosa refused to divulge.

"It's a secret," she said. "Besides, it tastes too good to question where it came from, right?"

"Well, don't think about poisoning me." Raquel joked. "I mean, go ahead and knock Zephyr the hell out—she needs to build more character. Just don't poison your mother-in-law, all right? I'm too young to die!"

Later that evening, when all of their stomachs were full of food and their hearts were filled with laughter, they bade good wishes for the coming slumber and retired to their beds. Zephyr had changed into an oversized white T-shirt, where its hem reached past her upper thighs. She wore a pair of navy-blue sweatpants that were loose and spilled over her ankles. Her hair was lazily pouring over her shoulders, with a few wide strands falling over the right side of her face. Her jewelry was off of her body, no makeup could be seen on her face, and she had showered off her fragrances.

Zephyr walked over to her mother's bedroom and gently knocked on the door frame. Rosa was reading another romance novel when she looked up and saw her daughter standing beautifully in her room. She shook her head and chuckled.

"How many times do I have to tell you that you don't ever have to knock when you visit me?" She smiled widely and patted the mattress to let Zephyr sit next to her.

"It's a habit," Zephyr replied. "You and *Abuela* were the ones who kept teaching me these things."

"And I'm glad you remembered."

Zephyr smiled. She and her mother were more of a pair of close friends than mother and daughter. They would always talk about everything: clothes, life, men, how to be confident, professionalism, men. Zephyr and Rosa were practicing this ritual even tonight, on the quiet eve of Zephyr's ascension.

"So what do you think I should wear tomorrow?" Zephyr asked with an innocent tone to her voice.

"Well, you have a neutral skin tone—courtesy of me, of course. Wear blue . . . why not?"

"Maybe. I think I have jewelry to match it. Somewhere."

"I like how you say *somewhere* as if you have a messy room. I mean, geez, can't you just leave a pair of shoes lying around, just to make it look like you actually live in it?"

"I thought parents liked kids with cleanliness."

"Normal kids, Zephyr."

They both chuckled; they looked at one another with smiles in their cheeks and stars in their eyes. The laughs died off into echoes as they suddenly found themselves in silence. Zephyr was staring at a spot on the bed. She was nowhere near normal, and she figured that it was a fact unintentionally mentioned by Rosa.

"I remember that one time," Rosa interrupted the quiet, "when I bought you those books. The classic ones. I think some of them were abridged. I mean . . . what ten-year-old reads *War and Peace*? Yes, I know you would—don't even think about giving me that look, silly." Rosa snickered. "Anyways, I remember when I gave you *The Count of Monte Cristo*, and for some reason, your eyes just...lit up! You snatched the book out of my hand and you flipped open the pages like they were on fire! I saw how fast you read those words and . . . you were so happy, Zephyr. I'd never seen you happier . . ."

Rosa trailed off her words and looked away from Zephyr. She kept replaying the memory of her giddy daughter holding the book in one hand and hugging her mother with the other. Her white eyes glimmered with joy. Zephyr thanked Rosa at least half a dozen times, and then she finished off the rest of her glee later that same night, when she gently knocked on the doorframe and had the book in her arms. "Can I read a paragraph for you, *Mami*?" Rosa had been dead asleep when Zephyr knocked, but she was always awake for her only little girl. "Sure, honey," she would answer. Zephyr screamed, "Yay!" and immediately flicked on the light switch. Rosa ignored the sudden glare of yellow light that beamed on her pupils, forcing them to dilate prematurely. Zephyr jumped on the bed and opened the book where she had marked the page she wanted to read. Rosa was surprised at how quickly little Zephyr had read the book—it was the last page.

"Wait and hope!" Zephyr exclaimed.

Rosa felt her eyes heat up and her lips quiver. She was hoping—praying—that Zephyr did not notice her tears. But her daughter was not normal, just as they both said earlier. Zephyr knew everything. Rosa knew this, but she still kept her face turned.

"*Mami* . . ." Zephyr placed her hand on Rosa's.

"Oh, Zephyr! I wish there was another way! There has to be! We never meant for you to be raised this way! There had to be some other way!"

Zephyr felt her lips form a deep frown. "It's . . . the only way, *Mami*. This is what I—"

"But, Zephyr! You could've had a happy life! Oh God, I'm so sorry! I'm a horrible mother!"

Zephyr grabbed her mother's shoulders. "You're not a horrible mother!" Zephyr said sternly. "You're not!"

Rosa sniffled. "It's just . . . your father . . . he—"

"He would not have wanted me to be this way, I know . . . but . . ." Zephyr's voice became increasingly silent. "It's what I need to do. We all know that."

"You need to be happy, Zephyr! I want you to be happy! To have a normal life, get married, have kids! To smile more! You don't smile anymore!"

Zephyr lowered her head as if she was humbled by a harsh punishment. She had nothing to say; Rosa was right. She did not smile anymore, and if she did smile, it was a brief moment of refuge into bliss.

"Baby," Rosa said, "I'm so sorry . . . I didn't mean to say that."

"No . . . you're right. I don't smile like I used to anymore. It's like . . . I don't know . . . I forgot how to smile. But I am happy with you and *Abuela*, even if I don't show it often. I promise that after everything is done, I will be okay."

Rosa wiped her face and looked into her daughter's eyes. She could always tell if Zephyr was telling the truth or not. Her silver eyes twinkled with joy when she was being truthful and remained the same if she was lying. Rosa read her eyes as she did for years and years. She stroked Zephyr's cheek with deep sadness and caution, as if she was worried that she would disturb a skin cell. She hugged Zephyr. Zephyr held her as tightly as she did, eyes closed and mouth clenched.

"No, you won't," Rosa whispered.

*   *   *

Emmanuel woke up from a miserable sleep and proceeded to walk downstairs. He looked out of the window, counting the water droplets and the sparkles of moonlight that trapped themselves inside that clear bubble. He opened the window and inhaled the moist air. It reminded him of his younger years where he wasn't called a Don. He sighed. He knew that those years were long forgotten and long destroyed. This is who he was, and he accepted it.

Her eyes still haunted him. They were so ethereal, so ghastly that he swore they spoke to him. "Accept her, Emmanuel Elizondo. She is true. Better than anyone else." Emmanuel knew that she truly was the best. Her ambition preceded her words: the way she walked, the posture she adopted, even the whisper in her voice that showed her calculated and calm attitude.

Emmanuel walked toward the front door and grabbed his car keys. He needed to drive away, purge those eyes away from his mind. Even as he walked outside, they followed him, studying his actions. He was still in his nightwear when he entered the car and turned on the ignition. The car started, and he backed out of his driveway.

He chuckled. He was so terrified of car bombs that he had a remote on his car key that unlocked the car door and started the ignition. Before the technology was available, he would reach his car, get on his hands and knees, and inspect the underside of the vehicle. He never found a car bomb, but he never took the chance of starting the car without proper inspection. And yet here he was, driving the car like he did before, before he became a don.

After a half hour had passed, he returned home. The image of Zephyr was still in his mind but not as menacing. The rain was falling hard. He looked around and noticed a pair of red lights leave the horizon. He tried to make out the image and realized that it was a car that had just left his driveway. A shadow brushed past a front window and disappeared deeper into the house. Without thinking, he reached underneath his seat and pulled out a small pistol. He did not need to check if he had bullets; this gun was so personal to him that he knew the amount of ammunition in it by weight alone. He hid the gun behind his back and snuck toward the door.

He walked around the perimeter of his home and carefully looked in each window. He found no silhouette of anyone present. He quietly entered a side door and swept each room on the first floor. He reached the staircase. He knew which step creaked and which one did not. He skipped certain steps, his gun still firmly clenched in his hand. He reached the top floor and hugged the wall toward his bedroom.

It was the first room that sat on the second floor. He designed it this way in case an intruder entered his home—such as tonight. He figured that a murderer would naturally head for the largest master bedroom at the far end of the hall. Emmanuel could exit the room, stab the bastard with a thin stiletto, and call a friend to dispose of the body. He crept down on his knees, took a deep breath, and swiftly entered the room.

A slim figure sat at the edge of his bed; he only saw the person's back. His eyes adjusted to the darkness, and he could see the figure of a woman. She had long hair, a slender back, and a pair of gentle shoulders. He hands were folded in front of her in a solemn prayer. She remained still, even as she heard the faint breath of Emmanuel behind her.

"I haven't been in this room for almost thirty years . . ." she said.

She turned around and looked at Emmanuel. His mouth dropped in shock almost as fast as he dropped the gun on the floor. He was frozen. The figure smiled at him in an innocent manner.

"*Dios mio* . . ." Emmanuel whispered.

"Hi, Manny . . ." whispered Raquel.

*   *   *

Raquel never knew how right she was when she had mentioned her past residency in Emmanuel's home. They both stared at each other in such a way that no one could ever doubt their years apart. Raquel was smiling shyly. Emmanuel could only hold back hot tears from his eyes when he studied the figure before him, to make sure that he was shedding them only for her and not for an imposter.

She moved closer into the light and slowly walked to Emmanuel. He did not blink, nor did he attempt to move away from her. She had cast a spell on him, some sort of black magic that forced him to stay still and become captured by her joyous spirit.

"Raquel . . ." he muttered. She kept smiling at him, even as he tried to understand her arrival. He felt the side of his mouth quiver, to match her smile with his, but he immediately forced it away from its moment of joy. "What are you doing here?" Emmanuel said it as if he hated to see her here, in his bedroom, after all these years.

"I came to see you . . ."

"You shouldn't be here," he said sternly.

Raquel sighed. "You're still as stubborn as ever! You know why I needed to come!"

"I told you why! Years ago!" Emmanuel's eyes squinted in the night light. "What part of that did you not understand?"

"Bullshit, Manny! You're always trying to push me away! Why? Is it because of you?! What you're doing now? Tell me!"

"I don't have to explain a goddamned thing to you! Why did you come here?"

"You idiot . . . you are such an idiot."

"Why did you come here, Raquel?"

"Because of your granddaughter!"

Emmanuel felt his jaw drop and freeze midway down its descent. He felt his body suddenly wishing to perish. He wanted to fall on the floor. He even willed it. But his body refused to obey his wish. His body told him to remain standing, to remain speechless, and to quiver under Raquel's command.

"You knew it, didn't you?" Raquel started. "You knew Zephyr was your granddaughter from the moment she walked into the room. You listened to her speak, you studied her face . . . you remembered her last name. My last name. Didn't you?"

Emmanuel was still frozen. Only his eyes moved, and its movements were confined to shock.

"Answer me, Manny! You knew it, didn't you?" Raquel felt streams of tears running down her face. "Zephyr told me what the bosses said today. What they all asked her . . . you were the only one who asked her about her father. How he died. Who killed him . . . you were the only one!"

Emmanuel felt his heart shake. His eyes started to get hot. His body let more parts of him function. But he was still frozen.

"Fucking answer me, Manny!" Raquel was sobbing.

"Oh God . . . no. No, no, no, no, no. Not Luis. Not my son . . ." Emmanuel finally felt his knees buckle. He dropped to the floor and ignored the sudden sharp pain that bolted up his legs. His volitional avoidance of reality was now too massive to carry. "Not our son . . ."

"Do you know what we went through all these years? Do you? You know how hard it was to see Zephyr grow up with so much hatred? She was an innocent child! She was such an angel, and now look at her!"

"Luis . . . my son . . ."

"He was my son too, Manny! He was our son! Oh God . . . why did this happen to us?"

Emmanuel grabbed Raquel's hips and brought her down to the floor with her. She wrapped her arms around him and let him feel every tear that dropped from her chin. She was angry at herself for letting herself cry like this. Raquel never allowed sadness to happen to her. She cried because she was spiteful of her own despair, and she wanted Emmanuel to feel every drop.

"I denied it, Raquel! I tried to! I refused to accept . . . oh, damn it! Let go of me!" Emmanuel pried himself away from her, but she felt a hole of air between them, and immediately she pulled him back to her chest. "I said let me go! Let me die here! Let me go to hell! I deserve it!"

"Oh, Manny . . . don't say that. Please. Don't . . ."

"I never wanted this for him! I never wanted this from him!" Emmanuel kept repeating these words as Raquel held him tight. She waited for his voice to exhaust itself before she could speak. He went on and on about how much of a wretched being he was. How he begged God to damn him, for ignoring Luis's full name. For allowing himself to watch as his only son became a leader himself, a title that Emmanuel never wanted. He kept praying every prayer he could imagine, for a red hole to open up beneath him and let oblivion's claws swallow him whole.

When he calmed down and reverted to sobbing, he heard Raquel's soft voice soothe his agony. "I know, Manny. I know. I prayed for the same thing to happen to me . . . but I never blamed you. I never blamed you."

"I . . . I never—"

"Shut up. I just want to love you right now. Please. Let me do this."

Raquel bent her head over and gently kissed Emmanuel on his forehead. She kept her lips there for a long moment, and then she released her grip. "I still love you," she said. "Always."

"Raquel . . ."

The two lovers still huddled in one another's arms, exchanging kisses whenever Emmanuel lifted his head. Raquel felt his lips, as sweet as ever. She remembered how they danced down the hallways enraptured in their shared euphoria. She had not felt his strong hands hold her back in so long, and now they were afraid of letting the other go.

"I . . . never wanted to divorce you." Emmanuel wiped his face. "Please . . . know that much."

"I know. I know you did it to protect me, but . . . you know I can take care of myself, you fucking idiot."

Emmanuel chuckled. "Still the comedienne, huh?"

Raquel felt herself smile. "I loved seeing you smile. Oh, sweetie, I still want to be with you. I didn't mind taking my maiden name back, but I still want you as my husband. If I have to wait another half century, I will. Just come back to me. I . . . can't stand to lose you. I don't want to lose anyone anymore. I'm tired . . ."

"I know . . . I know." Emmanuel forced himself to stand up, but he held onto Raquel's body close to his as she stood up with him. "You will never lose me. I promise."

Raquel smiled. She kissed him on the lips once more, and then she wiped thin tears that were still on his cheek.

Emmanuel swallowed hard. "So . . . Zephyr."

"She really misses her father."

"Yeah, you know what this means. If I do what she wishes, then there is no turning back for her. Any innocence she still has, any . . . remnant of a soul left in her . . . it's gone."

"She knows."

"Is she serious about Pedro?"

"Yes," Raquel said plainly.

Emmanuel looked at her with wonder on his face. "And that doesn't bother you?"

"He shot our son. That is unforgivable. But . . . oh God, I shouldn't say that. He's our grandson too . . ."

Emmanuel stared at the floor, briefly losing himself in thought. "I remember Zephyr said something about Pedro. Something . . . heavy. She said, 'He revoked his birthright when he pulled the trigger.'"

"Manny, I—"

"I know. I don't want to agree either. But I know it's hard to disagree."

"Yeah . . ."

"She is a beautiful young woman."

"I know. She really is."

"I still love you, Raquel."

She chuckled. "Random, but okay. I love you too. Dearly."

Emmanuel chuckled and kissed his former wife, as if they were married once again. He held her tight, tasting her wet lips. He let go of her and stared into her eyes.

"Stay safe, my love."

"I will, Manny Elizondo."

Raquel kissed him a last farewell and left the room. She made her way downstairs and exited her home. Their home. She decided to walk down the road and breathe in the sweet moments she had just shared. She hoped that one day, they would be able to share those moments again, under a bright and peaceful moonlight. As she returned home, she crossed herself and said a prayer. She prayed for Emmanuel's arms to wrap around her again as they accompanied each other, no longer bound by their bleak rules of separation. When she finished her prayer, she smiled. She snuck into the house and blew a kiss in the air for Emmanuel to catch with his heart.

*   *   *

The afternoon that followed such a momentous night proceeded as smoothly as it did the day before. Zephyr found herself sitting in the same chair, facing the same trinity of men in the same room. The only thing that had changed was her outfit. She saw herself still as a young and ambitious woman. Zephyr thought it fitting to wear a pair of deep-blue dress slacks pleated down the middle of her legs. The pleats were as sharp as the earrings in her ears, the same icicle streams that forever pointed towards the floor. She covered herself in a single-breasted blazer and completed the look with a pair of shoes. The heels were subtler in their incline but still showed off her attractive ankles. Her cleavage could still be seen peeking through her tops, but she kept it quiet in style, like noticing the stars in the sky without bothering to count them all.

Another thing that had changed was the company she kept. Raquel and Rosa stood in the back of the room as an audience. They stood in place like soldiers in formation, with whispered speech and quiet giggles. The men acknowledged their presence, especially Emmanuel, who nodded and smiled at them both. He remembered Rosa when she was younger, when Luis had taken a strong interest in her. She was young in youth, but he saw the sad wrinkles around her eyes, the same that Raquel had during their marriage.

"Do you think Zephyr knows, Raquel?" Rosa asked.

"Hell if I know, I didn't say anything to her, so she probably doesn't know. I doubt she does."

"Yeah . . ." Rosa became quiet for a brief moment. She snickered and covered her mouth in case she was too loud. Zephyr noticed and looked at her with her snowy eyes. She smiled the first real smile that Rosa had seen in a time that was too long to count. Zephyr turned her head back onto the men, and kept her cold gaze on them until they were ready.

"What's so funny?" Raquel wondered.

"I was just thinking . . . you were gone for quite a while last night."

"And? Am I on a curfew all of a sudden?"

"Oh, I don't know. Just saying . . . you were out late."

"Oh God!" Raquel kept her surprise whispered. "I didn't screw him, if that's what you're thinking! Jesus!"

"Uh-huh."

"I swear!" Raquel giggled under her breath. "But I have to tell you—all joking aside—he was very upset when I told him about Luis."

"I can imagine . . ."

Zephyr lost herself in her thoughts as the men conversed with each other. They talked about her, in front of her, in low voices. Her character, however, was built to such an extent that she cast aside any adolescent curiosity that may lead her to inquire about the subjects of their discussion. After a few minutes, they turned their attentions to her.

"Welcome back, Zephyr." Emmanuel spoke first.

"Again, thank you for this audience," answered Zephyr.

"Our decision was tough, but it has a conclusion."

"Yes?"

Emmanuel paused for a moment and gazed into his grand-daughter's eyes once more. For the first time, he saw a glint of hope, a silent prayer that lay deep within her soul. He saw a little girl who hugged her father for the last time, tears streaming down her cheeks as he kissed her softly on her forehead. Emmanuel's brief venture into Zephyr's spirit revealed to him all her power. Her anguish was now clear to him. He looked deeper, but Zephyr blinked and blocked his temptation to journey further.

"Based on what I have considered and per the counsel of the other members of this . . . committee . . ."

Zephyr did not show any emotion. She remained poised and confident. Emmanuel took notice of this and realized that she was a true Estrada woman—calm, luxurious in personality, and self-aware of their worth in this horrible world.

"You are an exceptional young woman. You have beauty and a seemingly incomparable intellect. You exhibit qualities that would make anyone, even myself, feel insignificant. You truly are a woman of ambition and passion, and at such a young age, I think that you are a rare species.

"But, Zephyr," he continued, "because of these qualities you hold dear, I am saddened. They could all be useful for other situations: politics, medicine, law, anything. I feel that these talents of yours are wasted in a business such as this. We do not need another ambitious soul—we have plenty to use and spare. We have people such as you who claim to change their own world. And yet, they fail. They end up accepting the world they live in rather than rebelling against it. The spirit they once had burned out. Why? Because they tried too hard. They did not plan. They did not discard the life they chose for something better, more meaningful. Although I am convinced that you will surpass the pitfalls so many have failed to avoid,

I feel that you force yourself to look in the mirror every morning in order to appreciate the beauty you hold dear. And not just physically but the spiritual beauty that you wish to reclaim. That is why you take such great care of yourself. Your clothes are of high fashion, your face is flawless . . . in a sense, you are Lady Absalom. Even your heart, damaged as it is, is still as pure as snow. You can be so much more, Miss Estrada . . ."

Zephyr cast her eyes on the floor once Emmanuel paused his speech. She did her best not to show any signs of defeat, or even sadness. She had her hands folded the whole time, and she clenched them when Emmanuel spoke those words to her. Despite his words, she still remained controlled and peaceful.

"I therefore reject your request for acceptance as a starting member of our organization . . ."

Zephyr remained stoic, surprisingly so. No tears, no open remarks, no outward actions that demanded an affirmative answer from the council. She, Emmanuel realized, was truly an unstoppable and focused force.

"Instead, I hereby grant you the title of boss."

Zephyr lifted her eyes from the floor and stared at Emmanuel. She could not say that it was all in shock, but it was an emotion that caught her off guard. It was an inexplicable feeling of relief; she no longer had to endure emotional defeat or spiritual suffering. Immediately her face felt content. The air surrounding her was now calmed. Everyone present in the room could feel a cool breeze brush against their faces, even though there were no windows present. This windless air was just a testimony to Zephyr's joy that was silently expressed.

Rosa had her mouth agape in shock; she exhibited every emotion Zephyr could not show. She covered it with her hand and chuckled under her breath. Raquel almost dropped the drink she had in her hand. She caught the small glass, letting a few drops of wine spill onto her fingers. She quickly placed the glass down on the bar counter, and then she reached for two sheets of tissue—one for her hand and one for her tears.

"So," Emmanuel continued, "do you accept this title?"

"I do." Zephyr remained confident and poised. She basked in the decision and felt herself attain a new level of sophistication.

"Then kneel before me."

Zephyr uncrossed her legs and gracefully stood up. She gently whipped her hair around her shoulder and approached Emmanuel. He marveled at her calm walk, not as stiff and practiced as a supermodel, but relaxed and smooth. She stopped a few inches from Emmanuel. She briefly looked at the men who sat next to Emmanuel, the two bosses, and gave them a respectful nod. They answered her welcome rather hastily, perhaps to avoid staring at her eyes any longer. She then turned to Emmanuel, who smiled at her. She knelt on one knee and bowed her head. Emmanuel stood up and placed his hand on her warm forehead. He kept his hand there for a short moment, and then he took it off. Zephyr made the Sign of the Cross and stood up. Emmanuel nodded and motioned his colleagues to exit the room. Once they left, he smiled at Zephyr and turned on his heel to walk.

"Sir." Zephyr stopped him. "One moment, please."

Emmanuel turned around and watched Zephyr as she moved toward him. She opened her arms and gave Emmanuel a large, comforting hug.

"Thank you, Grandfather."

Emmanuel, Raquel, and Rosa stared at her with pure shock.

"How did she know?" Rosa exclaimed. "Did you tell her?"

"No! I didn't say a thing!"

Emmanuel shook his head with a smile on his face. "It's okay . . . you truly are an Estrada woman. I am proud of how you turned out, Zephyr."

"Thank you." Zephyr let go of her embrace and turned around to meet with her surprised family. Emmanuel took a glance from Raquel and held her attention while Rosa hugged her daughter. Raquel kissed her palm and blew it to Emmanuel. He caught it with his own lips and placed his palm on his heart. He then left the room and disappeared through the doors.

"Now she can begin," he whispered.

II

A beautiful young woman stared away from him during the whole flight. He had taken a long nap and was happy to awaken next to someone that jumped out of a dream and claimed herself into this world. She wore a pair of typical Audrey Hepburn-styled sunglasses that seemed to have an indescribable sparkle of white light that beamed beneath them. She was wearing a short sleeve cardigan bathed in a cloud white color, with a tiny silver necklace that draped down to her cleavage. At the end of the necklace hung a single diamond small enough to match the size of a raindrop. He stared at her chest as she breathed softly, watching the hair move up and down as it flowed down to her breasts. He took a break, a brief one, to study the rest of her body. Her legs were crossed underneath a clutch purse and a simple white dress that accentuated her poise as much as her body. They were a pair of creamed, sexy legs—a pair in which he could see his face shoved. Feeling their warmth. Her muscles clenching on his neck . . .

The ding of the intercom slapped him out of his daydream. The stewardess spoke clearly into her microphone, but he was so enthralled in his seatmate's beauty that he listened to a few words here and there: "Good afternoon, ladies and gentlemen . . . making our descent . . . remain seated . . . electronic devices are . . . thank you."

The woman looked down at her waist and saw that her seatbelt was never taken off. She closed the window with the plastic cover and took off her sunglasses. Her eyes were closed, and she sighed deeply. When she swallowed, her throat rose and fell with a pulsing grace.

"Wow . . ." he whispered out loud.

"Say that again?" The woman spoke without opening her eyes.

"Oh . . . n-nothing," he stammered. "I didn't say anything."

"I heard your lips move, but if you say so. My mistake."

"Sure . . . no problem." He could not help but continue to stare at her. He glided his eyes up her entire body. He felt his pants get tighter and tighter. He shifted his body in his seat to hide his growth. "By the way, I'm Josh."

She sighed in annoyance. "Hi, Josh."

"And . . . what's your name?"

The woman did not say anything. She kept her eyes closed while she covered her mouth to yawn.

"Tired?"

"Bored, really."

"This your first time being here in the States?"

"I was born here," she answered plainly.

"Oh really?" He feigned enthusiasm. "Wow! That's really nice! Visiting family?"

The woman paused. "Yes, I am."

"That's pretty cool. Yeah, I'm going back home. I live in Ellipses."

"That is nice," she answered, with a chill in her voice.

"Cool, cool . . . anyways, ah . . . would you like to grab a cup of coffee when we land?"

"I do not drink coffee."

"You're kidding!" Josh was genuinely surprised. "You're the first!"

The woman smirked.

"Well, I will treat you to lunch. Not everyone drinks coffee, apparently, but everyone eats, right?"

"Yes," she answered coldly. "Fortunately, I will be eating alone."

"Oh, c'mon! Why not?"

The woman took off her glasses and hung them inside the top of her cardigan. She turned her eyes toward Josh. He flinched and held his fearful gaze when she looked at him. His body felt weak, his heart beat faster, and his lips quivered on its own. He was completely paralyzed.

"For one, you are such a pervert. I know they are beautiful, but you are not to be their beholder. So tell me, how is your wife?"

Josh's eyes widened. "How'd . . . you know?"

"Your ring finger is missing." The woman turned her white eyes away from Josh and stared at a spot on the seat directly in front of her. She lifted her finger in the air. She checked her nails and squinted at their small details. "I hope that you did not take it off for me. I specifically remember you having it on when you sat down. You do not want to betray your wife. Believe me."

The plane landed on the ground and taxied its way to the gate. Josh kept his eyes in front of him; he was afraid to look at her again. Her eyes were so . . . frozen. At the corner of his right eye, he saw the woman whip out a small hand mirror and comb her hair back with her fingers. He was still enthralled in her beauty, but it was a different wonder. It was like a person gazing at a mountain eagle—awestruck by its majesty but hoping that it does not attack its audience.

When the plane finally reached its gate, everyone on board seemed to arise from their seats on cue. Some immediately stood in line while others reached for their carry-on luggage that sat above their heads. Josh rose from his seat the fastest, letting his defeat goad him into letting the woman exit the plane before he did. They both stood in line, and he was as silent as a soldier in the Royal Guard.

The woman only had her clutch handbag to carry. She slipped on the long shoulder chain and opened the handbag. She gazed at a thick piece of paper and deeply, almost depressingly sighed. She closed her eyes and recalled how her mother entered her bedroom, sat down next to her, and gave her a small box without a word. Words were unnecessary then. They both looked at each other and held one another for one more time. Her mother then left the room after a while and let her daughter be. She recalled how she opened the box and found two small items: a jewel and a letter.

Dear Zephyr,

God has truly blessed me when you were brought into this world. For a man like myself, I'm not worthy of seeing your purity and your joy. The way you looked into my eyes when I held you for the first time brought me to tears. Your laughter has kept me alive and strong, so I could protect you from my sadness. This world's sadness. You're probably too young to understand what I'm saying right now, but just know that you are the greatest gift to me and your mother, and God forbid that I ever lose you.

The only fear I have is that I lose the most treasured soul in my life. I would beg God for Him to take my own life to preserve yours. I will always trade my happiness for the rest of my life in order to keep you from crying for one minute. And if I ever made you sad, please forgive me. I love you, Zephyr, and Papi was the happiest man alive when you were born.

In all my years, I never would have thought that those I love would be away from me. My son is sad. He is angry with me. I gave him all that he deserved but gave him nothing he wanted. Yet I still love him.

There will be a time where you will be angry with him. Zephyr, I love you. I love your brother. I do not want to see two of my own blood fight each other. I do not blame him for who he is; I blame myself. It is my entire fault. I have failed him as a father and let anger raise him in my stead. But promise me to never hurt him. He is still family, and we must take care of our family.

Even as I write this, I remember how your eyes sparkled when you smile, how those dimples buried themselves deep into your cheeks. I remember how my heart breaks whenever you cried, and how I wanted to make you happy again. I wanted to give you this necklace as my apology to you. I wanted to wait until Christmas to give it to you, but I know that your soul is too sweet for me to prolong this gift any longer. It is called a diamond tear. Please remember this name. It represents the tears of joy I shed when you became a part of my life. I will never forget your hugs and kisses. Thinking about them right now is making me smile. You were always a breath of fresh, clean air.

Zephyr, you have a tremendous gift. Promise me never to waste it. Use your talents to protect your mother and your grandmother when I am not around. More than anything, Zephyr, take care of yourself. Never worry about how Papi is doing, I will never leave you. Never.

May God bless you as he has blessed me. I love you.

Love,

Papi

Zephyr sighed and pulled the sunglasses from her dress. She placed them on her face in an almost poetic manner. Her posture was flawless as she walked down the path and exited the airplane. Once she was inside the airport, she cruised along her momentum and moved forward toward the baggage claim.

She stood next to the conveyor belt and rested part of her body weight on one leg. Her pose was as dignified as a countess, ready to have a suitor greet her on bended knee. She could feel dozens of pairs of eyes study her every being, but she paid no attention to their stares. The men caught quick glances of her body. Some even attracted the jealous attention of their wives. One little girl, however, walked up to Zephyr with a wide smile on her face. She had hair as long and as dark as Zephyr's, except her eyes were colored brown and she had a cute round face. She must have been at least five years old.

"Am I ever going to be as pretty as you?"

"Listen to your mother," Zephyr replied, "and you will be."

The little girl curiously looked at the floor. She held the sight of the discolored tiles for a moment, and then she lifted her innocent eyes at Zephyr. "She keeps telling me to eat my vegetables, though. They taste like grass!"

Zephyr chuckled. She bent down on one knee and addressed the little girl, who saw her reflection on Zephyr's wide sunglasses. "I felt the same way. I thought they were disgusting. But you know what? I learned a trick. Want to know?"

The little girl's eyes brightened. "Yeah!"

"Okay, but you have to promise not to tell anyone."

The little girl held out her hand and extended her pinky. Zephyr held out hers and wrapped it around the girl's. "I promise not to tell anyone, even Mommy!"

"Beautiful!" Zephyr whispered in her ear. The little girl was perplexed as Zephyr kept whispering. When she was done, the little girl nodded her head.

"That's it?" she asked.

"That's it," Zephyr replied.

"Wow . . . that's easy!"

"Imagination helps, my dear."

"Okay! Thank you!"

The little girl skipped around the conveyor belt and disappeared. Zephyr raised her head to see if her parents were around. She breathed a sigh of relief when she saw the girl holding hands with her father. Zephyr then made an expression she thought would never occur in this city.

She smiled.

*   *   *

Zephyr exited the taxi cab later that night and ventured up the old stone steps. The restaurant was slightly dilapidated but still maintained its ground. She looked up at the sign that hung with the neon red nostalgia that engulfed her the moment she stepped in its concrete. Her white eyes took notice of a large man with blonde hair that touched his shoulders. She approached him and made him stare into her cold eyes. His face held no expression, but she did notice that he fiddled around with his hands and his fingers were trembling.

"I am here to see Vladimir Kandinsky." She spoke with the coolness of the night air.

"Who the fuck's asking?" His voice was deep and hinted an Eastern European accent.

"Is that any way to talk to a lady?" Zephyr raised her eyebrows and stared at the guard. He walked down a couple of steps and stopped inches away from Zephyr's face.

"I talk however I fucking want!"

"You are sure that you do not want to watch your mouth?"

"Get the fuck outta here, you bitch!"

Zephyr kept her silvery gaze at the doorman and smirked. "I am actually glad you said that, *comrade.*"

Zephyr spread apart her fingers and shoved her nails into his crotch. He let out a bloody yelp as she hooked her nails around his scrotum. She squeezed hard, making sure that the doorman's testes crushed under her palm. His voice was hoarse from wailing, and it brought the attention of the men inside the restaurant. She turned him around and guided him toward the door. She squeezed slightly to hint that she wanted to enter the restaurant. His breathing was stuttered, and his face was drenched in tears. Zephyr slowly walked up the steps and waited at the door. She could see shadows moving through the red-stained windows. The shadows all converged into one spot, and then they spread out throughout the entrance. Zephyr made the guard open the door with a slight twitch of her finger. He flinched and let out a loud gasp of pain. He opened the door. Zephyr stepped inside with him blocking her front and smiled at each gunman who pointed their weapons at her.

"Good evening, gentlemen," she said coldly, in Russian. "I know this man here is like a brother to you all . . ." Zephyr's eyes narrowed. The men looked at her eyes and wondered if her body was devoid of a soul. "So if any of you wish to become the uncles of his children, then I suggest you stop wasting my time and allow me a private audience with your employer!"

The men cast quick glances at each other. They kept their guns aimed at Zephyr and her human shield. But their hands were shaking from fear so much that any bullet fired would surely miss its target. Zephyr rolled her dismal eyes.

"For the love of God, while I am still young." Zephyr kept her grip on the doorman's genitals. She rested her head on his shoulders and closed her eyes. "My hands are getting tired. Please make haste. I would hate for a bloody mess to spill on this floor."

One of the men reached for his cell phone while he kept his gun pointed at Zephyr. He punched in some numbers as Zephyr smiled at them. A sliver of white teeth peeked through her lips, which suggested both a facetious action and a sinister motive.

"Hey, boss," the man said, "you better come see this . . ."

Less than a minute later, Zephyr opened her eyes and saw an old, slim Russian emerge from the staircase, with tattoos and old scars on his hands. He displayed a look of confusion when he saw half a dozen of his men pointing their weapons at one gorgeous woman. But when Vladimir "the Impaler" Kandinsky looked upon the woman's eyes, his own widened in shock.

"Oh my god . . ." he whispered.

*   *   *

Vlad quickly signaled everyone to holster their weapons. Zephyr, in return, dropped her shield, and watched him grab his testes and roll on the floor. He gasped in pain as Zephyr ignored the doorman and wrapped her arms around Vlad. He held her as if she was his daughter, a ghost of joy that had departed from his life long ago. He let her go and bent over to kiss her hand.

"It is . . . truly an honor to embrace the daughter of my dearest friend."

"You are still the same man I remember years ago."

"*Da*. But this man has become old and frail."

"All I see is strength and integrity."

"You flatter me. But come with me! Let's sit in my office. We have much to discuss." Vladimir hooked his arm toward Zephyr, and she locked her own in his. They walked upstairs together, leaving the guards to tend to the doorman. He was still on the floor, holding his testes and groaning in pain.

"Look on the bright side," one of the men said, "at least you got her to touch your balls . . ."

*　　*　　*

Zephyr sat down in a soft leather chair and scooted over to invite Vlad to sit next to her. "You were my father's best friend," she said, "and I want you to be mine. Sit with me."

"Thank you, angel." Vlad approached his spot and slowly bent his knees. He gradually slowed his drop, and when he felt it was safe to let himself fall, he plopped himself right next to Zephyr. She felt the wind of his tired body brush across her face. She stared at the floor and remembered the face of her newest companion: exhausted eyes with wrinkles sitting atop more wrinkles, pale skin, and a slightly emaciated body. But Zephyr noticed his hands and how young they still were. They were still strong and immortal, with traces of scars on his knuckles during his days when he had to physically fight his way to the top. She admired his wide palms and imagined how he used them to either comfort a damaged soul or crush a neck. Zephyr knew that she must mimic the power of his hands with the power of her mind. Therefore, her intellect had to be almighty.

"These old bones age faster than I do," he lamented.

Zephyr smiled. She stared at the floor when he massaged his knees and reclined in the seat. She turned to him with her colorless eyes. He stared at them and breathed slowly and calmly.

"Your eyes have not changed a bit, Zephyr Estrada."

"Thank you. Oh, and I do apologize for your associate's shortcomings."

"Do not even mention it," Vlad said with humor in his voice, "he was always short on manners."

Zephyr smirked. "If it helps, he'll eventually heal."

"No rush."

Zephyr chuckled. She noticed how Vlad's face lit up when she smiled, as if he was not lying when he called her an angel. Her face was flawless; she had a thin amount of eyeliner that settled itself as a background for her infamous pupils. Her cheeks formed dimples whenever she talked. He wanted to kiss her forehead so bad to remind himself of what it was like to touch someone of pure beauty, someone of valor and dignity. But he had to wait.

"Vlad." Zephyr broke him out of his thoughts. "I wish to speak with you about past events. I need to absolutely know everything."

Vlad did not even bother to ask if she was sure. Her soul was felt when he first hugged her. He felt hot and uncomfortable. He thought that he was floating atop a flame from hell. When Zephyr had released him, he felt his body gasp for health. She was determined, and he felt it all. "As you wish, Miss Estrada."

Zephyr giggled. "Zephyr."

"Of course." He smiled. The joy he felt, thought it was brief, was a cruel and false precursor to what he was about to say. He closed his eyes and began to relate the events after Zephyr's flight from her own personal Egypt. "Your brother allied himself with the Forty-Second Street Gang after your father . . ."

Zephyr sensed his reluctance. She placed her gentle hand on his knee. He opened his eyes and met Zephyr's pure face, which bade him to continue.

"After your father died," he continued. "It was easy for him to do this, since his friend and partner Slim helped orchestrate the merger. Mr. Mal was more than happy to accommodate . . . but, my sweet angel, it is not your brother who is Don. No . . . it is just a title he gives himself. The true Don is Mr. Mal. He is an opportunist, you know this. He already had the largest gang in the city, even before the merger, and he saw how merging with your brother would increase his influence and reputation throughout the city. This city is his . . . Pedro and Slim are just fucking figureheads. After a while, Mr. Mal became greedier. He wanted more than just power, he wanted *complete* power! He took his gang and crushed anyone who wasn't Forty-Second Street. No criminal organization survived, small or big."

"Even you," Zephyr noted.

"*Da*. Even me."

"How did you survive?"

Vlad became quiet. Zephyr stared at him, not with disgust or blame but with kindness.

"Tell me."

"I . . . make deal with Mr. Mal."

"I see." Zephyr nodded and stared at Vlad's chest. She could see that his heart was beating fast and hard. He was silent, but his heavy breathing did little to hide his fear. Zephyr realized why he was afraid and quickly spoke to alleviate his sudden attack of phobia. "I will not ask you as to why you made the deal. I know you had two choices: stay alive or become dead. You value life, Vladimir, and I would never ask you to fall on your sword for someone as abhorrent as Mr. Mal. Pedro and Slim are worthless to me and they to you. Don't feel guilty, sweet comrade."

At that moment, Vlad smiled and inhaled deeply. He let out his stored breath and chuckled. "You had me worried that you would chastise me."

"I chastise myself for not coming here sooner," she replied. "In any case, what kind of deal was it? A percentage of profits?"

Vlad nodded.

"That must be extremely arduous, considering that you are already making ends meet with little progress."

"It is . . . but I have survived this long. I will not give in to them."

"Good." Zephyr nodded her head and contemplated. "Let us take a break from my dysfunctional family—how is yours?"

"I could not bear to watch my daughters witness this city being consumed by hellfire, so I sent them to Russia where they'll be safe. My wife . . . died of cancer a little over ten years ago. Our anniversary is in November. Forty-five years . . ."

Zephyr took Vlad's hand and kissed his knuckle. She held it in both of her palms. She looked at Vlad with her cold eyes and paralyzed his face so that he could read her intentions. "You are still with her tonight. Her spirit is in your heart—I can see it. I can see a lot of things, and I can tell that you are a good man. You will see your daughters soon, I promise you." Zephyr smiled at him. He returned with a slight smirk. He did not believe her—she knew this—but

Zephyr remained steadfast in her influence. "I keep my words as truth. You will see them, but only if you believe in me."

"I believe in you, sweet angel, even though I don't believe in anything anymore . . ."

"Then allow me to break that pattern."

Vlad smiled. He looked down at Zephyr's hands and saw that they were still holding his. He felt calmer the longer she held them. A breath of fresh air entered his lungs. He suddenly felt rejuvenated and awake. A spring of energy filled his heart, and he spoke livelier than earlier.

"What else do you wish to know?" he asked.

"Do you still own that nightclub?"

"Yes . . . well not soon. I am in the process of shutting it down. The lease is getting expensive and I have little to pay. I can't—"

"Give me ownership."

Vlad was confused. "What?"

"Give me ownership of the nightclub. I need it."

"For what?"

Zephyr smiled, her silver eyes shining with the faint light in the room. "Trust me. I have the funds necessary to finance the lease. Eventually, I will purchase the nightclub once I get things started. I also need a construction crew to renovate it and make some amendments. I need men to work around the clock."

"I can do all of that, *da*. When would you like to start?"

"Exactly two days from now. I predict that everything will be set in place toward the end of this month. Until then, place your complete trust in my strategy. I will not fail you."

"I will."

Zephyr let go of Vlad's hands and stood up. He arose with her and gave her a hug. She wrapped her arms around him, holding him tight and squeezing any doubt left in his soul. She released him and immediately saw an improvement in his spirit. "I will visit you in a couple of days," she said.

"I will await your return."

Zephyr bade him a comforting farewell. She walked toward the back of the room, but before she exited, she turned to Vlad, who was still watching her leave. He wanted to make sure that she would leave in a safe manner, much like a father drops off his only daughter to school and waits for her to enter the building. Once that happened, she was as safe as he was comforted.

"I have one more question," Zephyr said.

"Anything."

"Mr. Mal has the largest gang in the city, and yet my father barely has enough men to call a squad. What was it that made Mr. Mal fear him so much? He could've staged a coup anytime he wanted, but he didn't. Not until Pedro and Slim made that deal with him . . ."

Vlad nodded. "I asked Luis the same question years ago. He said, 'Much like a virus lays silent in a body and multiplies when ready, I have viruses throughout the city that will strike when I give the command.' He had always favored plan over assault."

"Assassins . . ." Zephyr replied.

"One does not need an army to raze another. One only needs to find a weakness and exploit it."

"'There is no terror in the bang, only in the anticipation of it.'"

Vlad laughed. "You are a fan of Hitchcock?"

"Immensely." Zephyr thought for a moment and smiled at Vlad. "I've learned a lot tonight. *Spacibo.*"

Zephyr gave a slight nod and exited out into the alley. She felt Vlad's presence follow her outside, letting her know that he let himself fall into her hands. She last saw a pair of joyful eyes that held a glimmer of lost hope. As she walked on the sidewalk, she could not help but remember the way Luis looked at her when he kissed his daughter for the last time. She narrowed her frigid eyes in anger and sped her gait.

Suffer, Pedro, she thought. *Suffer.*

*   *   *

She kept these words in her mind even after she arrived in her hotel suite. Zephyr had researched every hotel room in the Four Seasons and discovered one that matched her personality. It was, of course, a lavish hotel room that basked in modern design, created by someone who would add substance to an empty shell with just a glance. This, she felt, was a room that matched her personality—the ability to see a skeleton of a plan and fill it with something infallible, like building an impenetrable fortress with only a pile of logs. The room was a deluxe one-bedroom suite that had a tall window next to her bed that led out onto a terrace. Zephyr smiled once she took off her white cardigan and threw it on a nearby chair. She ran her fingers through her dark hair as she closed her eyes and breathed in the silent atmosphere. She reached into her white clutch purse and grabbed her cell phone. She then walked toward the terrace and slid open the glass doors. Her eyes matched the silver moon that beamed down onto the city. She stood with an arrogant and royal demeanor, looking down on the streets below as Julius Caesar looked down upon democracy, feeding his lust for supremacy. Zephyr knew that this city, with all its twinkles, cars, and people, would be hers.

Zephyr saw a nearby chair and table that almost begged her to sit and keep them company. She obliged and rested her elegant body. She crossed her legs and felt a subtle breeze tickle her face. Her hair rose and fell with each passing current. She shut her eyes and allowed the wind to bid her a fond welcome. It became stronger but only with enough strength to float her hair within its breeze. It was a cool night, maybe forty degrees, but Zephyr was not cold. She embraced the chilly wind as if it were warmer than her heart. Once a sigh passed through her mouth, she dialed a number on her cell phone. It rang on the other line until a gentle voice answered.

"Zephyr?"

"Hi, *Mami*! Were you sleeping?"

"No, no, I'm wide awake . . . I was worried about you. Is everything okay?"

"Yeah, I'm sorry . . . I'm just getting settled here."

"Oh, okay." Rosa fell silent for a moment. "How is it over there?"

"It's pretty much the same over here." She sighed. "Nothing really has changed."

"That's a shame. After all these years . . . I guess I shouldn't be surprised. But let me tell you, I heard that it used to be a nice area!"

"Oh, really?" Zephyr asked.

"Well . . . seven decades ago."

Zephyr laughed. "Not too long ago, right?"

"Right!" Rosa laughed. Zephyr heard her mother sigh with joy, and such an image of her smiling mad Zephyr smile in return. "By the way, have you seen Vlad?"

"Yes, I did . . . about a half hour ago."

"My God . . . how is he?"

"Sad . . . but still alive."

"Yeah . . ."

Zephyr tried to brighten the mood. "He still has the dance club you were telling me about. It needs funding, so I decided to purchase the rights of ownership."

"Wow, that sounds good!"

"Yeah!" Zephyr spoke with excitement. "I think that people will like it. Gives them a chance to forget about this city's problems."

"That's good, sweetie. I'm glad . . ."

"Are you okay?" Zephyr asked. "You seem quiet."

"Oh, I'm sorry. I was just thinking . . . you sounded just like your father right now."

"Really?"

"Oh, definitely. You know he felt the same way about music." She jokingly mocked his deep and calming voice. "'True democracy and complete unity.' Something like that." Rosa chuckled.

"I think so too."

"Yeah."

Zephyr paused for a moment and listened to the silence that came between her and Rosa. It was such a quiet melody in that it muted their voices and gave a clamor to their thoughts. "How's Grandma?" she finally asked.

"She's fine," Rosa answered calmly. "Out like a light though."

"I thought so . . . well, I won't keep you up any longer. Just thought I'd check in."

"Oh . . . okay."

"*Mami?*"

"I'm sorry, Zephyr. I really am. I just . . . be careful, okay? I don't want to lose you. You're all I have left."

"I will, *Mami*. I promise. We'll all be together again."

"I know, baby . . . I do," she said. "I will say some prayers for you. Get some rest, okay?"

"Thank you." Zephyr closed her eyes. She slouched in her chair as she felt the comfort of the wind blowing atop the high terrace. "I love you. I will keep in touch."

"I love you too, Zephyr. Take care."

Rosa hung up the phone. Zephyr placed her phone on the table and watched the light of the cell phone blink, letting her know that the call had ended. She watched the screen fade to a soft light, and then it turned to black after a few seconds. Once she saw her reflection of her face on the screen, she closed her eyes and let the sky carry her spirit to her mother.

*   *   *

III

Rebecca turned her key and stepped into her apartment. She dropped her duffel bag full of workout clothes and gear just to embrace the lonely air that surrounded her. She sat down at her kitchen table that also served as a dining table and also a small desk. The entire place was versatile in function and design: her living room was also her bedroom, but she was thankful for the futon in case she had to entertain any guests, which never happened. Regardless, she had a habit of being prepared, even if there was nothing to expect.

It was a lonesome apartment, but she did not care. Rebecca was so accustomed to being on her own that anything devoid of company did not faze her. There was a kettle sitting on the far end of the stove, a small countertop space next to the refrigerator, and a metallic sink full of a handful of plates and a single mug. In her bedroom/living room was a single end table with a lamp and a Bible sitting on top of it. It was the largest room in the place, and yet it was not big enough to house Rebecca's frustrations.

She flicked on the television and threw herself onto her sofa. She had a miserly expression on her face that seemed to wrinkle around her nose. She hated the television. Passionately. But it was necessary to update herself with local events, most of it laden with ninety percent murder and ten percent joy. One minute, it was a story about a family who adopted a basket full of German Shepherd puppies abandoned on the side of a highway; the next minute, it was yet another story of a beached corpse.

"Yet another body has been found at what is now called Beelzebub's Bay. The body has been identified as a William Theodore

Glasson, a former inmate of Hanson Penitentiary recently out on parole . . ."

"Gee," Rebecca said sarcastically. "I wonder where he came from."

Rebecca turned off the television and rested her head on her fist. She closed her eyes to search for a moment of respite. Her body was wrapped by a cold yet comforting embrace of a man who had saved her from further agony. He was someone whom she had never met—a stranger who was her closest friend—holding her as she cried into his shoulder. She wished desperately that she could have him as gentle company just one more time . . .

A loud buzz awakened her from her night dream. Her cell phone was vibrating on her coffee table. She growled before she answered.

"What is it?"

"Jesus! Is that any way to answer a superior officer?"

"Yeah."

"Someone's been riding her broomstick longer than usual." Greg braced himself for an attack from Rebecca. Nothing. Maybe she was too tired to retort. "I called you earlier. Did you get my message?"

"Hold on." Rebecca glanced at her phone and saw a small envelope blinking at the top of her screen. "I did, but I didn't listen to it yet. What's up?"

"Well, I have something big for you."

"Ha!" she exclaimed. "That's not what your ex-wife told me!"

"Wha—? No!" Greg realized that he should have known that Rebecca was never, ever too tired to retort. "That's not what I meant and you know it!"

"I'm just teasing," Rebecca reassured. "I'm sure you're blessed."

"Officer Ortega . . ."

"Okay, okay. Yessir!" Rebecca's sarcasm lowered Greg's spirit. "So what's the big something that you have for me?" Rebecca snickered.

Greg stayed silent for a moment and sighed. "Okay . . . do you remember a Luis Estrada?"

*   *   *

Rebecca sat in Greg's car on the lonely city street. This was her second day in a row where she gazed at the restaurant through her binoculars. It felt so good to be out of her uniform with that damn utility belt—she felt like Batman with that thing hanging around her waist. She wore a simple black blouse with a pair of dark-blue jeans that she bought at the mall a month ago. She did her best to remember the name of the brand. After all, she only wore two outfits every day: the uniform and her pajamas. Rebecca would cast glances at her legs and see how snug they were in her new outfit. It felt . . . weird but at the same time comfortable.

She could count the patrons and tourists who decided to eat at a place with no sign. The uncertainty of what the customers expected from the food was just as strong as Rebecca's anxiety to find her target. She dared not shut her eyes, no matter how massive her eyelids felt. One slip-up and she could French-kiss her job goodbye.

It also did not help that Greg had to sit next to her in the car. Actually, no—he *slept* next to her in the car. He insisted that she drive so that he could get some undeserved rest. She could feel his warm breath tainted with coffee and potato chips. His stomach slowly rose and fell as he dozed. Rebecca could not help but notice how it protruded like a woman in her third trimester of pregnancy. She was afraid that he would wake up and speak nonsense into her ears. "A detective always knows what to expect before he expects it," he would say. "Makes no fucking sense," she would always answer, but Greg continued to spill false words of advice to supposedly bolster her ambition to become a detective.

Rebecca rolled down one window and smiled at the touch of fresh air that entered the car. The brief wind wisped through her dark hair, relaxing her and beckoning her to close her eyes. It was such a cool evening, she thought. Need to relax and enjoy it.

Images of the John Doe suddenly flashed in her mind. His head was hanging from a lamp cord, eyes wide open and his chin slumped in his shoulder. He swung back and forth in centimeters, as if a ghost had pushed the body ever so gently. Rebecca was walking toward him, just as she did those many years ago. Her hands were outstretched in front of her. She wanted to reach him and pull him from the abyss.

When she came to him, he was suspended directly above her. His dead eyes were looking away from her at some sort of spot on the wall. She touched his leg. Nothing. Nothing at all. Just a hanging corpse who was lucky enough to be one.

"Rebecca! Rebecca! Take me down!" He was shouting at her, his lips moving with a life in his voice. "Take me down! I don't belong here!"

She felt a sudden chill rush through her body. She was so terrified of his sudden burst of life that she could not move. Her mouth could not open to scream. Her legs were paralyzed. She no longer wanted to see him. She wanted to run away.

"Take me down!" His legs were jerking back and forth to try to loosen his noose. He choked and breathed with an asthmatic breath as he tried to free himself. "Oh, Rebecca! Do not join me! Do not join me!"

"I'm . . . I'm so sorry I . . . can't take you down! I can't!" Rebecca stared at his cold eyes.

"Why? Why? I helped you! Help me!"

"I can't! I can't! Don't hate me!"

"Yes, you can, Rebecca!"

She felt hot tears streaming down her cheeks. Her eyes were bloodshot, and it actually hurt to keep looking at him. She turned away from him, all while hearing his jerking get slower and slower. The sound of the lamp cord scraped against the wooden rafter. Then it scraped less and less until finally, it stopped.

"Rebecca!" he yelled out. "Rebecca!"

She felt her body shaking. Her shoulder hurt with each shake. She was still sobbing hard. "Stop it . . . stop shaking me!"

"Rebecca!"

She opened her eyes and saw Greg's hand shake her shoulder.

"Jesus, Ortega! You okay?"

"Yeah." She caught her breath. "I'm okay. Nightmare."

"You all right?"

"Yeah . . . fine." She wiped her face to check for tears. There were none. Thank God. "I'm okay . . . sorry about that."

"You were mumbling something," he said. "Like . . . take me—"

"Hey! Is that her? That woman you were telling me about?"

Greg forgot his sentence as he whipped his sight at the restaurant door. A beautiful woman with the figure of a Roman handmaiden walked down the steps and glided onto the sidewalk. She was wearing a black city coat that completely covered her entire body, but she did have on a pair of black heels that did justice to her exquisite legs. She had such grace as she walked, he thought. Something out of a dance studio.

"That's our girl," he said. "Let's go."

They both exited the car and followed her. They maintained a moderate distance away from her. Rebecca was nervous but was glad that she did not have to explain her dream to Greg. Privacy was precious to her, and it was bad enough that he knew she used to be homeless.

They followed the woman for three blocks, listening to the click of her heels against the concrete. The woman suddenly stopped and waited for Greg and Rebecca to approach her; there was no more use to continue following her if she knew she was being followed. Once they reached her, Greg sped around the woman and blocked her path. He tripped over his own feet once he glanced at her horrifying silver eyes. Rebecca covered her rear. The woman turned to her and showed her unique gaze, but Rebecca only flinched. She stoned her heart and made herself show no fear. She was the cop training to be a detective, and she told herself that she was not going to be intimidated by some twenty-something-year-old bitch.

"Care to join me, officers?" She spoke with a frosty air in her voice.

"Let's take a walk down here." Greg motioned toward a nearby alley. The woman respectfully bowed her head and followed his command. Rebecca stayed close behind her and remained silent as the three walked down the alley.

"I've never seen you around," Greg said. "Are you visiting?"

The woman had a content smile on her face. She was not afraid in the slightest, as if she refused to acknowledge their authority. "More than that," she answered. "I am working. My name is—"

"I know who you are," he interrupted. The woman rolled her eyes. Greg was paralyzed by the way those moonlit orbs moved.

"My name," she continued, "is Zephyr Estrada. I just flew in from Spain forty-eight hours ago."

"Really? I thought you were born here."

"Yes, I was. But I moved to *España* when I was a little girl."

"How is Spain?"

"Breathtaking."

"Maybe I should visit someday."

"It is worth the trip."

"Hotel prices okay?"

"Do not bother yourself with such petty worries. I will accommodate you myself."

Greg swallowed hard. Was she serious or being facetious? "And what compelled you to leave there for here?"

"Detective Bernini, right?" Zephyr then turned to Rebecca. "And Detective Ortega? Pleasure to meet you as well."

"It's *Officer* Ortega, *Detective* Bernini," he corrected.

"My sincerest apologies."

Rebecca felt her heart sink. Did he really have to be that assertive about their positions?

"So you haven't answered my question," said Greg.

"You have not asked me any questions besides the ones I have just answered."

"Miss Estrada . . ."

"I know about your father," Rebecca interjected suddenly and confidently. "Who he was and what had happened to him. I know that you stayed alive somehow by the grace of God. But Pedro Estrada and Guillermo Nunez are still here in the city. Doesn't that piss you off?"

Zephyr merely smiled, as if she was amused by Rebecca's statement. Her eyes seem to give off a sense of pride, one that had kept her spirit and her body alive. Zephyr kept her face on Rebecca, ignoring a nervous and frozen detective that stood beside her. She seemed . . . intrigued.

"What I want to know," Rebecca continued, "is why you returned here . . . of all the cities in the world, you chose this one. You want revenge, don't you? Who doesn't, right? But as officers of the law, we cannot allow that to happen, Miss Estrada. If you don't mind, we're gonna have to keep tabs on you."

When Rebecca finished, Zephyr expressed delight in Rebecca's speech. She was not intimidated—it seemed like she never was. However, Zephyr did not impose her valiance on Rebecca. She gave the young officer the respect she had currently earned.

"Wow," Zephyr said. "You surprise me Detect—Officer Ortega. I beg your pardon—I am quite exhausted, but my fatigue has not blinded my judgment of you. You are too smart to be a cop. I mean, hey, in all honesty, the male officers in this city are pompous idiots while the women tend to be borderline lesbians—present company excluded. But you, Officer Ortega, you have received training from a different manual, have you not?" Zephyr walked closer to Rebecca to acquire a deeper analysis. "Oh, yes . . . I see it in your eyes and especially that relentless chip on your shoulder. I suppose you can say that I see a lot of things. These eyes of mine are—let us be honest—unique. Terrifying. Demonic. Beautiful, according to this boy in high school who had a crush on me. Call them whatever you wish, but they do see more than what people want to be seen within themselves.

"But believe me, we all have stories, my dear officer." Zephyr turned her eyes away from Rebecca and focused them on the path down the alley in front of her. "Mine is a comedy, to say the least. I would only wish to enjoy the city and the joys it has to offer me. My stay is not permanent. But let me assure you—and I would place my hand on the Bible for this statement if one was made available to me—that I will not stroll down the path of vengeance, as you propose I am doing. I do not know how my father died. I was too young to even remember his face. My brother chose to stay here, I did not. Yes, we are estranged, but not in a status that warrants any violence on either of our behalf.

"That being said,"—Zephyr raised her delicate right hand as she walked to the end of the alley— "I will not kill anyone. Not a single person. I promise. I have always been an outstanding citizen, and I love the gift of life that God has bequeathed upon us. I dare not threaten its ability to imbue vitality unto a worthy individual. I seek to prolong, not curtail. Is that what you both want to hear?"

"We'll get you that Bible, Miss Estrada." Rebecca did not hesitate when she said that. "For now, it's what I want to hear. The question is: Is this what you want to say?"

"It sure is." Zephyr chuckled. "Oh, you have to forgive me. You are certainly a person of character. I hope one day that I will be able to call you Detective Ortega and not feel the need to correct myself."

"Aren't you the charmer?" Greg finally spoke up.

Zephyr inhaled the night air and smiled as she exhaled. She walked away from the officers as they both stood in their places, while she playfully twirled her finger in the air. "'You attract more bees with honey than vinegar,'" she quoted. "Oh!" Zephyr quickly turned around with such glee displayed on her face. "I am showcasing a dance club soon," she said with genuine enthusiasm. "It is a project long overdue for completion. The grand opening is in two weeks from tomorrow—that is Halloween. I would be delighted to have you celebrate with me, so do not forget to dress up, okay?"

Rebecca stood in place without speaking a word. She glanced at Greg, who was unusually speechless. He was too stoic to provide her with any answers. "I will," she finally answered.

Zephyr nodded and waved farewell to Greg. She turned back around and walked back out onto the sidewalk.

"I hear your birthday is tomorrow, Zephyr," Rebecca called out to her. "Happy birthday."

"Thank you!" she answered, without looking back.

*   *   *

"Just know that she is smart. Scary smart. Zephyr really is the daughter of Luis Estrada. I wouldn't touch her with a ten-foot pole—she might steal it from us and beat us senseless."

Greg listened to Rebecca's report over a cup of coffee. He felt very insecure and uneasy. He kept looking for a waitress to serve him.

He caught the eye of one of them, a girl who looked to be in her early twenties. "Can I just have a coffee? Black."

"You got it, babe." She turned to Rebecca. "And anything for you?"

"Do you have any soup?"

"Sure do."

"Thank you."

The waitress nodded and carried herself away. Greg chuckled once the waitress disappeared into the kitchen. "She called me *babe*."

"Greg, take your mind out of your pants and listen to me real quick. I'm glad that I researched her before we made the stake-out, but . . . I thought I knew everything about her, but it's like she knew more about us instead. Like how she knew our names before we even introduced ourselves. *That* worries me." Rebecca leaned back in her seat and stretched her chest. Greg watched her breast move up and down with her long sigh. He wanted to smirk, but Rebecca broke his illicit concentration. "By the way, how did you know that she was here?"

"Neighborhood snitch of mine. I trust him."

"Well, how did he know that it was Zephyr and not someone else?"

"Hey, fuck if I know. When I hear that the daughter of a dead crime boss comes here to visit, I don't ask questions. Besides, you should be thanking me for bringing you along with me, Officer."

Rebecca remained silent. She stared at the table, not in defeat but in annoyance. "In any case, she's a bitch."

"She must've been in good company."

Rebecca made a childish look on her face and stuck her tongue out at Greg. She giggled, and Greg silently breathed a sigh of relief. He was her superior, yet he felt intimidated by this young cop.

"She must be well-informed," Rebecca continued, "or psychic. I'm gonna go ahead and say it: she knew we were staking out the place, she knew that we were following her. And shit! She knew that we were cops!"

The waitress came back with a small tray. She placed a steaming mug of black coffee next to Greg and a warm bowl of soup for Rebecca. Rebecca thanked her, and she walked off to another table.

"Greg, what do you think?"

He was watching the waitress move and glide around the restaurant. She was cute, had to be a college student trying to pay for her books. Nice blond hair, round butt, a pair of smooth legs . . .

"Greg!"

"What?"

"Did you hear me?"

"Yeah, I don't know what to think either. But I suggest that you stick to your promise to celebrate Halloween with her."

"What about you? You're invited too."

"No, she didn't—she was looking at you the whole time. She's interested in you—"

"Don't go there."

"I'm not implying anything, just saying."

Rebecca sipped on her soup. "She's not a lesbian—my gay-dar didn't go off."

"Right. Okay. But don't skimp out on this, Rebecca. You're not going undercover really . . . it's more like you're being her friend. And *that* will help us get a lot of information from her, as well as keep her in check."

"I guess."

Greg sipped on his coffee. "Besides, this will look good to the captain if you still want that detective spot."

"Really?"

"Really."

"Then I'll do it."

Greg was surprised. "Just like that?"

Rebecca shook her head and sipped her soup. It was steamy and thick, hot enough to steam away any ounce of stress she had in her heart. The soup was salty indeed—almost too salty. But more importantly, it was satisfying.

"And what is it with you and soup?" Greg asked. "That's all I've ever seen you eat."

"Old habits," Rebecca answered. "There are some things you just cannot forget."

*   *   *

Zephyr slipped into her nightgown once the midnight chime sounded off from the small clock in her hotel bedroom. The silk material introduced itself in the moonlight, giving off its blinding shimmer as an acknowledgement of Zephyr's glory. She walked out onto the balcony and immediately felt a curious sense of calm once she admired the gentle blanket of the night. "Such a lovely city," she whispered to herself. Indeed it was, but it carried a profound sadness along with the millions of white and red streaks on the streets below. This city was beautiful, for it once had a past better than now. Its attractiveness lay in its history, although decorated with visceral provocation. The bloodshed used to be sprinkled on the city, but it now bathes in it. Zephyr nodded her head as she reflected on her domain. She will have to rule it someday, but first she had to conquer it.

Indeed, it was an easy job for her. Conquering a land required concentration on one's strategy. Numbers demand consideration, yes, but numbers mean nothing if they are decimated. Once the destruction of Pedro's and Mr. Mal's forces occurred, Zephyr could brandish her sword and shove her frozen blade through their throats. She knew that as of now, it would be wiser to leave the sword as it is; others need to realize that she is not someone to challenge.

But as of right now, she needed to rest.

Zephyr's cell phone rang inside the hotel suite. She blew a kiss to the city below and returned inside to retrieve her call. The screen blinked a light-blue color with the black text flashing across the screen. Zephyr smiled as she lay on the bed and answered the phone.

"Hey, *Abuela*!"

"No, don't you 'hey' me! You know what time it is? I'm losing my goddamned beauty sleep because of you!"

Raquel heard Zephyr laugh on the other line. She always started her conversations with Zephyr with a smile. Raquel figured that her granddaughter needed every piece of joy available if she was to stay in that horrid city. *The sooner she leaves*, Raquel often thought, *the better she will live.*

"How are you doing?" Zephyr asked.

"I've been okay. Nothing new, really . . . what about you?"

"Relaxing. I was enjoying the night air a little while ago."

"Alone, I hope."

Zephyr giggled. "Of course. I doubt anyone can handle me anyway."

"That's what I like to hear," Raquel replied. "Always remember, Zephyr, 'If a man tries to tie you down, kick him in the ass.'"

"Did you kick Grandpa's ass when you married him?"

"Oh please, I broke my heel off him. Then I got mad because my good pair of shoes broke, so I kicked him again!" Raquel laughed. "You know what? I'm glad you reminded me, that jackass owes me a pair of shoes . . ."

"I think he's scared of giving them to you," Zephyr joked.

"Whatever. He shouldn't be a wimp about it either!"

Zephyr chuckled, but she discarded her joyous tone of voice for a brief moment. "Do you plan on seeing him about those shoes?"

Raquel was silent. Zephyr knew that she was thinking of how to answer that question. When there was no answer, Zephyr decided to speak first.

"I'm—"

"Don't worry about it, Zephyr. I mean . . . all joking aside, I . . . I really miss your grandfather. It was such a joy to see him again. I wish I can use those shoes as an excuse to see him, but . . ." Raquel cleared her throat. "Zephyr, if you ever get a chance to be happy, please, for God's sake and for your own, take it."

"I will."

"And I want you to promise me something."

Zephyr sat up straight on her bed and listened attentively. "Yes?"

"Don't do what you're doing forever. That's all."

Zephyr dropped her hand and looked forward. She surveyed the city that lay before her, as Alexander the Great once did when he cried over the lands he had conquered. But she refused to let a memory of history repeat itself through her eyes as tears. She had to petrify her soul in order to survive under the pressure of her grand-mother's words. However, Raquel was right. Zephyr had to swallow her pride—but only once.

"I promise," Zephyr lied.

IV

Rebecca walked in the station wearing a dressed-down outfit. She wore a black wool coat with a golden belt buckle that hung down her waist, a simple white blouse that showed off a bit of her cleavage, and a pair of black slacks that fell perfectly over her black flats. She was allowed to discard the normal uniform—per the instructions of Greg Bernini. Despite her change in appearance, she followed her normal routine out of reflex. Open the door with the rusted hinges, wave to the desk guard as he buzzed her inside and cast a glance at her rear end. She knew it was a die-hard habit of his, but her mind was constantly occupied by future views that she rarely bothered to shove her middle finger straight into the air. She instead gave him a nasty look that made him avert his eyes and get back to his duties.

Once she walked through the door, everyone stared at her. Traffic cops, detectives, rookies. Hell, even the new secretary whose first job was to file folders and make copies of "Most Wanted" photos. He was a shy guy who looked young enough to be in his first years of college. He always stayed late until each copy was completed. Rebecca liked him for his work ethic; he was a prime example of what Greg should have been.

They all stared at her as if the scarlet letter was painted on her forehead. She decided to walk up to the new guy and ask him what the hell was up with everyone. He seemed innocent enough to cut the crap and tell her everything straight up. He saw Rebecca slowly approached him.

"Do I really look that tired, or is it just me?"

"No, you look okay," he shyly replied. "Actually, you look fantastic, it's just that . . . no one's ever seen you outside of your uniform, and . . . you know . . ."

Rebecca chuckled. "Don't get used to it, I'm only doing this for an assignment. Once that's done and over with, so is this outfit."

"That's a shame—I think it suits you very well." He cleared his throat. "In any case, you have a visitor, and . . . she gives us the creeps. Can you talk to her? Please? I can't make these copies with those eyes of hers staring us down."

Rebecca whipped her head away from him and immediately saw a young woman looking around the police department. She wore a white trench dress that looked too expensive to name and a pair of white stilettos that added to the brand name's mystery, as well as hers. She sat so easily in her chair that it could have morphed into a throne. She caught the image of Rebecca in her view and smiled.

"Surprise!" Zephyr called out to her.

Rebecca could only help but smirk. She was not too surprised, strangely. Rebecca expected something like this to occur, and yet she was wary of honoring a meeting with an Estrada woman who welcomed herself so calmly in here, of all places. As soon as she started walking toward Zephyr, everyone in the room seemed to breathe a sigh of relief. The noise of the department commenced, telephones rang, operators were speaking on the radios, and another sheet of paper was fed through the copy machine.

"Surprise, indeed." Rebecca took off her coat and sat across from Zephyr. She leaned back in her chair without saying a word. She folded her hands on her stomach and rocked back and forth. It wasn't even her desk—it belonged to Detective Bernini. Rebecca looked around for him, but he was nowhere to be found.

"The good detective is standing over there." Zephyr nodded her head toward the back of the office. Rebecca saw Greg standing near a fountain and sipping on a cup of water. He nodded to her. It was a sign of instruction for her to humor Zephyr. He then turned around and left the room.

"I felt it would be a pleasant surprise," Zephyr said. "Have I succeeded?"

"You have. What brings you here?"

"I actually have a favor to ask—do you have any pressing obligations at the moment?"

"Nope. I'm all ears."

"Beautiful!" Zephyr smiled brightly. "Believe it or not—and this is a strange inquiry—but I am on the prowl for a car. I need not a typical car for a family of four, but a *chariot*." Zephyr kept her stare on Rebecca, but she did not flinch. "Will you be able to accompany me?"

Rebecca was perplexed. "Zephyr . . . you can get someone else to shop with you."

"I could, but you are not just 'someone.' You are Detective—I apologize—I mean Ms. Ortega. I am sure that your taste is incomparable. Plus I would love the company."

It was at that moment when Rebecca saw something in Zephyr that she thought was impossible to notice. Zephyr had a glimmer in her eyes once she finished her sentence: she was telling the truth.

"Why me?" she asked.

"Why not?" Zephyr answered.

"Because, Miss Estrada, I have more important things to do right now. Unless you have something to tell me that doesn't involve car salesmen and test-drives, don't waste my time." Rebecca arose from her seat. Zephyr rose up with her. "Miss Estrada—"

"Zephyr."

"Miss Estrada," Rebecca continued, "this is a police department. We have no time for games. Now do you have something to tell me that's important?"

"Yes."

Zephyr's answer was so plain, so matter-of-fact, that it was impossible for Rebecca to ignore it. Zephyr's intent was evident in her stone silver eyes. Rebecca tried not to stare at them for too long, not out of fear but for politeness. She constantly took her eyesight away from her for brief moments to glance at papers on a desk or at the new guy busy making copies. But she always returned to Zephyr.

"What is it you want to say?"

"Accompany me."

"And then you'll tell me everything."

Zephyr shook her head. "Just everything I deem is important for you to know. Do not worry, Officer Ortega. What I will tell you is everything you want to know anyway. I just choose not to bore you with meaningless details."

Rebecca suddenly remembered Greg's words of advice. "Be her friend. Get to know her. Find out what she's after." After all, this was her ticket to having the "Detective Ortega" plaque on her own desk. *Don't push yourself away*, Rebecca kept reminding herself.

"Okay." Rebecca was reluctant to say it, but she knew it was necessary. "When would you like to go? Tomorrow?"

"Now."

"Now?"

"I do not see the confusion in my answer," Zephyr said with a giggle. She bowed slightly at Rebecca and walked away. Everyone averted their eyes as if she was a goddess too beautiful for mortal views. She gave a slight nod to the man at the copier machine, but he quickly turned away and fuddled with some papers, dropping a few on the floor and scrambling to pick them up. Some still flew from his arms, and a breeze carried one on its descent toward Zephyr. She caught the paper in mid-air and calmly handed it over to him. She smiled; he nervously smiled in return.

She turned around and walked out of the visitor's lounge, waved goodbye at the desk guard, and ventured outside. She looked at the city in its daylight with a content look on her face. Zephyr marveled at the sun's reflection on each building as it cast a golden veil on the office windows. She imagined the ghost of King Midas, with his glorious decadence flying through the downtown area and leaving a trail of dust behind him. She kept following the soar of the Midas wind as it crept up on the police station. She leveled her gaze toward the ground once Rebecca pulled up next to her in her police cruiser.

"Would you like to sit in the back seat?" she asked.

Zephyr merely chuckled. She walked to the front passenger car door with a grin on her face. Once she entered, she kept her eyes on the road ahead.

"Go down the street, take a left, drive for exactly five blocks, and then take a right. Once you get to the third stop light, take a right down an alley—it is a shortcut I discovered. This will take you to the dealership."

"You certainly know your way around a city that you're just visiting." Rebecca brushed her hair back with her hand and made a quick glance in the rear view mirror. She halfway marveled at the police department she called home and depressed herself when she thought of the misery oft-attached with law enforcement. The crying spouses, the screaming kids, the cursing gang members in cuffs—all of it contributed to a sort of funeral melody that Rebecca was grateful to play, despite the stage.

"Three blocks down the road," Rebecca began, "Ingel Street. There's a big-ass pothole that I'll have to bypass unless it's been fixed, which hasn't been for the past ten years. Right before the dealership will be a slowdown. Construction. Again. So it'll take us a good twenty-five minutes. Is that okay?"

Zephyr turned to her driver with a cocky look on her face. She smirked at Rebecca and turned her frozen gaze back on the road. "You certainly know *your* way around a city, Miss Ortega. In any case, darling, if there is one thing you should know about me, just know that I memorize every road that leads to my destination. But you, on the other hand, you don't memorize every road—you live and breathe with it. Don't you?"

Rebecca remained silent.

*　　*　　*

Rebecca followed Zephyr's directions (along with her own) exactly as they both intended, and sure enough, they found themselves at the dealership in twenty-five minutes. The cars featured on the lot were all muscle cars, furious in their power and dominance. Rebecca felt intimidated once she surveyed the lot, but at the same time, she felt exhilarated. She imagined herself being behind the wheel of one of those armored sleds, breezing through traffic, chasing down whoever was dumb enough to commit a crime while she was present. She always wanted a loud car that was different from the crappy police cruiser she had to use today.

"What do you think, Rebecca?"

Rebecca had forgotten she had company. She turned to Zephyr and opened her mouth to speak, but her vocal cords stopped themselves. Did Zephyr really just call her Rebecca? As if they were friends already?

But she had to be friends with Zephyr. This was an undercover operation, despite the fact that it was a false definition. She was investigating Zephyr in plain view. Strangely, she did feel a sense of goodness in Zephyr. She had a small glow of purity in her soul, she thought. Or maybe Zephyr was pretending to have a frozen heart all along. Perhaps Zephyr *wanted* people to think she had a good heart. Or a dark heart.

"I think this is great, Zephyr," she replied. She gave up trying to figure her out. She was too transient to predict.

"I think so too. I have always had a soft spot in my heart saved for a car as powerful as these. I wanted something . . . elitist."

Zephyr walked over to a black sports car whose suspension kept it close to the ground. The body of the car was shaped like a broad-head spear that was ready to impale an unwanted visitor. It looked incredibly menacing. Rebecca nodded her head towards it, acknowledging its reign over the car lot as a knight kneels in front of his queen.

The driver door was open and gave a view of the interior. The seats were covered by a smooth black leather material and dyed in a deep blue. The steering wheel had the car's logo in the middle and the controls to the head unit on both sides. The head unit itself had a large screen adorned with a multitude of buttons and dials. Rebecca deduced that it was the GPS or a movie screen or both. It, of course, had manual transmission; a system geared toward someone who enjoyed being in control. All accessories considered, it suited Zephyr's taste perfectly.

"This car is beautiful!" Zephyr ran her delicate finger on the door frame. "Remind me to purchase an outfit to match this car."

Rebecca laughed. "We will have to take you to Saks after we're done here."

"I knew you had taste." Zephyr took her eyes off the car and walked away from it. Rebecca strode along with her as they casually made their way through the maze of vehicles. "How do you feel about this one, Rebecca?"

Now *this* car made Rebecca's heart flutter. It was a blood-red car a bit wider than Zephyr's but just as reputable. It also rose higher above the ground, almost like a queen escorted in a carriage upon her servants' backs. Rebecca opened the door almost too quickly—she initially did not want to drop her guard in front of her guest, but she felt so comfortable around Zephyr that she cast off all reservations. She climbed into the car and felt her body melt into the tan leather seats. The modernized interior hypnotized Rebecca and captured her in the sight of the dials and buttons that were just as entrancing as the one in Zephyr's. She breathed deeply and almost proposed to the car.

"This one feels fantastic, Zephyr."

Zephyr giggled. "You seem to be at peace."

"I am." Rebecca realized where she was and quickly opened her eyes. She jumped out of the car. "They are both excellent vehicles, Zephyr. Do you want to look around some more?"

Zephyr shook her head. "No, I made my decision."

"Which one are you going to get?"

"Both."

"Say what?"

"I am purchasing both of them." Zephyr saw a dealer and waved him over as Rebecca stood there, perplexed. Once he came over with his typical seller's smile, she winked at him. The guy flinched at her ghastly eyes and quivered. He thought his soul died from the sight alone, but he slapped the left side of his chest and breathed a sigh of relief once he knew that his heart was still beating.

"Ah . . . w-what can I do for . . ."

"I would like to purchase this car."

"Oh, okay. This car has . . . features that—"

"And that one over there."

She pointed to the black monster that she had first visited. The dealer quickly turned around to get away from Zephyr's gaze. He stared at it longer than usual, in order to get a mental note of it and to also catch his breath.

"Let me get the . . . p-paperwork," he stammered.

"Thank you, darling."

The dealer quickly jogged back to the building. Zephyr snickered and looked at Rebecca.

"It happens to me all the time."

Rebecca smirked at her. Zephyr must terrify everyone just by standing there. "By the way, how are you going to get one of the other cars back to you? Are you getting someone to pick it up?"

Zephyr gently brushed a strand of hair that fell across her forehead. "Yes. You."

Rebecca took a large step backward. "Me?"

"Unless you know of any other Rebecca Ortegas around," she playfully remarked. "Of course it is for you."

"Zephyr, you're joking!"

"Not in the slightest."

"Zephyr! I'm serious! I can't accept a car!"

"And I am serious as well, and yes, please accept it. Consider it a gift."

"No! I can't!"

"Just say yes."

"No!"

Zephyr did not get upset. She only expressed stoicism. "Rebecca, I will not force you to accept this as a gift. I understand. Pride is something I have as well. I refuse to accept any handouts from anyone, and I sense you are the same way. Probably more than I realize. You must have been born with a wooden spoon in your mouth. Splintered, I imagine. But this is truly a gift. The vehicles will be paid for with cash, so do not worry about payments, loans, et cetera. I will cover insurance, maintenances . . . all you have to do is drive it."

Rebecca closed her eyes and sighed. "Zephyr, I can't . . . I just can't."

Zephyr nodded her head. "Then I will not coerce you."

Rebecca stared at Zephyr and read the truth in her eyes. They glowed with such a brilliant white aura, so pure and stainless. She saw Zephyr's honest request to gift Rebecca a brand-new car. Why she wanted to do it, however, Rebecca could not tell. The aura only let her see so much. Everything that lay deeper in her psyche was hidden by a silver wall. But for certain, Rebecca knew that Zephyr really wanted her to have that car. She was sincere.

"I'll take it," Rebecca answered.

"Thank you."

*　　*　　*

Purchasing the car was a lot faster than what Rebecca had thought. She knew that it took at least half a day to get all the paperwork in order, calculate fees that arise from God knows where, offer added accessories that was not needed but advertised as if they were the Golden Fleece . . . but Zephyr walked right into the dealership building, sat down in front of the salesman, and told him the exact cars that she wanted. The salesman shot out of his seat and tried his best to ignore those piercing pair of eyes. He started to walk away from her to fetch the information on the two vehicles. Zephyr stopped him mid-journey and smiled.

"Darling, I have all the information you need."

"M-Miss Estrada," he stammered, "I just need to get the—"

"I have it all in my head. Let me write it down for you."

Zephyr reached into her clutch and pulled out a long black fountain pen with a silver tip. She pulled off the cap and grabbed a blank sheet of notepaper from the salesman's notepad. Rebecca felt awkward sitting next to her, a young woman in her twenties scribbling some figures on the paper, just to buy *two* cars! She realized that Zephyr was just as nonchalant in her purchases as her personality.

"Here you go, love." Zephyr handed the salesman the paper. He read over it and raised his eyebrows in shock.

"Wow . . ."

"How much are they?" Rebecca asked the salesman.

"One hundred fifty thousand dollars, give or take a few—"

"Horseshit. They need to be priced at 125K. They've been on that lot for months, they've been damaged by rain, sun, indecision . . ."

"But these vehicles are prime! Some of them haven't even been on the streets yet. As a matter of fact, this is the only dealership on the East Coast that has these models!"

"So that means no one has bought them, right? You want us to buy them? Set some stones in history? We'll be more than happy to do that. One hundred twenty-five thousand—and I'm being nice."

The salesman thought for a moment. "One hundred forty."

Rebecca snickered. Zephyr looked down at her cell phone, trying hard not to laugh.

"One hundred twenty-five K," Rebecca answered.

The salesman sighed, but it was unclear whether it was exasperation or fatigue. "One hundred thirty grand, but I can't go any lower."

Rebecca stood up. Zephyr followed suit. "Well, thanks for your time. Zephyr?"

"Good day to you, darling," Zephyr said to the nervous salesman.

The women reached the doorway and barely touched the door rug with their feet when the salesman called out to them.

"Okay, fine! One hundred twenty-five! You're killing me!

Rebecca smiled, as did Zephyr. "You're awesome."

"I don't feel it . . ." he replied.

"We will wait for your return," Zephyr said. "Please make it swift." Zephyr and Rebecca returned to their original seats and relaxed. She spread apart her fingers and checked her nails. Nonchalant and a bit vain, Rebecca deduced. Once the salesman departed, Zephyr folded her hands as if she was in prayer. She seemed relaxed as she looked about the large show floor. She looked at Rebecca and smiled. "So tell me, what do you like to do with your spare time?"

"Huh?"

"What do you like to do with your spare time? Besides haggle the hell out of salespeople."

Rebecca shook her head. "Look, I just can't see paying full price for something that could be bought for cheaper. Just because you're rich doesn't mean you have to spend like it."

"True. But what you displayed just now told me a lot about you, love. So to my original question . . ."

"Why is that so important?"

"Because I want to know what Rebecca Ortega does when she is not working. I mean, we all have lives outside of work, right? Arduous is the struggle against insanity, so humanity takes up arms against monotony and births hobbies. So what are your weapons?"

"Well, I . . ." Rebecca paused. She honestly did not have any hobbies whatsoever. Her only hobby was her job. "I guess I like relaxing at home. You know . . . maybe read a book or—"

"You have no hobbies."

Rebecca was surprised at Zephyr's statement. It was so blunt that she almost felt her heart pang in her chest. It actually hurt. "I . . . you're right. I really don't have any hobbies. I just work."

"You poor thing!"

Rebecca laughed. "Zephyr, I'm okay with it."

"So you say." Zephyr sighed. "You are coming to my party right?"

"You mean your grand opening? Sorry, Zephyr, but I'm not much of a clubber."

"You will be. Besides, it is on Halloween! You must dress up!"

"Wha—? I don't even have a costume!"

"Oh, you will." Zephyr looked away from Rebecca and saw the salesman returning. "Oh, good. Here he is."

"Miss Estrada." The salesman turned away once Zephyr's eyes flashed before him. "And Miss Ortega. You are both set."

Zephyr smiled widely. "Thank you, darling. I gather the vehicles are outside?"

"Yes."

"Then *buenos tardes!*"

Zephyr and Rebecca stood up together. The salesman did not bother to outstretch his hand to bid them gratitude and a farewell. Once they walked outside, the two cars sat before them, waiting as if they were too intimidated to leave their sight. Zephyr walked with a gait that suggested supremacy over the city; Rebecca strode alongside her and matched her dominance. She seemed relaxed around her new Estrada "friend," mysterious and cocky though she may be.

Despite her concerns—well, that was the extent of what she admitted to herself—she knew that Zephyr had taste. The cars she had purchased were not beyond description, but Rebecca was afraid to attribute any titles and stain their reputations. She noticed Zephyr blowing a kiss to her own car. She turned to Rebecca with a smile on her dimpled face.

"Just blessing her is all."

Rebecca smiled back. Zephyr opened her palm and tossed Rebecca's set of keys at her chest. She caught them close to her heart and slowly studied the pair of jingling stainless steel blades that settled so comfortably in her grasp. She found herself feeling so blissful, something that she has not felt in a time too long to measure.

"Go ahead and laugh it out, *mi amiga*," Zephyr called out to her. "I will laugh with you."

"Zephyr, I'm just . . ."

"Speechless? Then my work is completed. By the way, you are still coming to my party, correct?"

"What's the age limit?"

"Silly."

They gave each other a respectful nod before they climbed into their cars. Rebecca felt her nose tingle once she inhaled that beloved new car smell. She looked around the interior of the car as she felt the warm leather seat massage her back. She adjusted the rearview mirror and checked her face. She wrapped her fingers on the steering wheel and felt the exhilaration before she even shoved the keys in the ignition.

Zephyr had already turned on her car and stepped on the gas to let it roar through the streets. "Show off," Rebecca said. She did not want Zephyr to steal any glory, so she turned on her car and pressed the gas pedal twice. Her engine screamed just as loudly as Zephyr's. Rebecca was proud of herself.

"Looks like I have competition!" Zephyr yelled out.

With no hesitation, Zephyr sped off toward the streets ahead of her, leaving Rebecca to sit in her own car. She really was comfortable with her new vehicle. She imagined what she could do with it, and where she could go. She was laughing to herself. A new car in one day!

Then it suddenly dawned on her that she had to report back to Bernini. This, she realized, was the weirdest assignment in any officer's career. But as long as it got her to where she needed to go, so be it.

She put the car into gear and drove off in Zephyr's opposite direction. She needed to head back to the station quickly. Rebecca would hear the detective bitch and moan about how she had forgotten the police cruiser back at the dealership and how could she had let the daughter of a dead crime boss purchase her a vehicle in the first place. Rebecca would not reply, nor would she give him the pleasure of a logical explanation.

Rebecca would still able to drive the car, but only for the duration of her assignment, he would say. Afterward, she would have to have it impounded. Rebecca would stick out her middle finger once Bernini turned around to walk away. Like hell she was gonna give up her new car. Zephyr never bought her the car, she would argue. Rebecca had earned it by earning her trust; Zephyr merely expressed her appreciation by buying her something that would get her to where she needed to go. Or something. This is what would happen, and Rebecca was hardly one to conceive mistaken thoughts.

"So be it," she said.

∗   ∗   ∗

V

Pedro was never one to enjoy pleasure unless Slim was present. They shared a strange symbiotic relationship that solely depended on the strength of their business or, rather, their sinister frivolities. The mansion was supposed to be some sort of fortress built to contain what needed to be hidden and repel what needed to be ignored. But whatever—he had more important things to think about. For once, he was concerned. Deeply. He felt true fear for the first time in years, ever since . . .

No, he told himself. *Stop thinking about it—don't allow those horrible echoes of blood spilling on the wooden floors to enter your mind. Just shut up. It's not important, why bother with it?*

But Slim kept grabbing his cigarette box with trembling hands. His forehead was bathed in sweat and his eyes were twitching. He pulled out his lighter and tried maybe three times to produce a sufficient flame. Once the bright orange wave shot forth from the lighter, he held the cigarette until smoke came from its end. He puffed for a long time. His breathing calmed down a bit, but his voice was still shaky.

"S-shit, man . . . you're serious, aren't you?"

Slim was talking to one of their soldiers, a tall Caucasian man with tattoos on his knuckles that spelled out "Fire." He was fidgeting around with his fingers as he answered Slim's question.

"I checked what he said. He's right. That's . . . the word."

"Yeah . . ."

Slim turned to Pedro who just sat in his seat in silence. It would be wrong to say that he was emotionless; in fact, he was so full of emotion that his body just had no way of expressing it. His

317

emotions were, and he identified these in his tortured mind: fear, anguish, agony, and suicidal. The last emotion gave him some comfort, although what he had just heard from his underling stole such a fleeting pleasure away.

Pedro pulled open his desk drawer and found a large blade slid underneath a stack of papers. He wanted to slit his throat right in front of everyone. *Actually*, he thought, it would be best to check the point of the gleaming blade on his finger. Once it bled, he would look at his reflection in the blade itself and stare at his own tired eyes. Then he would grab the blade firmly in his hand and shove it into his esophagus. He would then jam it in such a way that when his heavy skull fell headfirst on the table, the handle of the blade would catch itself (he almost said *himself* in his mind, as if it was a murderer whom Pedro begged to kill him) and further plunge the blade in his neck. Pedro wished that he could somehow see the tip protrude through the back of his neck. That would totally make him feel better.

Yes, whatever it was that frightened both Pedro and Slim, it was *that* bad. It was the way Zephyr had punished two of their soldiers.

*   *   *

Zephyr had been walking on the sidewalk, listening to each tap of her heels that echoed across the night. Her eyes seemed to glow a brilliant white during the evening, which caused a number of passers-by to cross themselves and look the other direction; very few people actually stared at her in marvelous curiosity. Those gentle few were usually children who were still within the age of innocence to smile at Zephyr and not suspect anything wrong with her. Zephyr always answered their wonder with a kind smile, sometimes giving them a gentle wave with her fingers.

Night had fallen in a swift descent upon the city. Soon, all the insomniacs graced the streets and those who welcomed the dotted black sky retired to their homes. Zephyr was betrothed to Night, her faithful and comforting husband. They were separated during the obliged presence of Day. Day was jealous of Night and wanted to have Zephyr accompany him while he hung atop the blue sky. Zephyr politely acknowledged his arrival, but kept her true love hidden inside her heart. This may have been seen as an affair, but it was a different infidelity where Night knew what Zephyr was doing when he was not available. It was more of an agreement than a tryst, much like Hades arranging a contract with Demeter to have her daughter for a season.

Once Day fell, Night had risen. Zephyr awakened to the crescent moon and embraced Night. She held him tight, even now as she walked along a lonely sidewalk. It had begun with clean and polished squares, then it transformed into rugged and discolored concrete plates. Eventually, the sidewalk ended. Zephyr found herself facing a rusted fence with weeds and unkempt grass growing alongside of it. Nature's tendrils had dominated this part of the city. Within this area stood two men with tattoos on their necks that peeked out of their coat collars. One of them wore a large white T-shirt that draped over his knees, which were covered by a pair of baggy black jeans. On top of this smock, he wore a puffy white jacket, and his feet were covered by large boots that seemed to be the cause of California's earthquakes. He looked warm, but Zephyr was convinced that her presence made him warmer. It was not arrogance that led her to think this fact; it was the truth of the matter that led her to think this fact.

The other man was a true model of the gang he represented: white baseball cap that hung over his eyebrows, a thick red jacket, black jeans (Zephyr was surprised that it did not swallow up his shoes), and a pair of black suede boots. He seemed to be just as curious as his partner. After all, how often does one see someone like Zephyr in this area of the city? *Maybe she was looking for trouble on purpose,* he thought. This idea worried him, but he pursued his curiosity in the end. Zephyr was way too beautiful to escape.

They were standing next to a waxed 1974 sports car that Zephyr admitted was of exceptional quality. It was so clean, in fact, that the men saw a beautiful Latina walking toward them in the car door's reflection. They both gazed at her with sinister attempts buried in their eyes.

"'Sup, girl? You look a li'l lost." White Jacket spoke first.

"I am, actually," Zephyr said. "I was wondering if you could direct me towards Nobe Avenue?"

"Damn, you are *way* off," he answered. His colleague walked behind Zephyr and blocked her escape. "I could give you some directions, but directions need payment."

Zephyr's mouth dropped. "Oh . . . no, it's okay. I'll . . . just be on my way."

She turned around and saw Red Jacket walk towards her. He studied her figure and concluded that she was someone who clearly took care of herself. It was a shame that she had to find herself in this situation. He felt sorry for her. Almost. She should have known better than to venture down this path. Both men were lonely, and she would provide exceptional company. Still, he felt something . . . off with her.

"This is a toll booth," Red Jacket said.

"Oh?" Zephyr nervously replied. "Look, I'll give you whatever money you want. Just . . . how much is it?"

"You," White Jacket answered.

Zephyr felt their body heat warm her back. They were so close that she could smell the lust on their clothes. She felt White Jacket's hot hand grab her arm. Zephyr smirked and narrowed her cold eyes.

"Thank you."

She whipped around and snatched White Jacket's wrist in such a fluid motion that he was too surprised to react. She twisted his wrist to the point where his pinky was aimed towards his ankle. The thought of one of their heads slamming onto the pavement made Zephyr smirk, so she decided to that thought into action. She stomped her foot on White Jacket's right knee joint and watched it mutate in an unnatural and agonizing position.

She left White Jacket moan on the concrete and watched Red Jacket. He lunged toward her with a knife in his hand, hell-bent on shoving the shining blade deep into those damning eyes of hers. She saw it coming miles away, and he soon learned this fact when she dodged each wide swipe he made with such ease, as if she wanted to dance with him rather than kill him. Zephyr subtly stepped backward toward their car, smiling at him and taunting him the entire time. He wanted to slash that pretty face so badly that he made one large lunge at her. Zephyr just stepped to her right and showed him her profile. She firmly gripped both his wrist and his forearm, and bent his arm into an abnormal locus. Zephyr looked up to see the grimace on his face. She knew that she was doing everything just right.

After Zephyr had cracked his arm and watched it swing back and forth on its own, she heard a scream coming from White Jacket's direction. No attention whatsoever was paid to it. She left him on the ground and casually opened the car door. She then held his collar in her hand and dragged his head over to the car. He was heavier than expected, and she promised to herself that she would slice out his intestines if her nail broke. Luckily for both people, she was able to position his right where she wanted. She placed his forehead on the car step, digging her sharp heel into his neck for stability. Once he was satisfyingly positioned, she lifted her sleek leg, placed it on the door, and slammed it directly on his temple. Her pushes were powerful, she realized, when she looked at his body quiver even after the blow was inflicted. She kept kicking and kicking the car door, squeaking with every brutal slam. Blood started to pour out of his head—so much that it seemed to emit an evil red hue once it combined with his jacket.

She studied his chest for a moment and waited for his lungs to expand and contract. It took a few seconds, but she recognized the faint rise of his stomach once he inhaled, albeit with a stuttered motion. Zephyr whipped her hair away from her face as she calmly waltzed over to him. She reached into his belt and pulled out a chrome pistol. Meanwhile, White Jacket managed to hoist himself up from his bloody ground. Zephyr saw every movement from the corner of her eye.

"Stay down."

Zephyr shot two bullets in total: one in each shoulder. She let the echo of the bullets crack throughout the night air and let it reverberate out into space. Her victim fell in an odd manner. He did not fall forward nor backward; he merely knelt down in front of her. All he could do was stare up at her. His prostration was that of a worshipper kneeling in front of God. Right now, Zephyr was his deity.

"I want you to deliver a message," she started, taking the gun in her hand and placing it in her coat pocket. She pulled out a small compact mirror and studied her hair as she addressed her humbled sycophant. "I want you to tell your bosses that Zephyr Estrada is the true heir to the throne. This kingdom is mine, and they need to be cognizant of that fact and execute themselves. Can you remember that for me?"

White Jacket was held in a constricting pain that subtracted his ability to speak. Zephyr nodded to him as she closed the mirror.

"Very good. And stay alive for me . . . I want that message delivered. And lose some weight—you made my forehead perspire."

His eyes suddenly became heavy. His friend had escaped from his mind. If he was alive, then God bless him. Or maybe he should have thanked her. She could have killed them both with too much ease. But the vision of the woman who had instructed him these things disappeared into a blur. The last thing he remembered, which he reported to a pair of terrified bosses, was how beautiful she was.

"She said . . . she said that she is the true heir to the throne . . . and that you two have to leave . . ."

White Jacket was bleeding all over the floor. He was less than alive but not dead, which was miraculous given his conditions. The river of blood etched itself between each speck of dirt on the floor, guiding it through some invisible stream. Red Jacket was missing. No one cared. Zephyr was here, and that mattered more than anything right now.

"Oh no . . . oh God . . ." Pedro murmured. It was the first time he called out to God since his father . . .

Slim slammed his fist on the table. The tremor shook everyone in the room. "What the fuck is she doing back here?"

Pedro was trembling in his seat. He did not answer his partner. He did not even look at him.

"Jesus Christ, Pedro! Answer me!"

"I don't know!"

"Fucking hell! How are we supposed to handle this?" Slim picked up a bottle of vodka and threw it at a nearby wall. He picked up another bottle and slammed it on the floor. Then he flipped over the table, grabbed its legs, and slammed it on the floor. He took out his rage on the furnishings in the same way that he wished to exert on Zephyr.

"Son of a fucking bitch!" Slim was panting and coughing on his saliva.

"Sir," White Jacket pleaded, "I need to get to a hospital . . . and Trent is still in the alley unconscious-"

"Shut the fuck up!" Slim pulled out a gun from his waist and shot White Jacket in the head. He hopped over to his dead body and shot him three more times in his chest. The splash of blood was not enough to calm Slim, so he decided to kick him in the sides until his leg got tired. Instead of stopping, his kicks just slowed down and became considerably weaker. The last punt made him drop onto the floor.

"Funny . . ." Slim said with a chuckle. "Just . . . funny."

"Just . . . find her." Pedro ordered to no one in particular. Slim, however, was sane enough to listen to Pedro's words and follow them.

"I'll send out the word . . . keep this quiet . . . don't want Mal to know . . . don't want her to know . . ."

Both men turned their heads toward each other. Non-psychics would have known what went on between their minds. They were angry with themselves and with each other. Their gift of retrospect was more powerful today than any other day. After all, it was a dead boss whom Pedro had killed. This boss had a son. And a daughter. One sibling had killed his father; the other was going to kill him. Their soldiers watched on as they almost worshipped each other's curiosity. None dared to ask what harm Zephyr could do.

However, moments later, someone walked in their office with a baggy suit on his back and a long frown in his face. He was followed by another gangster, who wore a sweat suit instead. Pedro could see the dark cloud hovering over their heads. No one seemed to notice the bleeding corpse that kissed the floor. Slim was still lost in his anguish; his forehead was glued to the wall. Suddenly, he lifted up his head and whispered the word "fuck" when the shadow of Mr. Mal spilled into the room.

"You don't come by to see me no more," he bellowed. He puffed on his signature cigar as he slowly stepped over to Slim. He opened his lips and blew a dark cloud into his eyes. "Especially you. But I have a heart. You're still my prodigal son . . ."

He walked over to Pedro and wrapped his gaunt arm around him. Pedro coughed in Mr. Mal's smoky odor: tobacco mixed with expensive French cologne that wafted throughout the room. Mr. Mal patted his shoulder and smiled.

"You too! Shit, I haven't seen you in a minute! My man!"

At that moment, Mr. Mal's arm slid into the crease of Pedro's neck. He squeezed that small chunk of flesh tighter and tighter. Pedro's pulse began to beat quicker; his face turned rose red. It was so fast that he couldn't scream. He opened his mouth to yell, but only a sliver of saliva poured out the corner of his mouth.

"I oughta kick your fucking asses!"

Slim tried to run to Pedro, but one of Mr. Mal's men kicked him behind the knee and slammed him against the floor. They held him down by his arms and forced a gun against his head. He never knew that he would feel the cool frost of metal rub against his temple. He tried to stand back up, but the weight of Mr. Mal's men kept him on the floor. His eyes turned up toward Pedro and the giant.

"I heard what happened in Third Alley! One of my boys here was takin' a li'l stroll down that way. He heard that pussy groan a fucking mile away! So he steps up. He says, 'Goddamn Trent! Who the fuck happened to you?'" Mr. Mal leaned toward Pedro's ear. "Zephyr . . . Estrada."

Pedro felt his vision flash and blur. Oxygen was escaping his lungs. His heart was beating too fast. Too hard. He was dying, and by God, it felt fantastic.

Mr. Mal released his grip and watched Pedro crumble to the floor. He hacked out the loss of life that had entered his body. He breathed in existence once his eyes readjusted. He sat up and pushed himself away from Mr. Mal. He chuckled as he approached him.

"I specifically remember you having a sister. I would've hoped she'd be six feet under by now."

"I . . . didn't know she would—"

"I remember she had a father that got his punk ass shot to hell. I remember she disappeared."

"I swear . . . on my mother's—"

"And I thought about it on the way over here. Hypothetically speaking—and this is just off the top of my head—what if the long-forgotten beloved sister of the present Spanish Don of this city knew that her brother shoved a few bullets into their father's chest, killed him, and sunk him in God knows where? Now I'm not saying that I'm the smartest man in the world, but I would *imagine* that she must be . . . upset."

"Just let me—"

"So let's say I'm right," Mr. Mal said, bending down on one knee to speak closer to Pedro's ears. "Let's say that she is pissed that Daddy dearest met his end a little too quickly. Do you think that she would come back and exact revenge and all that shit?"

Pedro stayed silent. He knew his words meant nothing to Mr. Mal. He was in control right now, as always.

"I think so," he continued. "I think she would go bat shit on all of you motherfuckers! She would wipe you all out like it was ethnic cleansing! She would slice of your dicks and feed them to dogs! And you wouldn't be able to do a goddamned thing about it!"

"Look!" Slim screamed out. "We will find her!"

"Shut the *fuck* up!" Mr. Mal suddenly stood up and stomped over to Slim. "You should've found her decades ago!"

"She fucking disappeared, man!"

"Oh, I think Mrs. Houdini reappeared. No, no . . . you will make her disappear for real this time. I want her alive. I'm gonna fuck that tight-ass pussy, and then I'm gonna put a bullet in her head. So how are you gonna make this happen?"

"We'll . . . fucking shit! We'll spread out our guys every-fucking-where . . . and we'll bleed the Russian to help . . . and we'll get her. I swear to fucking . . . we'll get her!"

"Now that's what I wanted to hear." Mr. Mal puffed another cloud of smoke into Slim's face. He looked over at Pedro and chuck-led. He ordered his men to let go of their hold on Slim and escorted

Mr. Mal outside. Once his shadow disappeared, Pedro summoned his speech once again.

"God help us," he said.

"I'm atheist right now, just shut the fuck up and let's handle this now." Slim stretched his lower back and stumbled out of the room, leaving Pedro alone with his thoughts. He could not believe that Zephyr had returned after all these years. He almost had forgotten about her. He was not ready to accept it. This was a dream. Of course it was! No way could she be here again!

He stood up and pinched his arm. His discolored skin gave him no clue to the absence of reality. So he grabbed a knife in his desk drawer and began to slit his wrist. Each drop of blood angered him more, until he started to hack away at his arm.

Nothing. At all.

He threw away the knife and reached into his desk drawer once more. A few minutes later, when Slim re-entered the room, Pedro was sitting in his chair with a rubber tube around his bicep and a needle in his arm. His face was peaceful, droopy but calm. Slim became jealous and rolled up his sleeve.

*　　*　　*

Rebecca knelt down behind an old brick wall that had not recovered its red hue in years. She controlled her breathing while everyone else around her was panting like dogs in August. She could smell the nervous sweat that dripped from their foreheads and saw how it glistened atop their terrified eyes. Their fingers were fumbling the pouches that hung on their waists. No one dared to leave their safe spot—they clung to their walls like a child grips a security blanket.

Another bullet chipped at Rebecca's wall. She closed her eyes only to shield them from any dusty residue. Once she opened them back up, she peeked around the corner and took a quick glance at her surroundings. The alley was a nightmare to begin with, never mind the skinny corridor that branched off into small pockets where a group of gang members—Rebecca counted maybe half a dozen of them—could pick off every cop that tried to advance.

Stupid goddamned anonymous tip.

Her hair was a mess. She had tied her hair into a ponytail and hooked it to the base of her skull. Greg told her that it was supposed to keep it from attracting those who like to pull things. She joked around and said that he must do the same down there. He gave her an evil look, but she refused to stop laughing. She later apologized after she had caught her breath, not because she regretted her words but because she did not want to receive a citation.

Rebecca wondered why she was thinking of all these things at a time like this. Maybe it was the rush of adrenaline that brought her a sense of . . . contentment. *Weird*, she thought to herself. This firefight reminded her of those video games some of the guys back at the precinct would play. She chuckled as she fired off two rounds into the alley.

"Don't you wish we had a God mode on right now?"

"Now's not the time to joke around, Ortega!" one of the officers screamed at her.

"Just saying! I'm out of continues right now! How many men do we have here? Four?" Another stream of bullets flew out of the alley and poured out into the street. "How many do we have in there? I counted six!"

The officer grabbed his radio and shouted some orders into it. "This is Officer Hamen requesting more backup! Corner of Thirty-Second Street Southeast! We have—oh fuck!"

One of the thugs had an Uzi and he knew how to use it. Rebecca could almost see the rain of bullets that sprayed out from the alley. She closed her eyes and inhaled deeply as she reloaded her gun from memory. She remembered how fast she disassembled and reassembled firearms like she was baking a cake. One officer once said to her that Colt was her lover and used the barrel other than firing bullets. She feigned laughter, and then she slapped him. Twice.

"On my mark, we fire."

"Are you fucking kidding me? We don't even know who else has—"

"I know these buildings! Just trust me!" she yelled.

The officer became silent. He saw Rebecca falling into deep concentration, for God knows why. He couldn't care less—he just wanted to go home. More rounds kept spewing out through the corridor. Chunks of rock and brick were flying past their feet. He may as well have built a sand castle with the debris in front of him and his brave new partner.

"Now!"

Rebecca dove toward the alley and fired off five shots at the man who had just run out of ammo. His body jerked underneath the force of Rebecca's noble boyfriend. The sheer velocity of her finger pulling the trigger was absolutely terrifying. Her double-taps never missed their targets. Once he started to descend, Rebecca used this opportunity to use his body as a blockade of anyone else who wanted to fire at her. She rolled to the other side of the alley and joined her teammates. She exhaled, but it sounded more like a sigh of relief than a sigh of fear.

"Five!"

Rebecca stood up on her feet and hugged the wall. Her colleagues watched her adjust her grip on her sidearm with the touch of a gentle seamstress. An endless stream of vengeful bullets shot out from the alley. Some of the gangsters were shouting out mournful curses at their deceased friend.

"Motherfuckers!

Rebecca reached around the corner with her hand and blind-fired at anyone who approached. She was surprised to hear one guy drop to the ground, followed by the screech of his weapon slide on the pavement. "Four! Where the fuck is that backup?"

"On its way!"

"What are they doing? Getting their nails done?" Rebecca whipped her head around the corner then retracted it once the gang members saw her pretty head. One of them took his friend's Uzi and tried to match his skill. The bullets were awkward, and if Rebecca remembered correctly, the bullets were few. She did not notice that her teammates were letting her do most of the work. They could not help if they wanted to; she was taking out the targets all by herself.

"C'mon, c'mon, hurry it up . . ." she whispered. "Okay, guys! On me!"

The Uzi spat out a handful of bullets before it clicked.

"Now!"

All four officers emptied their clips into the alley. Another heavy body descended to the ground with a loud thud. Three. *Big guy*, Rebecca concluded. She turned to her comrades and issued them silent directions. *Go around the block, cut them off on the other side, and flank them.* They already knew to notify her when they were in position. They all nodded and dispersed in opposite directions. Beautiful. Time to concentrate.

Rebecca closed her eyes again and reloaded her weapon. The empty clip dropped toward the ground, but she caught it midair to avoid any unwanted alerts in her direction. She waited for that distortion to pierce her ears. Why the hell was there always static? She heard her radio turn on. She opened her eyes and pressed a button.

"We're here," one of them said. "Waiting on you."

"On five," she answered. "One . . . two . . . five!"

Rebecca sprinted inside the alley and held her gun in front of her. A shadow crept out of the pocket. Rebecca smirked and fired four shots at the poor idiot who thought he could take her down. His body dropped in front of her. She leapt over him and continued down. She could hear the other officers approach her on the other side. They met each other midway, all with bewildered looks on their faces.

"I thought you said there were six!"

"Up there!" Rebecca was the first to point her gun toward heaven. She did not know how she knew where to point, but when she did, the last of the dead gang fell from the steel balcony and landed twenty feet below. Rebecca and her own gang approached him with caution. Blood was spilling from his neck and covered him in a small puddle. Rebecca holstered her gun and shook her weary fingers.

"Two," she said.

"We lost one," one of the sweaty officers lamented. He holstered his gun and wiped the sweat from his forehead. "They must have escaped from the back before we got there."

"At least we're all alive," Rebecca said, looking around the inside of the alley. She exhaled out of exasperation rather than relief. "The back leads to Dorow Way. Sidewalk camera should pick him up if he heads east. If not, there's another one at the Nigh intersection, if he goes that way. If not, we're screwed, but we live to fight another day." Rebecca wiped her forehead with her sleeve. "Fuck, this was pure hell, I'm glad we all got through it." She opened the holster and let her gun drop into its pocket. "Oh God . . . this was tough."

"You didn't seem like you were having a hard time," one of the officers said. "By the way . . . how did you know when to advance?"

"I counted the bullets."

"From an Uzi, Ortega?"

"Yep!"

"Horseshit."

"I just . . . knew."

"And how did you know about—"

"These buildings?" she interrupted. "I know everything, remember?"

"When it comes to Ellipses, you sure do."

"Bernini's gonna shit his pants once he finds out what went down here," another officer added.

"Don't worry," one of the officers reassured, "we got your back."

Rebecca smiled. "Thanks."

"Oh God! No! No!" He was laughing and genuinely happy. "Thank *you*!"

"How did those two assholes get out of there?"

"When I gave the order to encircle them, they probably had already escaped to the back toward Dorow Way before we had arrived."

Detective Bernini kept scratching the back of his neck as he listened to Rebecca's report. He would have had her type one out, but he said "Screw it" and gave her an interview—although Rebecca felt like it was an interrogation.

"What else?"

"So," she continued, "I saw our backup arrive. We all swept the area. Coroners had to call for extra gurneys. The men have yet to be identified, however, we all know they were Forty-Second Street."

"I see . . ." Bernini slouched in his squeaky chair and slightly rocked back and forth. "How do you it would be Dorow Way?

Rebecca sighed. "Because it's the only way out that doesn't lead to construction, and it would have slowed him down and get himself caught, thus my conclusion that he could've gone down another road, which he didn't, and no camera picked him up, blah blah blah—I know this city."

"Hmph. And that's that, huh?"

"Yep." Rebecca sighed and crossed her legs. "By the way, you need to get rid of that damn chair. It's driving me nuts."

"Hell no! I had this chair since I first worked here. This is a relic."

"It's an antique," she joked.

Bernini chuckled. "I won't rebut you this time, Ortega. Just know that the higher-ups took notice of today, so pretty soon you will have a squeaky chair yourself—if your other assignment goes well, that is. You're still going to her opening party, correct?"

"Like I have any choice. But this should be fun."

"I want you to make this productive. This is your ticket to the big leagues."

"I won't screw it up."

"Good." Bernini stood up from his chair and stretched out his arms. "I'm going to get a cup of coffee. And yes, I know you don't want any." He smiled at her. Rebecca merely smirked and stood up to leave. She nodded to him and began to leave.

"Oh, I almost forgot," he added. "A Forty-Second Street thug was admitted to the hospital late last night. Gunshot wounds in both shoulders. Fucking mess. Cops interviewed him, and he mentioned the name 'Zephyr Estrada.'"

Rebecca was shocked. "What?"

"You may want to talk to your girl. In the meantime, don't forget to type out the report and give it to whatshisname making copies over there."

Before Rebecca could answer him, her cell phone blared from her waist. She reached down into her pocket and checked the caller ID. "Unknown," it read. She let it ring a few more times, and then she pressed the Talk button to answer.

"Officer Ortega."

"Darling!" Zephyr's voice beamed from the other line. "How are you this evening?"

Rebecca looked at the detective and gave him a puzzled look. "Zephyr? Ah . . . I'm fine, how are you?"

Everyone within earshot of Rebecca quickly turned to her. The secretary, Bernini, a few colleagues, even the new guy who always made copies. Rebecca placed Zephyr on speakerphone so that her conversation was audibly recorded. Her breezy voice attracted the attention of all the men in the vicinity, most especially Detective Bernini.

"I am doing beautifully! I just wanted to call and confirm your company for my party coming up next weekend. I know you will be attending, of course, but it is proper to request your *respondez s'il vous plait* anyway."

"Oh . . . yes. Yes, I'll be there. I'll take some time to look for a costume—"

"I already have you covered."

"But . . . you don't know my—"

"I know everything!" Zephyr laughed. "I cordially invited you to my party, so you must allow me to accommodate you!"

"I guess I will have to accept your accommodations then."

"Of course you will. Furthermore, you have access to my personal VIP room, so we can chat for a while if you so choose."

"That sounds good, Zephyr."

"Lovely!" Zephyr became silent. Rebecca wondered if this was her cue to contribute the last words of the conversation. "By the way," Zephyr continued, "can you do me a small favor?"

"Yes?'

"Can you take me off speaker phone? I can feel the male hormones running wild over there."

Every man shrunk into their chests and calmly walked away from Rebecca. She could not help but smile.

"Thank you. Well, we shall keep in touch throughout the week. *Buenos noches!*"

"Zephyr, before you go . . . how did you get my number?"

Zephyr was silent on the other line. Rebecca briefly released the phone from her ear and checked the screen. The call did not drop, so they were still in contact. "Darling," Zephyr finally said, "I know everything."

The light on Rebecca's phone blinked on. Zephyr was gone, and so were any of Rebecca's intelligent guesses.

"Ortega," Bernini said, "I don't have to tell you to find out how she got your number. And how she is connected to the Forty-Second member that's bleeding his ass off in the hospital right now."

Everyone dispersed and returned to their duties. Rebecca knew that Greg meant more than what he said. But his implication did not bother her. More than anything, she was wondering what Zephyr was planning.

"Don't worry, boss man," she answered, "I'll get you answers."

She walked back to her desk and opened her laptop. She started typing her report on the blank screen in front of her. Her eyes narrowed in concentration. She was sick of the uncertainty, the inability to predict. She wanted to be psychic, but even if she were, she knew that Zephyr would always figure out her motive. Rebecca refused to let anyone outsmart her; she'd been through way too much to be defeated. Her independence was the source of her arrogance. Her strength was the soul of her drive.

These emotions poured onto the screen as she described each action in exquisite detail. The time of night, the number of alleged gunmen, the names of each officer with her. Nothing would be subtracted from that event. She wanted to put how grateful each of her comrades was, but too much fact could be construed as pride.

"Excuse me, Officer . . ."

Rebecca released her focus and laid her eyes upon the new guy. He sheepishly looked at her angry face with large glasses that reflected the ceiling lights. He had a stack of papers in his arms that seemed to shift out of order every time he breathed. He caught one piece of paper that slid out of his scrawny arms.

"I'm sorry," he apologized. "I get clumsy sometimes."

"No problem, what can I do for you?" she asked with a stoic tone in her voice.

"I'm just wondering . . . this Zephyr girl . . . why is she such a big deal?"

"Have you heard of Luis Estrada?"

"A little. Crime boss, right? Or . . .he was."

"He had a daughter."

"Oh . . ." He looked away from Rebecca, who kept her eyes on the young man. His innocence was still apparent, almost worthy of envy. "I . . . you know . . . overheard the detective saying that one of Forty-Second Street mentioned her name. The one that got shot. Do . . . you think she's really capable of doing that?"

Rebecca stared at the glare in his glasses. She focused on the bright squares that gleamed across his eyes. They were so damn perfect, so meticulous in its placement on his lens. They were laid like white cotton sheets on a palace bed.

"You know what, Mr. Xerox? That's a good question.

VI

Zephyr stepped out of her ominous chariot in front of Vladimir's restaurant. The bright neon lights shone on her car, casting a colorful mirror across the hood. The building reflected on Zephyr's colorless eyes and seemed to shrink in front of her. The guard—who previously had the discomfort of meeting her earlier—saw her, fixed his tie, and breathed in an extremely careful manner.

Zephyr studied the building for the first time. She was surprised that she did not do this in the past, but she was at her beloved Rubicon River and had to see everything that was in front of her before she could proceed. Her civil war was truly about to begin; the dice was in her hands. She just had to throw them.

She imagined herself sitting at a table. Nothing fancy, just a small wooden table with a fresh and polished shine. There were no walls, no evidence of barriers surrounding her. There was a black air. A frosty wind blew across her hair. Her white eyes shone through the dark and cast a subtle light around the rest of her face. Her expression was stoic; her emotions dead.

Zephyr blinked once. In an instant, the city of Ellipses rose out of the table and shot forth into Zephyr's view. She waited for the buildings to adjust themselves according to their scaled height and their wonderful architecture. Each street and tiny alley burrowed themselves within the metallic crevices, and then they were filled with small cars and miniature citizens. She chuckled. They reminded her of the dolls and sports cars she used to play with when she was a little girl. *Funny*, she realized. Many years ago, she was frolicking with effigies; now she was frolicking with the actual and the real. This time, the originals replaced the replicas. The distortion of reality was what Zephyr most dreamed. To control what used to be unaltered was . . . sexy.

She opened her hand and watched as the shadow of her palm flew over the entire city. Immediately, the city lights flickered on and dotted its personal black sky. The vehicles below turned on their headlights, and the people switched on their flashlights. Everything moved in a slow pace; no one rushed to his or her destinations. The city had finally reached night.

Zephyr retracted her hand, and opposite actions occurred: the city lights shut off, as did the vehicles below and the flashlights' owners. Movement accelerated, and life continued as promised to those fortunate enough to live it. The city on that little table continued on as if there never was a long shadow. The existence of darkness had long been forgotten.

Zephyr crossed her sculpted legs and spread out her fingers. The city model floated toward her hand and sat in front of her bosom. She waved her finger down to turn the city on its side and facing her. She now had a direct bird's eye view of the city.

She gently clapped her hands together as if she was in prayer and stared at the model. Everything was still in its place. No one seemed to notice her control over their physics. She separated her hands and the buildings surrounding a particular road separated themselves. She separated her fingers in a pulsing motion and further zoomed in on that road which captured her attention. She may as well have been controlling the city like it was a touch screen.

The road was the alleged headquarters of Mr. Mal. She knew the layout by heart and just wanted to make sure that the building had not been recently set aflame—at least not yet. She nodded her head and pinched her fingers together to zoom back out. A curious smile crept on her face.

Now she held the model in both hands and twisted it in a certain direction. After a few turns of the model, she came upon her old home. She released the model and let it float in the air. Her smile disappeared. Her cold, silvery eyes held a sense of longing for this morally abandoned mansion. She blinked once to keep herself from showing any signs of a tear welling up inside of her. She shut her eyes while she flicked the model on a random direction. She knew the home way too well to study it any further.

"*Papi*," she whispered. She knew that she would automatically think of him once she set her sight on her home. Or . . . what she thought was her home. But it was impossible for her to predict how forlorn she would feel for her father. An image of him holding her on the last night that he saw her made her heart . . .

Not yet, she told herself. *Almost*. She could think of him once everything was done. Once everyone had been brutalized, she could cry and sob and think of him all she wanted. Just . . . not now.

She held the model in her hand one last time and curled it into a ball. She placed pressure on it to shrink it down to the size of a tennis ball. She let it float for a moment, watching it spin on its own axis and the axis that she created. The city was hers to control: the phase of day, the view of the city. The specified dominance was her key attribute, and it was an ability she would exercise to its fullest.

Zephyr took the ball in her left hand and crushed it into a million sparks. It fell to the floor without her having to gaze at its descent. She was confident that her control was monopolized. It was just a matter of time before everyone else knew it as well.

As she sat up from her fantastic table, she approached the shy guard. He cleared his throat and awaited her.

"The boss, he's . . . inside waiting . . ."

Zephyr smiled. The sight of her deep dimples made him feel relaxed and calm. "Everything is okay. I will not . . . injure you again." She looked down at his crotch and snickered.

"Okay, because . . . I was worried . . ."

"What is your name?"

"M-Mikhail."

"Zephyr." She politely outstretched her hand. He reluctantly obliged her and shook her hand in a gentle manner. Her hands were as soft as butter and as warm as freshly baked bread. Her eyes seemed to be less frigid than before. Then again, she was not piercing his testicle with a manicured fingernail at the moment.

"No hard feelings?" she sweetly asked.

ANDREW COOKE

"You can say that again." Mikhail stepped aside and allowed Zephyr to enter the restaurant. She felt the warm air kiss her skin and the smell of hot food steaming from the kitchen. A number of tables were placed together that formed a sort of banquet table. A plethora of fine Spanish cuisine was ordered in such a sophisticated and splendid manner. Zephyr could not have planned this herself any better. Truly, he was grateful for her timely arrival.

His gratitude manifested itself in the form of hearty meals and expensive drinks. The wines that lined the middle of the table were imbued with noble antiquity. The candles cast a brilliant glow upon each glass that sparkled in front of Zephyr's eyes. She whispered a genuine voice of surprise once she saw the desserts that lined a table situated against the far wall. They were as delectable in sight as well as in scent.

Zephyr meditated upon the delicious after-dinner treats that begged her to indulge in her temptations. She scanned the room for a familiar face, or rather, a face she was expecting to find. She came upon a kindly old Russian man who looked to be in his late sixties wearing a suit that seemed to only see the light of night on special occasions.

The purpose of this special occasion answered Zephyr before she even questioned it. Vladimir had a number of men that stood behind him. They all looked to be middle-aged, but their wisdom had shone in their eyes, and it was a timeless perception. They were a racially mixed crowd, although Zephyr did find a Spanish majority within.

"So," she asked with a smile on her face, "what do you have planned?"

"Ah! You know already!" Vladimir walked over toward Zephyr and outstretched his elbow.

"Yes, I apologize. I hope I didn't spoil the surprise."

"No, my dear. I had a feeling that I could not surprise the daughter of a strategist. But please . . . come with me."

Zephyr took his arm and had him lead her to the group of men that stood at the end of the room. There must have been at least two dozen of them. They respectfully nodded to their guest and waited for her to reach their vicinity.

She truly was a rare beauty, a quality oft-mentioned to her implicitly more than the alternatives. She wore a taciturn little black dress, and she was glad to have worn such a coveted outfit during this evening. She wore a pair of Dior shoes that showed a peek of her toes. She nodded and gave them a comforting smile.

"Gentlemen," she started, "please sit with me."

"No, Miss Estrada." One of the men spoke up. "We are honored to stand for you."

Vladimir gently took her hand and had her sit in a dark leather chair. It cushioned her body and hugged her frame as a young child hugs a stuffed animal. Once her gentle body reclined in its throne, all eyes were on her own.

"Because of your devotion, I will protect you all with my life. My words will be your guides through these events. I swear to you that your souls will be rewarded in the afterlife, even if it means the damnation of my own. This is my first promise."

Zephyr witnessed the unanimous acceptance from all the men in the room. She continued with a light spirit in her voice.

"We all have been damaged by my un-brother, Pedro Estrada, and the miserable anathema he calls his partner. Though I flirt with the delight of slicing out their hearts in an immediate and warranted manner, I embrace wisdom. First, we must be strategic. We must exploit their weaknesses so that our cause will set an example to the mindless ones. We are a monopoly, and my reign will lead us into an immortal glory. This is my second promise.

"Let us never forget the benevolence in our spirits, for the abandonment of morality will give way to an unholy tranquility. To cast aside that which is good will only transform us into shallow souls. Always remember love. Remember that one emotion that has kept our gaze set upon wonder and hope. Never forget your childhood, that simple age of innocence where we did not know of death or what death does or why death exists. Though we will exact fatalities upon our targets, we must remain aware of what we are doing. We are ending lives, but do know that these are lives that require a quick severance.

"I ask you all to remember the last moments you have had with your loved ones." Zephyr took a quick vow of silence before she continued. "This purgatory in which we live has disallowed us a thought pertinent to retribution. And I assure you, our agony will finally disperse. I will give you entertainment. I will forcefully vacate all souls that resulted in the deaths of our happiness. I share your pain, I am the embodiment of your pain. Together, we will take our sadness as God's blessing, for He has given us weapons.

"With these weapons," she continued, with a growing anger in her voice, "we will slice their throats until their blood floods this city. Never again will we shed tears for our lost ones. Never again will we flee our homes and ransom our lives! We shall tear apart their beating hearts and feed them to the dogs, for we are magnanimous at giving them such a merciful death! We shall choke their souls into submission and watch as they burn in hell's flames! We have all lost our dearest, and so they shall lose their own! Channel your hate, gentlemen! Thrust your anguished blades into their sternums and twist! Never quit until they surrender their tarnished souls to judgment!

"Do this for me," she concluded, her voice returning to a gentle yet ominous tone, "and I shall reward you with a vengeance served warm. This is my final promise."

Everyone cheered for Zephyr once she had finished. Even Vladimir Kandinsky smiled and nodded his head in assent. She had their undying support, and they were willing to sacrifice themselves for her, as much as Zephyr was willing to sacrifice herself for them. She successfully garnered their devotion with her leadership. She motivated them with her words, and her commands would be followed without inquiry or reluctance.

What happened next was unprecedented. The men formed a line and knelt down in front of her, as a humble mortal offers his loyalty to his goddess. Each kissed her foot and tasted the soft flavor of her power on their lips. Zephyr felt it rude to halt their fealty, and so she sat with poise and respect. Simply, Zephyr was loved.

After the last man had finished, she saw Vladimir Kandinsky approach her. He slowly kneeled onto his withered knee and kissed her foot. He looked up at her with red eyes and a smile on his face. Zephyr smiled at him, her gentle sparkle comforting him as he stood up in defiance of his age. She looked among the men in the room. Her first order was to be spoken.

"Let us begin," she commanded.

*   *   *

Vladimir could not help but smile at the sudden hustle that occurred inside his quaint restaurant. Zephyr dictated orders to each person with such graceful leadership, and she also displayed a friendly character when she smiled at a job well done. She was such a motivating figure that the men seemed to smile when she spoke to them, as if she breathed encouragement into their lungs. Their spirits seem to resuscitate with every movement of her lips. Their energy was driven solely by her presence. *Yes*, Vladimir thought, she truly was the daughter of Luis Estrada. And she was right; she was the true heir.

"Marco," she asked in an amiable tone, "I need your expertise with architecture. Perhaps you could help expedite the construction of this part of my new club?"

"Certainly, *donna*."

She giggled. "Zephyr."

"Yes, Zephyr."

"Beautiful. Speak with Vladimir about the details. He already has his men at the site. The blueprints are there for you to peruse. Follow my notes, and your quest should be fairly simple."

"As you wish, Zephyr."

Zephyr grabbed his shoulders and stared at him with her cold white eyes. "Relax!" she said with a wide smile on her face.

"Ah . . . okay . . . you got it."

"Better!" Zephyr patted his shoulder and allowed him to depart. She turned her attention to one of Vladimir's Russian men and waved him over. He was enthusiastic in his approach. Zephyr knew that he had wanted to speak with her since her speech had ended.

"*Da?*"

"How are the stockpiled weapons?"

"We . . . do not have much."

"How much is much?"

"Twenty-five AK-47s."

"More than enough." Zephyr motioned with him to a nearby table. She grabbed a pen and note paper that lay in front of her and started to scribble on it. She tore off the page and handed it to him. "Can you deliver them to this address?"

"You sure that this will be enough? Pedro's men and the gangs are—"

"Darling," Zephyr reassured him, "strategy wins every battle."

"I . . . you're right. Okay."

"Thank you!" Zephyr watched him leave the restaurant and turned to Vladimir, who sat in a chair in the corner. He was relaxed, as if he took a night off to watch his men work under someone else's command. He trusted Zephyr so much that he contemplated retiring his position and casting aside his lackluster dominance over the city. She winked at him, and he winked back. She was unstoppable. Beautiful. Lustrous. The perfect woman, yet the most damaged. She never experienced joy, unless it was dying memories of her late father or the last moments of her faltering childhood. *Poor Zephyr Estrada,* he lamented. *Such a gorgeous mind corrupted by life itself, Pedro be damned.*

"Mikhail, my dearest." Zephyr laid her eyes upon the tall Russian who had the displeasure of meeting her during her very first visit. "How are your drug supplies?"

"It . . . is diminishing. We have maybe a million dollars' worth."

"Get in contact with distributors. All of them. Every low-life, every hobo, every young teenager trying to grow a pair. Give them exactly fifty percent of what you have and tell them to sell it at a lower price than what Pedro is selling. You will see the profit soon enough, I guarantee it. Give the leftovers to your comrades at the construction site. They already have a list of my instructions and will know what to do with it. Pretty please?"

"Yes, of course. I have all the information here." Mikhail pointed to his skull.

"Beautiful. Any sex slaves?"

"Y-yes." Mikhail was surprised by Zephyr's emotionless question. She had to be stoic, he supposed.

"Good. I realize it will be a bit pricey, but make them into prostitutes. Send them to this address . . ." Zephyr wrote another set of words on the note paper. She ripped it out and gave it to Mikhail. He read it with a perplexed look in his face.

"Are you sure?" he asked.

"Why, of course! Follow my instructions and we should have a solid foundation."

"Y-yes, Miss—I mean . . . Zephyr."

Zephyr gave him a polite nod and sent him off. She looked around the room and was pleased with the results of her ambition. She caught the eye of Vladimir, who admired her strength and her aptitudes. She accepted the evils of such businesses, and for that, he was glad for her understanding but bitter because she had to understand it. It was a requirement, a mandate, and not a mere suggestion or a "soft need."

Zephyr read the thoughts in his eyes. She smiled at him and walked out of the restaurant.

VII

Rebecca was surprised that Zephyr was able to keep up with her on the treadmill. Her strides were as perfect as Rebecca's, very graceful and disciplined. Rebecca thought she had the crown as far as endurance, but it seemed as though she had a rival in her midst. The platform was rolling at a moderate speed but tough enough to produce a warm glow on both of their foreheads.

Zephyr had called her a few days after her events with Vladimir and asked her if she wanted to work out together. Rebecca obliged, and then she phoned Greg and reported her plans. "Then you know what to do," Greg answered. Well, of course she knew what to do, but Zephyr was slowly becoming more of a friend than an assignment. They had so many parallels: the loss of a parent, the struggle of surviving, the ambition to be unrivaled . . . it was truly amazing how their lives were the same, though they were at opposing ends of the law.

But actually, Zephyr never did anything. Or never did anything that was *noticed*.

Rebecca and Zephyr had finished their two-mile warm up and cooled down. Rebecca grabbed her water bottle and drank about a quarter of the bottle. She looked from the corner of her eye at Zephyr and saw that she was doing the same thing. Thank God.

"Wow," Zephyr said between her heavy breaths.

"Look who's talking," Rebecca replied.

"Well, usually my warm-ups are not this hard." Zephyr took another swig of water. "But there was no way I was going to let you beat me."

"Funny, I was thinking the same thing."

They shut off their treadmills and stepped down to stretch their burning muscles. The gymnasium was a bit crowded. It was a typical Monday, so everyone was burning off weekend calories and Sunday football beer. Every cardio machine had been taken: stair-climbers, rowing machines, ellipticals, and stationary bicycles. Rebecca laughed when Zephyr sprinted toward a pair of treadmills that was recently vacated by a couple. She politely nodded at them as she climbed onto hers and frantically waved for Rebecca to join her.

"I'm surprised you didn't tackle them, Zephyr," she had joked.

"I thought about that until I realized that a cop was here."

"I wouldn't have arrested you."

"Uh-huh."

Rebecca stretched her lower back when she looked up and noticed an audience of sweaty men's eyes pointed at her. She sat up and waited for Zephyr to rise from her hamstring stretch.

"Those guys over there are checking us out."

"Aww, that's so sweet! We're giving them motivation!"

"Is that another word for a hard-on?"

Zephyr laughed heartily. "I can't top that! Brilliant!"

Rebecca laughed. She finished up her stretches and sat up to wait for Zephyr to finish. Suddenly, she realized something.

"Zephyr?"

"What? Did I just give Muscle Mike over there more inspiration?"

"You've used a contraction."

Zephyr's smile quickly faded. "Pardon?"

"You've never used grammatical contractions before."

Zephyr studied Rebecca's face with her lifeless eyes. God help her, Rebecca was right. "It happens. Are you ready to begin?"

"Yeah . . . I'm set." She knew that Zephyr had deflected, but she chose not to pry. It was the weirdest observation Rebecca has ever given, but holy geez, she was right.

The two women proceeded to the main weight room where they could smell the testosterone miles away. The scent made their noses crunch, so they hurriedly walked to a stack of small weights, picked them up, and almost ran to a private corner where they could work out in peace and relief. They ignored the stares, the whistles, most of all, the whispers. "What I wouldn't do to watch them squat," and more explicitly, "She could definitely curl my bar . . ."

Zephyr caught the attention of one bodybuilder who looked to be moving toward his mid-forties. His arms were still full of snakes and his chest was certainly monstrous, but his gut seemed to miss out on the hours and hours of punishment the rest of his body had experienced. His clean-shaven face and his needle-spiked hair were evidence to his struggle against age. He kept shooting quick glances at Zephyr, thinking that she did not notice, but in reality, she predicted his actions.

"Darling," she whispered to Rebecca, "would you like to see something funny?"

"I'm surprised you even asked."

Zephyr smiled and turned away from Rebecca. She looked at the bodybuilder and waited for his head to turn. Once he did, Zephyr gave him a frigid stare that made him flinch and drop his weights. Rebecca swore that she had just swallowed his soul; his face turned white, his eyes lost focus, and his muscles became weak. Zephyr inflicted him with atrophy without moving a single lip.

"How do you do that, Zephyr?"

"Natural gift."

"Well, it seemed to work."

Zephyr smiled as she started her signature workout routine. Rebecca looked to her right and saw a large heavy bag hanging from a chain. The leather was ripped and dented, and for some strange reason, she wanted it to burst. And she would be the first to do it.

She saw a man who looked to be in his early thirties sitting on the floor next to the bag. He was sweating heavily as he forced off his punching gloves, throwing them at the floor as if he was trying to punish them for his arduous battle. He was panting, too heavily for Rebecca's taste. *Novice*, she thought.

She approached him with a confident stride, keeping her eyes strictly on his duffel bag. She cared less for the tired boxer whose eyes had sparkled brightly once he saw this beauty approach him. "Excuse me?" she politely asked, making sure to breathe through her mouth.

"I was wondering if you had an extra pair of gloves in your bag. I wanna try out this bag here."

"Yeah!" His hand burrowed inside his duffel and pulled out a wide set of red boxing gloves. He handed it to Rebecca with a smile— more like a horny grin, actually. Rebecca nodded and turned around toward Zephyr. She gave her a look that screamed, "Oh my god, this guy is so freaking stupid!" Zephyr covered her mouth to silence her giggle. The boxer starred at Rebecca's chest as she put them on. He stood up and studied her body up and down, meaning that he stared at her face, breast, legs, and butt.

"Do you need help with those?" *Please say yes.*

"No." Rebecca closed them with a rotation of her hand. She tucked in her elbows and shrugged her shoulders. The boxer was surprised at her stance. Had she done this before?

Rebecca then swayed side to side, stopping mid-sway to dance around the bag. She jabbed at the bag and moved away with ease. She gave another jab, then a straight, followed by a cross. The bag was swinging underneath her powerful blows, and so was the boxer's disbelief. She was good.

Rebecca then stepped back a few inches and lifted her leg off the ground. She gave a round kick towards the top of the bag. The boxer caught his jaw as he watched Rebecca deliver a number of three-hit combinations to the bag: jab, straight, round kick, weave, and repeat. She felt her anger emanate from her fist and loved how powerful it was against this stupid hanging piece of leather. The sting of the impact only coaxed her bloodlust. The boxer scooted off a few inches away from her, this raging Latina, and never took his eyes off of her smiling face. Lust escaped his mind mere seconds after she landed the first punch.

Rebecca started to emit a blinding glow. Well, at least it was blinding to the boxer. He looked over to Rebecca's friend that sat alone. He saw the colorless eyes she wore and regretted his curiosity. If his testes shrunk, he thought, it was her fault.

Rebecca halted her slamming. The boxer and Rebecca both took a deep breath, but the former inhaled out of relief; the latter, out of victory. She smiled. She walked over to the boxer and handed out her fists to be unwrapped. He just stared at them, and then he looked at Rebecca and shook his head.

"Keep them."

He grabbed his duffel bag and sped away on nervous feet before giving Rebecca a chance to reject his offer. She shrugged her shoulders at Zephyr.

"You scared him off, darling," she replied.

Rebecca laughed. "Apparently. You wanna try?"

Zephyr held up her hands and showed Rebecca her silver fingernails. "I just had these done."

"You're so vain."

"And?"

Rebecca looked at the sincerity in her eyes. She had no answer for her. She held out her gloves to Zephyr. She nodded, and helped Rebecca take them off.

"By the way," Rebecca added, "do you know how to defend yourself?"

"Yes. I kill with kindness."

Rebecca did not reply. She tied the gloves by their strings and threw them over her shoulder. Zephyr walked alongside her in a comforting silence. They ventured through the gym floor and made their way to the entrance. Zephyr and Rebecca waved good-bye to the secretary at the front entrance and exited the building.

Once the afternoon sun settled into its cushioned earth, Rebecca whipped her hair around her neck and stared at the sky. It emitted such a colorful elegance that she looked as if she were sightseeing in Europe. She surveyed the blue and purple atmosphere that fell upon the earth. It seemed to comfort her.

"You were pretty intense in there, Ms. Ortega." Zephyr breathed the cool air into her lungs. "You fight like . . . a beast."

"Uh . . . thank you? I guess?"

"You fight erratically. No form, just substance. Your technique is brutality."

Rebecca shrugged her shoulders. "Yeah, well . . . I have a chip on my shoulder for show-offs."

"You have to admit he was cute."

"I've seen better." Rebecca chuckled. "Way better."

Zephyr smirked. Both women walked to their signature cars parked next to one another. The parking lot was a barren sheet of concrete, as if someone saw the two vehicles and ran away from them. Rebecca opened her car door and threw her gym bag in the back seat. She stepped inside, but she suddenly jumped back out.

"Zephyr, is your party still on?"

Zephyr folded her arms and rested them on the hood of the car. "Why, of course it is! Why do you ask?"

"This Friday, right?"

"Beautiful memory! Friday at ten. Please show up—fashionably, of course."

"And you're giving me a costume?"

Zephyr looked at her with a curious stare. "Yes, darling! I am having a costume party! You must dress in the themed garb for the evening. Do not worry, I have already provided you with one."

That's right. Rebecca remembered that it wasn't any party but *Zephyr's* party. She wanted to slap herself for forgetting that little detail. "Zephyr, you don't have to—oh, screw it, I accept."

Zephyr smiled widely. "Thank you!"

Rebecca nodded and entered the car. Once she saw Zephyr enter and start her horse, she stared at her, waiting for the Estrada heiress to catch her view. Zephyr saw Rebecca's inquisitive expression and rolled down her window; Rebecca did the same.

"Bitch, you better not mess up my measurements!"

"You worry too much! You are already set! Ta-ta!" Zephyr rolled up her window and sped off. She ran a stop sign, but Rebecca did not bother chasing after her. She figured it was not part of her deal to be a traffic cop.

Rebecca sat in her car and pondered the past hour. She swore to God that Zephyr contracted her words. Why did she? And what's the point of focusing on that little detail? It bothered Rebecca, and she despised it. It was a tiny ant that crawled underneath her armpit and tickled her with its miniscule legs. She felt it scratching at her skin, tearing apart her psyche and angering her with each microscopic stroke. She shook her head and started her engine. *Forget it. Nothing important. Too much sweating. Maybe.*

Then she realized something.

"She trusts me," she whispered.

*   *   *

Greg stood in front of Rebecca's apartment door. He did not pace in the traditional manner; he occasionally took a step to the right, stepped back, fixed his disheveled tie, and took another step. Rebecca was never one to be late.

The moment he finished his thought, the elevator down the hallway dinged. The green arrow that shot toward heaven gave him an incentive to look as if he had just arrived at her apartment. He feared that leaning against the wall or even sitting down on the carpet would make him look desperate. He had just arrived, he told himself. Been here for three minutes. No . . . five sounded better.

The elevator doors opened and interrupted his thoughts. A second later, an older woman with grocery bags exited the elevator. *Damn*, he thought. But his eyes gleamed with joy when he saw Rebecca exit the elevator with grocery bags in her hands as well. She noticed a tall, old figure standing in her doorway and, without even looking at him, addressed him with annoyance in her voice.

"The hell you want?" she angrily asked.

"Geez, I just came by to see you. We have some issues to discuss."

"Can it wait?" Rebecca set the grocery bags down to readjust her grip.

"Not really, Ortega."

"Well, *you're* gonna have to wait." Rebecca pointed her head toward the old woman who was walking down the hall. "I'll be right back."

"Sure. Okay."

Rebecca did not even bother to nod to him. She already sped down the hallway and caught up to the old woman. Her back was hunched over from years of untreated scoliosis. The results had shortened her stature and shot painful darts into her whole body. For how long, God only knew. Greg looked at his own body and wondered if he would be doomed to suffer as well. Would Rebecca carry his groceries for him one day?

God, yes.

He saw Rebecca politely take the keys from the old woman to open her apartment door. Greg saw them disappear inside. He looked down at his pants and brushed off traces of lint and cigarette ash. They seemed to be abundant, but then again, anxiety caused every unwelcomed thing to multiply. Soon, they were everywhere: his suit jacket, his sleeves, his hands, even on the tips of his shoes.

He found her suddenly standing in front of him. He stopped brushing off the dust on his clothes and cleared his throat.

"Lint roller, Greg. I mean, seriously. There's a convenience store down the street."

"Hardy har har," he replied. "Is she all set?"

"Oh . . . yeah, she's okay. She's new to this apartment complex, so I figured I'd help her get accustomed to it."

"Well, I salute you."

Rebecca did not smile or even smirk. She kept her eyes on Greg's face, reading him and trying to figure out why he would come here to "discuss issues" when it could have been done over the phone. Or even tomorrow, for God's sake. "So what is it?"

Greg was going to ask to come inside, but such a question terrified him. "How did it go with Zephyr earlier today?"

"Everything went fine . . . look, can this wait until tomorrow? I have to catch some rest."

"But I . . ." Greg paused. He did not have more to say. Rebecca just stared at him with a look of fatigue. She rolled her eyes and pulled out her apartment keys. She opened her door and kept it close to her so that Greg would refrain from looking inside.

"We'll just talk tomorrow, okay? Night."

She slammed the door in his face. He stood there for a moment and tried to recollect what just happened. He shook his head and walked toward the elevator. Once the arrow appeared—red this time—he reluctantly stepped inside.

Rebecca had her ear glued to her door the entire time she entered. Once she heard the elevator ding, she breathed a sigh of relief. She shook her head. If she had any trust of Greg left, it was now shot to hell.

She was not stupid. She knew that Greg wanted some. And he thought she would get it from her. All these years, she knew. She kept her distance when she did not need him. She followed his command only when it entailed her rise to detective.

"I knew it," she whispered.

She walked into her kitchen and pulled out a can of tomato soup and a box full of tea bags out of the cupboard. She opened the box and smelled the contents. She smiled. A small piece of joy indeed.

Suddenly, she opened her eyes in shock. She felt that someone was in the apartment with her. It was an odd feeling, but she refused to ignore it. Rebecca never believed in ghosts, but something ominous definitely accompanied her.

She pulled out a kitchen drawer and grabbed a .45-caliber pistol. She checked its ammo and held it in her familiar, almost reflexive pose. The barrel of her gun went wherever her eyes dictated. She checked the bathroom, making sure to become the smallest target possible. She knew that nothing was behind the curtain either; Rebecca was cautious enough to purchase a clear shower liner.

She was not hasty in her search. She wanted to be patient for once. She tiptoed through the hallway as she approached her bedroom. The foot of her bed was still there, and she saw no shadows hanging from the moonlight.

Rebecca stepped into the room and pointed her gun in every direction her mind could conceive. Nothing. She looked at her closet. It was wide open, and she could see a white glow shooting forth from the empty space.

"Wait . . ." she whispered to herself. "I never leave this closet door open . . ."

She lowered her gun and took a step closer. She saw a white piece of clothing decorated with tiny silver glitter that hung on an elegant wooden hanger. The rest of her clothes were pushed aside, as if they were unworthy of remaining close to it. It certainly gave off a sense of royalty. She pulled it out of the closet and inspected it further.

"Oh, wow."

She held it up and felt the silk pour over her arm. She could tell that it was expensive material, imported, and most likely custom-made.

"Zephyr, you've outdone yourself."

She marveled at the fine quality of the garment. It was almost as if Zephyr had succeeded in capturing a part of the sun's warming rays and bound it to Rebecca's outfit. There was an exquisite nature embedded in the tiny dots of glitter. It was necessarily subtle without being invisible.

Rebecca hung the garment in the same place where it had been found. She turned around and noticed a small purple box sitting on top of her window sill. She holstered her gun as she walked towards it. Rebecca chuckled when she opened the box and examined its contents.

"You just had to go out and buy a hundred-dollar bottle of perfume, didn't you, Zephyr?"

She pulled out the magical glass bottle and sprayed the air in front of her. She inhaled deeply and was amazed at how Zephyr could find a signature fragrance for her so quickly. It demanded attention but rightfully so. It was not overpowering; however, it was intimidating, almost too sensual to touch. And that was how Rebecca saw herself: a magnet with surges of electricity that jumped from one pole to another.

She could imagine Zephyr's breathy, vain voice agreeing with her. Rebecca looked around the room and wondered if there were any more Easter eggs she needed to find. She pulled out her dresser drawers and threw back her bedding. Nothing.

Rebecca shook her head. Now she was being greedy. Zephyr was spoiling her, and both women knew it. That silver-eyed Estrada must have laughed all the way home.

She felt tired. She needed to rest for the upcoming weekend. Zephyr's large, most likely grand, birthday party. The garment was the dress code for the gala. Rebecca smirked. What a narcissist.

She closed her bedroom door and saw a small blue note taped to it. She ripped it off and studied its words.

"Be sure to wear everything with love this weekend! Sincerely, Z."

*   *   *

Later that evening, Greg couldn't believe the sight before him right now. He clasped Rebecca's buttery thighs with one hand and his camcorder with the other. He wanted to capture every sweet and blissful moment. She was on top of him; she loved control, and she loved the fact that she had him eating out of her hands. What a bitch. She definitely could have him do anything for her.

But it just felt so damn good!

He closed his eyes and waited for that ecstatic build-up to start. Her toned, naked body breathed heavily in front of him. Her breasts arose and descended in such a lustful rhythm. God, she felt so warm inside. Her nails dug into his chest but he ignored the pain. He actually had hoped that she would draw blood. Funny. Masochism never came to mind until now. But who cares? It was her. Only her.

He found himself there, that beautiful place where he wanted to be. He grit his teeth and shut his eyes as he rammed himself further into her. She looked down at him and bit her bottom lip. She must have known that would turn him on. His skin started to tingle and his groans became louder. He was angry at her. She did this to him. So much pent-up anger and frustration. And soon, he was going to give her everything that he had: the agony, the fantasies, the addictions. She was going to get all of it inside of her, and he did not care how badly it would hurt her. She deserved it.

He felt his body release itself in a violent burst. He shoved himself deeper as it trailed off into a halt. The fatigue now set in. But it was at that moment that he forgave everything she had ever done to him. All the words, teasing, the attitude, the . . .

He still could not believe that she was on top of him. Such fire. The passion was in her eyes, but her face started to fade. Rebecca's succulent lips disappeared. Her body changed. Even her sweat mutated.

It was not Rebecca at all.

Greg had picked up a prostitute on his way home from his protégé's apartment. She was standing a few feet away from the entrance when he spotted her. She was beautiful, with long blond hair, narrow eyes, and a smile that would set the sun itself. Her name was Candace, and of course, Greg had to call her Candy. He said that he had a sweet tooth. She said that he could get diabetes if he had her.

After the bang, he dozed off and felt Candace's breathing move in motion with his own. They were there for at least two hours. It was totally worth it, every dollar, every minute. It wasn't the real Rebecca, but it was close enough.

He awakened from a dreamless sleep and sat up in his bed. He searched for his wallet and pulled out two hundred dollars. He placed it next to her naked body. She immediately awakened from her nap, grabbed the money, and counted it. Either she had an extremely keen self-awareness of money or she did not nap at all.

"You're giving me extra?" she asked.

"Mm-hmm."

"Thanks." Candace got off the bed and bent down to pick up her clothes. She slipped into her miniskirt and a silk blouse. Her outfit was way too cold for the weather outside, but then again, she often ignored it. "Later," she said, as she grabbed her purse and left his bedroom. He could hear her heels click against the wooden floor and soften at the area rug that was near the front door. He sighed once the door shut her outside and trapped him inside. He rubbed his eyes and sighed at the lonely, disassembled sheets that covered his bed. Alone and tired.

He regretted not asking her to stay with him. He wanted to be held, and not in a sexual manner but in the manner of a mother holding her son. He wanted to cry, yell, laugh, relax . . . anything but to be alone. Or tired.

He could just go follow her and ask her to come back. He could pay her some more money if necessary. Besides, she will do anything he wanted, so long as he exchanged part of his paycheck. She was worth it. Sweet Candace.

He dashed out of his apartment, fully naked, and yelled after her. "Candace!" He waited for a response. He heard her heels click repeatedly and then it stopped.

"The hell you want?"

That was the second time a woman said that to him in the same night. "I have more for you!"

There was a moment of silence before she spoke. "Of course, baby!"

Thank God, he thought.

*   *   *

An hour passed, and Candace was in a hurry to rush out of his apartment. He lay on his bed panting in a pool of sweat. She was tired, more than usual, and the money would never be enough if he asked for her to stay longer. No way. Shoot me first.

She already had the money in her purse, so all she had to do was tiptoe away from his bed without waking him up. She inched to the side and cursed every squeak that damned bed made. She winced whenever the old springs fell under her weight. The night needed to end.

She stood up almost too fast. She glanced at Greg and thanked God for his deep slumber. She closed her eyes and concentrated on her escape. Once she grabbed her things, she sighed in relief and continued to tiptoe out of the bedroom.

Once she was clear, she put on her clothes and flung her purse onto her shoulder. She gently twisted the doorknob with the very ends of her fingertips and opened the door. Before she left, she listened for his breathing. A faint blow of air emanated from the bedroom. She smiled and exited the apartment.

She walked downstairs and almost tripped over her anxious legs. She dug through her purse and whipped out her cell phone. She dialed as she pushed the door open. A cool breeze whisked away her fear, and so did the voice on the other line.

"Candace?" A young female voice answered.

"Naomi! Thank God you answered! God, who did you have me fuck?"

"Slow down. Are you okay?"

"Fuck no, I'm not! The guy I had was creepy!"

"All the men we screw are creeps."

"Not this one . . ." Candace looked behind her with terror in her eyes. He did not follow her. He was still knocked out—God willing.

"You should've seen the other guys I bedded the other day," Naomi reflected. "I'm beginning to really hate men, you know that?"

"Same here."

"I will gladly turn lesbian if the pay is good."

"Same here! Are you gonna pay me, by the way?"

"Of course. You can trust me."

"Oh, I know I can trust you. But my trust is expensive tonight."

"Don't worry, you'll get your money. And more."

"Okay . . ." Candace calmed herself down once she hailed a cab. It pulled up to her feet, and she opened the door to step inside.

"And Candy?"

"Yeah."

"Don't forget to see Dr. Marshall when you get here."

"Yeah, yeah . . . I'll see you later."

"Okay, take care, girl. See you."

Candace hung up the phone and thrust her arm out into the street to hail a cab. She saw that beautiful yellow chariot appear over the dark horizon and thanked God when it stopped in front of her. She trotted to the door and climbed inside. She closed her eyes and breathed a well-deserved sigh of relief.

"Going home, cutie?" the cab driver asked over his shoulder.

"Thirteenth Street, please. Frendon Hospital."

"You okay?"

"Not yet." Candace kept her eyes close. She welcomed the force of the cab drive away from the hellish place. Normally, she would plan on how to spend the money; how things suddenly change.

Can't wait to move out of here, she thought.

* * *

"She is impossible to find," Sean said to Slim as he quivered in front of the tattooed don. "We tried to ask our techies to find out where she may have used credit cards and . . . they can't find anything. They said that she must be using cash for every purchase. And they tried hotels, motels, malls, condos . . . nothing. She's a ghost."

Slim just stood in front of him with a blank stare on his face. Such stoicism frightened Sean. Only God knew what was going through his mind, and perhaps God was punishing him by not telling him. Slim did not have any weapons in his hand, but then again, Slim was a weapon on his own.

"But," he continued, "there's an opening of this new club that used to belong to that Russian. Apparently someone got the rights to it. Rumor has it that some chick owns it now. That could be her."

Slim looked behind him and saw Pedro playing with that damned knife again. But the mention of a woman owning a club attracted his attention. He stared at Sean with drugged eyes. Slim turned back to Sean with a look of satisfaction.

"That's her. It's gotta be her. Pedro . . . we need to move in now."

"Impossible, Slim," Pedro answered with dense despair in his voice. "You know how many cops will be there?"

"Shit, Pedro! We have her right where we need her, and you're telling me not to do shit?"

Pedro only shrugged his shoulders. Slim shook his head. He dismissed Sean and watched the shaken thug walk away in a hurried, almost desperate manner. Pedro chuckled. He really gave up. He almost wished that Zephyr would just end it already. Stop screwing around. Just do what you have to do . . .

"You're right," Slim admitted. "We're gonna have to wait. But that cunt will need to come out and play sometime soon."

"That's what worries me . . . I know she will."

"But that's fine because we have a whole army to come after her. Let's just wait for her to be alone, then we go in hard."

Pedro slouched in his chair. He stood the knife up on its hilt and stared at his reflection. His face was a mere shadow of what it once was. Depressed, ugly, and destroyed.

"She wants us to come to her," Slim continued. "Fucking bitch . . . she wants us to die in her hands. She's flawless. But she is stupid to think that she is untouchable. She knows we know where she is, but she doesn't have the muscle. She's bluffing."

Pedro sniffled. He seemed to catch his breath in order to speak again. "I say that we wait until . . . Sunday. Sunday night. The club will be closed by then and we can attack with Mal on our side." Pedro sighed. "I'm sure he would want to join in. We have to see him anyway."

"The fuck for?" Slim asked with annoyance in his tone.

"Money. We're almost dry, Slim."

"Oh, so he's the Count of Monte-fucking-Cristo now?"

"Slim . . ."

"All right! All right! Fine! Let me grab some muscle and load up for this weekend."

"Slim . . ."

"What? C'mon, c'mon, tell me quick, I have people to kill."

"Be careful."

Slim laughed. "You talking to me or her? Didn't you hear me before? Army. Forty-Second Street. Guns. Trigger fingers."

"She *wants* us to find her."

Slim thought for a moment. "Maybe you're right. But shit! We have her!"

"Yeah . . . just find her and kill her. Please . . ."

"Look, if it makes you feel any better, I'll cut off her head and bring it to you. Is that okay?"

Pedro looked at him in shock. For a moment, and for the first time, he questioned Slim's sanity. "You serious?"

"Damn dude," he chuckled. "I'm kidding. You know I wouldn't do that."

Pedro nodded. He sat up in his chair and pulled out his desk drawer. He took his knife and began to place it inside.

"I mean," Slim continued as he left the office, "I would much rather cut off her arms instead. Like that statue of Venus."

VIII

"The streets of Ellipses have never been this crazy! It is absolutely insane! It's like the whole world is in front of this building! Thousands of people are gathered here, crowding the doorways, trying to catch a glimpse of what's inside! Let's get at least a little bit of info from anyone who was lucky enough to see inside!"

The reporter nudged her way into the crowd and politely tapped the shoulder of a stander-by. She was a young girl, about halfway into her twenties. She wore what looked like to be a Roman tunic that draped over her shoulders and fell just a few inches above the ground.

"Hi! Any luck finding out what's going on in there?"

"Oh! My! God! This place is freaking amazing! Like I saw a glimpse of the inside and there are, like, statues of Roman gods on the sides and . . . I can't explain everything! It's awesome, that's all I can say!"

"Wow! And I noticed that you and everyone else here are wearing a Roman outfit. What's that all about?"

"It's the dress code! We all got this e-mail about the grand opening, and it said that we all had to dress like Romans! Everyone looks so sexy it's amazing!"

"Fantastic! Well, thank you so very much! Do you wanna give a shoutout to anyone at home?"

"I wanna shout out to my boyfriend, Ian, and my mom, and my li'l sister! I love you guys!"

"And there you have it everyone! Testimony from the crowd! For those of you just joining us tonight, we are just moments away from the grand opening of the new dance club called Olympus!" The reporter laughed at the sudden screams that emanated from the crowd. "I have to tell you, this place is absolutely enormous! This club is modeled exactly after the palace of the gods! From what I can see from here, if I can stand on my toes, I can see tall pillars with—"

The doors opened, and the screaming crowd poured inside like water bursting through a dam. They cheered louder than their initial screaming and clapped as they rushed through those monstrous doors. They passed by bouncers and security guards without paying them any mind. One of them could not help but smile.

The reporter managed to move alongside the ecstatic crowd. She was laughing with the microphone in her hand, occasionally glancing at her cameraman that followed right behind her. When she finally reached the main floor, her jaw dropped.

"My God . . ." She looked around and forgot that she was doing a news report. She reclaimed herself and spoke into the microphone. "Marble pillars covered with silver glitter, completely decked out with the best-looking sound system I have ever seen on the East Coast! Lights and lasers galore! The opening DJ . . . this place has acrobatic dancers and aerialists dressed in tunics themselves! Jesus, I . . . can't even describe everything in front of me! If you look to either sides of the wall, you can see what looks like to be thirty-foot statues of the gods of Olympus! The entire interior is made out of sandblasted stone to a glossy finish! The stage looks like a freaking throne for Zeus! I mean Jupiter! Sorry, sorry! You can imagine how everyone else is feeling! Channel Dance Radio Extreme will keep you updated throughout the night! We're not going anywhere! We're . . . hang on . . ."

The lasers stopped. The acrobats and the aerialists danced in a wavy motion. The DJ halted his set. The silence of movement made everyone's heart race.

"The lights are dimming, and it looks like the party is about to start—hang on—ladies and gentlemen, the owner of the club has stepped onto the stage! Let me just say that I am so jealous!"

Zephyr slowly walked onto the stage in a manner befitting her sovereignty. She glided toward the cheering and whistling clubbers with a gait that rivaled Botticelli's Birth of Venus. Everyone studied her from the toes up to her hair. She wore a pair of silver pumps whose brand could not be identified, only that it was truly—and only—hers. Her legs carried her in full splendor. She could feel the lustful eyes and the envious wishes of everyone inside the club. Her body would have been completely naked had it not been for her bright, platinum-colored tunica that fell down her body. A single strap was laid across her left shoulder and allowed freedom to her other side. The garment's style was a complete ribbon: the cloth reached from the shoulder strap and crossed her breasts (without sacrificing a view of her neckline) while falling down the left oblique. The garment then covered everything below her pierced navel. The garment seemed to spill halfway down Zephyr's left calf; on the other side, it only stopped an inch past her right knee. The dress was as windy as she was and probably just as frigid. She showed the world that she was truly bold.

And she succeeded in that endeavor.

Her earrings were cut into slim platinum rectangles that suspended from her earlobes. Zephyr had personally hired a European hairdresser to design her hair in an essence that evoked the styles of Ancient Rome. It was held up in a bun, and parts of her hair curled down the sides of her face. It was wavy and decorated with tiny silver jewels here and there. Her eyes were surrounded by a thin black eyeshadow, which formed small hooks at the far corners of her eyelids. Inside those hooks lay a tiny diamond stud that glittered only at certain angles. But when they were seen, they gave Zephyr an invulnerable aura, especially in a conjugal relationship with her soulless eyes. She stood at the edge of the stage and spread her spectral eyes across the thousands of clubbers that awaited her voice.

"Welcome."

Suddenly, geysers hidden in the ceiling shot forth their cooling mist that soon covered the dance floor and ascended to the torsos of the awestruck clubbers. The DJ blasted his music as the lights and the lasers beamed throughout club Olympus. The sound waves reverberated off the statues of the twelve, with Zephyr echoing a goddess herself.

The opening beat threw the crowd into a mesmerized state of euphoria. They jumped and moved in a pattern, a trait that was not learned but executed. Their arms held up the air as if they were pledging their fealty toward Zephyr. She answered their allegiance and raised one arm in the air. She then barely swiveled her hips in a smooth manner that matched the beat of the song. She smiled with the crowd as they stared at everyone and at no one. The beautiful luminous melodies added a rhythm to their stomps and shouts. They shouted in glee at the DJ, and they especially shouted at Zephyr and quietly begged to see her haunting eyes in full view.

Then suddenly, the music stopped. The melody froze in place, and the lights ceased their existence. This sudden time stop was completely new to novices, but experienced dancers allowed them to be taught on their own. There was no electronic malfunction. No natural storm or any acts of God. There was only a trance.

The silence was only a sign of things to come, and true devotees did their absolute best to trap their building emotions. Amid the quiet air that permeated throughout Olympus gave rise to tension. Their heart rates quickened, the blood raged towards their skulls, their breaths became hard and heavy, and their eyes widened. The silence had overwhelmed some; some screams could be heard erupting from anticipation. But the quiet lingered on.

At the last second, the melody returned and looped for a few more moments. A faint echo of a choir could be heard in the monstrous speakers than hung over the crowd. This echo soon turned into a beautiful harmony that seemed to make love with the original melody. The volume seemed to increase, but it was only the arrival of anxiety. A bass drum was heard in the background. It beat fast, then rapid, and finally it sounded like abnormally loud raindrops hitting against a windowpane. The reporter who was supposed to deliver news to the public ended up leaping into the air with her fellow clubbers, microphone in hand and all. The cameraman did his best to keep his equipment steady as he taped her.

Finally, all the elements of the song came together as one. They erupted in a fury and thrust everyone into a wild state of trance. That is exactly what it was. Trance. The music of the gods residing in Olympus, standing tall over the crowd as a king rules over his dominion. Everyone had a wide smile on their faces. Their hands were in the air, praising the blessed DJ that assisted their worship of the muse.

Even Zephyr smiled among them. Her hands were clapping in beat with the music. She gently moved her hips, in a sense dancing with the crowd as well as herself, without the former knowing how much she loved the music. She showed a little—never a lot. The DJ turned toward her and gave repeated bows to her. Zephyr blew him a kiss and mouthed the words "Thank you."

The lasers were erratic and beamed forth in all directions while discarding any semblance of a pattern. The dance floor was encased in a thick cloud. The crowd could feel the cool mist condense on their foreheads. The dancers danced in sequence with the music, although everyone could tell they were dancing out of pure joy rather than obligation. Olympus truly gave justice to its ancient name.

At least that was what Rebecca thought.

She admitted that the music was different. Rebecca never really had a genre that was "hers." However, she did like the ambience that surrounded her, and honestly, the music was definitely bad-ass. She could not help but find herself smiling with the crowd;

One patron saw her and said with a smile, "Your dress is gorgeous! Having fun?"

"I am!"

"The DJ is amazing! I've seen him play in Europe, and he's no joke!"

"Yeah!"

"I don't know how the owner got him to play here, but holy shit, thank God for her!"

Rebecca laughed. The music made a smooth transition to the next song, without any breaks in between. She could not tell when the first song ended and when the next one began. Yeah, he was *definitely* a pro, and Zephyr certainly had taste. Rebecca looked around the club for what seemed like the hundredth time. She was just purely amazed by the architecture and the arduous work that had gone into the building. Everything was a pure, celestial work of art. Rebecca could study the detail in the Twelve's creation: their garments, poses, even their faces were exceptional. She studied the row of deities until she reached Zephyr at the end of it all. How art imitates life.

The crowd exploded into frenzy when the song reached its climax. The music shook the dance floor, and Zephyr's performers matched the atmosphere. In this world, this small world that Zephyr had created; it was the only beacon of joy this city had ever experienced.

Rebecca took a look at herself finally. The dress Zephyr had picked out for her fit like a glove. Her gown was a glamorous white sparkled in tiny glitter. It was strapless and merely hung from her bosom in some divine grasp. The garment covered her torso but only the front—the back was completely bare. The hem was longer than Zephyr's, but it boasted a design where a single slit was placed toward her middle left thigh. Rebecca felt so comfortable in her outfit that she promised herself to thank Zephyr once she was able to speak with her.

Zephyr suddenly blew kisses to the crowd and allowed the DJ to carry them away on their journey. She must have read Rebecca's mind; Zephyr glanced over the crowd and caught Rebecca's eyes. How she did that was inexplicable, but it worked. Zephyr winked and made a subtle exit toward the left side of the throne.

Rebecca took that as a sign and proceeded through the crowd. She excused herself to everyone in her path. She soon realized that her manners were unnecessary; the clubbers willingly made a path through which she could walk. They saw how the fabric draped over her body. They saw how her heels raised her small ankles and transformed her calves into elegant pillars. At that moment, the same eyes that were once on Zephyr seemed to be on Rebecca. Both women had shone amid the dark club and the flashing glow sticks. Neon yellows and bright whites weaved in and out of reality, drawing numerous strings and ribbons in the black space in front of them. They disappeared when the dancers stopped moving their arms. They truly were alchemists in a modern realm.

Rebecca came up to a large silver neon sign with the words "VIP." The door had a metallic plate of what looked like a medallion of a woman's face. In front of the door was a large buff man who wore a Roman tunic that showcased his large arms and his wide chest. Rebecca smiled. She adored his masculinity.

Zephyr came behind Rebecca and startled her. Rebecca whipped around and breathed a sigh of relief.

"Zephyr! You scared me!"

"Hey! So sorry, love! You made it!" Zephyr smiled at her with a twinkle in her soulless eyes. Rebecca swore to God that they glowed.

"Yeah! Thanks for the invite!"

"Of course! Let's go upstairs to my office!" Zephyr nodded at the guard and stepped aside. Zephyr pushed a small red button. The door opened to an elevator. They stepped inside and waited for the door to close. Rebecca felt a slight jerk as the elevator made it ascent.

"You absolutely *must* see this view!" Zephyr commanded. "Breathtaking!"

Zephyr pushed a white button on a panel in front of her. It flashed for a second, and Rebecca heard a whirling noise through the elevator doors. She focused her gaze on the doors as they split apart to reveal a bird's-eye view of the entire club behind a window. She could see everyone clap his and her hands to the music the DJ spun. The marble dance floor shook with both the ecstasy of the clubbers and the flawless choreography of the dancers Zephyr had personally hired. Couples snaked around each other and moved with one another to create an erotic friction. Their eyes possessed one another as well as the music blasting in the air.

Everything was in sync. Balanced. Just like Zephyr Estrada.

Rebecca surveyed the pillars that enclosed every statue on both sides of the club. The architecture was gorgeous. She lost her breath for a moment when she realized how high she and Zephyr towered over the dance floor. She admitted that it was the most beautiful sight in the entire city that she had ever seen. However, she swallowed her pride and dared not admit it out loud.

"Wow . . ." she managed to say.

"I know," Zephyr replied. "It took forever for me to conjure up the concept alone. I am so indecisive."

"You did this?"

"Indeed. I enjoyed learning about the Roman mythos as a child. It stuck with me when I drew up the blueprints."

"You did a commendable job, Miss Estrada."

Zephyr chuckled. "I am not an old lady yet."

"So sorry, *Zephyr*."

Zephyr laughed. "I think I have the most unique name on this planet. It suits me."

"Did your parents name you after Zephyrus?"

Zephyr looked at Rebecca with a surprised expression. "You are well-informed!"

"Yeah, well . . . just enough to get by. You're lucky, my mother discouraged it. Said that it was a pagan religion."

"That is understandable. You are Roman Catholic, correct?"

"Born and raised. You?"

"Same." Zephyr breathed in deeply and grinned at the crowd below her. The elevator stopped and the door opened. Rebecca followed Zephyr as they exited. "If you do not object to my asking," Zephyr said, "will you tell me about your mother?"

"Only if you tell me about your brother."

Rebecca was hoping that mentioning Pedro Estrada would stir up emotions in Zephyr, but she truly was serenity personified. She was almost apathetic if Rebecca did not know any better.

"Follow me," Zephyr replied.

*   *   *

IX

Rebecca found herself in a long hallway decorated with God knows how much homage to Roman design: marble walls and floors that glittered with magnificent splendor, plants that were sheared to perfection, and pillars with the same look as the ones downstairs. Rebecca marveled at the beauty before her. She realized that the glory, the fashion, and the ambience all were mimics of the essence of Zephyr. She pursued such beauty and intelligence like a fox, and she succeeded in capturing them.

They continued down the hallway. Rebecca noticed odd signs on each door they passed.

"Hmm . . ."

Zephyr paused and turned her eyes toward Rebecca. "You're wondering about the signs on the doors?"

"You must be psychic," Rebecca answered.

Zephyr chuckled. "Maybe I am. Anyway, the first door that you have just passed on your left is Argus. This is my security room. One hundred-eyed monster, one hundred security cameras."

"Clever," Rebecca replied. "And is this club your Io?"

Zephyr grinned. "You can say that, although this venue is far from being bovine, wouldn't you agree?"

Rebecca smirked. Another contraction. She continued walking down the long hallway and allowed Zephyr to give her a tour of what seemed to be a palace.

"This room here is Thebes," Zephyr continued, "where everything happens: lighting, mechanics, sound . . ."

"Any lost, ancient kings I should know about?"

"You know what? Odysseus was here a little while ago!"

"You're something else."

"If you only knew, *mi amiga* . . . here we are."

Rebecca and Zephyr eventually came upon a massive door flanked by pillars on both sides. The overall design of the door teetered on fashionable ingenuity and exalted arrogance. It seemed that it was sprayed with a fine Lilliputian mixture of gold and diamond dust. Zephyr outstretched her arms and pushed the door open. Rebecca expected the jeweled dust to fly across the room and land onto the floor.

She found herself entering Zephyr's personal (and palatial) chamber. The main sitting area was comprised of marble seats with blue silk cushions. It smoothly blended with the plethora of thin drapes cascading from the ceiling. The floors were polished into mirrors that reflected the women's spectacular outfits and gave a treat for the ceiling to see. The walls were covered with beautiful bright paintings and classic statues. Rebecca recognized a miniature version of the Statue of David wearing a small white tunic. Rebecca chuckled. Zephyr had a whimsical side to her after all.

"Have a seat," Zephyr said. Rebecca nodded and sat across from Zephyr, who crossed her legs and leaned back in her chair or, rather, her throne. She continued to mentally congratulate Zephyr on her choice of décor. Tall green plants had been enthroned upon marble vases placed and arranged in an opulent manner. And here she was, in the presence of a boss's daughter sitting at a large desk that was cut from a brilliant marble worthy enough for a church altar.

Rebecca already knew Zephyr. She truly was an iron fist in a velvet glove. She also had eyes that could drive men and women into insanity as if they infected them with syphilis. However, she maintained her serenity without fail. Zephyr was a being of benedictions and curses—Rebecca wondered if Zephyr would ever give her an answer as to which ability she would use, and if so, how.

Rebecca reflected on the hundreds of people she had met, especially at headquarters. She could read every personality that entered the offices: the druggies, the prostitutes, their pimps, the robbed, and the robbers. She met a couple of murderers and tried to understand their minds' orders. She saw the light and the dark collide with each other and mix into a solution that drove them into a wall. Everyone noticed her talent of reading people, but she never knew if it was innate or gained.

"Comfortable?" Zephyr asked.

"Very."

*   *   *

Rebecca sped home later that night with a horrified look on her face. Her hands quivered on the steering wheel as her eyes jerked back and forth between the road and the rearview mirror. If a cop tried to stop her, fuck him. She just had to get home before she exploded. It was not fear that came upon her but anger. It was a heightened sense of militaristic passion that coursed through her and radiated from her flashing eyes. She stomped on the gas and dared any idiot (secretly wishing that it was a Forty-Second Street gangster) to walk in front of her car. The velocity was enough to splice the wind, but she felt the need to drive faster.

"Can't believe this. Can't *fucking* believe this!"

Rebecca muttered curses while the screeching tires complimented her irate silence. She saw the driveway that led to her apartment parking lot and drifted her bestial Mustang into the closest space. She turned off the headlights and yanked the car keys out of the ignition. She pulled the handle, almost tearing off the plastic wedge out of the door, and stepped out. She slammed the door with her foot and strode toward her apartment. Rebecca frantically searched for her apartment key and looked behind her shoulder. She still felt his presence facing her back—and she hated every memory of it.

She finally found her keys and stabbed it in the keyhole. She entered her home and immediately threw herself on the sofa. She titled her head back, closed her eyes, and recalled the events that occurred thirty minutes ago. The flashback materialized all around her. The image destroyed her living room and occupied her mind.

She was now in the presence of Zephyr once more, sitting across from her, telling each other their ambitions.

*   *   *

The two women sat in silence. Their calm moods suggested a necessity of this private conference. Zephyr nonchalantly examined her fingernails and gently blew away a tiny piece of lint. She set her hand down and leaned back in her chair. She smiled at Rebecca.

"So tell me," Zephyr spoke first, "what do you think? Overall?"

"I have to admit," Rebecca truthfully answered, "this is absolutely gorgeous." She glanced around the office and nodded her head. Zephyr had truly outdone herself.

"Thank you, I think it is very lovely indeed." Zephyr swung in her chair from side to side. "This took one extremely long night and a glass of wine in order for me to conceptualize the design. I have to admit, I had almost lost hope."

"Why?"

"I realized that it was impossible to capture beauty."

"But it looks like you did a great job."

"Thank you . . ." Zephyr looked forlorn. Her face lost her upbeat personality and her peaceful smiles. "I guess I have to swallow my pride and admit that beauty and perfection cannot be obtained. Think about it—what is true beauty? Everyone has an opinion on it, so a beautiful thing to one person is absolutely hideous to another. With this nightclub, I had to conjure something that was beautiful to the lover and the hater. Therefore, one has to find a common ground to suit one's peers. Please the crowd, right? And that's what I did."

Rebecca stayed silent. *Why is she using contractions all—never mind.* She continued to listen to Zephyr.

"I did not find true beauty. That's why I was up so late when I drew up the blueprints. I was searching for it, and then I realized that it is unattainable. That upsets me. It still does. Can I actually find a beauty that absolutely everyone loves? In search of that beauty, I suppose I was searching for a beauty within myself."

"What do you mean by that?"

"I don't think I'm beautiful."

"You're shitting me."

Zephyr giggled. "Not at all."

"Look at you!"

"That's the point," Zephyr sighed. "People shouldn't have to look at me."

Rebecca thought for a moment. Zephyr was right, in her own little way. Senses deceive. Beauty is not in the eye of the beholder but within intuition. She understood Zephyr's plight. She was stained.

"I was homeless," Rebecca started. Her words perked up Zephyr, who fixed her cold eyes on Rebecca. "I ran away from home because of my mom's boyfriend. Dad died when I was eight. A part of me died with him, of course. We were so happy with him around. When he died, my mom started drinking. Sometimes, it would get so bad that she would miss work because she had passed out on the kitchen floor. She eventually started dating this guy, Santo. He was nice for a while."

"For a while?"

"He raped me two days after I had turned nine."

Zephyr turned her head away and stared at a wall with anger in her eyes. They were shining a brilliant white, as white as burning phosphorous.

"My mom—her name is Melissa, by the way—caught him that night trying to force himself on me while I was dead asleep. She stopped him, but he threatened to kill her if she squealed. And that was when I had lost my virginity."

Zephyr looked at Rebecca with a combination of anger and pity on her face. Her eyes were still a flaming white. "Where is he now?"

"Prison."

Zephyr leaned back in her chair. "Well, that's a relief."

"My mom almost beat him to death."

"Good for her." Zephyr was frigid in her words. "How did she pull it off?"

"She told me that she beat him up while he was asleep. Ironic, huh? He took away my . . . when I was asleep, she took away his pride. After that is when I started to love her again. Now that I'm thinking about it, she never told me how she avoided prison time, but I'm assuming that she claimed…something. God only knows."

"I see . . ." Zephyr was silent.

"Anyway, I eventually went back to high school and finished early. I studied my ass off. I refused to get sent back out onto those damned streets. I went to a community college and received my associate in general studies, so I could avoid that 'take a mathematics course in order to graduate' bullshit." Zephyr chuckled at Rebecca's joke. She allowed her guest to continue. "I loved psychology when I had to take a science course, so I transferred to a four-year university and got my degree in it."

"Very interesting." Zephyr nodded. "You forgot to tell me how you survived on your own when you were homeless."

Rebecca chuckled with surprise. "Are you sure you're not psychic?"

"Positive."

Rebecca swore that her eyes saw more than what was physical. "Well, I was friends with this guy . . . he was very kind to me. When I first met him, he gave me soup. Tomato soup. It was expired as hell, which is saying something for a can of Campbell's, but my God, it was delicious. To this day, I can't eat anything other than soup, chicken if I'm feeling wealthy. And I'll have orange juice and vitamins and whatnot so that I don't catch scurvy." Rebecca and Zephyr chuckled. "In any case, when this guy helped me out, I said, 'Thanks, mister,' and that's what I called him: Mister."

"Where is he now?"

"Dead . . . funny how all the men in my life end up dead or dying."

Zephyr smirked. "You and me both."

"Really?"

"I'll tell you my story when you finish yours."

Rebecca smiled. "Okay."

"Wait one second." Zephyr stood up and walked behind Rebecca toward the front of the office. Rebecca did not bother turning around to see what Zephyr was doing. She trusted her, and Zephyr trusted

Rebecca. Zephyr was truly open to her, and Rebecca was glad that she was able to reciprocate.

"I had to bring this out," Zephyr said as she returned to Rebecca. She was carrying a tray with two wine glasses and a bottle of deep red wine. She set the tray on a nearby shelf, popped open the bottle, and sniffed the cork. She smiled as she poured the wine into both glasses. She set the bottle down, and then she took each glass in her hand and handed one to Rebecca. They held up their glasses to each other in preparation for a toast.

"A toast," Zephyr began, "to us. Two strong women who have experienced life in its ugliest moments but have emerged to successfully capture true beauty. Cheers."

"Cheers." Rebecca tinged her glass to Zephyr's. They both drank the wine and sighed.

"So," Rebecca continued, "one night I walked to Parish—that's what us homeless folk called home, Parish—and I found Mister dead. He was hanging from the ceiling by a lamp cord. It was . . ."

"Someone killed him."

"How did you know?"

"Good people are killed."

"Yeah . . ."

"Any idea who it was that had done it?"

"Yes . . .but I don't know if it's the right guy I'm thinking of."

"I'm willing to bet that you're right, love."

"Yeah . . ." Rebecca took a sip of wine. "I'm thinking . . . no . . . I know it's Guillermo Nunez."

Zephyr's eyes seemed to give off a spark. "Pedro's right hand."

"Right." Rebecca sighed and took another sip of wine. "I will never forget his face. I have his description and info at headquarters. Everyone keeps focusing on Forty-Second Street and Pedro himself . . . and even you, so everyone probably has forgotten about him already."

"Except you."

"Except me."

"Do you know anything more about Mister? Real name? Family?"

"Nothing. He only knew my name, but I didn't know his. I was his only family, far as I know." Rebecca swirled her wine in her glass. "The most he told me was that he was in the Korean War. Greg promised that he would find out more about him, but . . ."

"He never did."

Rebecca was silent. She froze her eyes upon the red liquid in front of her. It mimicked the blood she saw when . . . no. *Don't think about that right now*, she kept telling her mind. But she decided to share something with Zephyr, something that she has not shredded from her mind. Rebecca pulled out a small slip of paper with a little girl's scribbles over an old, wrinkled piece of paper. She read it over before giving it to Zephyr.

"What's this?"

"A contract. My contract."

Zephyr read the contents out loud. "'I, Detective Gregorio Bernini, do hereby swear to give Rebecca Ortega the information of a murdered victim, dubbed as Mister. She will receive this information upon completion of analysis and upon her return to her original place of residency. Any violations on my part or on the part of Miss Ortega will void this contract and result in penalties not yet outlined. Signed, Gregorio Bernini.'"

Rebecca mouthed the words as Zephyr read it. She gave it back to her, and Rebecca slipped it into her clutch. "I memorized that thing years ago. I always . . . I don't know. I was a silly girl back then."

"No, you were not. At all. This explains a lot actually."

"What do you mean?"

"Remember when we first met? You had this aura of strength that I couldn't place my finger on. Growing up on the streets—these streets especially—it will age Dorian Gray himself. And because of that, you knew these streets better than I do when we drove to the car dealership. The haggling you did was outstanding. I'm so used to paying full price for things, and then I saw the way you fought when you were kicking the shit out of that bag at the gym," Zephyr said with a chuckle.

"One hundred percent local geography, economics, and street fighting from the School of Mister. You can't imagine how hard it was to enroll into the police academy and have them teach you their grapples and strikes and bullshit. I threw it out the window and was never defeated during training. I actually won trophies in contests for the shit-kicking."

"I would never fight a street fighter, honest to God. You guys scare me."

Rebecca laughed. "You? Scared? You have a fear of real-life Capcom video game fighters?"

Zephyr laughed heartily. "Please, I'm scared of a bad hair day. And dirty clothes. And rats. Snakes. And . . . I think that's it."

"You would suck as a hostage, ha ha!"

"Which is why I will never get caught! Ever!"

Rebecca smiled. She remembered what the Forty-Second Street gang thug said. He knew her name. He was shot to hell. And he stated her name.

"I digress. I was just thinking that there may be a chance that Mister's DNA is still intact on his body," Zephyr said, with a slight joy in her voice. "And if you know that he served in the Forgotten War, then we may even find out everything about him. You never know."

"I need special permission to exhume his body. That would take a miracle."

"Do you believe in miracles?"

"I guess so . . ." Rebecca chuckled. "It's a miracle that I'm alive, I suppose."

Zephyr nodded at Rebecca and drank her wine. She set the glass on the table. "Everything else I can figure out on my own, Rebecca. Rest your lips. It's my turn to speak."

"Thank you, Zephyr."

Zephyr smiled. She stood up and walked to a wall behind her chair. She pressed a button, and the wall split open in the middle. The wall separated from each other and opened to a view of the dance floor. Rebecca could see the clubbers dance along with the music, throwing themselves into a high that no drug on earth could imitate. The lights were busy casting beams on the crowd, as well as the DJ that smiled throughout his whole set. The glows of the white tunics and the ominous statues of Olympus flashed before her eyes. Rebecca shook her head at its amazement.

"It's a soundproof two-way mirror. I just needed something to view."

"Of course."

"I guess my life is not as lustrous as your own. As you most likely know, I was raised by the late Luis Estrada. My life was safe and sheltered, but as you know, security is not everlasting. My brother, the creature whom you and the entire EPD is watching, is the—"

The phone on Zephyr's desk rang.

"Naturally," Zephyr lamented. "Excuse me, love."

"Oh, no problem, take your time."

Zephyr smiled and pushed a button on her phone. "Yes?"

"Sorry to bother you, Miss Estrada," said a rough voice on the other end of the line, "but a cop is here for you."

Zephyr and Rebecca shared a puzzled look. "You mean someone other than my guest?"

"Yeah," answered the guard. "And he's raising quite a ruckus. I think he's drunk or high. Want me to get a uniform in here and escort him out?"

"No. Send him up."

"You sure?"

"Positive, darling."

"You got it."

Zephyr pressed the button again and leaned back in her chair. Rebecca was completely boggled. She kept staring at Zephyr, hoping to find an answer within those soulless eyes.

"Looks like I'm popular tonight," Zephyr said. "Your friend is here."

*   *   *

Greg rode the glass elevator accompanied by three hefty security guards. He kept his badge clenched in his hand as a testimony to his supposed authority. He felt like a god with that gold-plated shield in his palm. He was unstoppable. He was almighty.

His tie was undone and plunged down his torso, past his crotch. His dress shirt was tucked in one side while the other grazed his slacks. His shoes were untied and dull. Sadly, he combed his hair back with his fingertips to provide himself with some semblance of a presentable appearance. This ironic gesture only added to his slovenly silhouette.

The elevator reached the top floor where Zephyr had been located. Greg shuffled his way down the long hallway. He passed by each strange door and tried to decipher their meanings. His failure to understand Zephyr's tastes increased his frustration and drunken anger.

"Where the hell is she?" Greg sobered up just to complete his sentence.

"Miss Estrada is behind these doors, sir," one of the guards said. "Go on in."

Greg pushed opened the large doors with a smidge of lazy strength. He entered the room and saw Rebecca's stunned face. Across from her sat Zephyr. She merely smiled politely at Greg.

Rebecca shot up from her chair and marched toward Greg. "What the fuck are you doing here?"

"I need to talk with Zephyr Estrada."

Zephyr gave Greg nothing more than a smirk. "I am she. What can I do for you, Officer?"

"The hell are you doing here?" Greg asked.

"I was having a rather intelligent conversation with Officer Ortega here." Zephyr poured herself another glass of wine and gently inhaled its decadent scent.

"About what?"

"Life."

"Bullshit!"

"No, we are not yet on that topic."

Rebecca clenched her teeth and blocked Greg from further approaching Zephyr. She stood in his path and tried to talk some sense into him without losing her own temper.

"Greg," she whispered as she controlled her ever-growing anger, "stop this shit right now!"

Greg spoke over her shoulder. "You listen to me, you little narcissistic bitch! I know why you're here, and I know who you want to kill! You better come clean and tell me everything! I'm not playing your shitty little game! Come clean now, and maybe I won't let your pretty little ass rot in prison!" Greg coughed. "You better fucking—"

"No, you listen to me." Zephyr slowly rose out of her chair and beamed her eyes on Greg Bernini. Her face was solid and ominous. Her gaze was absolutely terrifying. Rebecca caught a glimpse of Zephyr's furious eyes and forgot about everything that had happened in the past five minutes. Greg was a tall man, but he felt exceedingly shorter and weaker than the woman with the eyes of a ghost.

"Judging from your horrendous banter," she continued, "I would say that you have emptied the reserves of what is deemed your mind. What makes you think that I would ever comply with you? You are desperately delusional. You have absolutely nothing on me. How dare you attempt to harvest my intelligence for your starving, destitute masculinity!

"So fuck off, Officer Bernini. You cannot even begin to understand my exalted ingenuity; much less inquire about my future. Your presence is enough for me to envy the blind! I can throw you out of this building and have my security piss on your face! But I am a pacifist, so please, grant us the privilege of seeing you leave!"

Greg stood in his place, completely paralyzed.

Zephyr kept her chilling gaze on Greg. "Let me show you the door." Zephyr motioned her head toward the exit. "There it is!"

*   *   *

Rebecca stood at the foot of her bed and collapsed her face down onto her soft mattress. She let her feet hang off the end and kept her face buried within her sheets. They still smelled like the fabric softener she used the other day. It reminded her of the days when she came home from college and studied her textbooks all night. She secretly wished that she was transported back to those days once more. After all, she would already know what was going to happen, unlike certain past events. She was going to kill Greg—in her mind.

Entertaining the thought, she realized, would do nothing to change what had happened. The point was, it still happened. The embarrassment itself kept her petrified on her bed.

She turned over and stared at the ceiling. The small dots on that vertical wall stared at her as intently and as ferociously as she did. It seemed to swallow her whole. Suddenly, those dots turned into tiny stalactites. She created the shape of a gun with her fingers and shot at the ceiling—it did not collapse, damn it all. She closed her eyes, sighed away her agony, and finally fell asleep,

A few hours later, her phone vibrated inside her clutch. She did not hear it at first, but then she slowly opened her eyes and tried to decipher the source of that monstrous noise. The phone vibrated again and shot Rebecca a clue in her head. She rolled to her side and realized that she was still in her outfit from last night. She cursed under her breath. She forgot all about last night, and now those memories reared their ugly heads.

She grabbed her clutch and pulled out her cell phone. It was a number that she did not recognize. Something told her to answer the phone anyway. She also prayed that it was anyone other than Greg.

Rebecca cleared her throat. "Hello?"

"Good morning, darling!" Zephyr sounded cheerful and awake. Wide awake.

"Zephyr!" Rebecca shot up from her bed. "I'm so glad you called. Listen, let me just—"

"Oh please, you don't have to apologize to me. It was beyond your control."

"But I feel horrible that something like that happened on opening night. He was such a damned idiot." Rebecca paused. She searched through her mind for any professional way to say that Greg was an obnoxious dumbass. "Still, let me apologize on Officer Bernini's behalf. His actions were unbecoming of an officer and are in no way, shape, or form a reflection of what EPD does—"

"That was very nice," Zephyr said, "but you could've just said that he was a dickhead."

Rebecca laughed. It was the first time she laughed since the previous night. It felt good.

"See? I knew I could get you to laugh. No one is allowed to be sullen around me." Zephyr paused for a moment to yawn. She was not a morning person at all. Rebecca retracted her analysis of Zephyr being wide awake. "In any case, I didn't call to shoot the breeze concerning last night. I wanted to finish our conversation, if that's okay with you."

Rebecca brushed back her hair. "Ah . . . sure. Sure, we could do that. Where do you want to meet?"

"Back here at Olympus. One of my guards will unlock the door for you once you get here."

"All right, give me . . . a half hour to get ready and I will be there."

"Good lord!" Zephyr exclaimed. "You're an early bird! Can you take one hour instead? I need to at least put on my face."

Rebecca laughed. "You're so vain."

"Why, thank you! I will see you at eleven."

"Okay, see you later."

Rebecca hung up. Did she have a new friend? A new *best* friend? Zephyr was relaxed and informal around her but proper and dignified around others. Plus she still used those damn contractions around her. Silly, dumb-ass observation, but an observation nonetheless. She was going to investigate further, but right now, she had to take a quick shower.

*　　*　　*

Rebecca pulled up in front of Olympus in her form-fitting car. She shook her head. She still could not believe the idiocy that had occurred the night before. However, she was happy to know that Zephyr did not seem to be in a bad mood.

She stepped out of her car and allowed the valet to park it for her. She wore a simple black T-shirt with gray jeans and a pair of white sneakers. Her hair still maintained its altered style, but Rebecca couldn't care less. All she wanted to do was to eat breakfast and forget about everything that had happened.

Rebecca approached the entrance where a guard stood watch. He unlocked the door for her and watched her step inside. He closed the door back on her and locked it. He acted as if someone would have the strange idea to storm into the club during the day. Rebecca wondered where the hell he was last night.

She clenched her fist. "Stop thinking about it."

Next, Rebecca found herself standing in front of the same security guard who stood in front of the same damned elevator that carried the same goddamned Greg Bernini. He nodded to her as well and allowed her to step inside. Rebecca wondered if Zephyr kept them available 24/7. "Another question to ask," she supposed.

When the elevator opened up once more, she saw Zephyr down the hallway sitting at her desk. She wore a fluffy white robe with her hair still set in its style from last night as well. Her makeup disappeared from her face; however, her ghastly eyes remained intact. Zephyr yawned as Rebecca approached. Miss Estrada really did hate mornings. She also noticed that Zephyr actually *lives* here.

"Good morning, Zephyr."

"Good morning, Rebecca!" Zephyr stood up and walked toward her with open arms. She hugged Rebecca so tightly that Rebecca felt her eyes pop. Rebecca was not used to hugging. At all. But she did manage to pat Zephyr's back.

"Um . . . thanks, Zephyr."

"You're welcome! Come join me for breakfast."

"What are we having?"

"Scrambled eggs with French toast, bacon, sausage, hash browns . . . and a tall glass of OJ!"

"Wow, you've really outdone yourself. Again."

Zephyr chuckled. "I know it's not soup and all, but . . . I know you had a rough night."

"Yes . . ." Rebecca paused. "I need to talk to you about that."

"Look, no worries, okay? Besides, I need to talk to you first."

"About?"

Zephyr's smile faded. "Me."

Rebecca sat down at Zephyr's desk. She sat across from her host and waited for her to start.

"I have a favor to ask of you, Rebecca."

"Yes?"

Zephyr sipped on her glass of orange juice that sat in front of her and leaned back in her chair. She stared up at the ceiling as she pondered her next statement. Rebecca waited patiently for her to continue. It was the least she could do. "It is very simple actually," Zephyr began. "Avert your attention to two people."

"Which two?"

"Guillermo Nunez . . . and Pedro Estrada."

Rebecca's breathing stopped. "Zephyr, I—"

"I want *you* to concentrate your energies on them."

"Why me?"

"Because you give a damn."

"Zephyr, the fact that you're in the States constitutes—"

"I want him out."

"It's complicated."

"How?"

Rebecca chuckled. "It just is!"

Zephyr smirked. "I don't see it that way."

Rebecca sat back in her chair. She crossed her legs and turned her head away from her host. She had to think. She had a million questions, but she had to narrow them down to a few. "Why do you want to do this?" Rebecca nodded. She was still looking away from Zephyr. She stared at a painting on the wall and studied its intent. "Is it because of the last decade? He took over the business, right? And essentially took over the city. Murders, extortion, cartels, Forty-Second Street . . . it's all him. And you put a man in the hospital as a start. Is it because . . . he killed your father?"

Zephyr sat up and leaned forward. She rested her elbows on the table and stared at Rebecca with hellish intent in her eyes. "Now you know why I am here."

Rebecca turned to Zephyr. She finally saw the truth behind Zephyr's motions. Zephyr had cried just as hard as Rebecca once did. They both pursued their goals. They both put themselves through trials that would break any other normal person. They both should have been dead, but they terrified the Grim Reaper. Here was

Rebecca's mirror. She sat in front of a being from an altered dimension. These two women were as balanced as fire and air, sugar and cream, cloak and dagger.

"Okay," Rebecca answered. "I'll do it."

Zephyr smiled. "I knew you would." She gently patted her lips with a napkin. "You don't have to do anything special. Just continue to direct your attention to those two. Your colleagues will naturally keep their eyes on me, due to my unfortunate relationship with Pedro. Nevertheless, do not lose focus. I will handle everything else."

"What are you going to do?"

"Not too much." Zephyr folded her hands and rested her chin upon them. "But do trust me. I will most certainly return the favor to you."

"No, Zephyr. You don't have to do anything. You've done a lot as of now."

"Well, darling, it's too late. I already put everything in motion. So you will just have to accept my gifts."

Rebecca wanted to pry further, to get every little detail about Zephyr's plans. But she knew it would be fruitless. "Okay."

"Beautiful. And Rebecca?"

"Yeah?"

"Enjoy your breakfast. Believe me . . . everything will taste good. I prepare meals by my own hands."

X

Slim was seething with confidence. Too much, as a matter of fact. He wore an expensive suit as well as a smile wide enough to swallow a watermelon. He looked around the table and politely nodded to each of his colleagues. Forty-Second Street members recognized his joy, and they were terrified by it. Whenever Slim smiled, something bad either happened or was about to happen. God only knew.

"What you smilin' about?" one of the gang members asked. Slim did not respond.

Pedro was always the black sheep of any meeting. He wore pieces of a suit, but not necessarily a complete set. He already knew that he himself was not a complete set. He was just an amalgam of emotions and thoughts colliding together into one misshapen mass. What he constantly thought of, God only knew that as well. All he did was sniffle and wipe his nose on his sleeve. And good Lord, his nostrils were crimson, bloody red! Everyone took notice that Pedro sampled the commodity as much as he sold it, which was running dry at the moment. Pedro showed no shame for his actions; either that or he was just too ashamed to hide it. He was sitting next to Slim. He maintained his status as a shadow rather than a leader. He was just a dead spirit.

Mr. Mal sat at the head of the table and smoked on his large cigar. The room filled with a blue fog that smelled as sweet as spearmint. He surveyed the room and shook his head at Pedro. He was such a mess. Good. The more screwed up he was, the better.

Two young girls who looked to be in their early twenties entered the room with a tray of liquor in their arms and lingerie on their bodies. They served each man with whichever hard liquor they had available. When Mr. Mal called one of them over, he asked for a glass of wine.

"We only serve hard liquor, baby." She gave him a cordial, almost professional smile.

"So what are you going to do about that?"

Her smile faded to fear. "I could . . . run back to the kitchen and get you a glass."

"Merlot."

"You got it . . ."

Her partner watched her leave in a hurry. She served her last drink, placed the tray on a nearby table, and ran after her.

"As you know," Pedro began, doing his best not to sniffle the remains of his evening coke, "we've been planning to take out my sis—Zephyr." Pedro cleared his throat. "We've confirmed her location at Olympus."

"Well, no shit. What took so long to find her?" Mr. Mal interjected. "And how come you haven't taken care of her yet?"

Slim spoke up. "Well, as much as I *wanted* to storm inside and shoot her head off, we had to watch the place and kind of record her agenda. I stationed one of our boys to watch the place once it opened up."

"I see . . ." Mr. Mal puffed on his cigar. "And?"

"From what we've seen, she seems to be alone right after the club closes at—" Slim reached into his breast pocket and pulled out a notepad. "Four. She waves the guards good-bye, locks up the place, and walks home by herself. This has been the trend for about the past week."

"Nice . . ." Mr. Mal smiled.

Slim smiled back. He was proud of his report.

"It's a damn shame."

Slim looked puzzled. "About . . ."

"We had to hold a meeting for one damn person. This shouldn't have been a problem in the first place," Mr. Mal glared at Pedro, "but it is."

Pedro stood up. He wiped his nose and blinked a few times. "I've already told you—"

"Sit your ass down."

Pedro sighed. "I've told you, years ago, that it was impossible and, at the time, unnecessary to go after her. We already have her. That's all that—"

"I said . . ." Mr. Mal stood up. "Sit. Your ass. Down."

Pedro leered at Mr. Mal. His men stood up in unison and brandished their guns. Pedro raised his hands, but he did not take his eyes off him.

"See, something you have to understand is that I'm the big man in this room. Okay?" Mr. Mal pointed to himself with his massive finger. "I'm the big man in this city. You wouldn't be worth shit if it wasn't for me. My crew made you. You remember that."

"Fuck you!"

Mr. Mal stared at Pedro's nose. "I think you're sniffing too much shit, so I'm gonna let that slide."

"Pedro!" Slim stood up and tried to control his partner. "Chill the fuck out, all right?"

Pedro nodded. He inhaled deeply and allowed Slim to sit him down. He climbed into his seat and listened attentively.

"Good boy," Mr. Mal said. A minute later, the girl came back with a dark red bottle of merlot. She poured him a glass and handed it to him as he winked at her.

"Better," he said.

She thanked him and sped out of the room.

"It's that time of year again," he started. "We got a new shipment coming from overseas tonight. The amount we're getting is enough to carry us over for the next two years."

"Jesus, how much?" Slim asked. He wanted to direct attention away from the previous conversation and move on.

"Sixteen million."

"Not bad."

"Damn straight. Once the shipment gets to my garage on Thirty-Third, we'll unload everything from there." Mr. Mal burnt out his cigar on the table. "Now here's where everything gets complicated: Zephyr. I'll admit the bitch is smart. She took down two of my boys without any trouble. She needs to go underground."

Slim smiled. "Oh, I agree."

"So what I'll do is take her out myself. Tonight. I'll follow this agenda you gave me and I'll wait for her to come out of the club. I'm tired of having to do things with her narrow ass running around this city, taking out my crew and shit." Mr. Mal stood up and stretched his massive chest. "I'll do what Chicken Shit over here should've done years ago."

Pedro burst out of his seat and whipped out his gun. He aimed it at Mr. Mal's head with shaking hands. The men in the room jumped out of their seats and held their guns toward Pedro. Slim heard the melody of clicks and slides from each gun in the room. He remained in his seat without any intention of interfering.

"Pedro," Mr. Mal commanded with a smirk, "you better—"

"I am not a chicken shit!" Pedro jerked his gun forward.

"Relax, fellas, he ain't gonna do a damn thing."

"Fuck you!"

"He ain't gonna pull that trigger."

"You shut the fuck up! You hear me?" Pedro moved the gun around the room, but Mr. Mal only responded to his rage with a smile. Even if he had enough bullets in his clip, there was no way he could take out everyone in the room in his current condition, and Mr. Mal knew this oh so well. Although the thought of death appealed to him many times before, he did not want to die in someone else's hands. He would much rather swallow his own bullet. He lowered his arm and dropped the gun on the floor. Slim still kept himself seated. He yawned and looked at his watch.

"There." Mr. Mal motioned for everyone to leave the room. "Now why can't you do that to Zephyr?"

Pedro threw himself in his seat. He sat there staring at the bottles of liquor that lay on the tray. He counted them over and over in his head. What he wouldn't do for another snort of coke. He looked at Slim, who shrugged his shoulders as an answer to whatever questions Pedro may have had in his mind.

"Look on the bright side," Slim said as he patted Pedro's shoulder. "At least we don't have to worry about Zephyr anymore."

Pedro remained silent.

"She's up against Mal."

Pedro nodded.

"Not even the cops would go up against him."

"That's the whole point." Pedro stood up and walked toward the exit. "Zephyr's not the cops."

*   *   *

Mr. Mal entered his SUV and signaled the driver to meet with the second team at the venue. He always insisted on having someone else drive because, as he once selfishly stated, "In the movies, they always aim for the motherfucking drivers." He ordered his chauffeur to drive nice and easy in order to avoid unwanted attention. The car ride was painstakingly slow and unbearable, but no one dared voice their complaints. He pulled out his cell phone and barked orders to his secondary team.

"I want this over with quick. Take the other end of the alley, and we'll stay right here. When Zephyr walks out, we'll make her run down that alley, and that's where you'll pop her. Understand?"

"We got this," the team answered.

"Now remember, we gotta be smart. Zephyr ain't just a pretty face, she has balls hidden in that tight pussy of hers. You saw how she fucked up our guys. They were some hard-ass soldiers. Now one of them is in fucking wheelchairs, you know what I'm saying?"

"Yeah . . . that bitch needs to go."

"So we gotta use her own game on her."

"You got it, boss."

"The club closes at four . . . we have about five more minutes. Slim said that she sends her guards home first before she locks up. That's our cue to light her up." Mr. Mal brought the phone closer to his mouth. "I want this shit to go down perfectly. Check your aims, understand?"

"Yeah."

Mr. Mal hung up the phone. He sat in wait for his prize to exit the building. He shut his eyes. He was tired.

He imagined how it would all look, how it would all sound, when Zephyr would leave the club not knowing that she would be killed three feet away from the front door. He played the event in his mind, like an orator prepares for his speech and imagines the exceptional feedback he would receive after delivering his inspirational words. Mr. Mal wanted a standing ovation. He wanted to know what it felt like to kill again.

He imagined his reinforcements arriving at their designated position just as Zephyr walked out of the club. Only a few minutes would pass once Zephyr locked the doors and waved goodbye to her security. The guards would leave her behind. Alone. No large men to protect her, no screaming crowds to accompany her. It was just her and the early morning sky.

He would glance at his watch too many times to count. He would study every single person that walked by his car. Any other day, there would be nary a person around, but tonight, his car seemed to be a magnet for every drunk and horny couple in the city. They had better not let curiosity get the best of them and take a look inside. Shouldn't they be home by now or at least pass out in the middle of the sidewalk until dawn?

Mr. Mal kept his eyes closed. He smiled as he thought of the beautiful moment where Zephyr would walk away from the building without a worry in her head or a concern on her face. She would enjoy the cool breeze gently combing her hair. She would smile at the bright moonlight and wish upon the first star she saw. The innocence would behead her, and it would look so sexy!

He would get on his phone and order his men to move in. Zephyr would look up and see a mass of Forty-Second Street members rush her and block her path. Knowing her, she would run her pretty little ass off and venture down a nearby alley. And that's exactly where she would be trapped. The beauty of large numbers, of undefeatable odds.

His Forty-Second Street crew would make him proud once they grabbed her. He would let them smack her against the brick wall and throw her to the ground. She deserved it after all she did to his two guys who were minding their own damned business.

But he was a nice guy. She deserved better treatment than that. Instead, he would shoot her in her stomach and watch her keel over in pain. He wanted her to feel her hot blood spill over her hands as she tried to hold herself together. He would approach her with a sawed-off shotgun in his hands, probably do a little dance around her, and listen to her gasp for air and life.

He would wait for her to fall to her knees and grab at his ankles. He would laugh when she tried to pull herself up, but couldn't. She would look at him with painful tears in her eyes. He wondered if she would curse him out with her dying breath.

In that case, best to just shoot her and not find out.

It had been such a long time since he had participated in things like this. He was so used to having someone else "do it" for him. Did he remember how to even use a gun? No problem, it's much like riding a bicycle.

He opened his eyes and blinked himself back to reality. He saw the last bouncer leave. He picked up his cell phone and warned his teammates to keep their eyes peeled. "Here it is . . ." he whispered with excitement. "Wait for it . . ."

Mr. Mal sat up in his chair. He reached underneath his seat and pulled out his signature sawed-off shotgun. A little over the top, but it was his "fire and forget about it" weapon. One blast to the face and he could go home. He thought about the girl that served him the liquor earlier that evening. He promised himself that he would locate her once this was all over. He needed some company tonight, and dammit, she'd better give him more than just a shitty glass of wine.

Zephyr exited the club and placed her glittered hand on the door. She locked the doors and tugged on them to make sure they were correctly secured. She paused for a moment and took a long look at the starlit sky.

"Yeah, bitch," Mr. Mal chuckled, "enjoy that view while you can."

Zephyr turned her head in Mr. Mal's direction. No way she could have heard him, right? She kept her ghastly eyes on his car. Her face was stoic, almost dead. She blinked twice and ran off down the alley.

"Shit! Get that bitch!" Mr. Mal flung the door wide open and sprinted after her. He wanted to shoot her personally, even if she was already caught in the crossfire. One of his men saw her flying hair and took a shot at Zephyr. It struck the corner of the wall and ricocheted in the opposite direction. The spark that flew from the shot made Mr. Mal angrier. He wanted blood, not a spark of light.

He and his men chased after her. She was fast, faster than he thought. She ran in her heels like she was born wearing them. He thanked God that he had another crew waiting for her on the other side.

He was nearing the entrance to the alley. His heart thumped against his large chest. His breathing was nervous and erratic. He waited for the sounds of gunshots, but he only met silence. The hell was going on?

His men managed to run past him. Once they entered the alley, they stopped. They raised their hands and dropped their weapons to the ground. Mr. Mal knew exactly what was going on, but he was running too fast to stop himself.

"Put down your fucking weapons! Put 'em down! Now!"

Mr. Mal saw a small platoon of cops at the end of the alley. He glanced around the area and saw a medley of rifles pointed at him and his men. Flashes of blue and red painted the sky. He saw badges, blue uniforms, shaky hands, grim faces, and the ugly sight of his teams being thrown to the ground and handcuffed.

He saw Zephyr at the end of the alley with guns surrounding her, all pointed at him. She smiled an arrogant smile and shook her head at him. He could read her mind.

"Did you really think you could best me, Julius?"

Her mind spoke those words with such eloquence. Mr. Mal adjusted his eyesight and saw that she was slowly moving her lips.

"What made you think that you were smarter than I?"

Mr. Mal dropped his shotgun and fell to his knees. He was now at her mercy.

"Silence. That is rare for you. Well, you can be silent forever. I care less."

Mr. Mal's face was seething with anger. He wanted to choke her, smack her, and fuck her, anything but look at her living face. She folded her hands behind her back and gave him a polite nod. She had won.

Two officers handcuffed Mr. Mal and brought him onto his feet. He wanted to shoot those pretty little lifeless eyes out of her sockets. He saw her smile when she nodded at him. It was like daggers piercing his forehead. He couldn't do this anymore.

"Fuck this!" He muscled his way out of the officers' grips before they were able to lock the cuffs on him. He yanked the 9mm from one of the officer's holsters and held it at Zephyr's head. He squeezed the trigger with joy in his heart.

A shot was fired. He lowered the gun and chuckled. Zephyr stood in place and lowered her eyes. She took a deep breath, but it was Mr. Mal who slumped to the ground with blood oozing from his mouth. He gasped for selfish air. Zephyr turned around and saw Rebecca's smoking gun. She kept it raised in his direction, just in case he was more resilient than everyone thought. She walked toward his dying body. Zephyr walked one step behind her.

"Are you all right, Zephyr?"

"Lovely, darling." Zephyr combed her hair through her fingers. "*Gracias.*"

"*De nada.*"

"Best to call for an ambulance. He needs to live." Zephyr motioned one of the officers to come on over.

"How did you know he would be here?" the officer asked.

Zephyr and Rebecca stared at each other with a smirk on their faces. They both shrugged their shoulders. "Miss Estrada noticed some strange activity coming from those vehicles over there. She contacted our office, I showed up, and sure enough . . ."

"Good call," he said with a smile. Rebecca and Zephyr watched him assist his colleagues with arresting the crew that came with Mr. Mal.

"He asked a good question," Rebecca said with an air of curiosity. "How *did* you know he was going to show up?"

Zephyr smiled slyly. "Darling, I know everything."

"Will you share your knowledge one day?"

Zephyr chuckled as she walked back to her home. "If all goes well, I may get to tell you everything I know today."

Rebecca nodded. "I look forward to it."

"Relax for now, love." Zephyr said over her shoulder. "We have a big day ahead of us."

*   *   *

Slim paced the conference room for what seemed like hours. He kept looking at his cell phone to see if he had missed a call during his torturous mental escapade. He knew that Mr. Mal always delivered on a death sentence. Mr. Mal would make sure that Zephyr died from extreme lead poisoning. Everything was just fine.

It's just that he never took this long to call back after getting someone killed.

This much he did know: Mr. Mal has, literally, an army. On the other hand, Zephyr didn't need one. *She* was the army. If she was able to exact full militaristic agony upon Trent and what's-his-face by her own damned self, she could very well repeat her methods upon Mr. Mal and his men.

He cursed under his breath when he looked at his phone and saw nothing but the time and date. He threw the phone on the table and held his head in his hands.

"No word from him?" Pedro asked with a sound of defeat in his voice.

"No . . ." Slim sighed. "Nothing."

"Figures." Pedro laid his head on the desk. "Fuck it."

"Pedro . . ." Slim clenched his face in order to avoid losing his temper. "We have to do something."

Pedro lifted up his head and tried to compose himself. "He's most likely at his garage with the stuff." He rubbed his tired eyes. "Start there."

Slim stared out the window and lost himself in thought. "Okay . . . let me go with a few of our guys. You stay here with the rest, just in case."

Pedro surrendered his thoughts to a labyrinth that lay before him. The conference room lights hypnotized him, and he felt himself seduced by Lady Insanity. She bent down to greet his despair and gently kissed his hand. Her lips burned like acid, but he did not flinch. He wanted to lick his hand and taste the shameful flavors of regret. He wanted to swallow the Lady's tongue and set his soul aflame. Oh, how bad he wanted her to finish him off . . .

Suddenly, the horrifying event rushed back to the realms of his consciousness. The way his father's eyes bulged the second Pedro squeezed the trigger, the blood that trickled down from Luis Estrada's body, and the apathy he felt when he ordered First Degree—wait, his name was . . . Adam. When Adam was ordered to get rid of the body, everything came back like a vivid movie screen. The Lady held his head in her hands and kissed him. Her lips were rough and as jagged as broken glass. He screamed as it pierced his brain, the bringer of memories. He screamed because it felt so good to be hurt.

"More," he muttered. "Please . . . give me more."

"More what?" Slim had awakened Pedro from his trance.

"Say what?"

"More what? You asked for more."

"Oh . . . nothing. Go on ahead; I'll be here. Let me know what's up."

"Okay." Slim walked out of the room and left Pedro alone. He closed his eyes again. He wanted another kiss.

"More . . ." he said.

*   *   *

Slim arrived at the garage with half a dozen men. The morning sun peeked through a blanket of gray clouds that colored the city in a melancholic mist. He examined the entrance and saw nothing out of the ordinary. The door was still on its rusty hinges, the windows were shattered from a bullet fired over a decade ago, and old weeds still split the sidewalk. The only company that was present with Slim was his own men and a couple of squirrels.

"The three of you, check the back," Slim commanded. "Let us know when to come in."

They nodded and stepped out of the car. They cast quick glances around the area to make sure that no early risers were around. They disappeared around the corner and left Slim in suspense. He counted every second during their search, tapping his foot on the floor and biting his lip. He saw a trio of shadows appear on the other side of the building. Once their bodies followed afterward, he relaxed.

"All right, looks like nothing's up." Slim opened the car door and stepped outside. He walked towards the front entrance of the garage, all the while wondering if Mr. Mal would notice a couple of kilos missing from the stash. None of his guys would object, and what he didn't know won't hurt him at all.

He pushed open the door and breathed in the stiff air. His eyes fell upon a large storage container that sat on the far end of the room. He clapped his hands together as he hopped and skipped over to the container like a little girl on Christmas morning. This was a large stash, and too bad that Mr. Mal was unable to share the joy. He was grinning once he grabbed the handles and pulled the doors wide open. The sight in front of him made his jaw drop.

It was a stash of angry Russians with guns in their hands.

They approached Slim and his men with their weapons carefully aimed at their foreheads. Slim saw his men around him land on their knees with their hands on their heads. A curious shadow still lay inside the container. One Russian was behind him, in case he had a horrid idea of leaving his men behind and making a run for his car. He was completely trapped.

A curious shadow emerged from the container. He focused his eyes on the person that emerged from storage and walked toward him. The light finally shone on the figure. Slim felt his heart beat faster and faster. The sight of the figure made him want to turn around just so that he could be shot.

This was the second time he felt fear in his chest, and again, Zephyr was the source of his fear.

"Hello, Mr. Nunez."

"You . . ."

"Me."

Slim chuckled. "You're too damn smart."

"Thank you." Zephyr checked her nails. She noticed it was a habit of hers, to always analyze herself and to make sure she maintained perfection. Success once again. "How is Pedro? I am just dying to see him."

"Go to hell."

Zephyr glared at Slim with her eyes and ate his soul. He felt his heart stop longer than usual, and when it did beat again, it slammed against his chest. He had no clue that he had a soul to steal. Perhaps she did not either.

Zephyr nodded to her guys. They shot Slim's men like the dogs that they were. Slim felt his ears ring from the echoes of both the gunshots and the screams. He had never heard people die like that before, as if a pit of hell had opened up just for them. He could hear them shriek as they descended further into the pit. They landed on brimstone and immediately burned to an eternal crisp. He closed his eyes and waited for his turn.

"Oh no," Zephyr said as she walked closer to him. "Your time has not come as of yet. You and I are going to have a long talk."

Slim heard a metal pole being dragged on the ground. He turned around and saw one of the Russians approach him. He swung the pole and hit Slim on the back of his head. His eyes steadily blacked out before he fell to the floor. The last image he saw was Zephyr gazing upon him with a sort of sick passion in her eyes.

Trent's friend was right. She really was beautiful.

*   *   *

Rebecca stayed in the lonesome hospital until she was absolutely certain that Mr. Mal's vitals were stable. She paced the waiting room with her fellow officers. She felt herself thinking about Zephyr's mission—*missions*, rather. What would happen once she got even with her brother? All that intelligence, the strategy, the emotionless calculations . . . what of them? Would they wither and die when all was done, or would she use them for God knows what else?

She walked over to a water cooler. Her body was thirsting as much as her mind was thirsting for more knowledge. She felt concerned for her new and only friend. Sad. Zephyr was more than able to handle herself. Only God Himself could stop Zephyr, and knowing her, she would try to justify her actions.

As she stood up, a pair of doors that led to the hospital's exit swung open. Out of curiosity, she looked to see who had entered the hospital. She wanted to make sure it was not one of Mr. Mal's men trying to free the crime lord. When she saw a familiar face walk toward her, she immediately cast her attention back on her cup of water.

"Rebecca . . ." Greg approached her. She ignored his presence as she sipped on her water. "Ortega, I need to—"

"What the fuck do you want?" Rebecca was understandably cold.

Greg ignored her language. "What's going on here?"

"The head of the Forty-Second Street gang is in critical condition. Apparently, I have good aim."

"What? You put him there?"

"Yep."

"Why? What happened?"

Rebecca sighed. "He made an attempt to kill Zephyr Estrada. I intercepted him." Rebecca walked over to a nearby chair and sat in it. Greg followed her and sat next to her, in her dismay. "He managed to grab one of the officer's department-issued. Zephyr's head would have been part of the graffiti on the walls."

"Jesus . . ." Greg stood up and cleared his throat. "All right, just give me a full report this afternoon."

Rebecca sipped her water. "I'm not giving you a report."

Greg turned around with angered surprise. "Say that again?"

"Obviously, you didn't get the memo . . . but I have orders to report directly to the captain."

"Effective since when?"

Rebecca shot up from her chair and slammed her cup on the floor. "Effective since the time you barged into Olympus like a drunken fucking sailor!"

"Oh for fuck's sake, that—"

"I'm trying to solve crimes and you're not trying at all! So get out of my face and go fuck yourself!"

Greg swung his hand at Rebecca. She blocked it just in time and countered with a punch strong enough to knock him unconscious. All the hospital staff and the officers present stood in shock at the sight before them. She actually wanted to pull out her gun and make him wet his pants, but he wasn't worth it. She ignored everyone in the room because she was too angry to care.

"Escort Detective Bernini out of this hospital. Now!" Two nearby officers obeyed her order and grabbed him by his arms and legs. She watched them carry him outside. Thank God.

She stared at a trash can and wondered if she should throw away her hard-earned career. She shook her head. The godforsaken streets were behind her, so might as well focus on this case and wrap it up as quickly as possible.

The image came back. She had not seen it in years. The stranger hung in front of her from a lamp cord. The way he swung ever so slightly in the air never left her memory. She fought back tears and maintained her composure. "Right," she whispered. "Don't give up."

Rebecca heard a chime at her waist. She pulled out her cell phone and studied the screen. She raised an eyebrow at the text she received: "Good morning, Rebecca! Meet me at the street address that you should be receiving right now. *Ciao!*"

Rebecca chuckled. She received another text soon afterward: "And bring an umbrella!"

She looked outside and saw the torrential downpour. Things changed as fast as the weather. A nurse approached her with a tiny piece of paper in her hand.

"The patient is stable, *Detective* Ortega," she said as she handed Rebecca the slip of paper. "Don't worry—I will look after the patient myself."

Rebecca stared at the nurse's eyes for a long moment. She knew that the nurse's intent was anything but caring, that Mr. Mal would be another corpse to fill up the local graveyard. He would receive a mortal wound that no one would be allowed to close. He would die in an assassin's company that would stand over his perishing body, up until his last breath vanished in the cold hospital air.

"Okay." Rebecca took the note and smiled at the nurse. "Take care of him."

"Will do," the nurse answered. She turned on her heel and made haste toward Mr. Mal's hospital bed.

Rebecca did not feel ashamed, nor did she feel regretful of her decision. She was tired, and for the first time in years, she was glad that someone had died and deserved it. "Sergeant, take over while I'm gone."

"Yes, ma'am."

She walked toward the exit and unfolded the piece of paper that was given to her. She stared blankly at the address in front of her, a place she had not seen in years.

"Parish."

*　　*　　*

Rebecca never forgot about her once-upon-a-time home. How could she? It was her mother when she needed comfort. It was her father when she needed protection. It was her lover.

But like every child, she had to leave home at some point. It gave her enough nourishment to survive anything. Rebecca evolved from an innocent bud to a relentless rose because of Parish. She owed this empty venue everything.

So why the onset of dread?

She was a block away from her surrogate home, but she decided to pull over to a side street and park the car there. She turned off the car and stared at the entrance to the alley. She got out of the car and started walking. Parish deserved more respect than driving there, she concluded. She was to enter Parish in the exact same manner as she had first arrived there all those years ago.

Each step she made on the pavement brought about painful tremors in her heart. Rebecca saw a group of men huddled around a tiny barrel flame. The sky became darker by the minute. Zephyr did tell her to bring an umbrella, but she didn't give a shit. She did not have any umbrellas back then; why would she need one now?

Suddenly, she thought about Mister. She remembered the many nights he would cover her with a holey but clean blanket whenever it rained. She thought of his odor that was a stench to others, but to her, it was as sweet as honey. She had given him a daughterly devotion to him in return, as well as any sticks of French bread that she could gather.

Jesus Christ, how the hell did Zephyr know? Especially with the little bit of information she shared with her. Goddammit, she knows *everything*! Rebecca increased her walking speed as she entered Parish with anger in her eyes. Zephyr had now broken into both of Rebecca's homes with nary an effort, and this knowledge pissed her off, as if her life was under constant scrutiny. Her privacy was destroyed the minute Zephyr had entered her life.

Rebecca shook her head. She was getting angry at the only friend she had in the world, a friend who happens to know all of her secrets. But she knew Zephyr's as well. Both women trusted one another, and that made their friendship dangerous.

She saw Zephyr's car parked outside an old one-story apartment building. She carefully examined the structure with eyes that knew every detail like the back of her hand. It turned out to be worse than she remembered. If there had been windows that were cracked in the past, they were now completely destroyed. The gutters were broken in half, the tiles were balding, and the door swung off one hinge. She could smell the drugs that emanated from the doorway. Home sweet home.

Rebecca entered the old building and saw a group of mice scurry away from her. She sneezed from the dust in the air. "God," she muttered. Her nose was so used to the rest of the world that it had almost forgotten this one. She wiped her nose with the back of her sleeve and moved on.

She reached into her pocket and pulled out her cell phone. She scrolled through her last incoming text messages. She found Zephyr's odd number and dialed it. The phone rang twice before a soft voice answered.

"Hello, Rebecca." She sounded calm but serious. "I assume you're here?"

"Yeah . . ." Rebecca looked around. She began to hate this place with every passing second.

"Good. Come upstairs. I have a surprise for you."

Rebecca tightly shut her eyes. She was getting a little tired of surprises. "Okay . . . see you soon."

"Likewise, love."

Rebecca hung up the phone. She found the pitiful staircase that rose to the second floor. Each step squeaked underneath her weight as if they were annoyed that someone had the nerve to disturb them from their slumber. They screamed at Rebecca with each step they took. Eventually, they annoyed her so much that she ended up sprinting up the remainder of the stairs.

Once she reached the top, Rebecca saw Zephyr sitting in a chair in a nearby room. Her cold eyes pierced the darkness, and they were fixated on something in front of her. Rebecca could not see what Zephyr was concentrating on, but she was glad that it was not her. She politely knocked on the doorway.

"Zephyr," she said. "What's going on—"

"Come in," she replied.

Rebecca entered the room. She followed Zephyr's eyes and saw a tall, thin man standing on a chair on his toes. A lamp cord was tied around his neck, digging into his pulsing carotid artery. He was sweating quite profusely from maintaining his balance. Rebecca was in total shock. She studied his face and pulled out her gun almost instinctively. "Oh my god . . ."

"Rebecca Ortega, meet Guillermo Nunez."

XI

Rebecca couldn't believe that Zephyr managed to have Slim suspended in front of her. He was bleeding from the back of his head, his hands were tied by a leather belt, and his toes were strained from holding himself up. The strangest thing was that he was smiling the whole entire time.

"You . . ." Rebecca leered at Slim.

He managed to find a spot where he could stay still. "Who . . . who the fuck are you?"

"You don't remember me?" Rebecca was breathing heavily. Her rage grew with every tiny screech from the chair upon which Slim was standing, albeit partly and with difficulty. "That night! I asked you for a fucking dollar and you choked me!"

Slim chuckled. "So fucking what? I've choked a lot of bitches, especially when I fuck them. There's something about a pussy that struggles, you know?"

Rebecca pointed her gun at Slim. "You fucking bastard!"

"One second, love," Zephyr said.

"Fuck off, Zephyr!" Rebecca screamed.

"I understand that you are upset, but—"

"I said fuck off!" She aimed her gun at Zephyr, but she did not flinch. "You don't know the shit I went through with this asshole!"

"Slim, darling." Zephyr crossed her legs. "Do you remember what you did here?"

"Suck my cock."

Zephyr rolled her eyes. She reached for her thigh and pulled out a gun that was strapped to her leg. She shot near Slim's shin and grazed his skin. Barely any blood pilled onto the floor, but it was enough to make him curse out loud and stumble on the chair. He immediately switched sides and balanced himself on his other foot. His anger was just beginning to rise, and that's what Zephyr wanted.

"You fucking bitch!" he screamed. "I'm gonna fucking kill you!"

"You make things so difficult." Zephyr placed her pistol back in its holster on her leg. "Answer the question, unless you want me to blow off your only working appendage."

"Fucking hell! I just killed some old homeless guy 'cause he pissed me off! Christ, that was years ago—what does it matter to you?"

At that moment, Rebecca's eyes widened. She dropped her gun as she slowly walked toward Slim.

"What did you do?"

Slim laughed.

"Tell me what you did! Now!"

He snickered. "One night, I followed him here. Shit, it was awesome. I didn't have a knife or a gun on me . . . so I walked inside and snuck up on him. Bastard must have had eyes in the back of his fucking skull 'cause he turned around and punched me in the throat. But I grew up in the streets too, motherfuckers. We must've fought for a half hour, but I managed . . . I managed to knock him the fuck out with a lamp I found and I strung his ass high! If only you were there . . . you would've laughed too!"

Rebecca's eyes poured out tears, but she did not sob. She refused to give him the pleasure of sadness's sound. She remembered everything about him that she had grown to love. He was a saint, and Slim had made sure that he was martyred.

And as she cried, all he did was laugh. He became louder and louder, to the point that his voice echoed throughout Parish. Everyone could hear his demonic chuckle reverberate through the city. Rebecca turned to Zephyr, who just stared at Slim with anger in her eyes. She did not get up from her chair; she merely gazed at Slim's damaged leg as if she *willed* it to bleed.

Rebecca turned to Slim. Her tears were still pouring from her eyes. She could not bear to imagine how Mister had been killed, but her mind forced her to do so. She could see Mister walking up the stairs after a tired and fruitless day out on the streets, when Slim approached him from behind and tried to fight him. But Mister wasn't born yesterday, and he must have given Slim the worst fight he ever had. But age often comes with agony, and fighting did not regenerate Mister's speed nor did it grant him a brief repose. When that happened, after thirty minutes of punishment, Slim found that lamp and swung it against his head. She imagined Mister screaming out as he dropped to the floor. She imagined Slim dragging him across that same floor, occasionally kicking him in the side because he felt like it. Rebecca recalled every detail in the police report so many years ago . . . and now the inflicted injuries made sense. Slim had been the cause of his anguish. Slim was the reason for Mister's murder. Slim was the reason for everything.

She imagined the finale. She saw how Slim had tied the lamp cord around his neck and thrown the other end over a rafter. He had used it as a fulcrum to hoist Mister up, choking him as he ascended toward the ceiling. Slim had then stepped up to the ceiling and tied the end of the cord to the rafter to make it look like it was a suicide. Plus, Slim figured, he was homeless, and no one would give a shit. Except Rebecca.

She saw everything now, his jerking movements and his ill attempts for air, for a chance to live. But Slim wouldn't give it to him. Not at all. He wanted to make an example of him, so he fucking killed the only man in Rebecca's life that demanded nothing in return but a goddamned piece of stale French bread!

"Get him down, Zephyr."

"As you wish." Zephyr aimed her gun at the lamp cord and shot it so that Slim could fall to the floor, grab his neck, and gasp for air. For Mister's air. For the air of Rebecca's rage.

Rebecca was wearing her police uniform when she encountered Mr. Mal, and she took off her department belt and unbuttoned her blouse. She reached into her pockets and pulled out a pair of black studded leather gloves that she soon slid onto her hands. It was almost a holy movement when she embraced the thick hide wrapping around her fingers, as if they were the garb for a priest or a mansion's elongated curtain. She clenched her fists and raised them up in her unnatural fighter's pose.

"Take your time. I want you to heal up. When you're ready, get the fuck up and fight me. Give me your best, you fucking bastard."

Slim coughed. "Not gonna roll up your sleeves, you fucking cunt? Want me to smack your face and eat that sweaty pussy of yours?"

Rebecca slowly walked toward Slim and accelerated once he readied himself for the skirmish. She saw his right fist swing for a cross, but she slid underneath his intended blow and kicked his hamstring. She could have gone for his testes, but she wanted to fight, not win. Yet. This would be on her own terms, not his. Definitely not his.

Slim fell to one knee, but he quickly kicked out his leg to try to catch Rebecca as she stood up. She saw it coming and rolled away at just the right amount of distance for her to leap up in the air. She slammed her foot but only struck the hard concrete floor since Slim had already moved from that spot. She retreated, and he chased after. They were both approaching a wall, and Rebecca jumped on the wall, pushed off with her right leg, and kicked him in the face. Slim stepped back, rubbed his face, and laughed.

"Don't fight a guy on drugs," he said. "He won't feel shit."

"Don't fight a girl who's been pissed off since she was ten!" Rebecca yelled.

Slim then resorted to wild punches. They had no form, no order, much like Rebecca's, but she knew that each connection would be dire for her health if she didn't block them. He made a left cross, but she ducked underneath it and blocked his knee that tried to make contact with her nose. He tried again and again, but Rebecca was too fast and blocked each of them. She jabbed at his stomach, to get his air out of his torso, but she was surprised at how strong and resilient Slim was despite his build.

Slim then tackled Rebecca and brought her to the floor. She gasped in pain, but she embraced the cold concrete and wrapped her legs around Slim. She thrust her elbow into Slim's side repeatedly, but he wouldn't budge. He picked her up with his enormous strength and slammed her on the floor. Rebecca held on as he did it again. This time, she felt her back give out from pain. She released her hold, and blocked Slim's attempt to kick her on her side. Each block moved her a little, and that was all she needed to create some distance. She summoned her strength and rolled away from Slim as he tried to stomp on her neck. She stood up and tackled Slim and pressed her knee on top of his larynx so that he wouldn't be able to breathe or get up. She pounded on Slim's nose, his face, and even his eyes. She then punched Slim from his left side so that it forcibly positioned his head to expose his temples. She clenched her leathered fist and hammered on this spot. Slim was choking, and Rebecca stood up and moved away from him. She fought like a beast; Slim fought like a demon.

"C'mon, Guillermo . . . can't you beat a girl?" Rebecca asked in between breaths.

"F-fuck you, bitch!" Slim grabbed some loose concrete and flung the dust at Rebecca. She almost laughed as she shielded herself with her arms from the small storm. Dirty tricks were part of Rebecca's curriculum. She opened her eyes and saw the lamp on the floor. She picked it up with the instep of her foot, flipped it in midair, and smacked it against Slim's bleeding skull. He fell to the floor, and for once, he stayed there. Rebecca walked over with the lamp—still attached to its cord—and kicked Slim in the head with her heavy boot. He was knocked out, but Rebecca shook him to wake him up.

"Don't pass out, you fucking asshole. Get up!"

Slim slowly opened his eyes and saw Rebecca's profile. When he realized who she was, he remembered the fight and urged on. He grabbed her neck, just like he had those many years ago, and squeezed in a nostalgic manner.

"God, I forgot how good this felt," he said.

Rebecca didn't black out—she recalled the vision of her neck being crushed, and she had to close her eyes to bring it to the surface of her mind. When it was there, when her hunger had begged Slim for something, anything, to feed her for that night, she recalled his long nails digging into the sides of her neck. And she remembered how much she disliked it then and how much she hated it now.

Suddenly, she heard Mister's voice echo from the floor, instructing her and guiding her. "Do not bend what is already bent," Mister once told her. "Break what is already straightened out. Now stop bullshitting and fight this motherfucker as if he were trying to rip your ass off."

She briefly took her hands off Slim's and used them to break his arm at the straightened joint. Slim fell to the floor and yelled in pain. He held his broken arm, but it was useless to try to heal something that was impervious to mending. Rebecca quickly grabbed the lamp and swung it at Slim's face. The tremors she felt when the porcelain met the skull made Rebecca lust for more carnage, so she kicked Slim to the ground and pummeled the bottom of the lamp right on Slim's forehead. She kept slamming and slamming, to the point where she wondered if brains would ever spill out of his head. Rebecca then moved her grip toward the lamp cord and, in one swift movement, wrapped the cord around Slim's neck from behind. Her makeshift assassin's cord made Slim attempt to gather anything to free him, but all he was able to do was kick wildly and grab at Rebecca's hot hands.

"Stop struggling and fucking die!" Rebecca yelled.

Rebecca watched closely and felt Slim's pulse beat slower and slower through the cord.

"How does it fucking feel now?" Rebecca tightened her grip and watched the cord dig deeper into his neck, crushing his vein and blocking any blood flow. His eyes bulged in pain and fear, just as Rebecca's eyes were showing agony when he choked her. She watched him die with a satisfactory smile on her face. He shook a few more times, and then he stopped. His eyes were still open, and finally, the color of his face faded.

Rebecca spat at Slim's head and turned away from him. She was heavily panting and rubbed her neck, less out of pain and more out of a long-forgotten habit. She stared down the hallway and swore that she saw Mister's spirit wave her goodbye. He had a faint smile on his face, as he always smiled, and held up a piece of French bread that she found for him. He disappeared into the hallway walls. He could now walk amongst Parish in peace.

ANDREW COOKE

"Zephyr . . ." Rebecca grabbed a nearby box and placed it in front of her. She sat down upon it and wiped her face. She felt her heart beat decrease in tempo, and her personality and nerves were slowly returning from the adrenaline rush. "I think you need to tell me everything."

Zephyr nodded. She sat so silently that if she were to have left that brutal combat, no one would have noticed. "Of course." She pulled out her phone and silenced it.

"I mean it," Rebecca said with a firm tone. "You need to tell me everything. I'm fucking tired and angry right now."

"Very well." Zephyr sighed deeply and closed her eyes. "I am omniscient in the sense that I have eyes everywhere, even in your office."

Rebecca gave Zephyr a strange look.

"You call him Mr. Xerox. Cute guy, really."

Rebecca suddenly remembered the new guy with the wide glasses and warm smile. "Oh my god . . ."

"I kept him around to keep tabs on you and the bad detective over there. I got all the info I needed: telephone numbers to your desks, your contact info, Detective Bernini's contact information—"

"That's how you knew where I lived."

"Precisely."

Rebecca nodded. "You mentioned Greg?"

"Ah, yes." Zephyr combed her hair with her fingers. "I like you, Rebecca. I wanted to make sure that you broke the glass ceiling. As of right now, Greg should be demoted by now. Or fired. I prefer the latter, personally."

"Because of what happened at the club?" Rebecca continued to stare at Zephyr in disbelief. "Are you shitting me? You had a hand in that, didn't you?"

"Yes. I hired someone to convince him to visit me. Amazing what a special additive to liquor can do to someone. She then, pardon the pun, pushed him to come to me."

"She?"

"Oh, you didn't know? He has a thing for prostitutes."

"What?"

"Well, only in this particular case."

"Holy shit . . ." Rebecca rubbed her face.

"I also had my girl give him a lovely little bug.'"

"Jesus Christ, Zephyr! Why would you do that?!"

"Because I care."

"He didn't do anything to deserve this!"

"Yes, he did." Zephyr leaned back in her chair. "He does a poor job of detecting . . . anything. You do a fantastic job. You and I both know that you would never have made detective while under his tutelage. How else was I supposed to promote you?"

"Goddammit, Zephyr! I wanted to be detective, but I never wanted it this way! He would never do crazy shit like that! Where's your proof?"

Zephyr reached underneath her chair and pulled out a folder. She handed it to Rebecca, who immediately grabbed it and opened it. Attached inside the folder was a small thumb drive. "Plenty of video there, darling."

"Where did you get this?"

"The same prostitute that your former superior enjoyed that night. He recorded everything. Future viewing pleasures, I suppose. *I* didn't even know that he would be into that. I hire people that are better than I thought." Zephyr looked out a broken window on the left side of the room. She could see the entire city decay before her, much like Parish. She made the decision that she really needed to redecorate. "The former detective had a neighborhood snitch who announced my arrival, right?"

Rebecca closed her eyes in defeat. She remembered Greg first mentioning Zephyr's arrival. "Yeah. Yours?"

"Yes. I needed everyone to know I was here to—well, you know the rest."

Rebecca sighed. She closed the folder and placed it on her lap. "I give up, Zephyr. You win."

"Win what?"

"You win. I just . . . quit. You already know everything. You knew about Greg, you had a mole in our department, you knew about Mr. Mal's visit to your club. You planned everything from the beginning. I used to think, *Oh, maybe Zephyr is psychic*. But you're not a psychic . . . you're just a calculating bitch."

"I take that as a compliment," Zephyr replied.

"I know you, Zephyr. I know that everything fell into place. You even used me . . . I thought you were my friend."

Zephyr sat up in her seat and stared at Rebecca. "I did not use you, and I am still your friend."

Rebecca laughed. "I find that hard to believe right now."

"Remember that time you told me that I used a contraction?"

"What about it?" Rebecca replied coldly.

"It's such a ridiculous observation. Any other person would have disregarded it, but you . . . you have a gift of discernment, much like me. In any case, it's because I trust you."

Rebecca paused. She had gotten at least one thing right about Zephyr.

"Remember that little skirmish you had a while ago? With a number of Forty-Second Street gang members? I was the one who tipped off the police concerning their whereabouts. I knew you would be with them. I trusted your abilities, and you did not disappoint. Another basis for a promotion." Zephyr smiled. "I look out for my friends, Detective. I want them to be happy."

"My God . . ." Rebecca stood up and paced the room. "I just killed him."

"No, you didn't." Zephyr stood up in front of her. "You received an anonymous tip that Guillermo Nunez was in the area, possibly to distribute drugs. You wanted to call for backup, but you did not want to risk losing him, nor could you take the risk of Slim spotting one of your darling boys in blue. Plus, you could not risk this chance of a lifetime. Once you had arrived at the designated location, no one was there. So you decide to return home and call it a night. However, a gang member saw Slim and then you and concluded that Slim was snitch, thus the profane injuries on his body."

"What about my blood? DNA?"

"I'll have someone move his body to another place in Parish. I trust you know a good spot?"

"Yeah."

"In the meantime, just to be safe, I'll have a treasured soldier of mine to clean up the area. Oh, and—"

"No. No one here gives a shit on what happened in Parish, so no one will talk. Trust me."

Zephyr nodded. "I already do."

Rebecca thought everything over. Zephyr was right. She could pass it off as a gang murder and get away with it.

"By the way, the little note my nurse gave to you is proof enough, just in case anyone asks where you received such a tip. I can provide you with more information, which I doubt someone of your caliber will need. You still get your promotion, Slim is dead, you lobbed off a leader of a crime syndicate . . . do invite me to your awards ceremony, okay?"

Rebecca reached in her shoulder pocket and pulled out the folded slip of paper. She had almost forgot about it. "Yeah . . ."

"Rebecca." Zephyr walked over and placed her hand on her shoulder. "I don't have to be a telepath to know what you're thinking. You are not a dirty cop. You just get things done."

"Just like you."

Zephyr chuckled. "Just like me."

"I already know that Mr. Mal is dead," Rebecca said. "Your nurse must've taken care of him already."

"Exactly."

"It was risky to make yourself vulnerable like that, opening a club in the heart of Forty-Second Street territory and all."

"A necessary risk. I needed my enemy to come out of hiding."

"Mission accomplished." Rebecca thrust her hands into her pockets and began to walk out. Zephyr followed close behind. "So what are you going to do now?"

"I need to finish this. I will see Pedro."

"Are you going to kill him?"

Zephyr stopped walking. She looked at Rebecca with emotionless eyes. "I made a promise not to kill him. It's bullshit, I know."

"But you're going to dethrone him?"

"For certain, yes."

"How?"

Zephyr walked past Rebecca with a smile on her face. "And therein lies the rub."

*   *   *

Zephyr met with twenty of her men two streets down from the Estrada mansion. She employed not only Vladimir's army but also her personal team that had served her father many years ago. The same men who had sworn allegiance to Zephyr were now loading their weapons and strapping on their Kevlar armor. One of them set a box of radios on the ground and instructed everyone to attach them to their shoulders.

"Stay on frequency nine, gentlemen," Zephyr commanded. She slipped an earpiece in her right ear and switched it on. She herself did not put on any Kevlar, nor did she help herself to any of the powerful weapons that lay in front of her. She did go back to her home to refresh herself and change into an outfit that she had saved for this moment alone: a silk black top with vertical pleats that ran across her breasts and reached about two inches past her waist. The hem itself was fitted and symmetrical in cut. Her stretch cotton pants touched her black heels—nothing noteworthy, but the objective was to be elegant without being extravagant or gaudy.

She also put on a pair of platinum stiletto earrings and let her hair fall upon her shoulders. She wrapped herself in a black Burberry trench coat with a belt that she loosely tied around her waist. She enclosed her hands with soft leather gloves, not as bestial as Rebecca's but just as thick. To everyone who saw her outfit, it was the plainest one she had ever worn but still very attractive. To Zephyr, however, it was her funeral dress.

As far as her weapons went, she merely reloaded the pistol that wounded Slim earlier. She read her reflection and saw a hint of sadness in her brilliant silver eyes. *Almost there*, she thought. She kissed the barrel and slipped it back in its holster.

"Miss Estrada," one of the men spoke with concern, "let me give you a gun."

"You are such a darling, but this will suffice." Zephyr winked at him and proceeded to address everyone. "Gentlemen, I will make sure that you all get home to your loved ones in a safe manner. I *implore* you to follow my every command. For this battle, my strategy is absolute—you can all trust me. Is that understood?"

"Yes," they all replied in unison.

"Beautiful. This will be a simple brawl." Zephyr whipped out a long scroll from her jacket and set it on the ground. She bent down to unroll it and placed a small rock on each side to hold it down. It was a blueprint of the entire mansion. She had circled particular locations on the blueprint with a black marker. "The circles here are the precise locations of Pedro's men. They hardly venture away from their spots, so it should be fairly easy to take them out. Groups one and two will cover the east and west branches of the mansion, respectively. Group three will cover the north side. Group four, I request the pleasure of your company. We will handle the entrance from the south.

"If you direct your attention here . . ." Zephyr pointed her delicate finger at a number of squares. "These areas are recent, in the sense that their tours are not cemented. Pedro and his currently deceased partner implemented a strategy to have these men change their routes periodically twice a week in order to remain static. Thanks to a certain pair of eyes of mine, I already know of their placements. Group four,"—Zephyr turned to her personal team—"I will direct the trajectories of your shots. Once again, you *must* trust me."

"Yes, ma'am," one of them replied.

"My God! I am only in my twenties! Call me Zephyr. Or Lady Estrada! Something classy, okay?"

The teams laughed. They felt their nervous energy lifting off their shoulders.

"Are there any questions?"

"Lady Estrada . . . what will you do once we secure the mansion?"

Zephyr smiled. She liked that title. She reminded herself to use it more often. "I will have you all wait for me. I will be with Pedro."

"I understand."

Zephyr grabbed her blueprints and stood up. One of the men gave her a lighter and she set aflame the map. "Gentlemen," Zephyr said as the orange flames engulfed her former home's blueprints, "we will be facing some of the most dangerous men of the Forty-Second Street gang, but you have me. I guarantee our victory. Shall we?"

Zephyr turned around and allowed her teams to disperse. Zephyr's personal squad consisted of four men, each of whom covered all directions in front of her. They walked when she walked, floating around her like electrons in an atom, and she was the nucleus that held everyone together.

Zephyr casually walked up to the front entrance with a smirk on her face. The guard posted at the head of the driveway saw her and immediately radioed her arrival. One of her guardsman, Salvador, inhaled and shot him in the head. His blood barely had time to spill on the ground when other shots were heard throughout the perimeter. They moved so fast that Pedro's men were not able to keep up with the commotion.

"Zephyr, this is Team Alpha. Come in. Over."

"Report."

"Back entrance has been breached. Two targets down . . . just like you said."

"Excellent. Make your way towards the rear sitting rooms and take out the three targets there."

"Affirmative."

Zephyr made her way down the long driveway that led to the mansion. She felt ill at ease with the rush of memory that came to meet her. She suddenly remembered the nights as a shy little girl staring out the window to see if her father's car had entered the driveway. But she refused to let her past emotions distract her from this current mission. She had a job to do; nostalgia would have to wait, impatient though it was.

"Loves," Zephyr addressed her team, "be ready."

She reached the front door and hugged the outside wall. She waited until her men were good and ready. When they were, she nodded, and they kicked down the door. Salvador and his partner, Oscar, moved in and took out two guys with well-placed shots: two in the chest, one in the head. She then followed close behind, and then she was flanked once again by her rear guard. They scanned the area as she moved along her planned path. She kept her hands in her pockets as she gave her team commands that were scarily accurate.

"One is on the northeast corner on the balcony."

Salvador shot the man once as came out of hiding, and once again, he fell to the floor below.

"Another one five feet ahead of him, behind the pillar."

Oscar shot him twice in the head. His blood spilled all over the pillar and left a stain that would take days to clean.

"Benito, some idiot is going to try to shoot me in the back, southwest corner."

Benito turned around and blew the gangster's hand off. He grabbed his wrist and screamed out, but Benito silenced him with a deathblow to the head.

"*Gracias.*" Zephyr reached the middle of the hallway just a few feet in front of the staircase. She stopped. She looked up at the ceiling and marveled at the intricate design at its corners. She looked in front of her and smiled at the pillars and the dusty wooden chairs that have not been used in years. "Amazing," she whispered. "We are to be ambushed: three in front, two on each side, and two in the southwest and southeast corners."

Salvador, Oscar, Benito, and his partner, Rene, readied their weapons. They placed their faith in Zephyr and did not question the veracity of her commands. The seconds felt like hours as they waited for her prediction to come true. The shots from the other designated sides of the mansion were the only sounds heard.

Zephyr closed her eyes. She shut out the silver orbs that saw everything that was hidden and everything that had yet to happen. "Now."

As if she was manipulating their movements, the exact number of Pedro's men leaped out of their spots. But they did not realize that Zephyr's planning was almost precognitive. They all jumped upon a rain of bullets from her team. They pierced their lungs and their throats, and one guy caught a bullet in his nose. He was saved from his anguish when another bullet lodged itself into his skull.

Zephyr could smell the dust and embers that were abandoned by everyone's weapons. The sweet sounds of the casings falling on the floor reminded Zephyr of the church bells that were rung by the little girls in church. Their golden shines reflected off the lights in the house and were mirrors to the pools of blood and bone that washed the marble floor. Heavy thuds reverberated throughout the hallway. Finally, there was silence.

"Any injuries, loves?" She examined each member of her own team.

"None here."

"Team Alpha, status report."

"North end is secure, Lady Estrada."

"Team Beta, what is your status?"

"East section is clear. We have the same result from Team Gamma. No trouble here."

"No casualties, I assume?"

"Negative."

Zephyr smiled. It was exactly what she wanted to hear. "Wonderful! Let us rendezvous at the foot of the staircase here."

"Acknowledged."

Zephyr sat herself on the second step and crossed her legs. She flung her hair back and set her eyes on a bloodstain. It resembled a paint splatter on a blank canvas that was spread out in one direction. Smaller dots emanated from the largest glob in the stain. Underneath it, she saw a Forty-Second Street member who lay slumped on the floor with his eyes still open. He looked right at Zephyr, but she did not waver. Rather, her eyes consumed him, and his eyes finally closed.

"Two in each room upstairs," she said to her teams when they all met up once again. "Let me know when they are put to sleep."

Her teams nodded and left her alone. Her eyes suddenly glowed an intense white as she surveyed Death collecting their damned souls. She did not feel any sympathy; the bastards deserved every single last gasps for air, every hot bullet that ripped through their goddamned ribs, every sudden outburst of tears and screams when they realized that their dinner and sex were to be their last. No matter how many times they yelled or how many times they begged to live, Zephyr would not listen. She was blind to their sobs and deaf to their wails.

She heard the satisfying exchange of shots and their subsequent bloody melodies. She heard the cries, the cursing, and the pleas. She chuckled at each gunshot that followed their begging. Just desserts. But Zephyr was a kind soul; she made everyone suffer less, although she often doubted her magnanimous decisions.

The sounds suddenly came to a halt. Zephyr listened to the heavy footsteps of her crew as they double-checked each room. She twirled her ankle and awaited their return. She slightly bobbed her head; she remembered a song that her father had sung to her.

> Let's dance until we sleep,
> No one knows how deep
> Our love is . . .
> Let's dance until we sleep,
> Our love always leaps,
> Always so deep...

Zephyr used to sing that song with an innocent voice devoid of depression and loss. She chuckled and shook her head. Strange. That song had never appeared in her mind until now. She was coming home, and she missed every bit of it. But at this moment, this place was not a mansion anymore; it was a dungeon.

"All clear, Zephyr . . ." Salvador called from the staircase. "The only place left is the office farther down the hall . . ."

"Thank you," she answered. She stood up and smoothed out her dress. She pressed a button on her earpiece. "Back to me, everyone," she beckoned. "We are almost done."

"Copy that."

"On our way."

"Affirmative."

After a few moments, Zephyr's teams arrived at her spot. They were not injured, but they were tired. It had been a long time since they had executed a mission, but Zephyr was extremely pleased by their actions. "You have all done well," she praised. "A great reward for each of you awaits."

"Lady Estrada," Salvador spoke up, "we should have told you this before, but . . . we all have agreed to do this for free. Your father . . . he meant a lot to us and our families. We owe him—you—our lives."

Zephyr walked up to him and placed her hand on his shoulder. "Gentlemen, you all have precious hearts. I had figured that you would refuse my offerings. But no matter—I have already distributed the amounts to your special ones days ago."

Salvador chuckled. "You are always three steps ahead."

"Always." Zephyr reached down her thigh and pulled out her silver pistol. She stared at the door that led to the office where Pedro sat. She knew that he would soon be alone. Strangely, she almost wished that he was not alone at all. It would have given her an excuse to "accidentally" have him caught in the crossfire.

Sadly, a promise is a promise.

"Salvador, darling, do you have a field knife?"

"Of . . . course." He untied a leather sheath that was strapped to his waist and pulled out a beautiful grayed kukri that had a subtle Damascus design flourishing throughout the blade. It held smeared remnants of rain that crystalized on the flat end of this hand sword, and the tip was as microscopic as she expected. She examined the hilt and smiled at the sturdy black handle that balanced in her hand no matter where she flipped it and switched from one hand to the other.

"I said I wanted a field knife, not Excalibur! This is breathtaking!"

"It's yours," Salvador replied. "Please take it."

Zephyr sighed, but it was not a sigh of disgust but one of appreciation. "I will use it to the best of my abilities. I shall return and collect its scabbard. For now, hold on to it until I wipe off the blood from this . . . soul blade."

"For you, we will wait forever."

"*Gracias.*" Zephyr nodded to her men. She gave them all a look that said, "I shall return with blood on me, and not mine." She held her gun at her side on her right hand and held her new blade on her—her hand of dominance. Her grip was different from traditional holds in that the hilt was pointed toward the sky and the blade was facing the ground. This reverse clasp was her favorite and something learned many years ago. She, admittedly, was anxious to apply erudition to practice.

She walked down the hallway, passing by every empty spot that used to house paintings and family photos. The walls were plastered with blood and bullet holes, almost as if the whole house was meant to be blown to pieces. Zephyr wondered if it would be best to just burn the place down. That bridge would be crossed when she got to it, but right now, she had to burn one last bridge before she could move on.

She reached the door and breathed in the solid wood that separated her from her unfortunate sibling. She was excited to see him, of course—not from a sense of familial longing but from the knowledge that her brother would be forgiven through death. Wait . . . can't kill him. She sighed and welcomed her frustration.

"Death is too nice anyway," she whispered.

*   *   *

Pedro sat in the dark twirling a knife in his hand. The desk where he sat was covered with punctures; he often stabbed it thinking that Zephyr's beating heart was lying in front of him. He was going nuts. He heard the gun shots, the screams, and the heavy thuds that shook the top floor of the mansion. He knew that there was no way that one of the bodies belonged to Zephyr.

He stared at the floor and saw the blood of his father erupt out the floor and ooze toward Pedro's feet. His heart quickened as he watched the blood pulse between red and white. He felt mesmerized by it and wanted to touch it. But the minute he outstretched his hand, the blood slid away from him.

"Do you see that?" Pedro asked his guards. There were four of them, and they all had their guns pointed to the door. They could sense Zephyr was nearby, but they were too terrified to look and see. They had heard the rumors—a beautiful, soul-stealing sister of their boss who was out to reclaim her throne. Brutal, cold, manipulative . . . they knew her before she arrived here to kill them all.

"See what?"

"That!" Pedro pointed at the floor. "Don't you see it?"

"I don't know what you're—shit!"

The door blew wide open, and a cloud of smoke immediately entered the room. Pedro stood up and watched for Zephyr's cold eyes to pierce through the thick mist. His men opened fire through the hallway. They emptied their clips with their overanxious trigger fingers into nothing. They hit air. Once the firing stopped, they waited for something to happen.

"Did we get her?" one of the guards asked.

"Shh!" They waited a few more seconds. They tuned their ears for any sound that was coming from the hallway. Nothing. They only heard their own hearts beat in their chests.

"I think we got her."

"Shut the fuck up!"

"Go check the hallway," Pedro commanded.

They carefully tiptoed their way outside the office and closed the door behind them, locking Pedro as a prisoner in his stolen home. Their guns followed their eyes, which darted at every corner and every dead body that they saw lying on the floor. Their friends and colleagues were now bloodstains and an ill memory. Zephyr was so cruel with her executions. She didn't even bother wounding them or shooting them in their legs. They were all killed by headshots, some by two in the head. One guy had one in his neck. The blood dried all over his shirt collar. It was too much for their eyes to fathom.

"Where the fuck is she?"

"Right here, loves." Zephyr exited one of the adjacent rooms and held her gun at Pedro's head. They dropped their weapons the instant she addressed them. They were paralyzed by shock; they could not even raise their hands for mercy.

"Hmph," she muttered. "I specifically remember this room having a soft carpet. A light beige, if I am not mistaken, and I hardly ever am." Zephyr tapped the floor with her heel. "At least you had the decency to substitute the carpeting with dark brown hardwood. Or perhaps it was already underneath the carpeting, and you just ripped what was old and substantial to reveal something new and just as ample, am I right?"

Everyone stayed silent, especially Pedro, who only heard the voices in his fear as he cowered behind the doors, although a small part of him was happy that it was his men who were getting punished, and not the alternative.

"Take those words with wisdom, gentlemen." Zephyr kept her eyes on Pedro and successfully paralyzed him; she would address him when she was ready. Everything would be done on her terms from now on. "I am considerably bored. I wonder . . . could you entertain me and drop all your guns while I discard my own? I would like to fight you until your blood separates from the plasma." Zephyr grinned. "Pretty please?"

Each of Pedro's men obliged, almost laughing when they did so. They kicked their guns aside and raised their fists for battle. They were roughly two hundred pounds each, and they were interested to see how a young woman who barely weighed half their weight would beat them.

"You sure you wanna fight *all* of us?" one of them asked. "You'll lose and we'll run a train on you."

"Jesus, that is a horrifying image," Zephyr said as she took off her heels and glued her delicate feet to the floor. She took off her trench coat and threw it on to a nearby desk. She quickly tied her hair into a bun before she responded. "Well, I had better win, correct?"

One of them lunged at Zephyr. He raised his right fist to punch her in the throat, but she tightened her grip on her borrowed knife, ducked underneath the intended blow, and sliced the brachial vein on his arm with discerning accuracy. He grunted in pain and held his bleeding arm, and he could not see the blade thrust into his neck and slice open half of his jugular. He grabbed his neck to stop the flow of blood, but he might as well have used a picture frame to halt the rush of the Atrato River in Colombia.

"Next," Zephyr said.

This time, two of Pedro's men split up and attacked Zephyr from both sides. She weaved out of the wild punches thrown at her from her left side, staying mere inches from their knuckles. The other guard tried to kick her on her right side, but she pushed away from the kick with her legs and did a backflip. Once she landed, she hurled her blade at the guard who tried to kick her, and it flew right into his right eyeball. He gave a blood-curdling yell, and put both of his hands on the hilt to try to pry it out. The guard who constantly missed her face with his punches decided to tackle her instead and sprinted toward her torso.

"Really?" Zephyr asked. She stood in place and waited for her assailant to build confidence when he reached closer and closer to her. At the very last moment, Zephyr jumped straight up with amazing agility and gently touched his shoulder to hoist a few inches higher off the ground. He decelerated and turned around to see a chuckling Zephyr.

"I apologize," she said while trying her best to stop laughing. "Sincerely, I really am sorry. I just wished you did something more . . . intelligent? Would you like to retry?"

"You fucking bitch!" he screamed. He charged at her, faster this time, and saw Zephyr turn back and run away from him. She ran toward the guard with the knife still in his eye socket and pulled it out. He shrieked in pain and fell to his knees. Zephyr was still sprinting and was closing in on a wall. Her assailant was doing the same. Once she reached that barrier, she ran upward on it and used her powerful legs to push herself off into another backflip. The guard was smart enough to slow his chase, but he did not turn around fast enough to face Zephyr again. She used this split-second opportunity to fling her kukri at the soft spot between the base of the skull and the neck. The guard turned around and held the knife with a strong grasp and pulled it out. Besides the excruciating pain that poured out of his body, Zephyr kicked the back of his knee and grabbed his weakened forearm. With one swift movement, she bent his arm and thrust the kukri into his temple and dug it deeper until she guessed when, and if, it pierced his brain.

Zephyr unclenched his fingers and retrieved her prized weapon. His body jerked toward the floor, and she checked to make sure that his soul left his body before she spoke to the guard who was blinded by her attack.

"Ah, yes. The half-blind mouse." She slowly walked to him and plunged the blade into his other eyeball. He screamed, but Zephyr covered his mouth and muffled the noise. "Oh, shut the fuck up," she said.

"Impressive, Ms. Estrada." The last guard was found leaning against the wall with his arms crossed. He was smart, Zephyr realized. He had stood off to the side while he witnessed the onslaught of his associates. "You fight with technique, unlike my . . . coworkers."

"And you do?" Zephyr asked while she wiped the blood of her kukri with her gloves.

"If you want to know, come here and I'll tell you."

"Oh, I like you already."

The last guard snickered and took off his suit jacket. He rolled up his sleeves but kept on his tie. He slowly pulled out the knife that was always close to his heart. He twirled and flipped it in the air and held it in the same grip as Zephyr did.

"Die, bitch," he said.

"Shame," Zephyr began. "You wear nice clothing."

Zephyr and the guard slowly walked in a semicircle. She studied his eyes as they both encircled their territories, exerting governance and testing to see which of them would claim them.

And as they surveyed, the last guard standing moved closer to Zephyr. She felt led by his dance and shortened the space of air between them. Soon, they were locked in combat without flinching. Only their chests moved up and down as they breathed, and their eyes blinked. Zephyr saw a slight blink in his eye that was out of rhythm with hers.

"Mine," she whispered.

At that moment, the last man pushed Zephyr off and whipped his knife at her face. She dodged it in time and deflected it toward the ground, but his grip was just as firm as hers. He swung it at her breasts, and she swerved backward to protect her radiant torso. She retreated back into his space and swiped at his body. Circular flashes of steel and fury were seen in the atmosphere, and a musky aroma could be smelled from the flurries of both blades as they touched each other for that brief moment. With each touch came a feeling of disappointment that no scent of blood was sensed with each strike.

Sparks could be seen when Zephyr's kukri kissed Pedro's blade, that dull, lifeless sword that twirled upon an unseen target.

Zephyr and the nameless guard stepped back for a moment and assessed each other's attributes. Zephyr, in a long time, was actually breathing harder than usual. And she did not like it.

"I am not bored anymore," she said with a deep breath.

"I am," he replied.

Zephyr raised her eyebrow. He was good.

Before she could finish her accelerated thoughts, he threw the blade at Zephyr's head. She studied the knife's velocity and repelled it with her kukri's edge. It spun in the air with more revolutions than she could count, and she caught its hilt effortlessly in her right hand.

She turned her attention back to her opponent and saw him charging full speed at her. She knew this would happen, and she readied herself as he quickly approached her. Zephyr smirked and vaulted over him. She aimed her feet on his shoulders and pushed as hard as she could. Although he was impervious to her push, she was able to secure a safe distance between herself and her adversary, who stopped and slowly turned around to face her. Zephyr threw the knife at him, but he caught it in mid-air and smiled.

"I'm surprised you didn't just stab me in the carotid artery and call it a night," he said. You didn't like my knife?"

"Not really," she replied. "Besides, mine is bigger than yours." Zephyr placed her kukri between her teeth and patted her hair. "Let us end this, shall we? My coward brother requires my attention. Stay there, Pedro!" she yelled.

She kept her eyes where her ungodly sibling would be found and sensed his guard approach her at a speed as fast as she expected. She dropped the knife into her hand and imagined how anxiously his knife wished to plunge into her cold, deathly heart, but she dodged every swipe he made: throat, right shoulder, legs, chest, chest again, and even her hair. She engaged him again with blade strikes against his own, but this time she placed the weight of her body into her next block and managed to loosen his grip on his knife. She sliced his wrist, caught the knife as it dropped to the floor, and cut his femoral artery. He knelt down in pain, and she hopped onto his shoulder. She juggled both knives and used his own weapon to repeatedly stab him in his neck, while her victorious blade made certain that it matched the speed of the other.

Zephyr stabbed like a slow jackhammer. Each plunge traveled deeper than the other, almost as though it was a cathartic murder. She turned into a machine with no emotion, only external inputs that elicited an action. She kept stabbing him until he finally fell back, and her movements started to decrease. She was tired, and it was her way of conserving energy. Zephyr was not finished, even though her body tried to inform her otherwise.

"You know what, Pedro?" Zephyr called out. "I have to admit, I am glad that you had hired this gentleman to protect you. He failed to do so, but he gave me quite a workout. I have not been entertained until now. I hope to do this more often. and yet—"

This time, Pedro swung open his door, and he had heard every single decibel that transpired during Zephyr's coup. He pulled the drawer open and shuffled through his papers and drugs to look for his gun. He was growing increasingly angry when he couldn't find it.

Zephyr's men were already upstairs when they heard the commotion and saw the Forty-Second Street gangsters bleeding on the floor. Salvador shook his head when he saw their weapons on the floor. Zephyr must have manipulated them into dropping them. With those eyes, he concluded, and her family history, he would have done the same.

Meanwhile, Pedro found an old rusty cartridge of snuff. He smashed it on the table and dug his nose into the powders. He inhaled so much that he felt a trickle of blood enter his nasal passage. It felt so good . . . his eyes were bloodshot immediately after he lifted his head. He saw the imaginary blood reach up his leg, and then it crawled up to his chest and latched onto his neck. He screamed as he felt its cold claws burrow into his neck. He tried to pull it off, but it felt like strong glue that crept into his pores and entered his bloodstreams. The blood formed into a large glob and spread out his skin. He grabbed his knife and sliced the side of his neck, hoping to carve out the bloody amoeba. It finally attached itself onto his knife and he flung it on the floor. It completely evaporated before his eyes.

He breathed a sigh of relief, and then he grabbed his handkerchief to close his wound.

"You are a sick man, brother dear."

Pedro dropped his handkerchief and let his blood and skin fall onto his shirt. He saw Zephyr sitting across the table from him. She had put back on her trench coat and let her hair down again. She whipped it in a circle to open her face toward fresh and lustful air. She was examining both knives that she had acquired and marveled at the leather scabbard that wrapped itself around the blood tongue inside. The scabbard itself was nothing special—plain black leather with white stitching and a silver cap at the very tip. But to Zephyr, it was all that was necessary. Its luxury came from the wrathful soul that was clothed by the body and not the other way around.

The door behind her was closed. They were both trapped in the room together. Well, actually, *he* was the one who was trapped. She was so relaxed and so laid-back about his suffering. It was like she *asked* for this to happen. She was suddenly alone, and she wanted it that way. Zephyr gently placed both blades on the table, almost seductively, and smiled.

"Z-Zephyr . . ."

"Before we begin," she said as she crossed her legs to holster her gun back on her thigh, "I should tell you that Slim is dead."

"H-he's dead?"

"Yes, dead. Quite gruesomely, as a matter of fact."

Pedro exhaled with a force that blew the cocaine away from his face.

Zephyr's cell phone rang. "One second." She answered the phone call and let Pedro sit in fear. He could tell she was enjoying this. "Lovely. Thank you." She hung up the phone. "I have just received confirmation that Julius Mal is deceased. It truly is amazing how quickly vitals plunge when your face is smothered by a hospital pillow."

"Zephyr, you—"

"And of course, his garage was raided by the police. They received a rather propitious and anonymous phone call concerning its location. How much was the shipment worth? Mr. Mal said sixteen million, correct? I believe that is a record for the EPD. I wish I were there to see their faces, but I could not miss this family reunion."

"But how—"

"You and Slim have a tendency to have constant company. The prostitutes you bring over to fuck?" Zephyr leaned in close to make sure that Pedro understood every word. "They are my girls. They provided all the information I needed. I have to admit, that was a very simple task. You brought them over for a few fun nights, they got you drunk and high, and then they surveyed the entire mansion. They took photos of every room in this house, and then they sent it to me through a lovely text message. *Messages*, rather. That is how I knew the routes of every guard you have here.

"Do keep in mind that every female you have been bringing over in the recent past are all mine. Remember the girl who served Mr. Mal that cheap glass of Merlot? Mine. Oh yes, and the serving tray was bugged. That is how I knew about the shipment, Mr. Mal's ill-conceived plan to take me out, Slim's arrival at the garage . . ." Zephyr chuckled. "I am actually amused that you all thought you could kill me. Amused . . . and offended."

Pedro's hands were shaking. He remembered every prostitute, sex slave, and anything with a vagina. They were all Zephyr's. All their conversations, all their plans, everything. They were all shot to hell.

"I built the club both to satisfy my lust for the arts and to pull you out into the open. I have patience, Pedro. I believe in war of attrition. I wanted you to live in constant fear of my arrival because we both know that you saw it coming, you just did not know when. Once that phobia grew inside you, your resources were poorly executed and were directed away from normal routines. Understand this—instill enough fear into someone and he will falter, do you not agree? I also wanted you to see my nightly routines. 'Zephyr waves the guards goodbye after she locks the doors at around four in the morning.' Does all of that sound about right? I admit it was a tad bit bold of me to build the venue right in the middle of Forty-Second Street territory, but look on the bright side—I raised the property value ten percent."

Pedro was speechless. He just sat there with tears in his eyes. He wanted to die so badly.

"Are you tired? I understand. Truly, I do. I would have felt exhausted if I were in your shoes." Zephyr stood up and slowly walked toward Pedro. "To summarize, all your associates are dead, I have eyes everywhere, and everything I have planned is flawless." She sat on his desk and crossed her legs. "*Mami* and *Abuela* are both fine, in case you were wondering. As for myself, I have been absolutely fantastic. Especially today. It felt good to . . . take out my frustrations on your men." Zephyr combed her fingers through her dark hair. "I have talked too much. Are there any questions you have for me?"

Pedro sat in silence. He glanced at his former employee's knife on the table. It gleamed in such a beautiful manner. It asked him to take it. It wanted to be held. Caressed, actually. "Drive me into her beating heart," it said to him. "Don't glide me against your everlasting skin." Pedro glanced at the woman sitting on his desk who looked at him with those vampire eyes. He lunged for the knife, grabbed it, and swung it at Zephyr. She jumped off the desk and smiled at him. He kept adjusting his grip on the handle. He had never used it before, but damn it all, he would learn.

Zephyr stood in one place. She placed her hands in her trench coat pockets and waited for Pedro. Pedro knew she was planning something, but he was sick and tired of her always having a plan! "Come on, Zephyr!" he screamed. "Stop fucking around!"

Zephyr did not move. She just stood there and smiled.

"Fuck you!" Pedro lunged at her and stabbed air. She moved backward, dodging every swipe he made. Her arms were still in her pockets. She even laughed at him.

"God, another knife fight? You are pathetic!"

"Fuck you!" Pedro drove his blade into Zephyr, but she grabbed his hand before he could make contact, broke his wrist, and grabbed the knife before it fell on the floor. Pedro fell to his knees, grabbing his crushed wrist.

"Actually, this is a nice blade," she said. She examined the knife and twirled it around her finger. She threw the blade to her left hand

and impaled Pedro's hand to the floor. She twisted it in a full circle. His screams were beautiful notes in a song she had composed.

"Do you know how much it hurts now?" Zephyr yelled. "Do you?"

Pedro flinched from her screams more than the pain from the knife. Her words were the blade that froze him into his place. She finally had him petrified.

"Look at me! I said, *Look at me!*"

"I-I'm sorry—"

"*Sorry?*" Zephyr grabbed Pedro's hair and slammed it on the floor. She dragged his face across the wood and white powder that lay on top of it. She wanted his nose to bleed out of his own head. Oh, how she cherished this moment.

"Is this what you want? Fucking drugs? The empire? Is this shit worth it?"

"I'm sorry," Pedro sobbed. "I'm so s-s-sorry!" His head was violently pulled by his hair. He found himself staring into Zephyr's glowing white eyes. They were covered in tears that refused to fall down her cheeks. Her teeth were clenched and her nostrils filled with rage. The powder blew all over the floor in a dusty, drugged cloud. Zephyr watched each molecule fall ever so gracefully onto the same floor that had housed Luis Estrada's dead body.

"God . . . what am I doing?" She released her grip once he became silent. His breathing stopped, his body lay still, and his nose was bathed in his own blood and mucus. "This isn't like me . . ."

Pedro let out a loud and agonized groan. He stumbled as his arms gave way underneath his dead weight. He blinked his eyes, but they would not stay open. Zephyr figured that it was better that way.

"He told me not to kill you, Pedro." Zephyr stared out the window that was behind his desk. It was the same window through which Luis had observed the world so many years ago. He must have felt the same way that Zephyr was feeling then. Sadness. Disappointment. Regret. He had passed on his dark cognitions onto his daughter, the best one out of the whole family. "He knew you wanted the business. He tried to save you from it, but . . . I suppose things do not always go as well as planned, right?"

Pedro finally opened his eyes. He saw his hand still pinned to the floor. He tried to move toward it, but he was afraid that Zephyr would see him and stomp on his head. For once, he actually did *not* want to die.

"I cherished this night for years. I watched you act with a wide smile on my face. I mapped your associates' schedules. I know where you go to eat. I know how much you make a month. I even know how long it takes for you to take a piss. I had so many of your men killed. And do you think I feel sorry for them, after what they did? Oh, I am positive that they have girlfriends at home with a handful of children running around the house, wondering if it is finally time to eat and when Daddy is coming home. I am sure their mothers are calming them down and telling them to be good for daddy when he gets home.

"You want to know something, Pedro? I do not care how long they wait for their fathers to arrive home for dinner. I do not care how many times they stare at the clock, counting down the minutes until the car headlights shine through their windows. I actually want them to cry when they realize that Daddy is not coming home. I want to see their mothers put them to bed early and make up some excuse like 'Your father had to work late' or 'He had to take a last-minute trip to the grocery store.' I want to see their mothers hysterically telephone all his friends in a vain hope that maybe he *really* is working late." Zephyr smirked. "I wish I could see them look out their living room windows for days and days, realizing that every evening spent without him will be permanent. I want them to wail, I want them to scream out his name when they find out that someone made sure that there will always be an empty chair at the kitchen table. I want them to attend a funeral. I would love to see them cry over an empty coffin! And I want to walk up to every single last mother and child, look them in the eyes, and say, 'My name is Zephyr Estrada, the daughter of Don Luis Estrada, and as I have lost my father due to your men's doings, so shall you lose your men due to my own doings.'"

Pedro knelt upon his bruised knees as he listened to Zephyr's hellish speech. She still looked out the window with no emotion in her eyes, as they always were. She had no soul left, and he started to cry because he was the cause of it. He opened his mouth to speak, but his tongue could not will itself to move.

Zephyr bowed her head and folded her hands in prayer. Pedro could see her lips move in a hurried manner. He could hear the soft sounds of her voice reciting her prayer. He tuned in to hear her words, but all he could make out was "Amen."

"I just prayed for you Pedro," Zephyr said as she turned around and walked past him. She stopped right in front of him and glared down at him with condescending eyes. "I asked God to make sure that you burn in hell."

Pedro closed his eyes and heard her footsteps fade away from him. Suddenly, he opened his eyes and felt his mouth move again. "Zephyr! Come back! I've found him!"

Zephyr stopped walking. She did not turn around to look at Pedro. He did not deserve the luxury of seeing her face once more. She merely stopped to listen.

"He's right there! I found Dad! I found *Papi*! See? Look! He's just lying on the floor!"

Zephyr heard Pedro squirm himself off the floor. He ignored the searing pain in his hand and tried to get up. He was cognizant of the blade that impaled his right hand, but he was ignorant of its placement—he couldn't figure out why he wasn't able to move.

"Zephyr! Stop standing there and help me clean up the blood! It's everywhere. You've sure made a mess, Dad! No more bleeding, okay? Wake up! Wake up!"

Zephyr shook her head and walked out of the room. He had lost it.

"Oh! Okay! So you'll go ahead and get the ambulance? Good thinking! I'll stay here with him!" Pedro laughed hysterically. "C'mon! Stop that! This isn't funny, Mom is gonna be so mad at you if you don't wake up!" He repeatedly slapped the floor with his free hand. "Hey, Zephyr! Try getting some ice water, like the cartoons we used to watch together! You remember, right? Pour it over his head and wake him up! Wake up! Wake up! Wake up . . ."

XII

Vladimir sat in his office, listening to his voicemail over and over. Zephyr had called him to thank him for all he has done for her and to say that she would like to visit him in person and celebrate with him. He ordered his men to wait outside when she arrived. A few moments later, a beautiful angel graced him with her presence.

"*Privyet*, my lovely princess!" He stood up to greet her with open arms.

"I see you've received my message!" Zephyr hugged him and kissed his wrinkled cheek.

"Yes, I have!" Vladimir pointed to a seat. "Come! Sit with me! Sit!"

"Thank you." Zephyr took a seat next to him. "I must show my appreciation for everything you have done for me. I admit, I had absolutely no clue what to give you, other than the news that you don't ever have to worry about Forty-Second Street, Julius, or Pedro and Slim."

Vladimir breathed a sigh of relief. "That's good news indeed. Tell me . . . is Julius really dead?"

"Indeed."

"Slim?"

"Yes."

"And Pedro? He is dead as well?"

Zephyr became silent. She looked away from Vladimir with a disappointed look on her face.

"He is still alive, I can tell by your eyes."

"Yes . . . he is."

"Zephyr, a father would rather die than to see his own child dead. Please understand this."

"I don't think I can, dear friend. I . . . cannot fathom why my father would ask me to show mercy on the primary cause of his . . ." Zephyr shook her head.

Vladimir looked at Zephyr with pity in his eyes. "Promise me you will try to understand. One day."

"For you,"—Zephyr turned her face to Vladimir—"I will try."

"Thank you, sweet child." Vladimir smiled.

"In any case, Forty-Second Street is a faint remnant. There are still some members out there, but I will hunt them down and exercise my wisdom upon them. I plan on monopolizing on this trade . . . with your backing of course."

"Zephyr . . ." Vladimir grabbed a bottle of vodka and poured himself a shot. He downed it in one gulp. "You have taken down the heads of the largest gang in the city with only a fraction of necessary manpower. No one has done that before. Not even your father, and he was the best out of all of us. Just . . . don't do this forever. Please . . ."

Zephyr chuckled. "My grandmother told me the same thing the other day."

"Listen to us old folk," he laughed. "You are too pure to be in this business. Too precious. You have a chance to get out."

"You and I both know that there is only one way out of here."

"*Da* . . . such is the life of constant death. But, my angel, if you have a chance to get out, take it. Your soul will last longer."

"Mine is depleted."

"Oh, but that's where you're wrong." Vladimir held her hand with a gentle squeeze. "You have so much left to give. Your potential is limitless. What you've just done in a matter of weeks is unprecedented. Imagine what else you could use your intellect for. You think your eyes are lacking a soul. That they're empty and without love or fear. But your eyes are beautiful, Zephyr. They have the potential to hold *anything*! You are able to *carry* anyone's love, anyone's fears, and anyone's souls in them. The storage in your eyes is not empty. Do you see?"

Zephyr smiled warmly. She truly appreciated his words. "Your words give me comfort . . . they really do." Zephyr sighed with a smile on her face. "I will do as you say. I just need time to finish what I started."

"I understand, but do not take too much time. This city is brutal." Vladimir smirked. "But it is nothing you cannot handle."

"Thank you."

"No, Zephyr . . . thank *you*." Vladimir took another shot of vodka. He sighed as he felt the burning liquid slide into his stomach. "Zephyr, I must ask you something."

Zephyr smiled. "By all means."

"What is your philosophy?"

"That's an interesting question." Zephyr sat up in her chair and rested her elbows on the table. She looked around the room to give her a brief moment to answer his question. "If I were to pick a philosophy . . ." she paused. "I would probably be inclined toward consequentialism."

"Why?"

"I firmly believe that my actions will bring about results that are pertinent to my desires."

"Have you done so?"

"Yes." Zephyr motioned for a waiter. He walked over with enthusiasm and honest interest in the beautiful woman sitting in front of him. He was more than happy to accommodate her. "A glass of your best pinot noir please."

The waiter nodded and sped off to the kitchen. A minute later, he returned with a burst of energy in his step. He held Zephyr's glass and poured a generous amount of wine. She thanked him and gave him a warm smile. That made his day.

"I desired that Pedro and Slim be—*eradicated* is not the word I'm looking for, but it's the word that immediately comes to mind. Granted, my actions were not worthy of a Miss America contest, but I know that it got the job done." Zephyr took a sip of wine. She set the glass down on the table and stared at the deep red liquid. "I will never forget that night when my father held me in his arms and I *begged* him to let me stay with him. I *wanted* him with us. I wanted him with me.

"I will be honest," Zephyr continued as she ran her finger up and down the stem of the wine glass, "there were many nights where I wondered if this was my entire fault. Indirectly. If I hadn't been born, would all of this nonsense have taken place? Those were a series of suicidal thoughts—not the thoughts of killing myself, but the thoughts of halting my own birth."

Vladimir watched Zephyr speak of herself. She was so dignified with her words. And she was so honest with herself. He had a feeling that she had never related this to anyone, not even her mother or grandmother. He dared not interrupt.

"You see, during these reflections, I realized purpose. I was born for a *reason*. This is my reason, my friend. It's impossible for me to identify a higher being's plans with my humble human logic, but I am smart enough to know that whatever talents I have, whatever drives me, I will use them for benefit."

"Whom have you benefited?"

"My family, my father, and this city. No particular order, although I will admit that this was mainly for my family."

"So you're an altruist."

"Not fully. I derived some pleasure out of this whole ordeal."

"I see." Vladimir looked to the side. "What do you plan on doing now?"

"In regards to this industry?"

"No. For yourself."

Zephyr paused. "I . . . honestly haven't thought of that."

"Your biggest weakness is that you forget to think about yourself. And if you do, it's in relation with some other thing or person. You've felt bad for having selfish thoughts, haven't you?"

Zephyr chuckled. She did not have anything to say to that. He was absolutely right.

"Have you ever thought of leaving Ellipses alone?"

"No . . . to be honest, I haven't."

"I think you should." Vladimir held out his hands. Zephyr placed her hands in them and felt tickled by his rough palms and dry skin. They were so brittle and worn but so warm and loving at the same time. "I'm trying to save you, Zephyr. Please, let me. Your father would have wanted this."

Zephyr stared at his eyes. His light-brown irises were swimming in a pool of tears. They did not fall down his cheeks; he had been in this business for so long that he had forgotten how to cry. They were dammed up, and there was no way they could ever escape.

"Your father is dead because of someone else's forced refusal of him to leave this demonic business. Please honor his original wish. I beg you."

Zephyr squeezed his hands. "You want me to leave?"

"Yes."

"Then . . . I will."

Vladimir smiled despite his tears. One finally fell down his right cheek. "I want you to be the last young soul to join us in this hellish venture and the first to leave. Zephyr, that will be your legacy. Not taking over the gangs and the mobs and the mafias but *leaving*. Not all battles are meant to be fought, my angel."

Zephyr raised her silver eyes and read Vladimir's mind. He was truly exhausted from all those years of torture and struggle. The wrinkles were set in so deep that any gentle reminders of a youthful age were gone forever. Any signs of vibrancy were darkened and bleak. He needed the rest so much. She stood up, and he slowly followed her. She walked over to him and gave him a large hug. He clasped his hands around her back and held her close to him. She smelled of roses and gentle raspberries. She felt so soft to the touch. It was hard to believe that this very woman in his arms was the same person who had brutalized the entire Forty-Second Street gang. An iron fist in a velvet glove, indeed.

"*Da svydanya*," she said. She gave him a kiss on his cheek, on the spot where his tear had fallen. "May you be happy once again."

"Zephyr . . ." Vladimir kissed her hand. "I already am."

She walked away and held his hand until their arms could reach no longer. She kept walking toward the exit even as she saw Vladimir's men waiting outside in the cold. The door closed behind her, and she felt an overwhelming sadness overcome her. She kept her head bent low, and her mouth was tight and frowning. A gunshot was heard inside the restaurant, but no one made any haste to check inside. Instead, they took off their hats and bowed their heads in prayer. Zephyr crossed herself before she left.

*　　　*　　　*

Zephyr came out of a rather long shower, longer than usual. She was notorious for taking long showers, to the point where Raquel once joked, "You're the reason why there are droughts in the world." But this one was different. She was trying to wash away her past sins. She tried to baptize herself by burning off her deeds with hot water. But when she exited the bathroom and put on a soft cotton robe, she did not feel forgiven.

She threw herself onto the bed and stared at the ceiling. She was often warned as a child to never think while staring at the ceiling, for her thoughts would be warped. But she could not help it tonight. The one person she wanted dead was still alive, albeit in a mental institute by now. On the other hand, the people she wanted alive were dead. Life sure was funny. Too bad she wasn't laughing.

She analyzed every angle of that ironic format. The novels and classical literature with which she learned her tricks never taught her the emptiness that remained buried in her heart. Her silver eyes were pure in the sense that they held nothing; they held the void, the abyss, everything that had something to do with lack or depletion. She needed to fill her eyes with something, but sadly, she never became satisfied.

No wonder they were always frozen.

Zephyr grabbed her cell phone and began dialing a medley of numbers. The line rang for a few moments until someone picked up.

"Hello?"

"Hi, Grandma."

"Zephyr!" Raquel's excitement erupted. "Oh, sweetie, how are you?"

"I'm okay . . . just tired."

"Is it over?"

"Yeah . . ."

"Okay, let me get your mother."

Silence.

"Zephyr, honey," Rosa answered, "are you okay?"

"No."

"I understand, sweetie."

"*Mami*," Zephyr began, "I know you and Grandma have warned me countless times that nothing I do will make things better. And that's true. But I feel . . ."

"Empty."

"Yeah." Zephyr sighed. "What should I do?"

"Go to church." Rosa paused to let that sink in. "It's time to go."

"You sure?"

"Trust me, it's time. You'll feel so much better once you go."

"Okay . . ."

"Trust me, Zephyr. Your father would want this."

"Once the afternoon starts, I'll do it."

"I love you, sweetie. Let me know how it goes."

"Will do. Bye."

Zephyr hung up the phone. She shut her eyes and mentally prepared herself for the trip to church. It had been a long journey to get up to this point, and it was time to end it. One last thing. Just one last thing.

Epilogue

Zephyr sat inside that tiny confessional stand all afternoon and well into the evening. It was way past closing time for the church, but the good Father did not make haste to have Zephyr summarize her sins. He sat and listened with so much attentiveness, so much honest interest and a yearning for healing her hurting soul. She was such a kind-hearted woman, but her voice was tainted with loads of regret.

The radiators had been turned off automatically a few hours earlier, so the church was colder than usual. However, the frigid air did nothing to deter Zephyr from pouring out her every action. Her cold ambitions were dispersed out onto his ears. She held nothing back. Every sentence she uttered lifted her soul higher to heaven. Her mother was right in saying that she would feel better once she went to church.

"I've done a lot of things . . ." Zephyr cleared her throat. "I know that my actions were . . . cruel. And perhaps I did go over the top during some events. But . . . I didn't know any other way to handle everything. I've thought for *years* of different variations of my deeds. I even considered abandoning my war on my brother, can you believe it? I was thinking, 'Oh, just let him be, Zephyr. He'll make sure that he digs his own grave without your involvement.'

"But then I thought, 'What if he doesn't? What if he actually enjoys his ill-gotten reign? What if he just makes himself stronger?' I couldn't let that happen." Zephyr spoke with a bottled fury. "Because of him, I had to watch my family suffer! He was the reason why I can't even share a decent laugh anymore! He didn't have to do this! And because of that, I'm not at all sorry for what I've done!"

The church echoed with her raised tone. She cleared her throat and sighed. "I'm sorry . . . I'm just angry and upset and sad all at once. I just . . ." Zephyr shook her head. "I just wanted to be happy. I still do." She paused. She took some time to concentrate on her next set of words. "To be honest, I wish none of this happened. But such is life, right? What did God say again in the Bible? 'Vengeance is mine,' right? Have I sinned against God, or was *I* His vengeance?"

There was dead silence on the other side of the screen, but she knew that he was still there listening.

"In any case, I . . . just wanted to talk really. I constantly have to maintain some form of composure, to be in perpetual control of my emotions. Which is true, but there are times where all I want to do is crawl in bed and cry. I'm only human, right? I'm not some princess or an emotionless robot. I have feelings as well. I just choose not to express them in public. I mean, I can see my biography now." Zephyr raised her hands as if she was painting a billboard. "*Zephyr Estrada: The Source of All Winters!*" She laughed. "If they only knew . . ."

The church lights were dimming. The lighting system had begun to shut down the church for the evening. The little light bulb in the confessional was the only source of light in the entire building. Zephyr and Father Bonaduce were alone.

"I'm sorry," she apologized as she crossed herself. "I lost track of time. Figures . . . I have no sense of it whatsoever." She giggled. "I'm always late, but I'm working on it . . . gradually. But . . . thank you."

Zephyr was silent. She had really missed her father, and she felt it showing on her face. She smiled. She was always a sensitive one.

"I just have to know something," she said with tears in her voice. "Why did I have to do this, *Papi?*"

Her confessional door suddenly opened. She kept her gaze on the small fenced window in front of her. She looked ahead with a river of tears flowing from her eyes. She could see that the shadow that had accompanied the priest's spot had disappeared. She slowly turned her head to meet the one who had opened her door.

She saw the tired, remorseful face of Luis Estrada.

He had almost forgotten what it was like to hold his daughter in his arms. She still felt innocent and precious, even as she poured herself out into his embrace. He shook his head as she cried. He would never forgive himself for doing this to his one and only daughter.

All the years of sending her letters much like the one she read on the plane to this circle of hell they have the nerve to call a city, all the years of remote communication between him and his family in Spain, the pages and pages of wise words to his little Zephyr, who was to be the best leader in the city. She was to be the little girl who would rise to supreme power, with no hindrance from anyone. He taught her strategies, logic, presentation but not how to cope. It was a lesson impossible to teach.

Yet here she was, learning the subject firsthand. He held her tight as she sobbed in his arms. She reminded him so much of Rosa. Oh, how he missed her. So many nights he wanted to leave the city and see her for one minute. But he was dead. Ghosts do not travel on planes, nor do they sail on boats. He felt hideous. He told himself that he was not a good father.

"I'm sorry," he kept saying. "I'm so sorry."

Zephyr sniffled. She wasn't ready to talk. She did so much talking tonight that he didn't blame her at all.

But he thought of the past as well, and wished that things were different. He will never forget waking up inside

Adam's car, gasping for air and holding onto that precious element as long as he could. He scared the hell out of Adam, who honestly thought he was transporting a dead body. Luis had awakened in the back seat and saw Adam's tearful eyes in the rearview mirror.

"A-Adam . . . I—"

"Don't talk," Adam had said. "I'm gonna take you to a safe place where they won't find you!"

He took him to a local hospital that was far away from any gang territory. The emergency room was empty, thank God, so there were a number of available nurses and physician's assistants ready to help him. Luis had slipped in an out of consciousness countless times. He even medically died once. But by some God-given miracle or by innately blessed hands, he survived.

Luis would never forget that the true hero was Adam Stokes. If it was not for him, his whole family would have perished. No one was stronger than Adam when he carried Luis's dying body to the hospital. No one exhibited as much bravery as Adam did when he returned to Mr. Mal and lied to him about Luis. No one was mourned over as much as Adam was. God rest his soul.

The last memory Luis had of Adam was when he said, "I'm sending my grandmother away from this city, and I want you to stay alive." And that was that.

Luis wanted to thank that priest who baptized Zephyr. How else could he have hidden? The last place anyone would look for a Don is in a church. All those years of hiding from his own family. All those years of . . . un-living.

"Zephyr, I never wanted this. I swear to you. I never wanted this."

Zephyr wiped her face with her palm. "It's over. Let's just go home. I'm so tired of this place."

Luis nodded and kept Zephyr huddled next to his heart as they walked outside. The snow had stopped falling. They were both enveloped in one another's arms, as a father and daughter should. They looked at the ground ahead of them. No more looking forward. No more planning or waiting. Enough with strategies and Plan As. Just walk, for God's sake.

When they reached Zephyr's car, they released each other. She dug into her coat pocket and grabbed her keys. She stuck it in the door, but she did not open it. She looked over her roof and stared at her father. A faint smile formed on her face.

"You okay, Zephyr?" Luis asked.

"Yeah . . . this is the first time I get to drive my father home."

"Don't speed," he joked.

Zephyr smiled. She wiped her eyes once more and opened the door. She unlocked the passenger door and waited for Luis to enter the car. No way was she leaving him out of her sight ever again. "By the way, the money and items are in the statues at the club. It's safe."

"I know. I trust you."

"Looks like I'm not the only one with secrets, Zephyr."

Both Estradas turned around and saw Rebecca standing behind them. She was alone, only accompanied by her car, Zephyr's generous gift. She was not in uniform; rather, she wore a black slim cut jacket and matching pants with a white blouse, all covered by a warm black overcoat. A flash of gold was seen on her waist. Her badge was considerably shortened, but it still bore her calling. She looked content and satisfied.

"Rebecca . . ."

"Don't say anything," she replied. She looked at Luis and bade him a respectful nod. "Don Estrada."

"Evening, Rebecca," he answered calmly.

Rebecca looked at Zephyr and chuckled. "You really are something else, you know that?"

"I am, yes."

"All this time?"

"All this time."

"Wow . . ." Rebecca walked closer. Zephyr and Luis stood there and waited for her to approach them. "I just wanted to thank you, Zephyr. You're the best friend a girl can ask for."

"Thank you . . . you too."

"And I'm sorry for earlier . . . for yelling at you like that."

"It's okay. We've both . . . been through hell."

"Just one thing . . ."

"Yes?"

"What are you going to do now?"

Zephyr looked at her father, who smiled at her as he entered the car. "My dearest *Detective*, that's for me to know and for you to find out."

Zephyr outstretched her arms and gave Rebecca a big hug. They both held each other for a few seconds before they released. It was hard for Rebecca to leave. She had had quite a bit of fun with Zephyr, but they knew that they had to go. As far as the law was concerned, they were on opposing ends.

Zephyr and Luis entered her car and closed the doors. She turned on the vehicle and revved the engine. *Such a showoff*, Rebecca thought. Zephyr rolled down her window and waved Rebecca over.

"Does this mean that I have a detective in my pocket?"

"Maybe. Only if it means that I have a crime lady in mine."

"Deal!" Zephyr smiled. "I will text you my number. My real one. Call me if you need anything, okay?"

"Okay! You got it!" Rebecca cast her attention onto Luis. "You take care, all right?"

"Always," Luis replied. He closed his eyes and smiled. It was good to be with his daughter once again.

Zephyr rolled up her window and sped off. Rebecca waved them both a fond farewell. She thought of everything that had transpired in the past few weeks. She laughed. What a family indeed.

Rebecca felt her phone vibrate. She saw the phone blink from an unsaved number and a text message from her friend: "Check with Mr. Xerox about a letter he is supposed to give you. Be ready to give Mister a more proper burial. And a name. I will be back soon. Remember me!"

Rebecca chuckled. *Very hard not to, Miss Estrada.*

House of E

Greg flashed his badge to everyone that stood in his way at the hospital. He was deeply depressed; his clothes did not hang on him anymore. They were just . . . there. They were just as unflattering as he was. His badge did not help his status much, although everyone did move aside. Perhaps he wasn't too worthless after all.

Then again, his own protégé had his job now.

But why should she have it? After all, it was he had who found her in that damned slum! He didn't have to take her underneath his wing. He didn't have to overlook everyone else's applications and focus on hers! He could've very well thrust her application through his desk shredder and move on to someone else. Yeah. That's what he should've done. Move on to someone else who was just as smart, just as ambitious . . .

Just as hot too.

But Rebecca was not his to command anymore. Now he had to answer to *her*. Such is life.

"I'm D-Detective Bernini," he said to a nurse behind the desk. He flashed his badge once again, but she seemed unfazed by it. Even the glory of a police badge diminished along with Greg's dignity. "I need to see a patient."

"What's the last name of the patient?"

"Estrada."

"One moment . . ." The nurse began to type on her keyboard. Greg marveled at the speed of her fingers gliding and slamming on certain keys. "He is in room 29. Past this desk, to the right."

"Thanks."

"He has neural syphilis," the nurse warned, "so don't be surprised if he says something weird."

"How did he get it?"

"Most likely from unprotected sex with prostitutes. His immune system has been shot to hell with all the narcotics we found in his system."

"Jesus . . . okay, thank you." Greg walked down the hallway and followed the nurse's directions. He saw a posted guard sitting in a chair right outside the hospital room. He was reading a small newspaper in one hand and had a cup of coffee in the other hand. He looked like shit. He must have been there all night.

"You've been here long?" Greg politely asked. He flashed his badge again. No satisfactory response.

"Yeah, since freakin' nine. I missed the game. You know who won?"

Greg ignored the officer and walked straight inside. He saw one patient behind a half-drawn curtain who looked to be in his sixties. He had so many clear tubes poking out of his arms that he may as well have been a pincushion. He looked terminally ill to Greg. But then again, what did he know anymore?

Greg turned to his left and saw a fully-drawn curtain, with steady beeps emanating from the machine. He walked over and pulled back the curtain. In front of him lay the battered and almost-massacred body of Pedro Estrada.

Pedro was not sleeping. He just stared at a spot on the wall without noticing Greg standing over him. His right hand was extremely crippled; he had thick bandages wrapped numerous times around it. His hair was wet from sweat and blood. His nose had dried blood that flaked on the oxygen tubes that were shoved up his nostrils. He was a complete mess.

Admittedly, he looked better than the victims of the bloodbath started by Zephyr Estrada.

"Pedro," Greg said.

Silence.

"Pedro, my name is Detect . . . Greg Bernini." He sighed and shook his head when he corrected himself.

"Yes? How may I direct your call?"

"Good Lord," Greg muttered. "I need to talk to you about some things."

"Oh, *everyone* talks. It's like no one knows how to keep quiet, right?"

"All right, I'll get to the—"

"Wait, wait, Gregory. Greg. Gregorio. Greggy." Pedro sat up from his bed, still staring at that spot on the wall. "What did you say?"

"I said I will get—"

"Shush! Don't interrupt Slim when he's talking!"

Greg looked around the room. Oh God, he had really gone insane. *Zephyr . . . what have you done?*

"Yes, I know he's a cop! I'm not stupid! Say what? Oh . . . you sure? Okay, okay, fine." Pedro looked at Greg. "Slim says that I can trust you."

Greg was puzzled, but he brushed it off. His proposal was much more important. "Pedro and Slim . . . we're interested in the same people, right? Right. I think we can . . . work something out. Let's talk about Zephyr and her friend, Rebecca Ortega."

Pedro, for the first time since he was admitted to the hospital, formed such a wide smile that it brought chills down Greg's spine. His smile was just as disheartening as Zephyr's eyes.

"The three of us should get together then," Pedro answered.

To be continued in the next book of the Zephyr series, *House of E*.

If you enjoyed reading this novel, please feel free
to leave a review on Amazon.com!

www.andrewdcooke.com
www.twitter.com/andrewdcooke

About the Author

Andrew Cooke was born and raised in Hartford, Connecticut. He was introduced to classical literature as a child when his mother gave him a small stack of literary classics, including *The Count of Monte Cristo* and *A Tale of Two Cities*.

Andrew holds a bachelor of arts degree in philosophy and a master of fine arts in creative writing. He wrote *Zephyr* when he was twenty-one and has not stopped writing since then. He currently lives in Maryland.

CPSIA information can be obtained
at www.ICGtesting.com
Printed in the USA
BVHW03s0536170818
524767BV00001B/1/P

9 781641 385923